Light Heart

Jessica Santi

To my husband—
You are the reason I write love stories.

THE TELACIEN
WRENFAST
QUEENDOM OF
LAEY
VEIL BETWEEN
WORLDS
STOALT
EVERLASTING OCEAN
ALONA
ISLAND REPUBLICS
The C

The Nest
Bascade
Naeryll
Fae Territories of Runne
Draconic Isles
The Dells
Artaxia
The Hold
Dom of Monstakar
tinent
N
W
E
S
Neverending Sea

Content Warning

Light Heart may include content that is unsuitable for some readers. This novel includes mild profanity, consensual sexual content, discussion of the death of loved ones, on page death, anxiety, grief, gore, self harm, and mentions of suicidal ideation. If any of these are triggering to you, please proceed with caution. Feel free to reach out to the author if you have questions.

CHAPTER ONE

DEMING

LIGHT DANCED ACROSS THE surface of the lake, glinting off scales of fish as they darted to and fro beneath the waves, winking in and out of existence as gentle swells of water lapped against the ice beginning to crust along the shore.

Light shone through the leaves of the trees, dappling the grove with patches of warmth.

Light played with the snow falling through the air, happy to have a companion in the sky, bouncing between the bright, white flakes with crystalline brilliance.

Everywhere, all around, light.

And yet, all Deming could feel was the shadowy darkness of grief pressing in on her from all sides, threatening to compress the world in on itself.

Some days were better than others.

Some days she found herself able to fake a smile. Some days she found her ears perking up, intrigued by the conversations the others were having. Once, she had even croaked out a laugh. A hoarse, sad sounding noise that felt unfamiliar on her lips. Though that had been followed by an immediate and all encompassing tidal wave of shame that hit her so hard she hadn't spoken to or looked anyone in the eye for two days afterwards.

Who was she to find joy when Miriam was dead?

Looking out across the lake was a dissociative experience. Deming was acutely aware of the individual strands of hair whispering across her chilled cheeks, red from the cold. She was also a million miles away. So far away from the scene before her that the clouds were pillowy companions offering their soft edges as blankets to curl up in and the winged male walking to the edge of the lake was a speck of nothing in the distance.

Grief was temperamental. It was a living thing coiled like a snake in her gut, strangling out needs, desires, emotions. Occasionally it brought a wave of nausea crashing into her, bile coating the tip of her tongue. More often, though, was the odd sensation of feeling like she was falling even though she was standing still. More often still, the unnerving ability she now had to exist in the world but not interact with it at all.

It was rare that anything felt real these days.

Nikita paused at the edge of the lake. His grand wings hung low, though he refrained from dragging them along the ground. A slight breeze wandered through the clearing, rustling the softer, downy feathers near his shoulder blades. He knelt to the ground, rocks surely biting into his knees, and placed a bouquet of winter wildflowers onto the small, ramshackle raft that floated at the edge of the water.

Though she was close enough to hear the words he spoke, they went in one ear and out the other. The only thing she heard was the wind telling her it's secrets. Coaxing her to unravel completely and join it in disappearing into the ether.

Nikita rose, gesturing across his chest in a tight circle once, then again the other direction. An ancient burial ritual to summon the Goddess of Death and Truth and ask for her help in ferrying the dead soul to the underworld.

Deming wasn't sure that particular ritual worked when the body was, at best, rotting many miles away in an unmarked grave. But she had said nothing when, one by one, all six of her companions made their offerings and called to Dorthrum.

Nikita returned to her side. Marking her turn to begin.

Her legs didn't seem to work. She asked them to move forward, yet her feet remained planted in the cold earth.

A soft hand rested on the small of her back. "You don't have to do this."

What a ridiculous thing to say. As comical as saying the sun didn't have to set or the moon didn't have to pull the tides.

Of course she had to do this. She was the reason Miriam was dead. Those around her, human and Fae alike, had all tried at various points within the last few weeks to convince her otherwise but she could not be swayed. Her uncle may have wielded the knife, but Miriam was dead because of their relationship and their relationship alone.

No, she wouldn't sully her memory further by abstaining from her burial ritual, however futile the rights seemed without the proper members of the temple or the body.

Deming said nothing to Nikita. She could feel him tense beside her, the beginnings of what would surely be another plea to not pressure herself into walking to the raft, but thankfully he thought better of it and stilled. He removed his hand from her lower back. A small, quiet part of her missed its warmth. A far louder part reminded her that even if she didn't deserve to be hurt and alone, which she did, he had hidden the truth from her for months.

If she was hurt and alone, he should be too.

The petty thought settled into her mind, cold and rotting like leaves caked together under snow in the winter, and she tried once more to move.

Her foot lifted. Her legs propelled her towards the lake. Every joint creaked against the unnatural stillness they had just endured.

The pebbles beneath her feet glistened with water and snow. If she squeezed her eyes tight enough, they almost looked like jewels. Rubies and emeralds. Quartz and peridot. Diamonds to match the stars in the sky that she stared at endlessly before falling asleep each night in hopes they would turn back time.

It was odd how specifically focused or dreamlike her thoughts could be. One or the other. Never anywhere in the middle.

The lake sprawled before her like the yawning mouth of some long forgotten beast. Waves kissed the toes of her boots and tugged at the raft, lightly straining against the rope tying it to a nearby rock.

She pulled out the ribbon from her hair, letting loose a flurry of pink and white and red to whip in the wind.

The satin was silky and soft. It fell gently in between her fingers like water.

They had nothing of Miriam's to offer her in the underworld save the locket resting against Deming's chest, and she couldn't bring herself to part with that. So instead they had gathered whatever bits and baubles they could find.

The smattering of flowers and bent coins and shiny stones seemed a pitiful offering when considering the sacrifice Miriam had unwillingly made.

Deming knelt and tied the ribbon around a jutting branch of one of the logs. The tails of the bow breached the surface of the lake and moved softly with the waves.

She pulled at the knot of the rope, giving the raft a push as she released it into the rolling clutches of the lake, and stepped back. Pressing her finger softly into the fabric of her overcoat, she mimicked the burial ritual and prayed the Goddess of Death and Truth was feeling sentimental today.

Silence enveloped the glen. The only sound was the waves jostling together as they pulled the raft towards the center of the lake.

Then, a swoosh of air sounded from behind and a flame-tipped arrow arced high above. It landed with painstaking accuracy and the wooden raft was ablaze in seconds.

The crackle and spitting and smoke of fire and wood and water filled the air.

The roar of the flames echoed the beat of her heart, tinging the despair raging inside with anger for a moment.

One by one, Deming heard the others leave. She was thankful that they left her alone. She had no energy to speak to them. No energy to reminisce. No energy at all.

"I'm sorry," she whispered once she was sure the only ones who could hear were the gods and the wind. "I miss you, and I love you, and I'm sorry, and it will never be enough."

She let herself collapse into the rocky shore, sobbing into her hands as the weight of her loss threatened to pull her under the waves.

CHAPTER TWO

DEMING

WHETHER THE GROUND BENEATH her was stiff with rocks and packed dirt or full of soft grass, she couldn't tell.

The sky was too curious for her to care about anything else.

Deming was laying on the ground at camp, far enough away from everyone that she hoped they would leave her alone for a couple hours while she contemplated the blue oasis above her.

Indeed, the sky was curious today. There were no clouds in sight. Not even a whisper of one. Only beautiful topaz and tourmaline swirling together seamlessly across the roof of the world. Near the tops of the trees the sky shifted closer to deep sapphire.

Winter in Laey was usually disparate and cold and gray down to its roots. But perhaps, she thought, perhaps they weren't in Laey anymore. They had been traveling via horseback for weeks now.

A pang of longing hit her chest. She missed Quintessential.

In what direction they were traveling, she surely couldn't say. Towards what city, a similar conundrum. Though, was it a problem to not know if she didn't care to know in the first place?

The sky certainly didn't care. It was everywhere, all at once. Knowing and unknowing. Ethereal and eternal. What a beautiful thing to be.

No wonder Kielle and Selene called it home.

Deming wondered absentmindedly why the High Deities didn't share the sky at the same time. It was rare for them to be seen together. Maybe they too, had decided that bitter loneliness was preferable to the sting of loss.

A scuffle beside her brought Deming out of her daydream.

"You know," Vallyn said, leaning against a nearby pine, "It would be helpful to talk about what happened."

Deming shifted onto her side, facing away from the dark-skinned warrior and her placating words. Unfortunately, this did not dissuade Vallyn.

"I find that movement clears my mind. You haven't trained with us at all since we left Arsaela. It's been weeks. I could walk you through the warm up?"

Some small mammal shuffled in the bushes beyond them.

"We all lost something that night, Deming. Mourn with us, don't push us away."

The wrong thing to say. Deming's blood boiled at the insinuation that anyone lost anything remotely comparable to her that night. They couldn't possibly know the strength of her sorrow. How deep it had burrowed into the marrow of her bones. How she desperately wished for the return of her nightmares because suddenly the burn of the flames was preferable to reality.

The death of two parents was preferable to the death of three.

Vallyn opened her mouth to say something else that would likely infuriate her further.

Deming held a hand up. "I'll do the movements. Just stop talking."

Vallyn released a sigh heavy with all the words left unsaid, but nonetheless offered a hand to the heir.

Deming ignored it and pushed off the ground on her own, not bothering to dust off her linen pants before moving seamlessly into the routine she was familiar with.

She reached skyward, the muscles in her back stretching and protesting.

Why couldn't they understand she was incapable of focusing on anything but the ragged hole in her chest? Why did they insist on pushing her to move on with her life?

Breathe in. Her fingers reached one inch closer to the clouds.

Breathe out. Delicate as a swan, she dipped her arms down to her toes, arching her back and pressing her forehead into her thighs.

Life ended all those years ago when the fire claimed her parents' lives. She had moved on from that, albeit reluctantly. And where had that landed her? Stewing in the same soul-tearing pit of dark emotions that she crawled her way out of a decade ago.

She unbent her spine and stepped forward with one foot, sliding the other perpendicular and bending her front knee.

Breath in. Fingertips to the sky.

Breath out. Palms to the ground.

Other side.

Repeat.

Why bother trying to get back to the surface now? No one was safe from death. Better not to love at all. Better not to care. Better, perhaps, to give in to the void altogether.

A tear fell to the ground. Deming watched until the singular drop of liquid disappeared completely into the packed soil.

When had she started crying?

Frustrated and annoyed, she stood. She wiped at her eyes with the back of her wrist in a jagged motion, rubbing hard.

Pain lanced across her cheek.

The sharp bite of injury felt sadistically blissful. She rubbed harder.

Vallyn said something but Deming was too consumed with pursuing the terrible, wonderful ache of pain to bother comprehending.

Feeling pain was better than feeling nothing. Right?

She twisted her wrist around and dug her nails into the soft skin beneath her eyes instead.

Why hadn't she seen the signs? Why had she trusted so freely? Why had she let any semblance of power she once had slip away? Why hadn't she told Miriam how much she loved her? Why was she alive while the pile of dead loved ones behind her grew and grew and grew? Why why why why why—

A scream ripped from her throat. At least, she thought it was from her throat. She didn't feel connected to her body. The world was black and wild and red and sticky—

Her arm was yanked away from her face sharply.

Deming blinked and reality rushed in.

Vallyn stood in front of her, gripping her wrist ferociously and staring at Deming with a mix of terror and pity.

Mostly terror.

Deming looked at her hand.

Blood streaked across the skin, coated her fingernails.

Lifting her other hand, she pressed it to her cheek, then held it in front of her.

Blood dripped from her palm.

"What happened?" Deming asked softly. She looked over her shoulder to find everyone in the camp looking at her.

Hartford looked up from the map of Runne she had been examining, mouth agape. Next to her, Ilysse's eyes flitted from Deming to Vallyn and back again. Her brow set firmly and lips pursed. She shook her head almost imperceptibly.

Paris had whipped open the flap to his tent, tears of his own glistening in the sun and hand covering his mouth in horror at the sight of her bloodied face.

Even the squirrels paused their skittering. The birds stopped their song.

Nikita approached her slowly.

It wasn't fear that slowed his steps. Deming tilted her head, taking him in. No, it was more that he was walking towards her as one might approach a doe in the forest. He didn't want to spook her.

"We should wash you up." He took her hand once he was close enough. Not flinching at the blood. Not taking his eyes off hers. "Can I take you to the water?"

She blinked away the remaining haze of panic and pain and nodded.

It felt odd, holding his hand. She felt vaguely like a small child. It would be good to be taken care of in that way, she supposed.

Nikita said nothing as they wandered through the quiet woods. Occasionally she could feel his storm gray eyes glance her way, accompanied by a gentle squeeze of her hand as if to remind her that he was still there. Or perhaps to remind himself that she was still there.

Either way.

It mattered not.

Deming's breathing was shallow but calm. Puffs of hot breath fogged the air in front of her, then disappeared as they walked forward. She wondered what it would feel like to walk through a cloud.

Cold, probably. Wet.

As if it appeared out of nowhere the river stretched out in front of her. Farther away to their left, where the head of the river cascaded down a mountain pass, rapids held frothing white peaks, swirling eddies, and currents that threatened to pull an unsuspecting traveler under. Here, the river ran calm. Any anger lay dormant beneath the waves. Here, they could cross it without fear of drowning, or kneel on its banks to wash blood from a mauled face.

Nikita pulled her to the ground with him. Deming let him adjust her so he was in between her and the water. Even though the river here was no threat to her life, he was taking no chances.

Discovering the stones in her coat pocket the other night had shaken him to his core. The fear that lanced through him had been palpable. His hands hadn't stopped shaking for hours. Deming had almost been able to scent his terror at the prospect of losing her. She was sure the other Fae had.

She hadn't bothered explaining that she wouldn't have been able to go through with it. That the thoughts echoing in her mind scared her too.

She hadn't protested the decision that Vallyn sleep in the tent with her from then on.

She had simply pulled a blanket tighter around her shoulders and softly cried herself to sleep.

How do you find the will to live when everything you love has been taken from you?

Nikita pulled a handkerchief from his breast pocket and wet it in the river.

"This may sting."

She looked up at him, caught off guard that he spoke.

"Can I touch you?"

Deming nodded.

He was right, it did sting.

Deming hissed and recoiled as the handkerchief pressed softly on her skin. The icy water was both shocking and a balm to the thudding pain of her wounds that was slowly creeping into her senses.

"Is it bad?" Her voice sounded far away and for a second she wasn't sure she had spoken out loud.

"You'll be okay. It looks worse than it is."

She glanced down at her hands, still covered in blood. Some of it was beginning to crust, especially under her fingernails. She used one hand to flick away the maroon chips on the other.

Nikita paused, pulling the handkerchief away from her face deftly enough that she couldn't see how soaked it was. There was no hiding the red and pink water that flowed away from where he wrung it out, though.

He returned and began work on the other cheek. Though she was prepared, Deming winced once more as the cuts screamed in protest at being touched.

"Will they scar?" She wasn't sure if she could handle more scars. More evidence of indiscretions leading to death. More physical portrayals of guilt.

Nikita slid a hand under her chin and tilted her face up to meet his gaze. "No," he said quietly, "They aren't that deep." Then, with a whisper of his old self, he added, "If I wasn't so worried about you I would make a joke about your pretty face remaining intact despite your best efforts."

Deming pulled back and looked down, but a small smile graced her face nonetheless. "You don't have to worry about me."

He didn't bother deigning that with a response. Instead, he washed the handkerchief once more and wiped her hands. When he was finished there was hardly any proof the panic attack happened at all, save for the angry, red cuts across her cheeks.

She let him pull her body into his, the warmth and comfort of his embrace outweighing any lingering mistrust. She was too tired to protest, anyway.

They stayed like that for a time. Deming couldn't be sure if it was minutes or hours. She counted her breaths in and out. Watched the sky deepen to indigo.

The sound of the river and the heaviness of Nikita's hand as he ran his fingers through her hair lulled her into a state of serenity she hadn't felt in quite some time.

She wished she could bottle this feeling. Take sips of it when the darkness threatened to pull her under.

The thought brought tears to her eyes. Her chest tightened.

No, no, no. She didn't want to cry now, everything was fine for a moment. She willed herself to go back. Go back, go back.

Deming squeezed her eyes shut as if tensing every muscle in her body could keep the emotions welling inside her at bay.

It could not.

A howl of angst and anger burst from her. She curled into Nikita's chest as sob after sob wracked her body. Her throat ached from the noises she was making, her eyes rimmed red from the tears pouring down her face.

How did she have any more tears to cry?

From far away she heard Nikita murmur into her ear. "We'll get through this." Over and over again he repeated, "We'll get through this, we'll get through this."

"How?" The word escaped between soul-rattling sobs. She was sure she sounded more animal than human.

He pulled her in closer, so no part of her touched the ground anymore. She was a ball of tangled limbs and sorrow in his lap.

"Together."

Though she wanted to, though she tried, Deming didn't believe him.

A soft touch brushed tears away from her bloody cheek. Her shoulders shook but he held her tightly, the protective cage of his arms holding her together when everything inside felt like it was coming undone.

Nikita took a deep breath. Deming's face rose and fell with the expansion of his chest. Something rumbled against her ear, then stopped. As if he had begun to say something but thought better of it.

Only when Deming's sobs quieted to pathetic sniffles did he speak.

"I have a hard truth for you, Deming." His voice was firm, but not sharp. He went back to running fingers through the lengths of her hair. "Dissociation is easy. Ignoring is easy. If you really think everything that happened in Arsaela is your fault, if you really want to commit some self-inflicted penance for Miriam's death, you know what you should do? Live. It's so much harder than what you think you're doing right now."

Every muscle in her body contracted. Her heart thrummed in her chest, beating wildly as if trying to escape his words. Live. Did she even know how to do that anymore?

She burrowed her head further into the darkness and warmth of Nikita's chest. A childish part of her wondered if she could disappear into him completely and leave all this hurt behind if only she closed her eyes tight enough.

He let her try.

They stayed there, silent, until the sky began to dim.

CHAPTER THREE

NIKITA

THE SWEEPING PINES OVERHEAD rustled in the wind. Water roared down a cliff in the distance, the falls plunging into a river so wild it wouldn't ice over even in the dead of winter. A dusting of white snow crunched under the hooves of their horses and occasionally the majestic screech of the eagle whose territory they had been traveling through could be heard. The melody of the forest was peaceful and inspiring but Nikita could think of nothing except the woman back at camp who was slowly drowning herself in regret and grief.

It was the worst kind of torture imaginable to watch Deming curl into herself until she was no more than a husk of the woman she once was. Her sparkling laugh, gone. The curiosity in her eyes, gone. The very warmth from her skin, gone. Vallyn had to coax her gently for days to get Deming to even brush her hair. The long lengths of gorgeous pinks and reds now hung limp against her pale face and sloped shoulders. Any and all vibrancy had slowly been leached from her until all that remained was a specter that barely spoke, barely ate.

In the early days, he had barely been able to restrain himself from scooping her into his arms and flying them across the Neverending Sea. His throne and hers be damned. He would leave the entire continent behind for her. All the mess and horror and bloodshed that drenched these lands didn't have to be their problem, couldn't be their problem if she was gone. If this continent was goddess-bent on breaking her down to dust and tearing her soul to shreds then they would simply leave it all behind.

He needed her to be okay like he needed to breathe.

In the end, it was Ilysse of all people that had soothed the flames. She knew loss intimately, though she rarely spoke about it, and she had withdrawn her walls for a moment to convince him that Deming would survive this and when she did, she would need to be here. Laey was her home, her birthright, and even though the possibility of reclaiming it was far out of reach at the moment, eventually she would want to try.

So he would keep her safe and alive until she was ready.

Which is how he found himself at yet another village in the middle of the continent. They had crossed over the Laey-Runne border a few days ago and were in desperate need of supplies.

Raellen leaned a bit more towards city than village, he supposed.

The road beneath his feet was wide and clear. Though they had joined it from the midst of the forest when no one was looking, this was one of the only roads that traversed the continent west to east and as such, was well traveled and many towns flush with trade markets sat on its path.

Towns like Raellen.

As he and Vallyn slipped through what were supposed to be city gates but in reality were planks of wood swinging on rusty hinges, Nikita pulled his hood up so it covered his eyes and pulled on the reins to slow his mare down.

Ramshackle houses with crooked doors stood next to shops built of stone with beautiful hammered glass windows. The road broke off into every direction like tributaries from a river and tufts of grass and weeds and wildflowers poked through wherever cracks in the patchwork cobblestone allowed.

Ahead of them lay the center of town. A small fountain spurted water erratically and clusters of people mingled. They spoke through scarves, their bodies bundled in wool coats and their breath coming out in foggy puffs.

Raellen was charming, but that wasn't the point. It fulfilled a purpose. This quaint town was big enough to have the trading and resources they needed. On the other hand, it remained small enough that any news of what happened in Arsaela had, hopefully, not yet reached the ears of it's gossips. It was also in Runne, which meant there were enough Fae around that his wings didn't attract unwanted attention.

It was a delicate game they were playing.

"Are you sure we don't need anything else?" Vallyn's rich voice pulled him out of his thoughts. She hopped off her horse and handed him the reins.

Loose curls of hair tickled the back of his neck as he shook his head. "We need to travel light. Only the essentials."

She dipped her chin then strode into the throngs of people weaving in and out of shops.

While she busied herself with finding flint, fresh arrows, and a few loaves of bread, Nikita eyed the surrounding building for a farrier.

How he had gotten stuck with the task of getting their horses new horseshoes was beyond him. The animals were too large, too strong, and too finicky for his liking. He actively despised riding to the point that more often than not, he flew and scouted ahead for the group rather than resting atop one of the horses.

It was his turn to go into town for provisions, though, and he wouldn't shirk responsibility for the sake of a childhood fear.

"Come on, ladies," he muttered to the mares as he led them down the street. "Let's get this over with."

Two hours and eight horseshoes later, Nikita walked towards the center of town.

Vallyn sat against the trunk of a tree, eating pieces of bread from one of the three large loaves poking out of her pack. She ripped off a hunk and handed it to him in welcome.

It was warm, freshly baked with a crisp crust and pillowy middle, and tasted absolutely divine.

"Got everything?"

"Mhmm. Horses are all set?"

Nikita nodded.

"Alright, time to go then." She stood, brushing away crumbs.

As she did so, Nikita eyed a small trinket in her left hand and raised an eyebrow.

Vallyn opened her palm to reveal a small wooden horse. Its features were painstakingly carved in incredible detail and then polished so the afternoon light reflected perfectly off of its mahogany surface. "Only essentials, I know, but...it's for her. It reminded me of Quinn."

His shoulders slumped, heavy with emotion. "That's," he cleared his throat, "that's very thoughtful."

Deming would love it, he was sure, and though a small part of him wished he had thought of the gesture, he was thankful she had so many people looking out for her.

Nikita bit his lip at the errant term of affection his mind was continually attaching to Deming. He knew she wasn't his, not really. There was something between them, a pull that he hoped she felt too, but they had barely begun to explore. After everything that happened the night they fled Arsaela, it was all anyone could do just to keep her alive. There was no room for romance, not now. No matter how much the very fiber of his being ached for her, he would give her time to heal. When—if—she came to him, he would allow his restraint to shatter. Only then. Only on her terms.

It was only when they crossed through the main square on their way out, packs full, that Nikita's eyes snagged on something plastered to the side of a wall. The parchment was fresh and bright, new. One corner had pulled away from the stone and was rustling in the breeze. The black scrawl jumped off the page loudly proclaiming the substantial amount of coin being offered for the delivery of a woman back to those she betrayed. And smack in the middle, clear as day and immaculately drawn, was Deming.

Nikita's heart jumped to his throat and he nearly tripped on air at the shock of seeing her painted as a criminal. They all knew this would happen, her uncle had all but said he was embarking on a mission to smear her name. But to see he would go so far as to say she could be brought to him dead or alive snapped something in Nikita.

"What?"

He jerked his head towards the wanted poster. Vallyn's eyes followed, then widened.

"Oh, fuck."

His eyes darted around the square.

A group of children were chasing each other around the bubbling fountain. Sets of what appeared to be parents watched from benches and beneath the shade of old trees. An old man smoked a pipe outside a dimly lit bar. The clop of hooves and raised voices bargaining told of travelers and traders in the distance.

No one was paying any attention to them.

Still, Nikita couldn't shake the feeling of dread slithering down his spine.

He discreetly tore the wanted poster down and shoved it in his pack.

"Let's get out of here."

"You're sure no one saw you?"

Everyone other than Deming was huddled around Ilysse's outstretched hand, peering at the wanted poster with varying levels of concern.

"No one saw us," Nikita told Hartford.

Vallyn huffed and he caught the end of an eye roll when he glanced towards her.

"What?"

"There's no way we can guarantee that."

"Then what do you suppose we do?"

Vallyn crossed her arms and sighed. "I don't know. I'm just saying we might have been seen."

"There's nothing we can do," Paris said, hand rubbing the back of his neck. "I don't see how this changes anything. We still can't go back to Laey and we still don't know where might be safe."

"What's going on?"

Nikita turned towards Deming's voice like there was a physical tie between them and the tug in his chest, the one that made him wonder if maybe she was his by fate, deepened.

She was curled in on herself like a burnt piece of parchment—shoulders slumped, head curled towards her chest. One hand clasped her arm, the other picked at a thread of her coat. The lack of fire in her amber eyes made him want to pull her into his arms and never let her go.

"Nothing—"

"Not nothing," Ilysse snapped at him. She thrusted the poster at Deming before turning back to everyone else. "We need to be more careful. No more towns."

"If we need food, we need food, Ilysse," Vallyn shot back.

The rest of their voices fell away as Nikita watched Deming.

She held onto the slip of parchment so softly he thought it might blow away. Her eyes took in everything—the image of her, the lies about what she had done, the reward for her return to Reynes Castle, dead or alive.

She stood mutely for a minute, then her hands started to shake.

He was at her side in an instant. "Hey," he cupped her elbow, "hey, it's okay." With his other hand he tilted her face up and away from the image of her. "Look at me."

She did, but her gaze remained worried and her hands still trembled beneath his grip.

"We knew this might happen, yeah?"

She nodded.

"You're safe, I promise."

"You can't promise that."

Her whispered words broke Nikita because she was right—he couldn't promise that. He would do everything in his power to protect her, to heal her, but he couldn't promise safety forever. Not in this world.

"You should all leave," she said dejectedly. "No one around me is safe."

Deming pulled away from him and he let her even though he wanted nothing more than to tug her into his arms. She hadn't wanted physical touch from anyone since Arsaela.

"Deming."

She halted.

"I may not be able to promise you safety but I can promise that I will never leave you."

Her eyes flicked to his and he could have sworn he saw the briefest sliver of curiosity flash across her amber irises. She stood there stoically and as still as deer. Nikita wasn't sure if it was his renewed promise or the shock of seeing a price on her head or something else entirely, but something had changed about her.

"Nikita?"

"Yes?" He waited on bated breath for her question.

"You told me that if I…that I should live. That living is harder than whatever I'm doing." She grew quiet, her voice trailing off near the end of her thought. "What if," she took a deep breath, "what if I can't? What if something is broken in me that I can't fix? I feel…I feel like all of the life inside me has withered away."

As the words fell from her lips, Nikita felt the duality of joy and pain. It was horrible to hear her describe the loss of life she felt. And in the same breath he felt like he could sink to his knees and thank the gods over and over for the small blessing of Deming opening up about her shattered heart. Perhaps this was the first, small step she needed to take.

He stopped, needing to look at her fully when he next spoke.

"You are more full of life than anyone I know. It's just lost right now, buried under your grief." He risked a gentle caress of her cheek and swept a few wayward curls behind her ear. "But anything lost can be found."

Chapter Four

Deming

AS SHE DID EVERY morning, Deming woke with tears on her cheeks and salt on her lips.

She sat up, rubbed the tears away, and flinched. First, at the tenderness in her cheeks. Then, at the realization that the desire to dig further into the pain wasn't there where she would have expected it to be.

There was something different about today. Something that filled her with a cloying mixture of interest and horror.

There, sitting in a tangled mess of blankets and swimming in the dissipating remnants of a nightmare, Deming realized that the grief induced fog she had existed in these past weeks was lifting.

Her fingers remained frozen, pressed gently on her cheeks, as some ray of long forgotten brightness reached out for her.

She searched her soul for the all too well known feeling of guilt, trying with all her might to dig mental daggers into the open wound of everything she had lost, and surprised herself by finding a kernel of something new next to the languishing emotions that lay there among the memories of her dead loved ones. Hope.

Small and delicate and lit only in her very heart of hearts, but it was there.

Hope that maybe she wouldn't have to feel this way forever.

What did that mean for her? Was the only other option to confront her trauma? Was she supposed to walk through grief with others now? She hadn't interacted with anyone in any sort of meaningful capacity in weeks. Did she even remember how to?

She should ask Miriam what to do.

The thought rushed in unbidden with the ferocity of a bull and the feeble strands of hope withered away as the reality of why that was impossible smacked into her. Visions of Miriam laying lifeless before her flooded Deming's mind. Over and over she saw the jagged wounds and heard slow, rattling, wet breaths and felt the sticky warmth of blood coating her hands and arms and lungs and she was drowning in it, drowning, drowning—

Oh, gods—

Miriam was dead because of her.

Forearms slit to the bone, dead.

Blood drenched and cold skin, dead.

Loving Deming to her last breath, dead.

Deming's breathing was ragged and her hands trembled uncontrollably. She buried her head into her sweating palms and clutched at the roots of her hair. Rocking back and forth on the hard bedroll, Deming tried to calm herself but panic and grief and deep, unending sadness swallowed her whole.

It took a long while for the images plaguing her to quiet enough for Deming to hear her own thoughts. It then took until Deming counted out loud to well over a thousand for her body to stop shaking.

She couldn't quite stop the trembling in her fingers, though.

They trembled as they brushed through her hair, folding the lengths into a simple braid that hung down the middle of her back. They trembled as she touched the locket resting against her chest. Trembled more as she laced up her boots. Trembled still as she pulled a wool coat on.

Deming's eyes snagged on the small wooden carving Vallyn had given her the other day.

She picked up the beautiful gift and turned it over in her hands. The wood was a rich, deep color. The mane and tail were detailed down to the individual strands of hair, the ripples of carved movement incredibly intricate. One of its hooves was raised as if about to paw at the ground. Its neck was arched, nose tipped down to show off the inlaid stripe on its forehead.

Exactly like her beautiful, brave Quintessential.

She set the horse back down with steady hands.

Anything lost can be found.

Deming stepped out of her tent and into the world. Even now, more clear headed than she had felt in weeks, the shadows called to her. They were still there, a comforting presence curled up in the corner of her mind like a cat. She felt as if she was walking along a rope, teetering over the edge of a darkness that called to her so sweetly.

She curled her hands into fists and let the bite of her nails digging into her palms bring her an odd sort of peace. Pain was useful, in that way. Grounding.

Across camp, Ilysse and Vallyn were huddled next to each other, speaking low enough that Deming couldn't hear their conversation. Vallyn said something and Ilysse burst out laughing.

The blonde Fae shook her head, still smiling, and turned to the edge of the forest. She flipped a dagger casually in one hand and then hurled it at a far off tree without much warning.

The dagger glinted menacingly as it shot through the air and sunk into the trunk with a satisfying thunk. The hilt wobbled wildly on impact.

It was then that Deming realized they had scraped the bark off in places to create a crude target. Ilysse's throw had hit the innermost circle, though it was not dead center.

The lioness frowned, then bared her canines halfheartedly at something Vallyn said.

Vallyn pulled a similar sized dagger from her belt and gave its blade a playful kiss before stepping in line with the tree. She gracefully drew her arm over her shoulder before stepping and releasing the dagger in one fluid motion.

Deming's breath caught in her throat as she watched it sail through the dawn air.

The ting of metal on metal echoed through the clearing as Vallyn's dagger narrowly edged out Ilysse's.

Ilysse swore, loudly enough that Deming heard the curse clear as day even from where she stood.

A whisper of a laugh tugged at her lips.

She walked hesitantly towards the pair.

Ilysse's ears flicked towards the sound of her footsteps crunching on the semi frozen ground. After seeing who approached, she elbowed Vallyn.

"Deming." Vallyn's eyes widened. Shock colored both her face and voice. She quickly quelled the emotion, but Deming saw it all the same.

She couldn't blame her friend. She hadn't been up this early since they left Arsaela. Someone usually had to drag her out of her tent in the early afternoon and even then, she was prone to sitting under a tree silently until it was appropriate to go back to sleep.

Deming nodded to the target. "Nice shot."

"Thanks."

Silence coated the clearing. Neither woman knowing quite what to say. Deming, because she truly felt like conversation was something she no longer knew how to partake in. Vallyn, because she didn't want to spook the traumatized woman back into the tent.

Ilysse, apparently, had no such worries. She offered another dagger to the heir, hilt out. "Want to try?"

Vallyn shot her a look, almost certainly referencing the utter disaster asking Deming to train yesterday turned out to be.

Deming didn't immediately reject the weapon. But when her hand twitched to raise itself, she was brought back to Miriam's chambers. The smell of blood and death. The weight of her own dagger that night. How miserable her attempt at throwing it at her uncle had been. How helpless she had been.

A stronger woman would take the dagger. A braver woman would train so she was never helpless again. But she was not that woman. She was sorrowful. She was broken. She was lost.

The idea of touching the weapon filled her with sizzling anxiety. She could feel her pulse beating faster just at the thought.

She took a step back.

"No," she said, softer than she intended.

She inhaled deeply and tried to ground herself in this moment. The crisp air filling her lungs. The solid ground beneath her feet. She blinked away the memory and focused only on the two warriors in front of her. Ilysse was draped in furs, golden eyes shimmering with violence and ferocity and wickedness. Vallyn's twisted white hair was piled atop her head, held together with a forest green ribbon. She shifted from one foot to the other, cocking her head inquisitively at Deming.

She was here. In a winter clearing with her friends. Reynes Castle was miles away. Nothing would hurt her here.

Deming's chest loosened ever so slightly.

To Ilysse's credit, the immortal didn't push her. She merely shrugged and slid the dagger into its sheath. "Your loss."

"Maybe—" Deming bit her lip too hard and tasted blood. "Maybe next time."

Ilysse nodded curtly. No one said what they were all thinking. A comforting lie is a lie all the same.

The sun had fully breached the horizon. Its rays flickered through the pines and washed their camp in a buttery glow. Soon the rest of their companions would rise and begin their day of traveling. To where, Deming was still unsure. Though she supposed today was as good as any to figure out where they were. First though, she needed some medicine.

"Vallyn?"

The warrior perked up and looked at Deming.

"Do you have any more salve for my cheeks?"

"Yes, of course. I have something in my tent that should help."

"Calendula would be best for shallow cuts like hers."

"Thank you so much," Vallyn shot at Ilysse with a heavy eye roll, sarcasm dripping from her voice. "I would have never thought of calendula without you. You are a goddess of knowledge, the smartest of us all."

"Glad we're on the same page." A playful smirk played at Ilysse's lips. She ran a tongue along her canine, biting back a laugh.

Vallyn grumbled something incoherent and turned away from the female, choosing not to respond to her provocation.

Inside her tent, Vallyn knelt beside her pack, shifting through its contents until she found what she was looking for. She pulled out a small tin and twisted off the cap. A plain looking substance lay within.

"This may sting a bit."

Indeed, when Vallyn brought her calendula dipped fingers to Deming's cheeks, the touch stung. Though the warrior was gentle, every circular motion her fingers wove across Deming's mauled face felt intense.

Deming inhaled sharply and balled her hands into tight fists.

Soon enough, the salve was worked into her skin and the pressure from Vallyn's fingers alleviated.

"Thank you." Relief flooded through Deming where pain had just been. The calendula would work its magic eventually, though she would have to reapply in a few days. But even just the application of the cooling balm released some of the tension her face had been holding.

She stretched her jaws. Wrinkled her nose. Yep, already her skin felt less tight and itchy.

"Of course." Then, after a moment. "I'm happy to see you this morning. How are you feeling?"

Deming nodded subtly, folding her hands in her lap. "I feel…"

How did she feel? It seemed impossible to pinpoint just one emotion. She felt unsure how to move throughout the world in the wake of loss. She felt terrified both at the prospect of never feeling fully alive again and at losing the companion of grief. She felt scared of how eager she had been only days before to never wake up. She felt an ache for the ability to appreciate beauty and joy once more. She felt betrayed, still raw and harsh and infuriating.

Most of all, she felt unknown. Even to herself. Her body and her mind and her soul felt incompatible. Who she was today felt like a completely different person to who she had been.

She settled on what felt the most true.

"I feel lost."

Admitting that brought odd sensations forward. Her anxiety spiked, fingers itching to pick at something, anything. They landed on the fraying ends of her coat. She couldn't look at her friend.

That's who Vallyn had become, Deming realized. Not the Captain of the Guard at Reynes Castle. Not her personal shadow, watching Deming's every move.

A friend.

Vallyn's hand reached forward and gently nudged her chin up. "I know." A soft, comforting smile pulled up one corner of her mouth. Pain and sadness and understanding swam in her brown eyes.

She lowered her hand, took Deming's hands in her own, and squeezed tightly. She said nothing else, to which Deming was immensely grateful, but the touch conveyed more than words ever could.

Together, Nikita had said to her. They would get through this together. Not just the two of them, but everyone.

The path forward may be clouded, but she wasn't walking alone.

Chapter Five

Deming

THE FIRE CRACKLED, SPREADING warmth and spitting embers at the cluster of six bodies that surrounded it.

In the days since Deming began clawing her way back to life, she had said little and done less. Thankfully, her presence around communal fires and the absence of death in her eyes seemed to be enough for her companions for the time being. She knew they would expect more of her eventually, but eventually was not today. Today everyone was content with her tracking conversation with her eyes, looking at whomever was speaking and nodding in agreement when applicable.

Perhaps they coddled her. Perhaps the bar was depressingly low. But the general air of relief at her interacting with the world again, however minimal, was too good a feeling to risk jeopardizing.

Deming pulled the blanket tighter around her shoulders with gloved hands. Its threads were rough but thick, and colored vibrantly. Winter had the wilderness firmly in its grasp and as such, the group had taken to lighting fires whenever possible. It was midday, the sun shining high above their heads, and still a fire roared in the middle of their camp. They had stopped an hour ago and would leave again in the morning. The pace they kept was clipped and her bones were weary from constantly moving around, but they had no place to go. A source of contention that was being argued over yet again.

"Bascade is the wrong choice." Ilysse's words were clipped, pushed out roughly as she shook her head. "The capital harbors no friends of ours."

Nikita looked at the female with steel in his eyes. "We have no other choice."

"Monstakar! The Island Republics! The Draconic Isles! Even Naeyell! We've been over this!"

Nikita's hands tensed and flexed, balling themselves into fists in an attempt to temper his frustration. "Yes, we have gone over how none of those options are viable. Monstakar is Laey's closest ally in the human territories—"

"Which is why we should go there. They will support Deming's claim to the throne."

Nikita shook his head. "We don't know that. They could just as well believe the lies her uncle is spinning. It's too risky to make any moves towards reclaiming Arsaela right now. We have no allies."

"How do you propose we make any if we don't go anywhere?" Ilysse growled. She looked to Vallyn and Paris. "Neither of you have changed your minds?"

Paris opened his mouth to seek but Vallyn beat him to it. "Until we have a understanding of what is happening in Laey, Arsaela specifically, it's not safe for us to announce ourselves formally anywhere. I still don't understand why we can't go to Runne." She flicked her wrist towards Nikita. "You're the Crown Prince."

Quiet and calm as ever, Hartford cut in. "As we have said several times, we would not be welcome in Bascade. Even the coastal city of Naeyell is a risk."

"I've been to Naeyell," Vallyn said, "If you have no reason to risk going, fine. But I can take Paris and Deming there without repercussions."

The three Fae exchanged a look.

Vallyn grit her teeth. "Even if Nikita is banished from the capital city, Naeyell should be safe for us. The king isn't going to go out of his way to hunt down his only son and heir."

"You clearly don't know my father very well," Nikita grimaced.

"It's our best shot—"

"He said no, Vallyn." The words slipped out of Deming's mouth before she realized she had spoken. Everyone's gaze snapped to her. The weight of their gaze felt heavy and uncomfortable. "Sorry."

"No, no," Paris said, finally able to get a word in edgewise. He placed a gentle hand on her shoulder, squeezed once, then removed it. "No need to apologize. You're right, arguing is going to get us nowhere."

"So will saying nothing and pretending everything is okay," quipped Ilysse under her breath. "At least arguing is honest."

Paris glared at the lioness but backed down.

"What we can't do is wander around—" Ilysse stopped speaking abruptly. Her eyes narrowed, her elegantly pointed ears twitched. She put a long finger to her lips, hushing everyone around the fire. She looked to Nikita, who was already locked onto the Fae captain with startling intensity.

Ilysse touched three fingers to the inside of her wrist, paused, then flipped her hand over so her palm was facing up and touched the back of two fingers to her wrist.

Vallyn leaned to Deming and whispered almost imperceptibly into her ear, "Three on the ground, two in the sky. Be ready to run."

Deming's spine straightened. Her fingers sparked with nervous energy as they slowly wrapped around the hilt of the dagger Vallyn had extended to her. She had no time to dwell on the fact that this was the first time she was wielding a weapon since Arsaela before the glen erupted into chaos.

A deep rallying cry shattered the silence and two men burst from the edges of the forest in Deming's field of vision. Nikita and Ilysse whirled into motion, sweeping out the legs of one and catching the other with an elbow to the face. The attacker's nose broke instantly in a crunch of crushed bone, blood pouring from his face and splattering the snow covered ground.

A feminine voice matched the cry from behind Deming, who whipped her head around just in time to see a woman with black paint smeared across her cheeks hurling a spear towards her with strength and speed that seemed inhuman.

Deming swore and flattened herself to the cold ground, rolling to her left without a second to spare as the spear collided with the hard earth and dead grass where she had been sitting moments before.

"Behind me, now!" Vallyn's voice cut through the clearing and Deming was more than happy to oblige, pushing up from the ground and lunging to where the warrior stood only paces in front of her. Vallyn had unsheathed her sword and was rocking on the balls of her feet, ready to launch herself into the fray as soon as she was needed, but not a moment before.

Protecting Deming remained her priority.

"Paris!" Deming yelled in warning as a winged figure rose from the tree line and dove towards her friend, the metal strapped to both his thighs glinting menacingly in the sun.

Paris was already moving. He darted away from the fire and towards where his own weapons lay, grabbing the hilt of his sword and spinning around to meet the strike of the winged male in a narrowly life-saving clash. The impact thrust him back, though, and within seconds both he and the attacking male had crashed into one of the tents, lost in swaths of collapsing fabric.

Deming's heart raced, her breath came in frantic pants and gasps. The speed of the attack was disorienting, they had come out of nowhere on silent footfalls. How had that been allowed to happen? How long had they been on their heels?

The woman with warrior paint on her face had not stopped running towards them to throw her spear and consequently was now rushing quickly into the space Vallyn and Deming occupied. The woman reached over her shoulders with both hands and drew matching swords, longer and thinner than normal. With a cry, she leaned to the left and used her body weight to slam the swords into Vallyn's own. The sound of metal on metal screeched through the air as Vallyn dug her heels into the frozen dirt to stop herself from skidding further back.

Deming leapt to aid her but was whipped around by something crashing into her shoulder, knocking her back and sending the dagger in her hand flying across the glen.

Pain shot through her body and a string of curses flew from her mouth as Deming tried to pick herself up and orient her senses to the attack.

She had no time to react as a second winged figure appeared above her and kicked her swiftly in the stomach.

All breath left her body as she curled over herself in agony, protecting her middle as she slid roughly across the packed earth and slammed, spine-first, into the broad trunk of a tree. Her eyes shot open on impact, the pain so intense it swallowed the gasp on her lips entirely and she was left heaving her chest erratically, trying to bring air back into her lungs.

Shaking, Deming braced herself against the tree and stood. She turned to face her attacker, who was stalking towards her with the deliberate pace of a predator.

"There's quite the bounty on your head, girl," he growled, "I'd prefer the purse offered if you're brought in alive but I have no issues delivering a severed head." The closer he approached, the clearer the malice in his eyes became. "Your choice."

"Fuck you," she spat between heavy pants.

"Dead, then. Fine by me." He balled his hands into fists and flared his wings out behind him.

Before he could take another step Deming rocked back on the balls of her feet then launched herself at his ankles.

The rocky, winterized ground shredded the skin on her forearms as she dove forward but she had little time to register the injury. Her arm looped through his legs, locking around him with the crook of her elbow, and her momentum swung her body around him. She let go and skidded back towards the middle of the chaos, palming the ground with her hands and trying to find purchase with her feet.

Her speed had caught him off guard, but it was not nearly enough to fell the man. He swore as he lost his balance momentarily but within a second he spun around and was honed back in on her.

This time, he took no chances, gave her no time to react. He pulled a small blade out and leapt forward, his movement faster than anything Deming could retaliate against.

With one beat of his wings he was slamming into her. Their bodies flipped over one another as they crashed against the ground—wings and limbs and breath and sweat colliding so aggressively it was impossible to tell which way was up or down.

When they came to a stop, the male was on top of her. He thrust one forearm on her neck, pressing dangerously hard against her throat and constricting her ability to breathe. With the other, he took his blade and buried it in the dense muscle of her upper thigh.

Deming's scream was fierce and full, despite the lack of air in her lungs, and it only increased in intensity as he pulled down on the weapon, slicing her leg open from hip to mid thigh.

Nerves and muscle severed in time with her sanity. The world collapsed in on itself and for a moment all Deming knew was sharp, blinding pain like she'd never known.

She was still screaming when the winged male yanked the blade out, looped a muscled arm around her waist, and shot them both into the sky with powerful beats of his wings.

She struggled to push the need to focus on her bleeding, burning thigh into a recess of her mind.

She struggled to regain her breath under the oppressive strength with which his arms had her pinned to his chest.

He smelled of sweat and blood and vile things.

"Get the fuck off me!" Deming ground out, beating at his chest with her fists, pounding as hard as she could against the cold, corded muscle that could be felt through the thin layer of leather he wore over his midriff.

Each shift of her body as she thrashed, each dip and sway of his as he flew them through the sky sent waves of renewed pain through her leg. The wound pulsed with a heartbeat of its own. Deming could feel warmth spread from the gash and knew without looking down that she was already covered in blood and would soon be at risk of passing out if she didn't escape and bind her thigh.

She grit her teeth and steeled her mind.

The metallic din of the battle below grew fainter by the second as the male tore through the air. The wind nipped at her skin as they rose, colder and colder until it felt like tiny pins digging into her skin with every gust. Her hair whipped at her cheeks, lashing out as if it, too, was ready to riot.

She had to get back to her friends. Had to find her way back to the ground. Hitting him wasn't doing her any good so she switched tactics and drove the knee from her uninjured leg upwards, hard.

"Bitch!"

His wings failed him and Deming found herself momentarily in a free fall, the sky and clouds blurring together into terribly beautiful chaos and the wind tearing at her skin before he righted himself and snatched her waist once more.

In the exact moment the world stopped spinning, she saw a glint of metal flash from his left thigh.

Deming tried to grab the dagger but her reach was limited by the male's hold on her. She needed him to loosen his grip.

Without thinking, she leaned forward as far as she could, bit down hard on the soft, exposed flesh of his forearm, and tore her head back with a viciousness she didn't know she was capable of.

White-hot pain from overextension shot through her skull, emanating from the point where her spine and her neck met and showering her vision with sparks, but her mouth filled with blood all the same. She spat the chunk of flesh out, not bothering to watch it fall to the forest floor below, nor to admire the blood that trailed like brilliant, red rain in its wake.

They careened off course as the male released one hand, shaking off the pain and lingering mauled skin. It was just enough release of tension that when Deming reached for the dagger again, she was able to grasp the hilt firmly and pull it from its sheath.

Still reeling from being bitten, the male had no time to defend himself as Deming slammed the dagger into his chest and twisted the weapon sharply for good measure.

She yanked the dagger out only to drive it into his chest once more.

It was only when he finally released his other arm from her waist and she kicked at his stomach to put space between them that she remembered where they were.

Hundreds of feet in the air.

And they were well and truly falling now.

Deming fell through the sky, uncontrolled and flailing. The wind ripped at her hair and clothes and skin as she hurtled towards the unforgiving earth that raced upwards to meet her with increasing speed.

Panic lanced through her like lightning, crisp and hot and wild and not at all like the fear that had coursed through her moments before. She could fight a man, she could not fight gravity.

An anguished scream tore out of her as she fell, frustration and anger reaching a breaking point as she refused to come to terms with the fruitlessness of her situation. Escaping one terror only to be immediately punished by the consequences of her actions.

Out of the frying pan, into the fire.

This couldn't be how she died.

The thought chased itself on a loop in her mind as she experienced the last seconds of her life in a blur of blue-gray color with the biting cold air snapping at her skin.

There was so much she still wanted to do—needed to do. So many apologies to make and paths of forgiveness to forge. She would never heal the wounds between her and Paris. She would never again ride bareback on Quintessential through wildflowers in the peak of summer. She would never get the chance to take back her throne. To honor Miriam properly.

She would never see Nikita again. Never get to thank him for the kindness he had shown her, for the friendship he offered her, for the small kernel of hope in her chest he had fostered.

We'll get through this.

Together.

Prickling tears budded in the corners of her eyes, only to be instantly whisked away by the wind.

She did not want to meet Kielle and Selene with so much of her life left unwritten.

It was there, with her body tumbling through clouds and her screams echoing across the expanse of cerulean sky, that Deming realized she truly, deeply, honestly did not want to die.

It was a shame she no longer had a say in the matter.

Blood poured from her thigh, scattering droplets in the sky like ruby stars. Her vision swam and her eyelids hung heavy.

Deming closed her eyes and sent one final prayer out into the world as the snow tipped trees grew larger. Not for her. For the ones she was leaving behind.

A prayer for forgiveness, and a hope for a peaceful life.

The world grew quiet and small as death became imminent.

And then, out of nowhere, she was not falling anymore.

All of her momentum shifted sideways in one, aggressive motion. Her head slammed into something firm and warm, her body was suddenly cradled by two strong arms, one around her chest and the other beneath her knees.

Her eyes snapped open, chest heaving, and for a moment the fog of blood loss lifted.

"You didn't think I would let you die, did you?"

Nikita.

Relief like ice water crashed into her.

Deming couldn't help the unhinged laugh that escaped her. She leaned her head back and howled into the wind, the narrow escape of death plunging her into a temporary fit of insanity. She laughed until her chest ached and the tears streaming down her face were from relief, not fear, and stopped only when the uncontrollable shaking in her fingers slowed to a gentle tremble.

The smirk in Nikita's voice was audible as he shook his head and said, "Just say thank you, you wicked woman."

Her heart twinged. It was like he knew.

"I'm not wicked," Deming breathlessly corrected, marginally collecting herself and the wild emotions of her beating heart. She wiped her mouth with the back of her hand, grimacing when it came away smeared wet and red. She leaned over Nikita's arms and spat, clearing out the metallic tang of blood as best she could.

The brutality of what she had done was undercut by the palpable release of tension that washed over at the realization that she was safe. She would not be whisked away and captured. She would not die on impact or snap her spine from the fall and languish before death.

Nikita was here.

She looked up at him. Sweat mingled into his hairline and dripped down his temple, his cheeks were flush from battle. A shallow, arcing cut had been newly bestowed on his face. It curved from his temple to his chin and was inflamed and puckered despite the thinness of the actual wound.

Deming reached a hand up and brushed the pad of her thumb underneath the cut. Nikita shivered delicately under her touch. He tightened his grip on her waist and legs, careful to avoid the jagged gash on her thigh.

They were a tattered, bloody pair.

"Thank you."

Then she felt her head roll back as the gravity of her wound reclaimed its hold and she lost consciousness.

CHAPTER SIX

NIKITA

HER HEART RATE WAS dropping.

With each second that passed he could feel it slow down, down, down until it was barely a feather's pulse keeping her tethered to life.

Nikita pressed her thigh tighter against him, trying to staunch the blood, but the pressure of one hand could do little against a wound of this scale. She needed cauterization. She needed sutures. She needed something—

A frustrated yell slipped past his lips and was instantly lost in the torrent of wind rushing past him. Panic held him in a vice-like grip but there was no time to give in to those emotions. Deming needed him to get her to safety.

So The Prince of Runne swallowed his fear like he had done his entire life, clutched the fading woman to his chest, and shot through the sky.

Never had he pushed the limits of his wings like this. His back ached, his wing joints screamed. The winter air clawed at his skin and hair and clothes as he flew towards camp.

If he was in the mood to thank the gods, he may have considered it at the sight of Vallyn and Ilysse piling up bodies, no longer fighting. With Deming limp in his arms, he was not.

He would thank them if she survived.

"Hartford!" His warning cry echoed through the thin winter air.

Tent flaps whipped open and dark skin and antlers nestled into tightly coiled hair appeared. Long strips of cotton for wrapping and their bag of ramshackle medical tools were already in her arms as the female darted on sure-footed hooves towards the center of camp.

Nikita threw open his wings and his upper back strained as both his and Deming's weight resisted the sudden halt. Feet skidding only slightly on the landing, he fell to his knees and laid Deming down with the grace one reserved for hand blown glass or flower petals.

"Serrated edge knife to her thigh. Roughly an inch deep and a foot long." Nikita nearly choked on the description. He had seen more than his fair share of gore in his lifetime but it was so much worse seeing Deming in this state.

He'd seen those he loved hurt before—Ilysse had more scars than he did—but this, seeing the amber eyed heir crumpled and lifeless, was like nothing he had experienced before. There was something about her that inextricably tied her to him. He had felt it since the very first time he laid eyes on her.

Then, too, she had been in peril. Clothes torn and stained, terror reflected in her glassy eyes before they slammed shut and her body tensed in the anticipation of death.

Would they ever get a chance to know each other in peace?

Would death follow them like a shadow their whole lives?

Vallyn crouched beside him, leaning over Deming. "She's still breathing!"

"Oh, gods," Paris whispered to himself from the edge of the chaos. "That's too deep. She's lost too much blood."

Her entire lower half was stained maroon. Blood seeped out of her, soaking into the muddied snow and grass she lay on. The blade had ripped her skin chaotically, leaving a jagged tear that spanned most of her thigh. Muscle protruded up and outward like some sort of twisted, fleshy flower opening its petals. Flashes of white could be seen from certain angles.

"He missed the femoral artery," Hartford said without looking at Paris. Her deft fingers traced the wound, alert eyes analyzing what needed to be done to save her. "If we can limit blood flow to the leg she might pull through."

"What do you need?" Nikita ignored them all, speaking only to Hartford.

"A tourniquet."

He spun around to grab something, anything, but Ilysse was already there with lengths of torn clothes.

She tossed the rags to Hartford who caught them in one hand.

"Lift her hip," Hartford commanded, "gently."

Nikita slipped his hand under Deming's hips and back. A breathy groan escaped her lips at the movement and his wings flared out at the sound. Was she waking?

"Watch it!" Vallyn growled, shoving feathers out of her face.

Hartford slid the fabric under her thigh, then up as high as she could towards Deming's hip. Once it was above the wound, she wrapped it fully around Deming's leg once and pulled so hard the skin around it bulged out under the pressure. After securing the tourniquet with a double knot, Hartford paused over the leg, watching it intently.

One second passed, slow as dripping molasses.

Two seconds.

Three.

Nikita stopped breathing, his lungs simply refusing to pull air into his body as he waited and waited for some sign of lessening blood loss.

Hartford's entire body leaned back. She closed her eyes and placed her bloody hands on her thighs. The softest smile of relief tugged at her lips and only then did Nikita let himself relax. That first inhale was crisp and chaotic and deep.

"Fire and a white hot knife," Hartford muttered, eyes still closed, "please."

Calm with the knowledge that if Hartford was content, Deming would live, Nikita left her side. His fingers brushed across Deming's forehead then cheek then bottom lip as he stood and heat tingled through his palm. Gods, he cared so much for her. She was soft but fierce, honest but careful with her words. She was as beautiful to talk to as she was to admire.

Even now, skin peppered with purple bruises and mud matted into her red and pink tangled curls, she was painfully beautiful.

"How did you know how to do all that?" Paris asked, face full of awe. "I thought you were in politics."

Hartford shot him a sad sort of smile as she began gently cleaning the wound. "I used to be a medic."

A fire soon flickered to life beneath Nikita's hands. He pulled a knife from one of the sheaths on his leg and placed it in the flames. The blade heated slowly in the caress of the flames, twigs popping and crackling beneath it.

"What's that?"

Suddenly, the world fell away.

Nikita didn't comprehend who had asked the question, nor what they were referring to. He couldn't possibly because at that exact moment, his world shifted so dramatically he nearly collapsed.

There was nothing—darkness and midnight so void of life he couldn't see, couldn't hear.

Then, there was everything.

With the speed and force of a lightning strike, fate snapped to life inside him. Stars sparkled within his chest, dancing along the thread tying him completely, irrevocably to another. Thin and delicate and golden and stronger than any tangible material, it urged—demanded—he find the other tether.

Nikita knew before he turned around where he was being drawn to.

Who he was being drawn to.

As if connected by some invisible string, his gray eyes found their amber counterparts.

Deming's lashes were wet with tears, her breathing erratic, but her eyes were steady as they bore into his.

Awake and alive, she looked at nothing but him. The dullness that had filmed over her gaze for so long now melted away as something clicked into place between them and Nikita felt more at peace than he had the capacity to believe possible.

Anything that wasn't Deming fell away, blurred into a background of white snow and green pines and blue sky.

There she was.

His mate.

Nikita was numb as the bond settled into his bones.

Could she feel it?

How could she not?

Hartford's voice broke the glassy moment. "She's awake!"

Deming blinked then, her face pulled as the pain registered and she screamed.

Without consciously moving, Nikita found himself by Deming's side. He cradled her head in his lap. Her skin was hot, feverish. The back of her neck was sweaty against his leg. His mind was swimming, rocking like a ship about to capsize at the magnitude of what had been revealed to him.

Why now? He had an inkling that Deming was more than just a girl he cared for but this...

This was something else entirely.

Were the fates that cruel? With all of the instability and the threat of looming war, was the reveal of the bond to taunt them with the possibility of what a future could look like?

"I wish she would have stayed passed out for this," Hartford said under her breath to no one.

"For what?" Deming grunted between the forceful, choppy breaths she was taking.

"We have to cauterize the wound now that it's clean. You aren't Fae, you'll heal too slowly to ride if we don't."

Hartford's words thrust Nikita down to earth, grounding him in sober reality. She may not have had the same experience as him. Only time would tell if she, too, could feel the bond. Humans rarely did.

And if she didn't?

Nikita's stomach dropped at the thought.

Would he tell her? Should he?

Ilysse brought the knife to Hartford. The metal was glowing with heat, smoke unfurled from the bits of leather on the hilt that had been too close to the fire.

"This is going to hurt," Hartford murmured, brushing wisps of white hair away from Deming's face.

Without any other warning, she placed the blade against Deming's thigh and the sizzling sound of skin crisping filled the air.

Nikita gagged on the scent of burning flesh. He curled his wings around them protectively as if he could take away Deming's pain by cocooning them inside the expanse of black feathers.

Nothing was that simple.

Tears rolled down her cheeks, her mouth hung open in perpetual agony.

Deming hands were gripping wildly at the ground. Her fingers clawed into the hard packed earth by her sides. Dirt and mud coated underneath the fingernails that hadn't cracked.

"Fuck!" She swore through sobs and the pain in her voice pierced Nikita's heart like she had driven a sword through it herself.

No one chastised her language as Hartford placed the blade against her flesh once more.

"Only a few more," Nikita said, coaxing her attention to him. He could barely get the words out. His throat was cracked and dry, his voice as shaken as the bedrock of his world. They had been gifted a mating bond and he had no idea how to process its existence or what it meant for them or their thrones. He had no idea what to think, how to breathe. And what pounded in the background of every thought like a drumbeat was the fear that this bond, however divine, would tarnish what they were already building.

Would she see it as another decision thrust on her? Another bead in the long string of choices taken away from her?

Nikita had no time to mull over any of these worries. Certainly not now, when Deming was in so much pain and they were surrounded by so many others.

He could do nothing but hold her and help her through the pain so as best he could, that is what he did. He spooled up the precious thread connecting them and wrapped it in the depths of his soul, then pulled Deming further into his lap.

"Here," he extended a hand, "Let it out on me when it hurts, not the ground."

"It all hurts," she whimpered.

"I know," he pressed a kiss into the crown of her head. He would place a real, jeweled one there someday. "I'm so sorry. Show me."

Deming locked eyes with him. Her chest heaved as she tried and failed to maintain steady breathing but she did as he bid. She clutched his hand and tightened her grip on his palm with feral ferocity as Hartford sealed sections of her injury once, twice, three times more.

Her face was contorted into twisted expressions of unimaginable pain. Her eyes bulged then snapped shut. The sound of her teeth slamming together sent chills up Nikita's spine. She would crack her jaw if she didn't release the tension another way.

"Scream it out," he commanded.

Like a banshee, she did.

CHAPTER SEVEN

DEMING

DELICATE SHADES OF ORANGE danced across the back of Deming's closed eyelids, beckoning her awake. Sunlight streamed in through the tears in the tent walls and she yawned, wide and restful.

She had managed only a few blinks before the events of yesterday came barreling into her consciousness.

She shot up, palms pressed to the bedroll. Her eyes darted around. Weather-proof fabric pitched upwards at an angle around her. Two rucksacks leaned against each other in the corner. A small, waxy bag was tipped over, spilling sweet stone fruits on the floor.

Her tent, she was in her tent.

Nikita had caught her and brought her back to her tent.

She was safe.

Chest heaving, pulse racing, Deming put a hand to her heart and begged it to slow its panicked beat.

Adrenaline still coursing through her body, Deming made to shift the blankets off her. The largest was twisted around her legs—

Her fingers stopped just above the thickly woven wool.

Like a deer before a predator, she froze. Confusion rippled through her. Why was she not in pain? Had she dreamt the knife wound?

Before she could consider anything else, Vallyn's head poked through the tent flaps.

"Hey, Ilysse heard you shuffling around. How are you—" One look at the distress in Deming's face had Vallyn flying to her side. "What is it? What's wrong?"

Deming considered the question carefully. She wasn't quite sure what was wrong. The fog of sleep had not yet fully dissipated. She was having a hard time grounding herself in reality. The whiplash of going from unconscious and nearly dead to awake and somehow in no pain at all had rattled her.

"I..." she licked her lips, eyebrows furrowed, "my leg doesn't hurt."

Vallyn cocked her head in question.

"I was stabbed, wasn't I?" Deming looked up, begging her friend to confirm she wasn't going insane.

"Badly." Vallyn's eyes narrowed. "You almost died from blood loss."

Deming breathed out heavily. The air puffed like miniature clouds in the cold. "You didn't give me any poppy?"

She shook her head. "We couldn't find any." Then, skeptically, she added, "Well, let's look. The bandage should be changed anyway."

Deming nodded and removed the blanket, pulling her slip up and away from her thighs so Vallyn had access.

The linen wrap was stained maroon. The evidence of how close she was to never waking up again was plain as day and yet Deming wasn't feeling the throbbing, jaw-clenching pain that should accompany an injury like the one she sustained.

"Prop your leg up, if you can."

Deming obeyed, putting a slight bend in her knee.

Vallyn untucked the end of the fabric and began unwrapping the wound. Around and around, until Deming's skin was finally visible.

The linen wrap fell from Vallyn's hands and time slowed to a drip.

Both women stared at the sight before them, frozen and unable to speak.

A thin, dewy, perfectly healed scar rested where mauled flesh had been only hours before.

The puckered skin laced up her leg like the delicate ribbons she once wore, twisting back and forth with all the chaos of the original wound but none of the blood and gore and agitation.

Deming couldn't find it in herself to look away from her leg as she whispered hoarsely, "Are you seeing what I'm seeing?" From her peripheries, she saw Vallyn dip her chin shakily. "How..."

"It's not possible..."

She pressed a finger gently down on the scar. Only the slightest twinge of pain flickered through her.

"Let me get the others." Vallyn fled out the tent without so much a backwards glance.

Catching her breath, Deming pulled her fingers away from the scar they traced and placed both palms on the ground. Praying this wasn't some elaborate illusion and she wouldn't be in a world of pain after attempting to do so, she tucked her legs underneath her and pushed off the ground.

It was shaky and not without tenderness, but her legs were able to bear her weight.

Impossible...

Deming tested the strength of her muscles, shifting her weight back and forth between legs. There was definitely some soreness, it felt like the deep tissue in her thighs were bruised, but nothing more than she had experienced in the height of her training with Vallyn.

How—

Light flooded the tent as Nikita barreled into the room, everyone else hot on his heels. His gaze immediately scanning Deming from head to toe. His eyes flared wide when they saw the pink scar trailing up her leg and disappearing underneath the black fabric of her slip, then snapped to hers.

Her head tilted subconsciously.

Something was different about him, about the way he was looking at her.

Like morning light filtering through fog, a memory from the day before surfaced.

She had been lost, drowning in black nothing and pain, then, suddenly, he was there. Storm gray eyes boring into her own.

Nikita.

He had pulled her out of dreamless unconsciousness like she was a moth and he the flame.

It had been the most curious feeling.

"How is this possible?" Paris approached Deming warily, edging out from behind Nikita's flared wings. "That wound was," he grimaced, swallowing hard, "intense. You shouldn't be able to move that leg at all, let alone stand."

Unable to give him answers, her honeyed eyes roamed the room. Everyone wore the same hesitantly worried expression.

"I'll ask again, do any of you know what this is?"

Hartford's voice cut through the air, dragging all eyes to her.

Held between her thumb and index finger was something small, dark, and not quite round.

Deming cocked her head to the side. She leaned forward, trying to get a better look. It looked like a pebble.

"I pulled it out of you as I was stitching you up," Hartford told Deming before turning to the others.

Blonde braids swished through the air. Ilysse peered over Paris's shoulder. "What do you mean what is it? I told you yesterday, it's nothing. A rock or something that got stuck under her skin during the fight."

Vallyn scoffed. "What naturally occurring rock do you know that is perfectly round and smooth?"

"Something from the ocean, I don't know," Ilysse growled through bared canines. "What do you think it is?"

"Some kind of condensed healing magic?" Vallyn shot back.

"That only heals her when it's taken out of her body?"

"You're being purposefully antagonistic."

"I'm being realistic—"

Nikita held up a hand that silenced both of them with the exception of one, final, huff from Vallyn accompanied by an exasperated head tilt and flexed hands curling into fists by her side.

In the silence, the beginnings of an idea whispered to Deming.

Her face pulled on instinct, but there was a cruel seductiveness about it all that coalesced the whisper of thought into something more.

Nikita caught the movement, as he caught everything she did. He was attuned to her acutely so, curiously so. "What is it?"

She hesitated. If she spoke the words out loud, there would be no turning back, no denying the part she had to play. There could be no more wallowing in grief. She would have to face her fears and culpability if she were to truly take on what she was about to suggest.

"Deming?"

She looked at Nikita and a sense of quiet calm washed over her. Whatever was hidden within the tangled words of the seer for her couldn't possibly be worse than what they had already survived.

"Do you still have the prophecy?"

Nikita looked at her curiously. "Yes, why?"

Deming sighed, gathering her courage. "I'd like to hear it. Not secondhand," she clarified, willing her voice into steadiness, "the original prophecy as it was spoken."

"Are you sure?" Nikita asked.

There it was again, something different about his features, his voice.

Deming's eyes roamed the face she had come to know as well as her own. Was he hiding something?

She blinked, realizing she had been staring instead of answering him.

"Yes. I'm sure."

His question nor her answer mattered not. Hartford had already slipped out of the tent. Deming had sealed her decision the moment the words fell from her lips and she was fine with that.

Perhaps it was time to stop running from her fate.

Cool air wound its way from outside, brushing against her cheeks and ears and tugging at her unbound hair. To keep her hands busy while Hartford retrieved the prophecy, Deming reached back, gathered her hair, and twisted the entire length in on itself once. The loose knot was a swirl of shades of red, pink, and white and rested neatly at the back of her neck.

The distinct, clipped sound of hooves announced Hartford's return moments before she ducked through the flaps.

The unfamiliar object pulled from Deming's thigh remained in one hand. In the other was a bone white, conical shell. Bereft of cracks or impurities, the shell was impossibly smooth with sharp, needle thin points capping both ends.

Deming's heart fluttered.

"So impractical," Paris muttered.

Ilysse gave him a withering look. "I don't remember asking for your opinion on our traditions."

His hand jutted towards the shell. "The fate of the continent wrapped inside a shell?" He looked around the room for support. "I can't be the only one who thinks that's ridiculous."

"The prophecy picks its container," Hartford said calmly. She handed the shell to Deming. "For this one to have chosen something so…breakable," she inhaled deeply, "I don't know. Maybe it's more subject to change than others."

Deming held the shell in her hands with care. It was fragile, delicate, like many beautiful and terrifying things are. She had expected it to be cool to the touch but it was not at all. A pleasant warmth seeped from it into her palm.

"How do I—"

Nikita tapped his ear. "Lift it up."

The soft edge of the shell rested against her skin and like it had been spun into the air with magic, a melodic voice began echoing in her ear.

"To war and blood we will succumb.

What was lost will now be known.

Ash and dust from feather and plum,

Beware the festering throne.

Born of light, a savoir is near.

The truth forgives what you see.

For life to thrive she must adhere,

The uncrowned queen is the key."

Over and over and over, the seer repeated the prophecy.

The uncrowned queen is the key.

She had known those words already, known she was somehow inextricably tied to the fate of the continent, but to hear them in the seer's own voice sent chills up her spine.

Deming pried the shell from her ear and the voice fell away.

Paris leaned forward, eager. "What did it say?"

She repeated the harrowing words. The rhyme felt like both poison and honey on her tongue.

"The prophecy has been lingering in the fabric of our continent for over two decades now," Ilysse said, "laying in wait. Since the seer's vision, there has only been one female heir born in any queendom, kingdom, or territory on the continent."

"Me," Deming whispered.

"You," Nikita said, "and there has been no unrest that warranted our venture into Arsaela to watch and protect you until recently."

"What do you mean?"

"Stories here and there. Hunters coming back from the mountains with tales of animals acting out of character. Rumblings of dissent brewing in Laey. Just...oddities that piqued our interest enough. We couldn't risk anything happening to you, so we went to Arsaela and waited for things to unfold."

Deming scoffed at that. Pain and disbelief jarred the sound so it came out unnatural and gruff. "Unfold. Yeah. That's a nice way to put it."

Deming let the new knowledge float around them for a moment, then sighed. The reason she had asked to hear the prophecy in the first place hummed at the forefront of her mind.

She touched the pink scar on her thigh. "Could this be connected to the prophecy?" Deming tossed her chin towards the round, foreign object in Hartford's cupped palm. "Could that?"

Vallyn shifted her weight. The movement aligned one of the knives strapped to her thigh with a beam of light streaming into the tent. The metal gleamed as she spoke, her face furrowed in thought. "We need to know what it is, first, before we make any assumptions about whether it is or is not related to the prophecy."

"Well," Ilysse clapped her hands together, "I'm pretty sure there's only one female with the skillset and discretion we need to go to with this."

A soft, knowing smile pulled at the corner of Nikita's mouth, his gaze shifting to Hartford who was in turn looking at Ilysse. Her spine was straight in anticipation, her eyes glistened with hope.

"Hartford," Ilysse asked, tossing the ends of her braids over her shoulder, "does Soraya still live near Bascade?"

CHAPTER EIGHT

NIKITA

Nikita had thought of nothing else since the bond revealed itself. Even his dreams were full of her. Her face, her eyes, her gentle voice, her intoxicating smell, the warmth of her body against his. He laid down at night to sleep and mirages of her painted themselves against his closed eyelids.

He had thought of their bond when exhaustion had dug its claws into her and she fell asleep after Hartford cauterized her injury. He had thought of their bond when she blinked at him, fresh off the surprise of her healed leg. And he thought of their bond now, begrudgingly sitting astride his horse, Pascal, who was plodding along dutifully east towards Bascade.

Always, in every moment, he thought of her.

Even the dread of returning home paled in comparison to the awe he felt at the golden fate tie tethering him to Deming.

Hartford's mate, Soraya, lived on the outskirts of Bascade, the capital city of Runne, and was raised under the literal wing of a talented apothecary. She would have access to Fae literature that may be helpful, as well as ways to test the material of the object plucked from beneath Deming's skin for traces of magic, malignant and benign alike.

He hoped desperately it was benign.

She had gone through so much already, they all had. The last thing they needed was something else to worry about. Not when Deming, Paris, and Vallyn were still mourning all they lost. Not with the prophecy hanging around their necks like a noose. Certainly not when they were inching closer to the capital city of Runne with every step.

Nikita's grip on his reins tightened, leather biting into his palm. Pascal nickered.

He reluctantly conceded that the last bit might be an issue only for him.

Everyone else was eager to go, no one more so than Hartford. She was over the moon to be heading to Bascade. Her unbound joy at the prospect of seeing Soraya after so long was more than enough for him to put his own reservations aside. Let alone the fact that Soraya would almost certainly be able to give them some answers.

The poking at scars and reopening of wounds that he felt stirring within him with each breath could be contained, needed to be contained. The world did not revolve around him, and he had put that relationship in the grave a long time ago.

Warmth thrummed through him and he smiled softly as Deming urged her own horse forward to walk shoulder to shoulder with Pascal.

Her eyes were inquisitive, bright.

Gods, he had missed that look.

"Can I help you, princess?" The corner of his mouth pulled upwards.

"You've been quiet."

He glanced at her sideways through his lashes and lifted an eyebrow.

Deming rolled her eyes. "Is there anything you want to talk about?"

He sighed heavily. Such a weighted question, one she couldn't fully understand the implications of.

More than anything he wanted to talk to someone, anyone, about their mating bond. He wanted to know if she had felt it too, if she was tiptoeing around talking to him about it in the same way he was. He wanted to know what it meant for their lives, their reigns.

And like an undertow, there was the ever present pressure of his father.

What would his father think of his son being bonded to a human? Any children they might bear would be mages, infertile and unable to continue either the Magdalene or Elyachar lines.

He was getting too far ahead of himself.

There could be no thought of heirs now. Deming hadn't shown any indication she was ready for a relationship at all, let alone a mating bond. And she certainly hadn't spoken of children. Nikita wasn't sure she even wanted any.

As deeply as he felt for her, he could rationally admit they didn't know each other well enough to even begin thinking about anything like that.

Besides, his father would be a beast of an issue even without the reveal of the bond.

Nikita was not pious, but he had prayed every night since they decided to go to Bascade that they would not have to interact with that man. He asked every god and goddess in the pantheon that they could speak with Soraya and leave without anyone else noticing.

The drifting thought of Trevelyan Magdalene, King of Runne, across Nikita's consciousness was enough to make him shudder.

There was too much buried there. Too much history, too much hurt. As much as he had tried to let go of everything his father did to him, the fingerprints of rejection had burned themselves into his soul.

The mess of a father shunning a son for something he had no control over was not something easily untangled.

Did he want to talk about all of that?

With everything in him, yes. And in the same breath, he simply didn't have the words nor the energy to sift through it all.

"No, princess," he landed on wearily, "there is nothing I want to talk about."

He could see her face scrunch up from the corner of his eyes.

"That's not true and you know it."

Nikita's wings dropped slightly, feathers brushing the soft hide and legs of his horse. The stallion flicked his tail to and fro trying to rid himself of the sensation.

"You shouldn't keep to yourself like this," Deming continued.

"Deming—"

"No, I'm serious." She tried to make eye contact with him but he would not move his gaze from the winding road in front of them. "It's not healthy."

Nikita shook his head. He could feel the sharp point of his ear cut through locks of dark, wavy hair with the movement. "It's not that simple." His voice was strained. Every word she spoke pressed on the carefully constructed wall he had built to protect himself from his family. Again and again, her soft voice rallied against the stone in his mind, begging to be let in, begging to be someone he could rely on.

Unfortunately, he had learned long ago that relying on anyone but himself was a lost cause.

"It could be if you opened up. I know you're grieving your relationship with your—"

"And you are qualified to give advice on this, are you?"

The words snapped out of his lips before he could stop them.

"You, who refused to speak to us for weeks? You, who suppressed your emotions so much you ended up mauling your face when they escaped? You, who still cannot find it within herself to pick up her training again? I should be taking advice on how to grieve from you?"

The second his words settled around them like flakes of snow falling to the ground, he was filled with regret.

Deming recoiled as if his words had physically struck her. The sting of rejection and embarrassment flooded plain as day across her eyes. Her cheeks turned brilliant red. A cool breeze lifted strands of hair away from her face so every inch of hurt was visible.

She chewed on the torn skin of her lip, rough and cracked in ways it had never been before due to her sudden prolonged exposure to the elements. She winced as she bit too far.

Nikita could see blood well. He watched her tongue flick the ruby bead away.

He desperately wished to go back in time and scoop his words from the air before they reached her. The venom in them was not meant for her.

"I'm sorry—"

"You did nothing wrong—"

"I pushed too much, I—"

"Deming, please. Look at me."

Her eyes were laden with the same sadness that had filled her frantic apologies. Her lip wobbled. She was sitting stiff and still in the saddle, so unlike the way her hips normally rolled with the shifting weight of the horse.

Everything about the sight made Nikita's heart contract. He didn't think he had ever hated himself more than he did in that moment.

He could feel a tidal wave of emotion cresting in his chest. He was usually so careful about letting anything slip through the cracks of his facade. His issues with his father... those were to stay tucked away safely where they could hurt no one but him.

He didn't know what it was about Deming that thinned the veil between his two worlds. It couldn't just be the fate tie. Mating bonds didn't work that way. They were indications of equals, a perfectly matched pair with souls that bled together like ink drops in water. It was a nudge from the gods, but it could be ignored. And it certainly wasn't capable of peeling back layers of someone's past, leaving them raw to the world.

No, whatever it was about Deming that made him feel this way was something purely, solely to do with her.

"I was wrong to snap at you." He hoped she could see the sincerity in his eyes, hear it in his voice. "No matter how...irrational being this close to Bascade makes me, it will never be okay to speak to you like that."

Her chin dipped. She sucked her bottom lip into her mouth and bit down like she was on the verge of saying something but thought better of it.

He sighed, then pulled on Pascal's reins. The horse slowed to a stop, his hooves crunching in the frozen grass that poked through patches of snow.

Deming's mare walked a few more feet before coming to a stop. The two horses huffed and threw their heads.

"Can we start over," Nikita said, "please?"

The winter wind wound its way around Deming. She looked ethereal atop her roan mare in the forest. The white of her hair blending into the snow seamlessly while the pink and red danced wildly, bright as comets.

The thought of that hair against the backdrop of the clouds darted across the backs of his eyelids.

Nikita dismounted.

Deming peered down at him curiously.

He looked over his shoulder and made eye contact with Ilysse. He held up the reins and she nodded. She dug her heels into her own horse, jaunting up to them to tie their horses to hers.

With his second on her way, Nikita let the leather fall and closed the gap between him and Deming. He offered a hand to her.

"Will you fly with me?"

"Why?"

Her question was accompanied by her own dismount. Her hand slipped into his, accepting his offer regardless of his answer. His calloused palms snagged on the delicate latticework of her fingerprints and, like always, he felt her touch deep within his bones.

"I'm at my best when I'm in the air," he said honestly, "and I'd like to be at my best for you right now, for this conversation."

She lifted her free hand and tucked white tendrils of curled hair behind her ear. The air tugged at it relentlessly, and within seconds it was free once more, brushing across her cheek and nose.

Nikita felt his lips pull upwards at the inability of her hair to be tamed. No matter how she wore it—braids, ribbons, loose—it remained wild. He loved that about her, it felt like a subliminal representation of her spirit.

A ghost of a smile graced her features, mirroring his own. "Let's visit the clouds."

Nikita slipped his arms around her, one under her knees and one behind her back. It felt right to be this close to her. The subtle strain of the muscles in his shoulders and back as the weight of her settled into his was pleasant.

He opened his wings to their full length and reveled in the pleasure of seeing Deming's amber eyes flood with awe.

Then with a slight bend to his knees and two beats of his wings, he carried his mate into the sky.

They soared above the trees. His wings cut through clouds like butter. The air grew sharp and crisp the higher they rose but Nikita held Deming close and with her wool coat and his body heat, he knew she would be warm enough to withstand the cold.

The bite of the atmosphere had never bothered him. Conversely, with every crack of wind or flurry of snow that hit his cheeks he drew closer and closer to what he imagined freedom felt like.

When he finally leveled them out, they were high above the continent. The winding road below was a ribbon lacing through the patchwork forest. Their companions, flecks of barely visible movement.

"Everything is so beautiful up here." Deming's voice was full of wonder. "I feel so at peace."

Her hair wound around them both like extensions of the wind. It was exactly as he had pictured. Nikita smiled. He loved that she loved being able to see the world like this as much as him. Twin souls.

"I feel the same. It's easy for me to think clearly up here."

She rested her head against his shoulder. He allowed himself a moment of relaxed joy at the simplicity of flying with her.

"Do you remember what I told you during Midwinter? About my banishment?"

Deming nodded solemnly as she echoed his own story back to him. "You were given the mark of a Rider as a child," her hand pressed into his chest as if she could feel the faded, incomplete whorls beneath his vest, "but it faded over time. You never bonded with an amphithere and your father held it against you."

Her nails curled into his chest. Her voice could cut glass.

A small, vindictive part of him loved that someone else held vitriol for his father.

"You've heard the prophecy now," he continued, "but there is more to the story there, too."

Her neck careened upwards. Curiosity fell across her features like a curtain. "The seer's vision ties into your relationship with your father?"

"Intricately so." Nikita's back pulsed with each wingbeat. He let the calming motions of flight settle the nerves bubbling in his gut. He never spoke about this.

But he needed to—wanted to—with her.

"How much do you know about the history of Riders?"

"Not much," she admitted, "only that they are exceedingly rare and usually Fae."

"True on both accounts." As he spoke, Nikita pretended it was lore about someone else to ease the dizzying sensation of speaking about the King of Runne and the prophecy that laid waste to a family.

"Amphitheres have been the symbol of Runne royalty for as long as Fae have walked the continent. Like leodins in Laey or beathors in Monstakar, amphitheres are concentrated in our territories. There is the nest of amphitheres that reside in the Draconic Isles that have bat-like wings and horrid temperaments." Deming laughed and the vibration sent pleasing chills up Nikita's spine. He gave her a squeeze and ran a thumb up and down her arm. "And then there is the feather-winged nest that resides in the Telaciens."

Interested, deep golden eyes glowed up at him. "My Telaciens?"

He met her gaze through his bottom lashes. "Even future queens don't own mountain ranges. But yes," his lips pressed just below her hairline, her skin was soft beneath them, "your Telaciens."

She smiled shyly, dipped her head down, and snuggled into the warmth of his neck.

"The Telacien nest is led by the Crest Major—always the eldest amphithere and the only one able to grant a Rider bond. The current Crest Major, Daughlr, has reigned over the nest for three centuries. All those years, yet he had never seen fit to dole out a Rider bond until I came to the nest."

The Crest Major's name tasted like poison in his mouth. He hadn't spoken it aloud in years. Nikita wouldn't dare be disrespectful to the most powerful amphithere on the continent, nor did he want to. It was just that he had never understood why the amphithere had chosen to give him a bond and then peel it away so slowly and tragically it left scars.

What was the point? Was it a mistake? A test?

Nikita swallowed the emotion rising in his throat.

"My father only brought me to the nest because of the prophecy."

Nikita could tell by the way her body tensed that Deming was itching to ask questions, but she refrained, remaining still and quiet in his arms. He clutched her tighter and trudged onward.

"As you know, the prophecy speaks of war and bloodshed, of a future rife with conflict and an uncrowned queen being the key. The seer gave this reading on the night I was born."

At that, Deming's restraint broke. Her neck tilted upwards, brows furrowed and eyes hesitant. "The night you were born?"

"Nearly the exact same time I was pulled from my mother's womb, yes."

"That feels…important."

Nikita pressed his tongue into the back of his teeth to prevent emotion from spilling over his features. "My father thought so, too. The reason Riders are so rare is because bonds are only gifted during times of intense struggle or hardship—times when the fate of the continent is tipping on the edge of destruction or survival. So, when the prophecy was given at the same time as my birth, he took it as a sign that I would be the next Rider. The first Rider in four hundred years. It would be the highest honor to ever be bestowed on the Magdalene family and would secure our reign for centuries to come."

The night his father told Nikita about the prophecy and his perceived role in it he had been young, barely five. The memory was hazy and some details were lost to time, but Nikita could still remember the heat of the flames roaring from the fireplace, the warmth of the stone beneath his palms. He could still remember the way his father looked at him with hope as he wove the tale of how he, the young prince of Runne, would one day not only bond with an amphithere but save the continent.

Looking back, it was too much to thrust on a boy. But at the time Nikita had felt nothing but excitement and pride. He was chosen. He was honored. He was loved.

Until he wasn't.

"Soon after, he took me to the nest." Nikita scowled against the wind. "You know the rest. I became a stain on the family, a source of shame. My father couldn't look at me, couldn't stand to be around me. He banished me. A carousal of servants raised me. Friends were difficult to manage since I was always moving, which is why I value Ilysse so highly. I've been to every city in Runne, but never back to Bascade. I can return to the capital once I restore honor to the family name." He chuckled darkly. "Like I know how to do that. It's a fool's quest. Nothing more than an excuse to have me out of his sight and hide me from the world while he tries for another heir."

His words fell heavy from his lips. The sky swallowed them whole and he hated the way speaking them aloud made him feel worthless and ashamed all over again. This was why he never spoke about his father, why he didn't want to go anywhere near Bascade.

Those old wounds of his had a way of bubbling to the surface and making him feel inadequate despite rational sense telling him otherwise.

And yet...

"Despite all of that," Nikita's head hung low, his heart beat rapidly at the admission on the tip of his tongue, "I still want his love. I want him to be my father again."

There it was. The truth he had buried so far beneath the surface of his anger that he rarely remembered it was there.

He missed his father. He missed his love. He missed the rich tapestry of their relationship. The threadbare one they now tread on was a ghost of what they once were, what Nikita hoped in his heart of hearts they could be again.

It felt delusional to hope for that with the ocean of mistrust between them. Yet, here he was. Adrift on the sea with nothing to cling to except the woman in his arms.

Her hand squeezed his in silent companionship and Nikita was endlessly grateful that she didn't push him to expand further.

"Thank you for sharing, I know that was difficult for you. I understand what you mean," she said quietly, contemplatively, "about wanting your father's love despite everything. As much as I can, anyway. Miriam was as much of a parent to me as my birth mother."

Her voice cracked on Miriam's name and for the thousandth time Nikita wished he could take away her pain.

With a heavy sigh she slumped into his shoulder. "But that relationship feels tainted—murky—in the wake of everything she did."

This was the first time she had spoken about Miriam—about anything that happened those last days in Arsaela at all, really—since they had fled Laey.

"Everything she did was to protect you," he reminded her gently.

"Lies under the guise of protection are still lies."

That was true enough. Eager to keep her talking, Nikita asked, "You feel that she should have told you about the fog? About Khalil?"

Everything that was unveiled in the bowels of Reynes castle had been devastating to Deming. Miriam and Khalil being shadows mages—the former having created the fog that ensnared Arsaela and the latter turning out to be very much alive after a decade of Deming thinking he had perished in the same fire that took her parents—was a lot to process.

These were prominent figures in her life. Miriam had been as close to a mother as one could be in the wake of Samira's death. For Deming to find out Miriam had been withholding not only her own heritage but also the knowledge that Khalil was alive and wanted Deming for some twisted magical experiment of his was daunting to wrap her mind around.

As much as Deming had changed for the better since he had known her, there was a part of Nikita that doubted her ability to handle all of that information well, no matter when it would have been presented to her.

To no fault of her own. He doubted anyone would handle that well.

Reading his mind, she said, "I know, she had her reasons to keep it all from me. She wasn't sure what Khalil wanted with me yet. We still don't." She sighed again. Her body slumped against him as the air whipped at her hair. "It doesn't matter, I guess. The fire, Miriam's death. I'm a jinx. It wouldn't have mattered when she told me. I'm sure I would have ruined it all anyway—"

"You ruined nothing," he said fiercely. He needed her to know that, believe that. "You were made to feel guilty for something that had nothing to do with you."

Only the whistle of the wind could be heard for several long seconds.

Then.

"Just like you," she murmured.

His heart thudded so fast and heavy she must have been able to feel it. Blood pounded through his veins, calling out to her.

Mates. Equals. Twin souls.

Nikita swallowed down the temptation to tell her. It was not the time.

Instead, he echoed her. "Just like me."

Deming turned towards him and pressed her lips to his chest, right above his heart.

Shivers rolled down his spine and through the feathers on the tips of his wings.

They dipped in the air and he thought he heard the semblance of a laugh bubble from her, but it melted into a somber exhale.

"I miss her." Longing drenched each syllable.

"I know. I'm so sorry she's gone."

"I—" She cut herself off and stilled in his arms.

"What?"

"Nothing, I—never mind."

She hadn't pushed him to talk more about his father, and he wouldn't push her to bare more of her soul to him. They would learn about each other at their own pace. Mating bond or not, they were still just two living beings with hearts to be cherished and feelings to be honored.

So they flew through the clouds in comfortable silence for a time. Each passing whisper of wind or sunbeam or cloud remnant cradled their admissions, eased their guilt. To be above the world was to be known by the air and sky and sun and that was the most freeing experience Nikita had ever known. He was humbled beyond measure that Deming was here with him.

When she finally spoke, it was with a delicate fragility.

"I miss Colette, too."

Nikita made sure to still his muscles and keep his grip on her relaxed.

He had wondered about Deming's cousin. Specifically, he had wondered where Deming's head was at with regards to her.

Colette Penrose. Cousin. Best friend. Royalty. As beautiful as a rose. Brilliant red hair and whip smart at court.

Traitor.

How much Colette knew about her father's coup was unknown.

What they did know was that Dresden intended her to be heir. Being the other female in the royal bloodline, it would be permissible so long as the original heir was deemed unfit. Which, thanks to Dresden's machinations, was now believed to be true by the masses of Laey.

They also knew, thanks to the rumor mill in various towns they had stopped in, that Colette was, indeed, wearing a crown and sitting the throne in Deming's absence.

No coronation yet, but it was only a matter of time.

"She's your best friend. I would be shocked if you didn't miss her."

"She was my best friend. Not anymore." Deming tried to stiffen her voice, steel her resolve, but Nikita could hear the vulnerability in her words all the same. "She's a liar and a traitor and I shouldn't miss her. I should hate her." Her fingers curled into her coat, bunching the wool. Her knuckles were white with strain. "Why can't I hate her?"

The plea was desperate, sorrowful.

"I don't know. Because the gods are cruel. Because life is hard. Because we only get so much choice in who we love." Nikita shook his head and repeated himself, "I don't know."

So much heaviness surrounded them. Not for the first time, he wished they were less entangled with the motions of the continent.

"Can we go back?"

He was banking before she finished her request. "Of course."

The air was cooling as evening approached. It would be time to make camp for the night by the time they returned to everyone else.

Nikita thought that they had exhausted the conversation, but just as he caught sight of their horses she spoke again.

"I felt something," she whispered, "when I was dying." The last word was spoken so softly he could barely hear it.

His heart fluttered and he was thankful she was looking out at the forest because if she had been looking at his face, she would have seen the realization dawn in his expression.

Did she know after all?

Deming leaned in closer to him. Her fingers traced nonsensical patterns on his arms.

Wherever she touched, heat followed. Longing swam just underneath his skin like she was singing desire into his very veins.

He wondered if she felt it too, the energy that crackled between her skin and his.

"It asked me to open my eyes." She cocked her head at him, expression curious and tentative. "Was that you?"

His pulse quickened, breath hitched.

She had felt their bond. It had called to her despite her mortality, despite her humanness and lack of magic.

No sooner had hope flickered to life then Nikita pinched it off like a candle wick. The wisps of it sizzled through his veins, smokey and full of heat.

She may have felt the bond, but she hadn't recognized it for what it was.

He couldn't tell her.

Not now, not like this.

She was still healing, had barely begun. He wouldn't force this on her.

"That wasn't me."

Not a lie.

Not the full truth, though.

Deming frowned as if she had been expecting a different answer. She was quiet for a few seconds before speaking once more.

"Nikita?"

"Hmm?"

"I don't ever want to start over, not with you."

His confusion was short-lived, his own words spoken while they were still on the ground poking at his memory.

"I'm not going anywhere."

She shifted against his chest, peering up at him through thick lashes. "I mean I don't want to glaze over confrontation. I don't want to pretend like arguments didn't happen or we don't accidentally hurt each other's feelings sometimes."

Her hand touched the column of his neck and he shivered at her touch. So soft, so gentle. He ached for her hands to roam the rest of him. He pulled her closer as his wings propelled them through the clouds.

"This feels real to me," her voice was thick with vulnerability, "and real isn't perfect."

Emotion tightened around his throat, his voice. "Okay, no starting over." After a beat he added, "Deming?"

She smiled, bright and dazzling, at the sound of her name on his lips.

He would give anything to remain the reason behind that smile.

"This feels real to me, too."

Nikita pressed a kiss on the tip of her nose and her laughter pealed like bells through the air as he flew them back to earth.

CHAPTER NINE

NIKITA

THE MOST DIRECT ROUTE to Bascade was a trail that hugged the Laey border then cut through the easternmost section of the Telacien mountain range. Nikita guessed it would be about a week before they found themselves in the outskirts of Runne's capital.

The prospect of being so close to his father still unnerved him, but after the time spent in the air with Deming, his anxiety had leveled out. Like a tea kettle releasing steam, speaking the hurt and hope buried inside him aloud had eased some of the tension in his shoulders.

He swallowed his last bite of dinner, savoring the gamey flavor and wiping grease from his fingers onto cold blades of grass.

Hartford had found a small glen for them to set up camp for the night. They had fed and watered the horses, pitched their tents, and cooked a small dinner of rabbit and grouse that Ilysse had hunted for them.

Half of their party had dispersed after dinner. Hartford had ducked inside her tent some time ago. Vallyn and Ilysse were talking quietly together as they cleaned weapons.

Deming and Paris remained by the fire with him, though they sat across the pit, their bodies flickering in and out of view as flames licked the air between them.

Their faces were close together, knees touching, and they were speaking softly enough that Nikita could only make out a word here or there.

Jealousy poked and prodded at him, hot and slick in his veins.

Nikita clenched and unclenched his hands. He knew he was being unreasonable. He knew that Paris was not a threat. They had broken up months ago and Deming had been unhappy in that relationship before she had ever met Nikita. He knew that Deming wanted him, was attracted to him.

Still, unwanted jealousy crawled up his spine.

He hated the feeling, hated anything that felt possessive and he knew that Deming would hate it too. It was the recency of the mating bond, he told himself. That was where these irrational feelings were coming from.

The theory did not make him feel any better.

Nikita stood abruptly, grabbed a bandolier full of throwing knives and stalking towards the woods. He needed to clear his head.

"Hey," Vallyn called out, "those are mine."

"I'm borrowing them," he mumbled.

The forest engulfed him with the scent of pine and the quiet of wilderness.

Once the fire of camp was a distant flicker of light and no sounds other than the swish of needles and whistle of wind, he dropped the bandolier.

First knife in hand, he flipped it over and over, catching the leather hilt and letting the familiar weight of it settle his nerves.

Nikita flung the knife towards a nearby tree. It sank into the wood with a satisfying thud.

He had gotten through all twelve in the bandolier and was prying them from the tree when light footsteps crunched in the snow behind him.

He turned to see Deming leaning against the trunk of a tree.

"Hey," she said in greeting, "why did you wander off?"

He didn't feel like embarrassing himself with the truth. "Just wanted a little target practice."

"It's dusk, can you even see where you're throwing?"

Nikita looked from her to the trunk he was standing beside, gesturing to the knives embedded in it. "Does it look like I can see where I'm throwing?"

Deming laughed and Nikita felt any semblance of remaining jealousy melt away.

"Yes," she said, looking up at him as he approached her, knives in hand, "you're quite talented." She nodded towards the marred trunk in the distance. "Show me."

Nikita stepped up and eyed the target. Dark feathers rustled as he adjusted his stance, shuffling his feet with minute movements. He could feel the heat of her gaze on him.

Without any warning he sent the dagger flying. The sharp whistling as it cut through the air sounded in the seconds before it hit its destination.

One moment it was in his hand, the next the hilt was flexing back and forth rapidly from where it stuck out of the trunk.

Deming crossed her arms with feigned petulance. "Anyone could do that."

"Okay, princess." Nikita couldn't keep the amusement out of his voice. "Whatever you say."

"Can I try?"

Nikita nodded and took another knife from the bandolier.

As she raised her hand to accept the offering, Nikita's mind flashed to the last time she attempted training in any capacity. The panic attack that ensued. Nails biting into the soft tissue under her eyes. Hot blood seeping from the self-inflicted wounds.

He was lost in the memory for a moment too long, allowing worry to seize him. Nikita pulled the knife towards his chest and away from her outstretched hand. "You don't have to, Deming."

She met his gaze and smiled. Calmly she said, "I know. I want to."

Her hand did not shake as she grasped the hilt.

Pride and admiration washed over Nikita. So brave, his mate. So strong and resilient.

She twisted her wrist, getting a feel for its weight, then shifted her feet into a fighting stance.

She raised one hand out in front of her and lifted the hand that held the dagger over her shoulder—

"Whoa, there!" Nikita grabbed her wrist. "What do you think you're doing?"

Deming's eyebrows furrowed. "Throwing this dagger at the tree?"

The laugh that escaped his lips was carefree and joyful. "In that stance?"

Deming glanced down at her feet then up at him. "What about it?"

"It's horrendous. You wouldn't hit the broadside of a barn if you threw that right now."

"Rude."

"Truthful."

"Fine," Deming huffed. "What do I need to fix?"

"Wickedly impatient woman," Nikita said, chuckling as he stepped behind her. His hands gripped her hips and tilted them slightly. "Like this."

His chest was pressed into her back and the warmth of her nearly made Nikita forget how to breathe. It was primal, his reaction to her.

Never in his life had he experienced something like this. Common sense and rationality were foreign concepts with her proximity but Nikita managed one piece of advice before stepping away. "The edge of speed and precision is thin, but you need to walk it if you want to land this."

Deming nodded.

She was quiet, still. Her chest rose and fell with deep breaths.

Nikita signaled her to throw.

She whipped her arm forward and let the knife fly.

Nikita watched as it sailed through the forest, hit the dirt, flipped end over end, and skidded to a stop.

Far, far away from the tree.

She hadn't been remotely close.

Her shoulders slumped as she harrumphed in frustration.

Nikita shook his head, a joyous smile plastered on his face. "We'll work on it."

"It's dark out!"

"If thinking the lack of light is why you are a terrible shot helps you sleep at night, by all means run with that."

"Once more," Deming sneered, her nose pinching in feigned offense, "rude."

"My darling Deming, if you haven't figured out by now that I am quite frequently rude I don't know what to tell you." His wings flared slightly, preening under her inflamed gaze.

Beams of moonlight wove through the pines as silence settled between them and the air shifted.

"It's getting late," whispered Deming.

"It is," Nikita replied.

"We should get back to camp."

Nikita hummed softly. The shimmering bubble they were existing in felt impossibly fragile, like they were on the precipice of something grand.

"What were you and Paris talking about?"

The words slipped out unbidden. Her eyes lit up and Nikita knew instantly he had given himself away.

"Were you," she cocked her head to the side, a pleased smirk tugging at the corner of her lips, "jealous?"

"No."

He crossed his arms, then uncrossed them, then propped on hand on his hips.

Dammit, what was he supposed to do with his hands?

She observed him curiously. "Sure." After a moment she added, "I don't do jealous."

"I don't either."

She pulled her bottom lip into her mouth, biting it as thoughts swirled behind her eyes.

Nikita was hit with the overwhelming desire to take that lip between his own. He needed to know what she tasted like, what she felt pressed against him.

He took a step towards her. The air between them was thick with tension.

Her breath hitched and Nikita nearly let out a groan at the sight of blush staining her cheeks. He would give anything to know what she was thinking.

This time it was Deming who took a step forward. Then another. Then another. She moved to him as if he was the moon and she was the ocean and she could not help being pulled to him.

His fingers trembled with restraint, begging to be allowed to touch her, hold her.

"We were talking about you, actually."

"Me?" he questioned, barely able to focus on anything other than their closeness.

"He wants me to be happy."

"And what would make you happy, Deming?"

His voice was husky and low. He didn't know if it was the mating bond or seeing her so close to Paris or simply the innate attraction that had been simmering below the surface of his skin since they met but Nikita wanted to kiss her terribly.

"You."

That one little word was saturated in desire. Deming took the final step, closing the gap between them and placing her hand on his chest.

His eyes darkened, every muscle taut. "Don't say things you don't mean, princess."

Deming paused at his words, but only briefly. When she spoke, it was with more conviction than she had used in a very long time.

"I've spent too long saying things I do not mean. I've spent too long hiding from things I need not hide from. I do not mean to continue denying myself of you, too."

He cupped her cheek like she was made of glass. His calloused thumb stroked her skin absentmindedly and she shivered under his touch.

His wings curled around them and Nikita knew she could feel the butter-soft touch of his feathers graze her calves, the backs of her thighs.

Nikita leaned down. His nose brushed against hers, his mouth following shortly after with a soft, gentle kiss. His hand slid to her chin and lifted her face to his. His mouth hovered over hers.

"Is this what you want?" His breath mingled with hers in the space between their lips.

She nodded.

"Use your words, princess." He ran the pad of his thumb over her bottom lip.

"Yes," she exhaled, "yes, this is what I want."

"Be specific, princess."

"You. I want you. I want you to kiss me."

Hearing those words fall from her lips set his body aflame. Every inch of his skin was on fire with want, with need, for more of her. More friction between their hips, more of her hands on him. Anything as long as it was more.

He dragged his fingers up her back—teasing, slow, languid.

"Please, Kit."

Her whispered plea coupled with his clipped nickname snapped his final thread of restraint.

Nikita closed the distance between them and kissed her.

His lips crashed into hers, warm and fierce and soft and eager all at once and for a brilliant, shining moment time stopped and Nikita forgot who he was.

There was only the feel of her lips on his.

There was only the heat of her body pressed into him.

There was only her daisy and fresh linen scent everywhere, all around him, in him.

On instinct Nikita pressed his hips deeper into hers, needing to feel her against him like he needed to breathe. He was hard beneath his leathers and even the barest contact with her upper thighs sent waves of pleasure rippling through him.

They had spent months denying the fact that this is what they wanted and now they were frenzied with their deepest desires coming to fruition.

Her hands left his chest and though Nikita loved their pressure over his heart, he was eager for her to explore the rest of him.

Nikita moaned against Deming's mouth as she wrapped one arm around him, fingers splaying across his back. Slowly, she moved towards where his wings extended from his shoulder blades, stopping just short of the joint. His muscles flexed underneath her hand.

"Can I?"

"Yes."

Quick, breathless words for both of them. Enough for consent to touch one of the most vulnerable parts of him.

Her fingertips stretched upwards and met soft, downy feathers. Nikita's entire body shuddered at her touch. He knew the moments her fingertips spread through his feathers like they were made of silk that he would be forever ruined. Nothing would ever come close to this feeling.

Deming gripped his hip with her other hand, then slid her palm slowly across his stomach.

Nikita pulled his mouth away from hers and peppered kisses across her jawline, each one harder and breathier than the last as her hand edged towards where they both wanted her to be.

When her hand finally cupped him, he swore into her skin and bit her neck.

She felt so good he saw stars.

Literally.

The forest erupted in a flash of light, so bright and dazzling and out of nowhere that Nikita jerked away from Deming in shock, prepared for an attack.

Eyes wide and voice frantic, she asked, "What was that?"

His eyes darted through the trees, looking for any sign of danger, but abruptly stopped when he got to Deming.

Her hair was tousled, her lips were swollen. She looked so good he wanted to lay her down in the snow and kiss her senseless and he would have were it not for the soft light surrounding her like a halo, slowly dissipating into the night.

"I think...I think that was you."

Chapter Ten

Deming

"Me?"

Deming blinked away the flurry of confusion that consumed her. She looked around the glen once more.

A white dusting of snow blanketed everything. Bark and boughs reached towards a night sky that twinkled with stars. The moon swelled above them, large and luminescent. Selene's light flickered as an owl passed over it, wings wide and broad as it darted away quickly from where Deming and Nikita stood. As if it had been spooked by the sudden flare of light.

There was nothing and no one but them.

Her head hung and eyes fell as she tried to feel anything out of the ordinary inside her. Her heart was racing, her skin felt warm and tingly. But those stemmed from the intensity of the kiss, didn't they?

Her fingers skimmed her swollen lips. Heat spread across her cheeks and down her neck. Even the memory was enough to make her spine arch.

Her body was certainly alight with energy but that couldn't have transformed into...What even was that? Magic?

Humans didn't possess magic.

"That's not possible."

"No," Nikita's eyes roamed her from head to toe, looking for an explanation and finding none, "it isn't."

Seconds later, Ilysse burst through the brush, Vallyn on her heels.

Their eyes scanned the space with the trained, efficient vision of the warriors they were.

Vallyn was the first to sheath her sword. "What happened." Clipped, direct. A leader and guard that needed information.

"I...The light..." Deming stumbled over her words. Her tongue felt too heavy, the thoughts racing through her mind too loud.

"Speak clearly," Ilysse hissed through her canines. The Fae female had yet to retract the razor sharp claws extending from her knuckles.

"Watch your tone," Nikita reprimanded.

"I wouldn't have to watch my tone if someone told me what happened." Feral ferocity coated every word.

Nikita's wings snapped open. Their full length filled the small clearing so fully and so immediately Deming's breath caught in her throat.

"That was a command from your prince, Ilysse."

And just as quickly, the wings folded closed once more, tucked neatly behind his shoulder blades. A display of strength or an impulse, Deming wasn't sure, but it had the desired effect nonetheless. Ilysse stood from her crouch and pulled her claws back. The bone and cartilage slipping into the seams between her fingers just like they would if they had been on a natural lioness.

"We don't know where the brightness came from," Nikita explained, "it flashed out of nowhere."

"What were you doing when it appeared?"

Hartford and Paris approached from the edges of the forest as Vallyn spoke, drawn in by the commotion.

Deming met Paris's eyes and felt a stone sink heavy and fast in her stomach.

Gods, the sight of him made her feel instant regret for the kiss she and Nikita shared, and she hated the feeling. Nikita's lips on her felt divinely promised but she hadn't processed it at all and was certainly not ready to explain herself.

She would give anything for Paris to not know what had just happened, especially after their conversation around the fire. Their friendship was already holding on by a thin, twisting, delicate thread. They wouldn't survive another blow and she couldn't lose him, couldn't lose another friend, her only one left—

Deming took deep pulls of the cold air, tried desperately to quiet her racing heart. She was sure that everyone could hear the pounding beat.

A hand on the small of her back stopped the spiral.

Subtle, soft, and instantly removed.

Just a glancing brush of his fingers along her spine.

"We were throwing daggers." Nikita inclined his head towards the tree in the distance, its trunk chipped and marred from being sliced into repeatedly. "The light flared after Deming's attempt."

She cleared her throat. "I was frustrated that I missed the target and Nikita had said something that aggravated me—"

A scoff accompanied by crossed arms from Ilysse. "Typical."

Deming laughed nervously, still on edge. The half lie sat in her stomach about as well as spoiled milk but it was better than admitting their dalliance. "Yeah, exactly. And then the light flashed."

"Right after Nikita spoke to you?" Paris asked. When Deming nodded he followed up with another question. The one on everyone's mind. "And where did the light come from?"

Deming turned to Nikita, who was already looking at her. He shrugged, deferring to her to share his theory only if she wanted.

Deming bit her lip. "We think," she started, cautious, "that it came from me."

Ilysse straightened and though Deming thought it was in response to the oddity of the claim, when Ilysse spoke it became quickly apparent something else was afoot.

"Did you hear that?"

Molten gold swam in Ilysse's narrowed eyes. She looked directly to Vallyn, who cocked her head and squinted.

"I don't hear—"

Ilysse's nostrils flared. Her head pulled back. "What is that?"

"What?" The simple query from Paris was directed at Deming, not Ilysse.

The group had split into two conversations and it was becoming difficult for Deming to stay focused, to decide where her attention was needed. Unease spread through her.

"We don't know..." Deming turned to Nikita, then quickly back to Paris and Hartford when she saw the former was preoccupied with peering into the forest. "There isn't anywhere else it could have come from."

Hartford hadn't spoken since they gathered, but Deming caught a flash of recognition dart across her rich face. It vanished almost instantly and Deming would have let it go if it hadn't been for the fact that the stag-appointed Fae met her gaze then whipped her head away with speed only someone hiding something could wield.

Vallyn muttered something to Ilysse. The pair scowled and scoured the horizon.

Fully on alert, Nikita turned to them, hand on the hilt of his sword.

Deming stepped towards Hartford and opened her mouth but before she could ask the female what she was hiding a hulking form crashed into her, knocking her solidly onto the hard packed earth.

Her teeth clashed together and her head slammed into the ground, the snow doing little to protect her skull as it rang and rang and rang from the impact.

She blinked rapidly, trying to clear the blurry vision away. She kicked and rolled and desperately tried to get out from under whatever had pounced on her. Heat and growling and coarse fur suffocated her senses.

A mountain lion.

No, not just a mountain lion.

From underneath the ferocious chaos shafts of moonlight glinting off a multitude of sharp needle-like objects protruding from the animal's hide.

Quills.

A leodin.

The sound of steel rang through the air as weapons from every hip were unsheathed.

Deming had no opportunity to question what a leodin was doing this far east.

Not when a paw the size of her chest capped with claws that were more like talons swung towards her head.

She tucked her head to her chest with milliseconds to spare. Claws sunk deep into the winter earth where her head had just been and the leodin yowled in pain as it ripped the paw away.

Deming shimmied further down, breath coming out in pants. Her shirt caught on something, exposing her back to the earth. Skin scraped and bled, but the sting of pain was far away from her at the moment. The only thing Deming could focus on was getting out from under the massive cat before it attempted to take another swing at her.

The beast was too large. She was encased on all sides in muscle and fur.

Deming made the mistake of looking up and froze at the sight.

It opened its maw to snap her head off, hot, putrid breath spilled out. Teeth larger than her forearm and dripping with saliva took up her entire field of vision. Deming shut her eyes and braced herself as death incarnate careened towards her—

Then she was rolling across the ground, carried forward with the momentum from someone heaving the animal off of her.

The beast roared in pain nearby where it now lay, Paris's spear jutting out of its side.

Paris himself was charging at the wild cat with a war cry fit for a king. His mouth split open wide and face pinched with fury. With mere feet to go, he leapt over the yowling animal, pulled the spear out of its side mid air, landed in a crouch, and spun around to once more pierce its flesh with the weapon.

"Deming!"

Her head whipped to the sound of her name just in time to see the hilt of a small sword the length of her forearm sliding across the ground towards her. Deming screeched ungracefully and then swore as the leather-wrapped hilt crashed into her open hand, bending fingers back and pinching skin into the frozen earth.

Vallyn hadn't bothered to look to see if her offering had made it to the heir. The two leodins she and Ilysse were dealing with only allowed her attention to flicker momentarily.

They stood back to back, protecting one another and moving in tandem unlike any pair of fighters Deming had ever seen. Ilysse moved to strike and Vallyn followed. Light and dark, human and Fae, two sides of the same coin. They shifted and stepped in time with each other, flowing like twin currents.

Deming's appreciation of the ease with which they fought together sank like a stone as a realization hit her.

Two leodins. Not including the one that she had just been trapped under.

Deming whirled around, looking at the flashes of fur and claws and quills that darted through the woods like shooting stars.

Confusion rippled through her. Leodins didn't hunt in packs. They were solitary creatures.

Deming spun her body to the other side of the clearing just in time to see Paris take a swipe from a leodin's paw straight to his chest and slam into the tree behind him. His neck snapped to the side and blood splattered the bark as he collapsed to the ground.

The scream that escaped her was guttural. Instinctive and crazed.

She ran to him, praying to any gods that would listen that he would lift his head, move a muscle, anything. They couldn't repair the bond between them if he was dead and Deming knew deep in her bones she would never recover from such a permanent loss.

She flew across the snowy ground, eerily red from the spraying blood that fell from animal, human, and Fae alike. Her heart raced, her arms pumped at her sides. She was nearly to him when the ground behind her shook with the impact of a leodin and she spun to greet the beast.

Nikita had been taking on two leodins at once—a feat Deming would have marveled at had it not been for the impending demise of everyone left alive that she loved—but one of the cats had gotten bored of him, its attention drawn by the sudden movement of Deming darting across the clearing.

She found herself once more facing imminent death. This time, however, she was not yet pinned underneath the weight of the leodin. This time, she had steel.

It was still not exactly a fair match, to be sure, but one in which she had a fighting chance.

The flicker of confidence within her withered within seconds of taking on the predator in front of her.

It paced back and forth, its shoulders moving up and down with feline grace. It extended its paw, as large as a dinner plate, and dug its claws into the earth. It was playing with her, playing with its prey. A low growl rippled from its open mouth, its muzzle drawn back to expose a row of teeth as large as knives.

The animal launched itself at her, claws out, and Deming could only thank good timing and luck that she was able to juke to the left and avoid the mauling that almost occurred.

The leodin was done playing.

It advanced once more, swiping at her. Deming swung the sword and managed to catch the side of its face. It hissed at the measly cut, more enraged than ever, and lowered into a crouch. Its haunches wriggled, waiting to pounce, and Deming looked around for support.

She needed help, she couldn't do this alone. Where was Nikita? Where was anyone—

As if her thoughts summoned him, dark wings swooped across the field and the sound of metal slicing into flesh filled the air. An animalistic scream of pain sounded from the jaw of the leodin. It spun around to find what had caused the wound now gracing its hide, forgetting Deming as its prey long enough for her to scamper away from its reach and curl around Paris, protecting him feebly with the short sword outstretched.

The weapon trembled in her hand and she cursed herself for not continuing to train with Vallyn. If she was unable to protect the ones she loved, what good was she? If Paris died because she couldn't wield a sword properly, what was the purpose of all the time she spent grieving Miriam?

She vowed then and there that if she survived this, if they survived this, she would never again be defenseless.

Nikita's tactic had done the trick, luring the leodin away from them. Deming looked around in shock at the carnage littering the field. Two leodins lay dead. One lay where Nikita had just come from, its neck half severed and blood seeping into the snow. Another lay near Vallyn and Ilysse. The two warriors were now taking on the other leodin as a team.

Deming withheld a gasp as Vallyn swung her sword into the side of its head, knocking it off its feet just enough for Ilysse to slide to her knees and slice her own sword across the underbelly of the beast. Guts and muscle and blood poured over her like a horrendous, demented thunderstorm.

The female smiled wickedly at Vallyn, looking like she was something from a nightmare.

Vallyn grinned wildly back, offering her a hand.

Only one leodin left. With Nikita drawing it away and Vallyn and Ilysse now able to support him, Deming turned away from the battlefield.

She took Paris's head in her hands, ever so gently. Her eyes roamed his body and she felt sick at the sight of his injuries. The leodin had carved into him. Torn skin and muscle rippled away from his broad chest. The cuts were shallow, thankfully. The full length of its claws had missed their mark, but the attack was forceful enough to crack several bones.

Only good luck and the protection of his ribs had saved him from instant death.

If one of the broken bones had pierced his lung, though...

She swallowed her fear.

"Paris," she whispered, "Paris, open your eyes." He did no such thing. "Paris." His name came out as a desperate plea. "Paris, please. You can't leave me. Please, wake up."

She tapped her fingers against his cheek, softly at first, then with more urgency. "Paris, wake up."

Something moved behind her at the same time Nikita screamed her name.

"Deming!" His voice was pure, undiluted terror.

Her unbound hair cut through the air in a tricolored arc as she twisted around to see the last leodin leaping through the air towards her.

Time slowed to a drip.

Moonlight reflected off the extended claws, off the impossibly large canines, off the quills undulating across its muscled neck and chest.

Nikita was just behind the leodin, in flight with wings at their full length and his arm stretched reaching towards the danger. He would never catch the animal. Not in the seconds they had before the beast collided with Deming and Paris.

Closer and closer the leodin soared at her, mouth agape in a wild, ferocious roar.

Deming did the only thing she could do.

On instinct she pushed Paris as far away from her as she could then grabbed the sword lying beside her and drove it upwards, hard, at the exact moment the beast reached her.

Her senses flooded as time resumed and her body was thrust into the trunk of the tree as the weight of the leodin slammed into her. Her neck snapped back and head hit the trunk with a sickening crack.

Stars filled her vision. Yowling and bells and screaming rang in her ears.

Blood poured from the wound, hot and thick. Instantly, Deming's clothes and skin were soaked in it. She gagged at the sensation and smell.

The leodin thrashed on top of her in pain. Deep, cutting pain exploded in her arm as the dying animal sliced frantically into her forearm with a claw.

With one last screech, the leodin tried to clamber off but failed, collapsing in death directly on top of Deming.

Its massive body settled onto her chest. The pressure was so intense, she couldn't inhale at all. She shoved at it with her uninjured arm to no avail. There was no way she would be able to move this much weight.

She wriggled, trying to find some relief from the pressure. Nothing she did changed her position.

Her lungs burned.

She gasped for air but found nothing.

She was suffocating, suffocating, suffocating—

Then Nikita pulled the lifeless body off her and she gasped roughly, dragging precious air back into her burning lungs.

Her chest rose and fell erratically as Nikita fell to his knees before her. His eyes scanned her body for fatal injuries. "Hold still."

As if she could do anything other than regain her breath.

He tore the hem of his shirt and wrapped it around the gash on her forearm, winding the fabric taut but not violently so. Maroon stains appeared instantly, but quickly slowed as the pressure from the binding staunched the flow.

Deming looked to her right and nearly cried.

Paris sat, head bowed and chest heaving as he, too, gulped in air. One arm was wrapped around his waist, the other hovered over his chest, trembling. His hand prodded gently at the torn flesh of his chest. Blood ran in rivulets down his face from a gash on his forehead. His breath, while heavy, sounded blissfully normal.

His lungs were not punctured.

Anxiety and anger and fear and relief simmered in her blood.

He was alive. Paris was alive.

"Not me," she exhaled breathlessly, closing her eyes and leaning her head against the tree, "Paris."

Nikita's hand stayed on her arm for a moment longer, the pad of his thumb gently tracing circles on the heated skin above the wound. One look at Paris, though, and he yelled with authority to the others for help.

Hartford rushed over to them. Her hooves made the barest of sounds as she flew over the snowy ground. As quiet and lithe and delicate as the animal she embodied.

"Can you breathe?" she asked Paris, quickly assessing the slashes across his chest.

"Yes." His eyes were closed in pain.

Hartford nodded to herself then began wrapping long lengths of fabric around his torso. "You broke a few ribs," she told him, "and the cuts will be slow to heal. But as long as it doesn't get infected you should be fine."

"Great." He grimaced, teeth clenched together as Hartford tied off the bandage.

Deming collected herself, forcing her heart rate to slow. Her body was still sizzling with energy and fear. It hadn't yet caught up to the reality that she was safe and alive.

Everyone was safe and alive.

Something eased in Deming's chest as gratitude filled her.

She would be dead if it hadn't been for Paris. He had thrown his spear and distracted the original leodin to save her at the risk of his own life.

Deming supposed they all risked their lives to help one another in some capacity these last hectic minutes, but appreciation swelled in her chest all the same.

No one else had been there to save her in those initial moments. She had been without a weapon and trapped. The leodins had surprised them all, throwing everyone into battle before they could think or organize or get into formation. Even Nikita was too caught up in defending himself from one of the pack to get to her in time.

And still, Paris had been there.

Tears welled in her eyes then burst forth and she was crawling to him before she could think twice.

He held his arm out to her and she tucked herself in close, careful to avoid putting any pressure on the bandaged wound. They were both hurt and sore, their embrace was tender and gentle. Even in pain, though, he pulled her into him.

He held her close and she buried her face into his shoulder. He smelled like home. Familiar and safe. And alive. Gods, she was so happy he was alive.

"Thank you," she mumbled into his bloody shirt, "for saving me and for not dying."

She could feel laughter rumble through his chest.

"Why would I not save you, Deming?"

She wrapped her arms tighter around him. The man who shared so much of her history. Her last connection to her childhood. "With everything that's happened to us, what I did to us…" She trailed off, not able to speak directly to the ocean of pain that lay between them.

He placed a chaste kiss on the crown of her head. "I would save you a thousand times over, Deming. Whether or not we're courting, you're still my best friend. I would never let anything happen to you."

Deming bit her lip. Everyone loved her too much, put her on too high a pedestal. She didn't understand it. She was just a girl.

Perhaps, though, she could learn to accept the love others so freely gave her even if she didn't understand why. Perhaps she could let go of the doubt that tinged every corner of her mind, that whispered still she wasn't good enough for the people in her life.

One could be healing and still be worthy of love.

The thought sounded like Miriam as it skated across her mind.

Deming smiled softly.

She sighed, placing a feather soft kiss on the back of Paris's hand before turning to the rest of their ensemble.

They talked amongst themselves, wrapping wounds and wiping blood from weapons and leathers.

Deming made eye contact with Paris, who nodded his affirmation that he would be fine if she left for a moment.

She stood, brushing the dirt off her knees and gingerly cradling her injured arm.

Walking across the clearing was surreal, almost like a dream. Hulking, densely furred bodies littered the ground. Six in all. Quills lay scattered and snapped. If she hadn't known better, it almost looked like the pines surrounding them had shed their needles. Little snow had been left white. Everywhere, the winter forest floor was splattered with blood and mud and dug up earth from where boots or paws had sunk into it.

Why on earth had they been hunting in packs?

"We were just talking about that," Nikita said.

Apparently she had spoken her question out loud.

Deming took the damp cloth he extended to her and began wiping her face clean of grime and blood. The coarse fabric coupled with the cold water it had been dipped in stung the plethora of small cuts decorating her skin.

"And to add another layer," the male said, "look."

He bent down and gingerly plucked a quill from the ground.

Deming squinted at it, not finding anything out of the ordinary—

She recoiled in horror. "What is that?"

Crawling from inside the barb was a slithering, worm-like creature. So small she would have never noticed if Nikita hadn't pointed it out. Its body was clear and the internal organs could be seen, undulating as it squirmed, trying to bury itself further into the quill.

Nikita dropped the quill and pressed his heel into it, grinding it into the ground. "No idea. But they're in almost every quill."

Deming's mind raced through the possible scenarios. "A parasite of some sort?"

"Potentially. We have a couple trapped in a vial. We're going to bring it to Hartford's partner."

Deming heaved a sigh. "We're bringing her a lot of questions."

CHAPTER ELEVEN

DEMING

DEMING PRESSED HER HEELS into the sides of her steed, urging the horse forward. She relished the natural, comforting feeling of moving in the saddle in rhythm with the long, equine strides.

They were finally in the last stretch of their journey to Soraya's. There had been no other attacks, human or animal, for which Deming was eternally grateful.

The six of them and their horses had instead fallen into a comfortable albeit boring routine. They rose at dawn, filled their water skins, and rewrapped any wounds that needed tending to. They rode for most of the day, stopping near dusk to hunt, eat, and sleep. While Ilysse hunted, Deming trained. Sometimes with Nikita, sometimes with Vallyn. Always until she was drenched in sweat.

Each morning she woke up sore and aching, but the burn of her muscles made her feel alive. She had nearly regained the stamina she lost while in mourning. Her strength and accuracy with a weapon was another story, but she was committed.

Nothing and no one would come between her and her loved ones again. She would be prepared. She would be ready. She would protect what was hers.

Deming glanced back at Paris. He caught her eye and gave her a smile that quickly morphed into a grimace as he shifted too suddenly in the saddle. She gave him a soft smile in return, waiting until she was facing forward once more before allowing her expression to drop.

Hartford had wrapped his wound as best as she could after the leodin attack and Vallyn had stitched him up the next morning when she was able to clean it properly in the daylight, but something was deeply wrong. He was still in immense pain. Not that he had said anything, he was too proud for that. But Deming knew all the same.

Everyone knew.

He was not hiding it well.

And no one wanted to broach the topic when there was nothing to be done.

Soraya would help him when they arrived.

Deming, on the other hand, had healed within hours.

Exactly as she had after the injury to her thigh.

It was beguiling, the rate at which her wounds stitched themselves together. Terrifying, even. Her body felt foreign to her and no one knew what was happening to her or why.

Not to mention the burning, twisting guilt that prodded her like a metal poker whenever she thought about the fact that she was fine while Paris was not.

Deming's grip on the reins tightened at the thought. She closed her eyes and inhaled the scent of the forest around her, letting her fingers relax slowly.

There was nothing she could do about it except wait until they arrived in Bascade. Vallyn still held the small stone-like object that had been pulled from Deming's thigh. Ilysse held the samples from the unnatural leodins. They could do nothing until they arrived at Soraya's and then, hopefully, answers could be found.

Deming leaned back in the saddle, letting herself sway gently with the gait of the horse beneath her.

The soothing sounds of nature wrapped her senses in a cozy, pine-scented embrace. Light crackling from rabbits and small rodents skittering through the underbrush broke up the otherwise quiet morning. The wind that played with her hair and caressed her skin had lost its winter bite. In its place, the warm, renewed breath of spring whispered against her cheeks.

Nikita had told her long ago, when they were still in Arsaela, about the ever summer gardens of Bascade but it was surreal to experience the thaw of winter as they drew close to the capital city all the same. What magic dwelt in the bones and soil of the city to keep all seasons but summer at bay?

Nikita claimed it was a combination of being so close to the center of the continent, therefore the location of Kielle's first drop of blood, and the magic of the amphitheres.

The validity of his claim mattered not. Deming was more than happy to believe anything so long as it meant she could escape the creeping chill of winter.

She had always loathed the cold.

The forest was quiet and calm, until it wasn't.

A sound unlike any Deming had ever heard bellowed from the sky. Her horse startled, rearing up, and she curled herself close to its broad neck and shoulders to avoid being thrown off all the while looking for the source of the noise.

Nikita tilted his head back and let out a joyous whoop from the horse next to her, nearly lifting himself completely out of the saddle. Ilysse and Hartford echoed his cheer with matched exuberance. The laughter they shared after shimmered like soap bubbles with both childlike glee and boastful pride.

Whatever it was they recognized sounded again, like bird and beast and something superbly ancient. The very fabric of the air seemed to respond to its call.

Deming's skin prickled as she looked to the skies, all at once knowing what she would see.

Swooping into view through the peaks of the pines was the largest living being Deming had ever seen.

A body like a snake, scaled and muscled, weaved through the tips of the trees. Each individual scale seemed to be a distinct color of gray. Charcoal, slate, ash, iron. The smoke rising from a fire. The delicate shading of a dove's tail feather. The dark shadows of depths of the woods. Where sunlight refracted off scales, beauty was made incarnate.

All those jewels, soaring through the sky, carried by two sets of wings. Vast, expansive, intricately feathered wings. Twins in all but size, the back set was slightly smaller, though even they were still far and away larger than Nikita's wings.

Nikita's stories from earlier welled up in her mind. Of Rider's and bonds and the almost myth-like reverence the amphitheres demanded.

She tried to imagine what riding through the clouds astride something as great and mighty as the beast before her would feel like and came up short. Nothing in her mundane life could possibly compare.

Unlike the scales, the feathers were predominantly one color. A deep, dark, navy blue. And though they didn't hold the same myriad of colors as the scales, when the wings beat and the feathers ruffled and the light hit certain spots just right, the blue flickered between dusk and midnight.

The crown of feathers framing its ferocious head were ornate and slicked back as wind whipped over them. The beast was too far away for Deming to see what color its eyes held, but it was not too far away for her to see the razor sharp teeth and elongated canines that glinted as it roared, the ancient sound echoing through Deming's bones.

Deming eyes soaked in as much of the legendary beast as she could. She knew her expression was akin to a child seeing a rainbow, but she couldn't help herself. To see the magic and mysticism that was the symbol of Runne in the flesh was…

Indescribable.

The amphithere twirled through the sky, spinning in tight circles like a corkscrew before breaking the pattern and turning back towards the eastern edge of the Telaciens in the distance.

It opened its fanged mouth and let out one more roar, sending fear and awe coursing through Deming and setting her soul ablaze with wonder.

She turned to Nikita, who was already looking at her with eyes full of excitement. The first positive emotion she had seen him express about his kingdom since they began their travels.

It was all too easy to justify that joy, to understand how one could hate the king and his court but deeply love these creatures.

Nikita's voice held every bit of the smile that had his lips swept upwards as he spoke. "Welcome to Bascade."

CHAPTER TWELVE

DEMING

THE SUN CAST LONG shadows over the rippling hills, dipping behind the horizon and bathing the world in umber and orange, when they finally arrived at the rickety apothecary on the outskirts of Bascade.

Deming hummed in satisfaction, admiring the view as golden hour descended on the valley.

It had been nearly a month and a half since the fog had broken in Arsaela, the passage of time marked by the moon, but the glow of the sun still felt precious to Deming. The shadow magic that Miriam had spun, cloaking the city in grayscale for months on end, had given the heir an appreciation for every hue of light the sun could create.

Never again would she take a sunset for granted.

Though every one of them was weary from travel and full of angst with all that their journey had given them to consider, each back straightened as they crested the final hill. Each rider nudged their horse faster.

The eagerness to reach their destination was led by Hartford.

She was simply beside herself when they had decided on heading to Soraya. The female had forgone her horse half an hour ago, claiming that if she didn't jog lightly alongside them her bones would break from the tension. She had hidden the pain of being away from her mate from everyone these past few months. Tucked it away so carefully into a deep corner of her soul that no one was any wiser to the angst that tugged her heart every minute of every day. When the light at the end of the tunnel came into sight, though, and they had decided on their destination, the love she had for her mate unspooled chaotically in all directions.

To watch Hartford in these moments was to be both awestruck by the seemingly limitless extent of their bond and filled with sorrow for how hidden away she had kept this part of herself that seemed larger than life.

Upon learning about Soraya, Deming had quickly realized that she didn't know Hartford at all. The facade the Fae had put on while in Arsaela was one of necessity. One that protected her heart while it was miles away. This Hartford, the one that wore her emotions on her sleeve and quite nearly glowed in anticipation, was true and real and raw. Deming caught herself on multiple occasions feeling eager and honored to begin knowing this version of her.

Deming smiled at Hartford, her own heart melting a bit at the sight of prancing cloven feet and breathy gasps for air as Hartford deftly maneuvered the last hill.

And as soon as the apothecary came into view, its door opened on slow, creaking hinges. It swung open gently, as if the Fae standing behind it had only barely pushed it open. As if she couldn't quite comprehend what she was seeing.

The door revealed a tall, muscled female. Her blue eyes were striking, even at this distance, but what took Deming's breath away was the thick, white and gray fur that covered her legs from thigh all the way to huge paws. The claws were retracted, but they glistened nonetheless.

Hartford burst into tears and lost all sense of decorum, sprinting the remaining length to the steps of the house.

Soraya collapsed into a puddle on the floor, sobbing into her hands, shoulders shaking violently as emotion crashed into her quickly followed by Hartford herself.

Hartford half ran, half fell into her mate, scooping Soraya into her arms and nuzzling her face into the other woman's neck.

"I'm here," Hartford said with a softness unknown to this world, "I'm here. I'm home."

Soraya wept into her mates arms, shaking her head and not look-ing up at Hartford as if she believed this to be a dream and couldn't bear to let it go.

"I'm here, I'm home." Hartford murmured the phrases over and over again planting kiss after kiss everywhere her mouth could reach, from the thick brown hair that tumbled around Soraya's shoulders to the tips of her wolf-like furred ears that had dropped from the perked up position they had started in, relaying the intense emotion coursing through the female.

Ever so slowly, Soraya pulled her palms away from her face.

Hartford cupped her chin and tilted it up, forcing Soraya to meet her gaze.

When their eyes met, tears were shed anew.

"Let's give them some privacy."

Deming jolted in her saddle, unaware that she had been staring.

She turned to Nikita, who had brought his horse next to her and grasped her reins.

"We should make sure the horses are taken care of, then we can go meet Soraya," he said. "The barn is around back."

Sure enough, as soon as he walked the horses over to the side of the apothecary, a small but sturdy looking barn appeared.

Deming dismounted and took her reins back.

Light shone in through both the windows on either end and the many cracks in the shoddy wooden walls. It smelled of hay and manure, a not wholly unpleasant scent for Deming, though she caught Ilysse gagging as she entered. There were two other horses already in the barn, tucked in with hay and water for the night. The space was not meant for company. There was only one more stall, but that was fine.

They were here.

They had made it.

"You okay?" Nikita raised an eyebrow at her heavy exhale. He had also dismounted and was stripping the riding gear off his horse. His wings were tucked in tightly in the enclosed space. If he moved too fast he risked swatting an animal or knocking tack off hooks.

"Mhmm," Deming affirmed.

He looked at her like he was going to press her, but then nodded and returned to his horse.

Deming looked over her shoulder.

Ilysse had taken her and Vallyn's horses and was getting the animals set up in the far end of the barn.

Vallyn was with Paris.

Deming's pulse quickened watching them.

Paris still hadn't dismounted. His face was pulled taut in pain, teeth bared, the edges of his hairline slick as sweat dampened the blonde locks. Vallyn had one hand on the reins of his horse, steadying the beast though it seemed to know to be still, and one locked in a bracing grip with Paris's hand.

Vallyn said something to the young lord but she was too far away for Deming to hear.

How had Paris devolved this quickly? He truly could not get off his horse by himself?

She found her breath catching in her throat on thick emotion. She swallowed the panic down but it lay in wait in her gut, curling and coiling within her like a writhing snake. Had he survived the attack only to succumb to his wounds days later? Was it an infection? The week of travel Nikita had predicted had nearly doubled because they had slowed down for Paris but they had been so diligent about changing his bandages and letting him rest as much as possible.

Deming was jolted out of her thoughts by a sharp pain on her lip. Her brows furrowed and she brought her hand to her mouth instinctively. Her fingers came away red. She had ripped the skin away from her lip in her anxiety riddled state.

She licked her lips then spat the blood out onto the dirt floor.

Nikita slid an arm around her waist and kissed the crown of her head.

"Go to him. He needs you. You need each other."

The words were spoken so softly and with such kindness that they threatened to break Deming apart. She tucked her head into his chest and inhaled a long, steadying breath of his cardamom and sea salt scent, then planted a kiss where her cheek had just been and walked towards Paris.

By the time she made her way to him, he had successfully dismounted with the heavy support of Vallyn, who was still by his side. One of her arms was around his waist, and one of his was across her shoulders. She looked to be bearing most of his weight. The pallor of his skin was a sickly shade that made Deming's stomach knot in fear.

"Hey," Deming put on a broad smile just for him, "are you okay?"

"Never better." His smile didn't reach his eyes. In fact, his lips had barely twinged upwards before they fell once more.

Deming slipped her shoulder under his other arm.

"You don't need to help, Deming. I'm fine, really."

She hushed away his protests and the three of them walked out of the barn and slowly up the dirt path to the apothecary.

The sun was in its final moments, setting over Bascade and nesting into the tips of the distant forest. The world turned dusky and dark.

The beauty was lost on Deming. The state of Paris threw a melancholy blanket over everyone. It was difficult to enjoy the view, to enjoy the end of long weeks of travel, when he had seemingly hit a wall physically and mentally.

It was as if he had delayed surrendering to his injuries until they arrived at their destination. As if he knew they couldn't afford to stop for him or deviate from the path to find a closer healer.

Tears pricked at the corners of Deming's eyes. This was just like Paris to be so stubborn. To put the good of the group before the good of the individual. If he healed fully she swore she would give him a tongue lashing.

They could have stopped.

His life was worth saving.

If not to the world, than to her.

Just as they were approaching the steps, the backdoor swung open.

"Hey, I was just about to—" Hartford's jubilant expression fell the moment she laid eyes on Paris. "Soraya!"

Introductions were thrown out the window in light of the state Paris was in. Soraya had taken one look at the haggard man, barely able to stand on his own, and ushered the group inside without commentary. They had gotten Paris into one of the chairs around the nearby table and Soraya had immediately leapt into action, darting from room to room collecting vials and herbs and a mortar and pestle.

It was her home, too, Deming realized the moment she stepped through the door, not just an apothecary.

A coat rack stood tall in one corner. Clothing ranging from shawls to jackets to scarves littered its branches. Through one of the arched doorways she could see a couch with blankets strewn across it.

They were in the kitchen now. A wood burning stove warmed the room, something bubbling in a cast iron pot on the singular grate atop it. The smell coming from the corner it sat in was...distinctive. Potent. But not unpleasant. It infused the air with a musky, woodsy aroma. Copper rods ran between the plentiful cabinets. Each one was full of pots and pans and mugs hanging from little hooks.

Soraya returned from another room and dumped the contents of her arms onto the table. She slipped a pot holder on, moved the cast iron from the stove to a stone countertop, and plucked a new pot from one of many hanging above her to set above the fire instead before beginning to concoct a tincture.

Her wolf ears twitched with each movement, flicking to and fro. "Someone get me boswellia from outside," she barked.

Ilysse ducked out the door without a sound and returned within moments with a handful of fern-y looking plants that had small white flowers budding in spots.

In any other situation Deming would have taken pleasure in seeing the fierce female taking direct orders so submissively, but all she could feel was gratitude for how quick she had sprung into action. Deming wasn't naive enough to believe that Ilysse would ever be empathetic about herself or Vallyn or Paris, but she knew the female had begun to genuinely care for them in their months of knowing each other. It was heartening.

Besides, Ilysse was a captain. She understood order and rank and Soraya was clearly in charge here.

Soraya took the plant and bit off leaf after leaf, chewing thoroughly but not seeming to swallow. Only once every leaf had been plucked from the stem did she pick up a small vial and spit the chewed up leaves into it.

Just as steam began to rise from the pot, Soraya lifted it away from the heat and poured it into a small jar sitting on the counter.

"Paris, your name is Paris, right?" Soraya's blue eyes darted to Hartford for confirmation. She nodded curtly. "Paris, I need you to take your shirt off and lay on the table for me."

His fingers trembled, whether from nerves or pain was unclear, but the buttons came undone nonetheless and the shirt fell unceremoniously to the floor. He made to get on the table but Soraya interrupted him.

"Actually, wait. Let me take off the bandage first. Can you stand?"

His knees knocked together, barely able to hold his weight, but he waved away help.

Soraya knelt before him, eye level with the makeshift wrap around his torso. Deft fingers began feeling for where the wrap began. Twice she pressed too hard and Paris groaned, his entire face contorting in agony.

Each flicker of pain that flashed across Paris's face made Deming's heart hurt a little bit more. Sweat beaded on her forehead. Her hands were balled so tightly under the table her knuckles felt like they might snap.

Nikita stepped closer to where she sat. He placed a hand on her shoulder, gently at first, asking silently if this touch was okay at the moment. She leaned into his hand to let him know it was and felt the tiniest knot of anxiety melt away as calloused fingertips began working slow circles into the back of her neck. Her fear for Paris was still raging, but she could breathe a little better.

Soraya finally found the edge of the fabric and began untwisting it from Paris's chest. She pulled on the makeshift bandage and collected it in her hand as she unwound it. Strips of shirts and rags and sheets balled in her fist. They had made do with what they had and what they had were the clothes on their backs and a few spare items in their packs.

Each rotation unveiled a little more of the wound. At first only puckered skin and thin red lines could be seen. Simple scratches. But as the bandage on his chest dwindled, the full extent of his wound was revealed.

It curved like a bloody smile from his shoulder all the way down to the bottom of his last rib. The tail end curled up sharply, caused by the leodin being knocked away abruptly. It was deepest right below his collarbone.

Though most of the blood had been staunched, any movement caused minuscule tears to reopen and as such, the wound still looked very fresh. Rivulets of blood dripped from the open wound. Maroon and crimson stained the skin around it despite their best efforts to clean in and around it. The swelling had not calmed and the smell was the sickly sweet scent of death and decay. It was inflamed and angry and horrific to look at.

Bile coated her tongue. She felt as if she might retch.

Deming had seen it before. Every time they put a new bandage on while traveling she had been by his side. But for some reason this time it took her breath away. She had been so worried about getting him here that she hadn't truly processed the extent of his injury. In her mind, if they made it through the forest and to the apothecary unscathed he would be fine. The journey was the dangerous part, not the destination.

Looking at the mauled flesh crossing his skin she realized just how wrong she had been.

Soraya's eyes widened for only a second before she regained her composure. Her voice was calm and cool when she spoke. "It's infected, which is to be expected after days of travel instead of rest."

Deming cringed into the back of her chair. They should have stopped more. They rode too far and too hard.

"It's not your fault." Nikita's voice was quiet, murmured softly for only her to hear, though both Ilysse and Soraya's ears flicked to him too. "He chose to keep riding. He knew the importance of getting here. Not just for himself, but for you. For all of us."

The truth did not bring Deming any relief.

Soraya handed the vial full of boswellia to Paris. "Drink this."

He took the vial from her and tilted it from side to side. The chewed up leaves climbed slowly up the glass, like sludge. His nose crinkled. "How am I supposed to drink this?"

"Drink it, eat it, spoon it into your mouth with your fingers, I don't care," Soraya said with an eye roll, "just get it into your system."

"It's full of your spit."

Soraya gave him a look that reminded Deming vividly of Ilysse. "It helps with pain relief. Trust me, you want it."

Deming took Paris's hand in hers and smiled at him.

He looked from her to the vial to her again. Then in one swift movement brought the vial to his lips, tilted his head back, and tapped on the bottom lof the glass until only streaks of green remained.

He keeled over and gagged.

"Bitter, isn't it."

Paris glared at Soraya. "A warning would have been nice."

"Get on the table. Please," she added when he continued to look at her incredulously.

Paris shook his head, but prepared to climb onto the table. He got almost nowhere as the second he tried to pull his body onto the table he cried out in pain, unable to access the core strength he needed.

Deming stood abruptly, the legs of her chair scraping against the hardwood floor. Nikita grabbed her hand, pulling her back.

"I..." He cleared his throat. "You'll be no use trying to lift him. Let me."

Vallyn had been on her feet instantly, too, and the pair of them lifted Paris as gently as they could onto the table.

His blonde hair fell limply around his too pale face as he lay down. Deming pulled her chair around to his uninjured side and took his hand in hers once more.

"Since you're a fan of warnings," Soraya said grimly as she took her place next to the torn flesh, jar of whatever tincture she had whipped together in hand, "This is going to hurt."

Paris dipped his chin in acknowledgement. His gaze clouded over, his mind going somewhere far away.

"I'm right here," Deming said.

He gave her hand a squeeze.

Then Soraya began.

CHAPTER THIRTEEN

NIKITA

MORNING LIGHT SHIMMERED IN through the window of Soraya's living room. The light refracted chaotically through the stained glass, bouncing hues of blue onto skin and fabric and stone.

Nikita admired the glass, a true work of art. It depicted no one important. No god or goddess or king or queen. Instead, this window was etched and welded and pieced together seamlessly to become a bluejay.

The bird's wings were outstretched, each wingtip a hair's breadth away from opposing corners. White and black glass was threaded delicately throughout and the blue glass that made up the majority of the bird ranged from sky to ocean to indigo.

Counting the individual pieces of glass, 287, and sipping the chamomile tea that Soraya had prepared for everyone had calmed Nikita's nerves.

Waking up this morning in the city he once called home, in the kingdom he was set to inherit, had finally caught up to him now that they were no longer on the move. He had awoken with an ominous, twisting feeling in his gut. There was something whispering to him in the dark that they were all on the precipice of something grander than they could imagine.

That, coupled with Paris's dubious infection which Deming had been handling poorly, had Nikita feeling frayed and on edge.

Paris was, thankfully, still soundly asleep upstairs. He and his body needed rest.

Soraya had hedged masterfully around commenting on his recovery, complimenting the wound care they had done while traveling and saying how positive it was that he was sleeping. Nothing about the current state of the wound. Nothing about how long it would take for him to heal. Nothing about what regaining strength and mobility would look like.

Sweet words like honey to cover the bitter truth.

Soraya was hedging because things were looking dark.

At least they were somewhere safe and warm. Somewhere Paris could be taken care of by someone who knew what they were doing.

Deming set her cup of tea down, turning her gaze from where it was trained out the corner window to the quiet room before her. "What now?"

Nikita looked up from the chaise he was lounging in but it was Soraya who spoke.

"If you're ready," she said, drawing out the syllables, "I would love to know why you're here. I mean, don't get me wrong, I am overjoyed to be with you again, my love." She kissed Hartford on the cheek. The pair of them were a tangle of limbs in the oversized, plush chair sitting next to the fireplace. Wood crackled and embers glowed, casting them in deep, warm colors. Despite everything they'd been through and everything on the horizon, joy was written across Hartford's face like the stars in the sky. Like all the problems of the world melted away when she was in her mate's presence.

Seeing Hartford and Soraya so at ease sent soul-deep longing thrumming through Nikita. It plucked at the golden bond tying him to Deming. The muscles in his chest tightened and he felt physically drawn to her across the room.

His eyes drifted to his mate and found she was already looking at him.

There was something in her shining eyes that Nikita couldn't quite place. Pining? Desire?

His wings shifted and flexed under her gaze as if each individual feather remembered how her fingers felt threading into them.

"But," Soraya continued, "I imagine any of you would be curious if your mate showed up on your doorstep with the Prince of Runne, the Princess of Laey, her Captain of the Guard, and another human on death's doorstep."

A snarl came low and slow and menacing from the floor.

"Sorry, Ilysse. It's not my fault you are the least interesting person in the group."

Vallyn choked on a laugh, trying and failing to cover it up with a cough. Ilysse's face furrowed with fury and she kicked a foot hard into Vallyn's shin, which only made the woman laugh harder.

Deming smiled into her teacup.

Nikita took it upon himself to answer Soraya. "It's a long story. To say the least."

"I've got time."

They had all been too tired last night, physically from travel and emotionally from sterilizing Paris's wound and watching as Soraya cut away swaths of infected flesh, to explain to her why they had shown up on her doorstep. But now, refreshed from the first good night's sleep in ages and bellies full of soothing tea and fluffy eggs Soraya made for them, it was finally time.

As Nikita recounted the tales of their journey he had a difficult time keeping the disbelief out of his voice. He was just as baffled by the events now as he was at their onset. Each claim seemed wilder than the last. They had been attacked by bounty hunters, during which Deming had almost died and they found that odd stone in her thigh, she had woken up the following morning to her horrendous knife wound completely healed over, and leodins had attacked them. Leodins that not only acted out of the ordinary by congregating in packs but that had been infected by some sort of parasite, too.

Soraya had gawked in horror at the quill Hartford produced to punctuate Nikita's story. A shudder rippled through her at the sight of the worm-like creatures crawling around the broken quill and up the sides of the glass vial.

The silence was as loud as any roar when Nikita stopped speaking.

After a long moment passed with no one offering anything more to the conversation, Nikita prodded, "Where would you like to start?"

Soraya inhaled deeply, shaking her head. "Hard to pick."

That got a soft laugh from more than one person in the room, Deming included.

Soraya bit her lip, brows furrowed. The speed at which the thoughts raced through her mind was plastered on her face for all to see. Then she looked to Hartford. "I want to get half of those," she wiggled a finger in disgust at the parasites, "in a preservation solution. After I'm confident they won't disintegrate or rot, I'll run some tests on them. In the meantime I'll experiment with some live ones. I want that," she pointed to the stone retrieved from Deming's thigh that had been brought out by someone during Nikita's monologue of their past few weeks, "soaking in lukewarm water. It isn't a stone, I can tell from here. If I can loosen the material I can figure out what it's made of. In the meantime," she turned to Deming, who froze like a deer in the woods under her gaze, "I would love to work on the curiosity of your healing."

Nikita was no novice to scrutiny, growing up as a banished heir had made sure of that. But even in his wildest interactions with nobility and commoners alike he had never experienced the attention to detail that Soraya paid to Deming in the hour that followed.

The female clung to her every word like it was gospel, taking copious notes and asking questions with such specificity that Deming looked at her in awe on more than one occasion before trying to answer with as much honesty as she could.

Soraya closed her notebook, tapped the excess ink off her quill, and pushed everything to the side. She clasped her hands together, elbows on the table, and looked at Deming with a face that looked like she was about to ask something unpleasant of her.

Nikita leaned forward in anticipatory apprehension.

"No getting around it, I suppose." Soraya cleared her throat. "I would like to see this in action, if I could."

Nikita was out of his chair before Soraya finished speaking. Protectiveness gripped his heart like iron manacles. "No, absolutely not."

His posture was rigid, his wings taut. He knew his eyes were wild and wide and that he looked slightly manic but his body was reacting viscerally on instinct to the suggestion that Deming voluntarily hurt herself.

Deming opened her mouth to speak, reaching her hand up to touch his arm, but she was cut off as Vallyn entered the room, closely followed by Ilysse and Hartford.

"Oh, everyone's here now," Soraya said, rolling her eyes and leaning against the back of her wicker chair. "That seems unnecessary."

"If that's what it takes to ensure you don't carve her up," Nikita said low and slow, "I'd say it's pretty necessary."

"Okay, prince, I'm not going to carve her up. Don't be dramatic."

"Not to burst your bubble but I absolutely think she should demonstrate for Soraya," Vallyn interjected.

Nikita, Soraya, and Vallyn raised their voices as they spoke, trying with each decibel to be the loudest. Within seconds the kitchen went from being peaceful to the battleground of an argument over Deming in which Deming herself had not said a word yet.

"I'm sorry," Nikita turned to Vallyn, "what? You want to take a knife to the rightful heir to the Queendom of Laey?"

"That's what I said, yes."

"Aren't you supposed to be her Captain of the Guard?"

"I am," she growled.

Ilysse shot Nikita a look to cut it out. He ignored her.

"A pretty big part of that job is keeping her safe, wouldn't you say?"

Vallyn sucked her bottom lip in, shaking her head and taking a deep breath, presumably to cool the flames beginning to burn in her eyes. She put a hand on her hip, an incredulous look accompanying the eye roll she gave him. She clearly tried to lighten her tone when she responded, but her attempt was in vain. Each syllable cut through the air like a hot knife through butter. "It's a small, contained injury for the better of the group. She'll be fine. You'll be fine, right?"

All eyes darted to Deming who looked incredibly irritated.

"Nice of you all to discuss what I should and shouldn't do as if I wasn't right here." She crossed her arms across her chest. "I am more than capable of deciding what to do or not do with my own body. That is my choice and my choice alone."

Vallyn raised her hands in defeat, bowing slightly before taking a step back.

Nikita felt his cheeks heat with shame as he mumbled an apology.

With a curt nod, Deming said, "I'll do whatever you need me to do."

The most peculiar mix of horror and pride swirled in Nikita's stomach at her proclamation. There was no part of him that wanted to see a single drop of her blood shed, no piece of his soul that tolerated her being in pain. And yet, there was a wonderful satisfaction at seeing her take control of her life, her decisions.

She was more queenlike by the day.

With every day, every choice, she was coming into her own.

A vision of her on coronation day flooded Nikita's mind. Deming in a fur-trimmed cloak, staff in one hand, orb in the other with a crown studded with jewels sitting amidst tricolored curls pulled back by silver pins. Regal and resplendent.

If it took his last breath he would ensure that future came to fruition.

Soraya smiled in thanks, then drew a sharp paring knife from the knife block on the counter behind her. "In order to understand what's happening, I need to see it happening in real time. A cut on your forearm will do, nothing too deep."

Deming took the knife and placed the tip to her skin.

It pricked her, blood welled, and Nikita gripped the edge of the table harder than necessary.

"Across the arm, not lengthwise," advised Soraya.

Deming turned the angle of her wrist in response.

Nikita's heart beat faster with every second that passed. She agreed to do this, she wanted to do this, so why was it so difficult to watch her run the knife across her skin?

A tug on the bond.

His heart skipped a beat.

Deming's eyes were trained on his. Worry etched lines into her forehead, her mouth was downturned.

It was in that moment Nikita knew she understood. Whether she felt the bond or not she understood. Any pain to her, no matter how small or self-inflicted, was pain to him.

He softened his expression and nodded encouragingly.

That was all she needed.

The knife flashed in the candlelight as it sliced through delicate layers of skin then clattered to the kitchen table.

Deming inhaled so sharply that she coughed and Nikita lost his breath entirely.

"Uncurl your fingers if you can."

She obeyed Soraya's gentle words.

The cut Deming made was deeper than necessary. Blood trickled down her arm and pooled onto the table.

"And now we wait," said Ilysse, pulling up a chair to the table and plopping down unceremoniously. She unsheathed a claw and picked at something in her teeth.

It was a droll experience, in the beginning. The trails of blood leaking from either end of the cut slowed to a dribble, then stopped all together. The streaks on her arm dried and crusted, falling off in flakes when she adjusted herself. No one left the small kitchen, though. The two other times her body had healed herself had been over night while they were sleeping. Everyone, not just Soraya, was eager to see what exactly happened to the wounds on her skin to cause them to heal so unnaturally fast.

Had Nikita not been wildly alert the entire time, Soraya's gasp may have surprised him.

Wings and fur and bodies and heat crowded around the table, everyone leaning in at the exact same time.

Slowly, as if moving through molasses, the skin at one end of the cut was stitching itself back together. It moved on its own accord, as if an invisible string was weaving itself through the sliced skin and sewing it shut.

Despite expecting the injury to do exactly what it was doing, Nikita's jaw dropped. How was she doing this?

A shiver skated down his spine. Watching it was a surreal, out of body experience.

He searched his mind, trying to find a thread of understanding or story of similar feats but came up short. It was foreign. Unknown. To stand there and watch as something completely unbelievable happened to Deming's body without her own volition made Nikita feel nauseous and out of control.

Under all of that, though, was the slightest spark of whimsy and awe.

This was magic in action. What magic, specifically, was yet to be discovered.

Ilysse leaned forward. Her nose was so close to Deming's arm that her skin pebbled under the female's breath. "Is that...a light?"

If at all possible, everyone bent closer around Deming's arm. Nikita's wing was completely draped over her shoulder at this point, his black hair mixing with hers.

Sure enough, if he looked close enough, there was a faint glow emanating from where Deming's skin was healing. It pulsed, as if it was alive.

Deming shuddered.

Nikita placed a hand on her shoulder. "What's wrong?"

She lifted her lashes and whispered, "Reminds me of the parasites."

"It's possible..." Soraya's thought trailed off as she furiously wrote down notes.

Nikita looked back at Deming's arm.

No scar was left in the wake of the knife wound. No red or irritated skin. Nothing. What came after the soft glow was skin perfectly fresh and clean and unmarred.

He had to admit that as jarring as it was to watch, it was beautiful. Something so wondrous couldn't be caused by something as invasive as a parasite, could it?

"Does it hurt?" Vallyn's question was a whisper.

"No. No, it...it feels numb but...tingly? Like when your limbs have been in one position too long and then you try to move them." Deming stared with rabid curiosity at her arm. She flexed her fingers and slowly moved her wrist from side to side, gently pulling and twisting the skin on her forearm. "And warm. It feels warm."

Soraya's eyes flicked up to her, recognition flooding her gaze. "Warm? Can you tell me more?"

Deming tilted her head, staring intently at the oddity of her arm. About a half inch of the cut had mended itself at this point. "Mmm I don't know. Not really, I don't think. It just feels warm."

"Warm like a fever or warm like a blanket?"

Deming shook her head. "Not like a fever. It doesn't feel bad, just weird. Unusual. Warm like the way hot tea heats you from the inside out. Why? Have you seen something like this before?"

Soraya hummed noncommittally, though she still looked incredibly intrigued. "No, I've never seen anything like this. Sensations can tell a lot about an ailment, though."

The room fell into strained silence as they watched the rest of Deming's skin knit back together. The progress was slow, but steady, and within the hour her entire arm looked as good as new.

After the last thrum of energy dissipated from the cut and the afterglow of whatever light that had trailed across her skin faded away, Deming poked at the healed skin with her finger.

Once, twice, and a third time, harder than the first two.

Completely healed, just as her other two injuries had been.

Deming had lied and Nikita could tell it was eating her alive.

Earlier that morning, Soraya had asked question after question about the manner of Deming's injuries—how long it had taken them to heal, the weapon used, and a hundred other details. She had also asked about the burst of light from Deming that preceded the leodin attack and Deming had told her what she and Nikita had told everyone else—it happened after she failed to land a knife in the tree.

This was, categorically and without a doubt, false.

The light had come forth during their kiss. More specifically, when he had bit her neck while her fingers were intertwined with the down of his feathers.

Nikita had stifled a smile when she purposely misled Soraya.

Deming was a horrible liar. She had adjusted her posture and her eyes darted to Nikita as the lie fell from her lips. Her voice wavered.

He supposed another male might be annoyed that she wanted to hide what they had done.

Not him.

No, Nikita loved that their midnight kiss was theirs and theirs alone. If he could live in that moment forever, alone under the stars with Deming's mouth on his and their bodies pressed fervently into one another, he would say yes in a heartbeat.

He couldn't care less that Deming had lied about the light and their kiss. What he did care about was that she was clearly wracked with guilt.

She had gnawed at her lip through lunch, remained thoroughly distracted while training with Vallyn under the sun that afternoon, and pushed the roast duck and root vegetables that Hartford and Soraya cooked around her plate at dinner.

So Nikita was relieved when, once everyone was winding down for the night, she tugged on his hand and motioned with a quiet nod for him to follow her outside.

The air was cool and refreshing as the moon crested the tips of the pines. Deming took a steadying breath before facing Nikita.

He ran his thumb across her jaw, her skin felt like porcelain. "Is everything alright?"

"I lied to Soraya."

He cocked his head and remained quiet, waiting for her to elaborate.

Pleading eyes peered up at him. "Should we tell her? Should we tell everyone?"

He cupped a hand under her chin, tilting her face to his. "I'll tell the entire world about us. I'll yell it from the top of the tallest mountain on the continent." She inhaled sharply and Nikita resisted the urge to lean in further. He tucked stray white strands of hair behind the curve of her ear. "But only on our terms, only when we're comfortable."

She leaned her head into his hand and closed her eyes. "And Soraya?"

It was Nikita's turn to inhale. The releasing breath was heavy. "I do think it best that Soraya at least knows the full story. We don't have to tell anyone else, but if we're asking for her help it's only fair that she has all the information."

As if summoned by the mention of her name, Soraya opened the back door and poked her head out. Her eyes lit up when she saw them, though she did not look entirely happy.

"There you are. I've been looking for you."

Deming stepped out of their embrace and cleared her throat. "I was just about to come and find you, too."

Surprise flashed across Soraya's face, covering up the odd emotion she wore before.

A slick, sticky kind of worry began spreading in Nikita's stomach.

"I wasn't fully transparent with you earlier," Deming said, "when you were asking me about the light that burst from me the night of the leodin attack."

"Oh?" Soraya's voice rose an octave as one eyebrow arched delicately.

"It didn't happen because I missed the target. It happened because we," her eyes darted to Nikita, who gave a soft nod of encouragement, "because we shared a kiss."

Astonished was the only way to describe the way Soraya looked in the wake of the news. Quickly though, she packed away the curiosity clearly bubbling at the surface of her emotions for another time and got back to the matter at hand—the light.

"The burst of light happened directly after you kissed the prince?"

Blush crept onto Deming's cheeks. "Yes, in the middle of it, actually."

"Well, that makes sense, I suppose." Soraya said the words to herself, under her breath, but Deming still caught them.

"It makes sense?" she asked.

The worry grew as Nikita saw Soraya's face pinch.

He stepped closer to Deming.

"Ahh, yeah." Soraya's voice wavered. "An emotional response can be typical..." She pulled a hand through her hair. "It's been documented that if magic goes unchecked for too long it can be explosive or unpredictable. Heightened emotions can trigger things..." She trailed off and shook her head. "Sorry, I should start over."

Her face twitched. She shifted back and forth from one paw to the other. The anxious energy she exuded was palpable. It was putting Nikita on edge. His palms felt sweaty, his wings itched.

Deming wrung her hands. "What is it? Is it Paris? Is he okay?"

Soraya held up a hand. "Paris is fine. He's still sleeping." The concern stayed firmly on her face, though, as she opened her hand to show the stone that had been found in Deming's thigh. "I figured out what this is."

Deming's brows furrowed. "That's good news, isn't it?"

"It is..."

"Get to the point, Soraya," Nikita cut in, voice sharp and clipped.

"Yeah, okay. You're right." She took a deep breath and closed her eyes. When she opened them, her body had stilled and her voice was level. To Deming she said, "You should be sitting for this."

Fear flooded Nikita's senses, instantaneous and all consuming.

Soraya moved away from the steps up to the door and motioned for Deming to sit.

Nikita followed, walking on feet that didn't feel connected to his body. He sat down behind Deming in a haze, panic coursing through his veins like lightning. What could possibly be bad enough that Soraya was this terrified to tell them? That Deming had to sit down to hear? Was something wrong with her? Was she dying?

He was normally rational but the thought of losing her so soon after finding her was enough to make Nikita spiral. If something was truly wrong, he would have felt it through the bond, wouldn't he?

His hand flew to his chest. The thundering beat of his heart pulsed against his palm. His lungs wouldn't fill no matter how deeply he tried to breathe. Had the air thickened?

He grasped for Deming's hand and she clutched it back desperately.

Then, everything quieted as Soraya spoke.

"This is root of hawthorn, condensed tightly and imbued with shadow magic. Something like this has only one purpose—to tamp down elemental magic. You are a mage, Deming."

CHAPTER FOURTEEN

DEMING

"YOU ARE A MAGE, Deming."

Mage.

Mage.

Mage.

The word rang in her ear until the syllable became a bell instead. Ringing, ringing, ringing.

She felt dizzy, confused. She blinked rapidly, trying to clear her vision that had fogged over momentarily.

Soraya's mouth was moving but Deming couldn't hear anything the female was saying.

Ringing, ringing, ringing.

Suddenly Nikita's face filled her vision.

She let the expanse of clouded sky and swirling storms that were his eyes ground her until she could hear the words he was saying.

She knew the flicker of recognition had been visible in her own eyes because he said, "There you are," and pressed a palm to her cheek.

Deming looked past the dense feathers peeking from behind shoulder blades and addressed Soraya. Her voice cracked pathetically. "That can't be true. My mother and father were both human. I can't be a mage."

Soraya's paws were soundless on the dirt as she stepped closer. Every move calculated and careful, slow and patient. "I know its a lot to process—"

"It's not a lot to process. It's not true!" Her palms slapped the stone steps in emphasis. The impact stung.

Soraya looked at Nikita, silently asking what she should do or say.

He looked just about as shocked as Deming felt.

"Don't look at him, I'm right here!"

Soraya held up her hands. "You're right, I'm sorry."

The initial disbelief and shock had quickly boiled away into anger. It was infuriating to watch someone act like she wasn't right there, like she was acting crazy. Soraya was the crazy one! Deming? A mage? That was so utterly nonsensical that unhinged laughter threatened to bubble up her throat. She could do nothing to stop it and the chaotic sound crackled through the evening.

It was ridiculous, the notion that she was a mage. She was her mother's daughter. She was the queen's heir and the realm's princess. She had grown in her mother's womb and countless servants and ladies of the court bore witness to her birth. And if she was of her mother's blood but also a mage, then that meant her father was not her father. That meant her mother had been unfaithful, that she had lain with someone other than the king.

No, not just someone.

Lain with a Fae.

Mages were half human, half Fae.

Deming was half human, half Fae.

The thought sent her spiraling once more.

Soraya spoke, but Deming was once again lost in the fog of her own mind. Unable to make out the words that were clearly leaving the female's mouth, Deming simply stared at her and then through her. Her gaze fell to the woods behind them. Focusing on something so far away was the only way for her to focus on anything at all.

Something warm touched her shoulder, then slid down her back. She couldn't be bothered to question what it was.

It couldn't possibly be true.

Could it?

A whisper of doubt snaked its way into her mind like a tendril of mist. Only the smallest hint of possibility was all it took for the pieces to fall into some semblance of place in her.

The way her body healed was utterly unnatural. It was not possible for any human body—any body—to heal with the efficiency and accuracy with which hers had done over the past few weeks.

And the explosion of light. There was no way to rationalize what had happened that night.

The only explanation for any of it was magic.

The magic that healed her, that caused sparks and light to shine, could only have come from one place.

Her.

Her magic that had been hidden and suffocated and suppressed for decades.

The root of hawthorn that was pulled from her. Soraya had said it was condensed with shadow magic.

Shadow magic like what Miriam wielded in life.

Deming could feel her heart physically contract at the reminder that Miriam had withheld that vital piece of information from her for her entire life.

And now...

She bent at the hips, chest nearly touching her thighs as she struggled to breathe.

Another deception? An extension of the same? Where does one betrayal end and another begin?

Would Miriam have made this suppressant? She had no memory of an injury on her thigh, nor a surgery to implant such a thing. Would Miriam have stitched it into Deming when she was so young memories couldn't take root in her mind?

Deming didn't have to think twice.

Of course she would have.

Before Miriam was Deming's maternal figure, she was Samira's best friend.

If Samira had asked her to hide a transgression, to make it so there would be no question Deming was the heir, Miriam would have in a heartbeat.

Except, of course, they couldn't hide everything.

All this time, she had assumed her tricolored hair was an oddity. On her worst days, she fell into the belief held by others at court that it was a sign from the gods that she was unfit to rule.

But no.

Gods nor goddesses nor deities of any kind had anything to do with it.

The brilliant red hair of the Reynes-Elyachar line had faltered in her because she was not a pureblood Reynes-Elyachar. She was not human, not completely. Not in the ways that mattered to the crown and throne.

Her heart began to beat, faster and faster like the pounding of Quinn's hooves on cobblestones.

It was suddenly impossible to breathe.

Her chest rose and fell erratically but she could feel no air in her lungs.

Something hot and breathy caressed the side of her face.

Words murmured into her ear. Words she could not, or would not, hear.

Someone offering a tether, trying to bring her back to earth with kindness or distraction or rationality. She didn't know the content of whatever was being spoken to her. All she knew was the rising panic and the weight of the claim that had been made.

The feel of it was heavy and slick and terrifying as it sank slower and slower into her until she knew it was true.

In her skin and marrow and sinew, Deming knew.

She was a mage.

Only when she allowed herself to feel the truth of it settle into her bones did she collapse to the ground completely and scream. The sound tore at her throat and scarred the natural serenity around them. As her fury and pain and despair rippled across the valley, something broke free inside her soul and the dusk sky erupted into a shower of stars.

CHAPTER FIFTEEN

DEMING

A COOL BREEZE SKATED across Deming's face, cooling her cheeks and tickling her nose.

She rubbed the back of her hand against the itch, then sighed and went back to her counting exercise.

Five things she could see. The moon hung high in the sky. A million stars—though she only counted them as one thing now, counting them individually had proven too difficult. A bundle of wildflowers nearby. The tips of trees in the distance. A candle flickering in the window of the apothecary, far enough away she couldn't make out which room it belonged to.

Four things she could hear. Leaves and needles rustling above. Chittering animals. An owl, somewhere. Her own steady breathing.

Three things she could feel. The cool earth beneath her palm. The scratch of the grass against her skin. The wind.

Two things she could smell. Pine, as strong as ever thanks to the forest. Lingering lavender soap from the bath she took this morning.

One thing she could taste. She tore another piece off the ramp laying beside her and placed it on her tongue. The savory flavor was fresh and wild all at once.

She frowned, looking down at the ramp. It was nearly gone.

She had been methodically repeating her exercise for almost an hour now. It was the only thing that kept her heart rate under control and her mind at ease.

Deming stood, brushed her skirts, and was about to go look for another ramp to pick apart piece by piece when a swath of stars above her winked out of existence.

"I want to be alone."

The near silent footfalls behind her paused, but only for a moment.

"If you truly wish me to leave, I will."

Emotion throttled Deming's heart, her throat suddenly thick with everything she had tried to shut out while sitting alone on this hill. She didn't want him to leave, not truly. She wanted, needed, someone to help her find herself again. It was impossible to know where to begin, though, when one's entire world was flipped on its head. Everything Deming knew to be true—about herself, about her parents, about her ascension to Laey's throne and her rule—was tainted now.

Nearly two decades of trauma and growth and power and love and building her life up brick by brick only to realize that the bricks she used had crumbled beneath her without her knowing.

A sob rose in her, heavy and unannounced. She tried to swallow it but her chest heaved and it came out strangled and sad.

"Oh, Deming," Nikita's arms wrapped around her, warm and solid and grounding, "come here." He turned her around, one hand firmly on her back and the other weaving upwards through her tangled mess of hair.

She cried into his chest, burying her face into the soft linen of his shirt and letting her tears fall freely. She was not built for this. She was not strong enough to handle so much change and heartbreak. Her body felt like it would simply cease to exist if one more tragedy struck.

Her legs wobbled, then gave out, and Nikita sank with her to the forest floor.

"It's too much," she whimpered, "I'm not strong enough for this."

"You are stronger than you know, Deming." His voice was soft but sure. He wiped away lingering tears from beneath her eye.

Deming shook her head.

"Yes," he said, "you are. Do you want to know why?"

Every muscle in her body stilled.

Desperately. She desperately wanted to know why he thought her capable and strong, but she didn't trust herself to believe his words. Could something be true about yourself if only others believed it?

He tilted her chin up so she was forced to meet his gaze when he spoke. "You are strong because you feel. You do not block emotions out, you embrace them fully. You feel everything fiercely and deeply and that is a strength. That is what you have brought to your friends, what you have brought to every trial you've faced, and what you will bring to your rule." He kissed the tip of her nose. "That is what you have brought to me."

His words broke her heart and healed it all at once. How could he have such soft thoughts about her when she was such a mess?

"I have never been one to wear my emotions on my sleeve," he continued, "but you have shown me what it is to be honest and true and how wonderful it can feel to let people in. Midwinter was...utterly cathartic. The male I was that night is who I want to be and you are the sole reason for that epiphany."

Deming sniffled, adjusted herself slightly in his arms. "I'm not controlled with my emotions though. You said it yourself. When I was grieving Miriam," her throat tightened as she spoke her name, "I shut everyone out. I'm not one to look up to."

"I never said you were perfect, princess. Only that I admire your strength. Even the fiercest river bends and flows and crashes into banks from time to time."

If Nikita could have grace for her, maybe she could have grace for herself. But that still did nothing to soothe the brokenness of her soul in the wake of what Soraya had told her.

"My uncle was right."

Violence flashed in his eyes like a lighting strike. "Your uncle was right about nothing." His lips pulled back into a snarl, each word held more venom than the next. "He is a vile man who stole your life and crown and I will make sure he feels every bit of pain you experienced tenfold when he meets his end."

"And if I want to be the one to take his life?"

"He is yours to do whatever you want with, Deming. Though," wicked mirth wound around the words he spoke next, "it would be a lie to say my hands don't itch to personally rip him limb from limb for what he did to you."

Deming didn't like possessiveness, but it turned out she did like whatever this was. Something fluttered back to life at his proclamation. He would go to the ends of the world for her. He would kill her enemies for her. And, most importantly, he would allow her to kill her enemies herself if she so desired. The choice was hers. Always.

"He was right about my rule, is what I meant." She twisted a finger into a lock of her hair, wove it through and watched the strands fall and tangle in a chaotic mess of red and pink and white. "About my hair being a sign that I was not fit to be queen." His hands tightened around her as if he had a visceral reaction to her saying that, but he let her finish. "It may not have been a sign from the gods, but it is a sign of my blood. I'm not..."

She couldn't bear to say it out loud. It wasn't that she had any resentment for mages or Fae. She certainly didn't think humans were better than either of them, quite the opposite, in fact. But she had spent her entire life believing she was one thing and to say out loud with her own voice that she was not human felt terribly definitive. "I'm not who I thought I was. I'm not—I can't be queen like this. I'm not worthy of the crown. I never thought I was and this..."

She huffed in annoyance at herself for stumbling over her words, then got to the point. "I've always been curious about my hair, wary. Me being a mage justifies that it's something to hate. Proof of what I am and what I'm not."

Nikita waited one second, then two, to make sure she had completed her thoughts before responding. His hand tucked stray hairs behind her ear, his fingers intertwined with the white pieces that framed her face.

"You resent your coloring, why? Because it highlights some supposed shame you're to feel? It matters not whose blood you share. What matters is the contents of your heart. The desires of your soul. Do you know what I see when I look at you? Fire and snow and flowers. Ferocity and softness. Beauty both bold and gentle. There are multitudes within you that should be celebrated, not suppressed. You are magic, Deming. The only shame in this is that you don't see it."

Her breath left her. "You can't mean that." Her voice was so quiet she wasn't entirely sure she had actually spoken the words aloud.

"I could never lie to you."

They remained tangled together, the steady beat of Nikita's heart and his deep breathing lulling Deming's stress and anxiety away.

Only when the moon had fully risen and the air took on the chill of night did Nikita break the silence.

"Do you remember what I said by the river earlier this winter? After you hurt yourself?"

Deming nodded, smiling at the memory that was so muddled with pain and sadness and grief but also, softly, hope. "That we would get through this together."

"Yes." He tugged her further into his lap. "Exactly. We will get through this together, as we have since we met. Not just you and me, but everyone here with us. We are with you, and you are with us. Family is blood, yes, but family is also who you choose it to be. I choose you, we choose you."

Warmth filled Deming all the way to the tips of her toes. She knew more than most that chosen family is just as important as blood. She had more memories with Miriam than she did with her own mother and father.

She winced briefly. Could she still call him that? A contemplation for another time. She reached out for the warmth of Nikita's words and held onto them.

"We survived Arsaela together and we will survive navigating your new sense of self. We will survive everything that Kielle and Selene throw at us."

"Together," Deming said, letting the word be an ember in her chest.

"Together," Nikita repeated.

CHAPTER SIXTEEN

DEMING

DESPITE FALLING ASLEEP IN tenuous comfort thanks to Nikita's words the night before, Deming woke up with frayed nerves and sweat trickling down her spine.

It was like a pendulum, the way she swung from feeling settled to feeling shattered.

She had padded to Paris's room and sat beside his bed, needing a tether to her old life, but the proximity to Paris only made her feel worse. Seeing him lifeless and limp made her skin crawl and hands clammy.

It was there, head in her hands and knees pulled up to her chest sitting on the floor beside Paris's bed, that Ilysse and Vallyn found her as dawn broke.

They exchanged a glance and firmly guided Deming to the kitchen, where they watched as she drank a full glass of water, then outside to train because, as Ilysse put it, there was nothing so grounding as a good spar.

So, here she was, pulse pounding and jaw clenched.

Deming had her feet firmly planted on the packed earth outside. Her knees were loose. She wiggled her fingers to ease her muscles.

Blonde braids lashed at the air as Ilysse advanced and Deming sank into her stance to absorb the blow rather than dodge.

Ilysse swung sideways and her fist connected with Deming's rib cage with a crunch.

Her breath momentarily gone, Deming drew her fists close to her belly and condensed herself as they both slid against the gravel.

The pain was instant and intense. It bloomed like a rose. She had been prepared for that though, had allowed Ilysse to land the blow on purpose. It may have hurt, but it also cleared her senses. The thorns of pain prickled through her.

Ilysse knew Deming would take the first hit and had pulled back just enough that a bruise would be the only damage done.

Deming exhaled. Strands of pink hair fluttered with her breath in the moment before she attacked back.

She threw an elbow into Ilysse's shoulder, then spun deftly around her back and landed another blow to her side.

Ilysse barely seemed to register the blow. She spun around quickly, her eyes sizing up Deming with the speed and dexterity of someone who fought for a living.

A fist shot out at Deming and connected with her shoulder. In the time it took Deming to recoil and gather herself, Ilysse had put space between them.

Deming rolled her shoulder to ease the pain. "Need a break?"

Ilysse laughed, the sound harsh and barking. "You shouldn't goad me, princess. You're lucky I'm taking it easy on you."

They circled one another like wolves. Each footstep precise. Every sweep of the eye meaningful. Deming had learned the dance, Vallyn had taught her well.

"You and I both know I don't want that."

"Very well."

The words were not yet out of Ilysse's mouth before she was advancing once more. Her body sliced through the air and it was all Deming could do to absorb the three blows Ilysse landed on her shoulder, ribcage, and thigh. The latter came with a fierce kick of Ilysse's leg and knocked Deming to the ground.

Deming hit the ground with a grunt and swiftly rolled away before the female could pounce further. Dirt clouded around her, clogging her breath and gritting against the soft tissue of her eyes. She spat out what had gathered in her mouth as she pressed her palms to the earth and leapt to her feet.

The air was hot and heavy, thick with sweat and panting breath.

The second Deming was on her feet she was moving, flying across the ground. To the left, she almost landed a punch to Ilysse's stomach. To the right, she dodged a counter attack and spun.

Ilysse's own feet skidded across the stones. She was on the defensive.

Deming's heart soared.

She could do it, she could pin her. This is what she trained for. She was better, faster, stronger than she was in the fall. The smack of her fist colliding with Ilysse's body. The sureness in the movement of her feet. The ease of her breathing despite the sweat dripping down her neck.

She threw an elbow and caught Ilysse on the chin. She could have sworn she heard Ilysse's teeth rattle in her jaw. The sound both frightened and invigorated her. This was it. One more blow and Ilysse would be down.

Braids whipped chaotically and sharp canines flashed as Ilysse lost her balance and Deming bounded forward to finish the fight. She cocked her arm and let it fly, aiming straight for the same spot her chin had just landed.

Her knuckles were a hairsbreadth from Ilysse's face but they did not make contact.

Ilysse ducked under the forceful swing and locked arms with Deming, twisting their bodies so Deming was suddenly and surely at the mercy of the warrior as they fell to the ground.

A frustrated yell escaped her as Ilysse's knees pressed into her arms, pinning her into the dirt. Ilysse's hand lay gently on her throat.

"Lose the battle, win the war."

Deming bit out a nasty response, to which Ilysse laughed.

Deming relaxed her body, tipped her head back against the ground, and laughed in return. The sound was sparkling and clean.

Close. She had been so close to winning. Closer than she ever had before. Pride blossomed in her because she knew that while Ilysse may have deceived her with that last sequence, she could not and had not been pretending to take every blow. She couldn't beat Ilysse, but she could hold her own.

"Get off me." Deming pushed against Ilysse's chest.

They untangled each other but didn't rise from the ground.

Vallyn leapt off the porch railing and joined them.

A breeze wound its way through the valley. Birds chirped and sang in the distance. Deming let the haze of the fight wear off and the sounds of the evening seep in. It was peaceful.

Deming was peaceful.

"Thank you," she gave both women an honest smile, "I needed that."

"I'll take any excuse to knock you on your ass."

Deming huffed out a half laugh. She whipped a pebble from the ground at Ilysse, who dodged and flung another one right back. Deming was not so quick and the small rock smacked her in the forehead.

"Hey!" Her admonishment was colored with jest.

The sun was rising, beginning its journey across the sky. Most of it was already peeking over the horizon of pines. Selene and her moonlight had fallen already, but the soft glow of stars still speckled the dawn.

The variety of light cupped in the sky at this moment sung to something deep within Deming. Her very bones hummed with anticipation or recognition or understanding… she wasn't sure.

"Deming?" Vallyn's voice was gentle.

"Mhmm."

"Do you want to talk about it?"

The awe Deming was feeling towards the view before her dimmed. The warmth in her blood was still there, still shining, but Vallyn's question drew her back to reality.

"No use in talking about it. There isn't anything to be done."

Stones and earth shuffled and scraped against each other. Vallyn propped herself on her side, holding her head up in one hand. Ilysse was strewn casually across the ground beside Vallyn, sweat and stray strands of blonde hair clung to the skin on her forehead, her neck, behind her ears.

Deming looked away and focused on the sky above her.

"Laey needs its rightful ruler on the throne," Vallyn said, "the continuation of the line matters not."

Deming closed her eyes against the emotion flooding them. "You know that isn't true."

The revelation of Deming's parentage was one thing, her being a mage another. But the true issue, the real reason her claim to the throne was in jeopardy now, was that mages could not bear children. No one knew how, or why. Perhaps it was because the gods had never intended for Fae and humans to procreate, so their offspring were incompatible with further life. Perhaps it was the way of the world, to balance power with pain. Mages had more control over magic than anything else on the continent—more than Fae, more than mythical beasts. Perhaps the inability to have children was their payment for magic living in their veins.

Whatever the reason, Deming would never produce an heir. The Elyachar line would die with her. Deming shoved down the turbulent emotions that accompanied that thought.

Whether or not her uncle knew that or guessed it or was simply lucky when he decided to overthrow a queen that conveniently offered no future to Laey they may never know. But the truth of that matter stands. Deming may be the rightful queen, but she would never give the queendom a red-headed, goddess-blessed princess.

The people of Laey wouldn't accept that kind of affront to their traditions.

Deming told the pair next to her as much.

Ilysse cracked her knuckles. "Maybe it's time for Laey to find new traditions." Classic condescension coated her muttered words.

"All I know is that you belong on that throne," Vallyn said firmly. "You are what our queendom needs. We can figure out your successor later."

Deming swallowed hard. She absentmindedly picked at the skin around her nails. "I don't—it's not—The matter of succession is an issue but," she sighed heavily, afraid of admitting what she was about to, "I don't know what I'm supposed to feel about my father."

Was she supposed to mourn Silas? Was she supposed to want to find her birth father? Was her opinion of who raised her supposed to change?

There weren't rules for this kind of revelation.

"King Silas or...?" Vallyn prodded gently.

Deming's head fell into her hands. "That's the whole issue. Who am I supposed to think of as my father? The man who raised me? Some enigmatic figure I've never met? Is it wrong to be sad that I'll never know whose blood I share? Any chance of knowing who he was died with Miriam." Her fingers grasped at the locket around her neck. She groaned, pushing hair away from her face. "I don't care, really, who he is. It wouldn't make a difference. I loved my dad, Silas. His are the footsteps I want to follow in. I just wish they hadn't lied to me."

Hot, fat tears rolled down her cheek.

"Oh, Deming."

Warm arms scooped her up. Vallyn pressed a kiss onto her temple and began combing her fingers through Deming's hair. The gentle tugging on her scalp felt calming. Deming let Vallyn comfort her for long, quiet minutes before shifting to give her a hug.

"I know it's silly to mourn over something I never even knew I had," she said into Vallyn's shoulder.

"You mourn your choice being taken from you. There is nothing more natural. And there is no right way to feel, so long as you're feeling something. If you want to be sad, be sad. If you want to be angry, be angry. Just keep feeling, okay?"

Deming nodded into her chest. Vallyn's body was warm and steady and Deming was hit by the feeling that she was deeply, tragically, truly undeserving of love and protection and yet, here she sat, basking in it all the same. Here, in the middle of the Runne, Deming found herself realizing that she was more than the sum of her parts. Did her blood matter? To some, surely. Not to her friends, though. Not even...

She laughed, a small, sputtery thing that caught in her throat and was accompanied by the breaking of some long anchored chain in her soul. Not even to her. The contents of her blood did not matter to her. She was Deming Sofia Reynes-Elyachar, Crown Princess to the Queendom of Laey. Her mother was Samira Reynes-Elyachar, Queen of Laey. Her father was Silas Reynes-Elyachar, King Consort of Laey.

Blood did not make a family, love did. And her father had loved her more than life itself.

The door creaked open behind them.

"Is everything okay?" Hartford asked, Soraya looking on from over her shoulder.

"Yep," Vallyn said, starting to stand up, "just a bit of early morning training."

Deming brushed the stray tears away. No more came.

She reached for Vallyn's hand, holding her back for a moment more.

"Thank you," she said, "I don't always know what I need, but you seem to."

Vallyn smiled. "It's my job to protect you. Sometimes that means from yourself."

Deming took a deep breath and for the first time since the revelation of her heritage, for the first time since leaving Arsaela, truthfully, the air felt fresh and clean and full in her lungs.

CHAPTER SEVENTEEN

DEMING

THE CONVERSATION IN THE kitchen came to an abrupt halt the second Deming walked through the door the next morning.

She paused mid step in the doorway, appalled at the speed at which every head swung in her direction and every syllable on the tips of tongues were instantly cut off. Where vibrant chatter existed only moments before now was barren save for the whistle of a kettle on the burner.

Everyone was clustered around the kitchen table with the exception of Paris, who was still fast asleep upstairs. Instead of addressing the fact that they all had either just been talking about her or were too jarred by her sudden appearance, Deming spoke directly to Soraya.

"Paris is still sleeping—Is that normal? His forehead is so hot."

Soraya didn't attempt to cover the concern laced in her voice. "No," her face contorted into a grimace that set Deming's nerves aflame, "it's not."

"Can you wake him up?"

"I wouldn't want to disrupt the healing process."

To no one in particular, she whispered, "He isn't healing, he's dying."

Soraya took a breath and the voice that she spoke with was calm but blunt. "Yes, he is."

Fear sizzled through Deming's veins and pain bit into her palms. She had balled her fists too tight.

The silence was oppressive. There was nothing to say, nothing to do. They could only hope for a miracle, though the gods had never been keen to answer Deming's prayers.

Flexing her hands, Deming smoothed wrinkles out of her skirt. The plain cotton fabric was soft with age and dyed a pale green that she knew complimented her complexion. The feel of it under her palms and in between her fingers helped settle her. She continued to play noncommittally with it as she sat in the only open seat and tried to restart the conversation.

"You've done so much for us already between researching the parasite and," she swallowed hard, trying and failing to keep her voice steady, "enlightening us about my heritage. I'm sure that eventually you'll break through with Paris, too."

Soraya dipped her chin, her eyes softened. "I promise, I'm doing all I can."

Deming's head tilted ever so slightly. The emphasis Soraya placed on those words felt off. The insinuation crested like a wave and crashed into her. "All you can do? Is there something that I could be doing?"

"Soraya! Why would you do that?"

"It's all conjecture—"

"She doesn't know what she's talking about—"

"You've gone through too much already—"

The screech of wood sliding abruptly across the floor screamed through the room as Deming pushed up and away from her chair.

She slapped her palms on the table as she said loudly and firmly, "One person, one," she held up a finger to emphasize the point, "is going to tell me what in Kielle's name you were talking about before I walked in. Now."

The last word came out more growl than speech but it had the desired effect. Spines straightened. Mouths snapped shut. Eyes flew to her. She raised an eyebrow and Ilysse was apparently the unspoken delegate to explain what they were talking about.

"We were discussing your magic."

The sentence collided into Deming. She felt the physical urge to recoil from it. She knew that with time she would learn to accept her heritage. That everyone at this table would help her forge a new path forward. But right now she still felt weak at the reminder that she was not who she thought she was. She was not even human. Her mother and Miriam had lied to her and the queendom for decades and now with both of them gone, it was unlikely Deming would be able to find any answers to the swell of insecurities and curiosities that plagued her.

"What you've demonstrated doesn't follow the traditional wheel of elemental magic," Ilysse continued, oblivious to the chaos in Deming's mind, "nor is it shadow magic. Hartford was saying that her best guess is that you possess a rare form of light magic."

The spiral of thoughts came to an abrupt halt.

Light magic? Deming had never heard of such a thing.

Nikita rolled his shoulders, easing the tension from them, and then responded as if he had heard Deming's thoughts. "There hasn't been a light mage in," he shook his head, sighed, "half a millennia at least. But there are records of them."

"Sparks, making items glow," Ilysse waved a hand flippantly, as if she was talking about the weather and not an ancient magic no one had seen in five hundred years, "that sort of thing."

"That seems rather uninspiring." Deming's quip was well received. A handful of smiles cracked around the table. Vallyn covered a laugh with a cough. "How is that supposed to help Paris?"

"Well," Ilysse leaned back and crossed her arms, "you clearly also have the ability to heal. If you can do it to yourself, you can do it to others."

Deming instantly felt foolish for not thinking of that sooner. Whatever magic flowed through her veins had healed her injuries on multiple occasions without her having to give it a second thought. If she could wrangle whatever part of her instinctively knew how to do that, she could use it to help Paris.

To help everyone.

Deming's heart brightened. Could this disaster of a revelation actually be a blessing? Her hand flew to the heart shaped locket around her neck. She had seen so much death in her life, so much hurt. She had been so helpless to those around her for so long. If what they were saying was true, if she did indeed possess light magic and by extension healing magic, never again would she have to sit idly by while her loved ones suffered.

The words flew out of her mouth on their own accord.

"I'll do it. Whatever it takes, I'll figure it out."

"Deming," Nikita warned, "you only found out about this part of you recently. No one would judge you if you needed more time to decompress. To wrap your head around what this means."

She shook her head, hair whipping violently. She appreciated his concern for her wellbeing but they didn't have a choice. They needed momentum, they needed a breakthrough. Maybe this could be it.

"Something sinister is creeping through the wilds if the leodin attack and those parasites are any indication. Every second we wait my uncle sinks his claws deeper into my queendom. We don't know what is coming, but we need to be prepared. That means Paris needs to be healed and I need to be in control of myself instead of letting the decisions of others lifetimes ago dictate who I am.

"There is war on the horizon. Your seer saw that much and everything we have experienced leads me to believe she is right. I want us to be at the forefront of that, not running from the tidal wave because we were caught off guard. If we will not be granted an audience with the king," she looked to Nikita for confirmation, who shook his head adamantly, "then we will do what we can here for the time being."

As Deming spoke, the effects of her words were tangible. Everyone gathered around the table, warriors and princes, humans and Fae, sat a little straighter. Heads bobbed in affirmation. Eyes glowed with purpose.

This is what it meant to lead, Deming thought. To inspire. To make decisions not unilaterally, but with the support of those around you. To take action.

Her heart fluttered at the realization that she enjoyed this. That maybe, in time, she may even be good at it.

"Soraya."

"Yes?"

"I need you to pour all of your focus into the parasites. Hartford will support. We need to understand what they are before we can send warnings to anyone who may need one."

Soraya's tail swished across the hardwood. She nodded then pressed a kiss to Hartford's temple.

"And you?" Vallyn looked at the lost heir with admiration, knowing as she asked the question what the answer would be.

"If I am to be a mage, then I must learn to wield magic."

CHAPTER EIGHTEEN

DEMING

WIELDING MAGIC WAS EASIER said than done.

Her magic lived within her. Now that she knew it was there, she could feel it flowing beneath the surface of her skin. It swam in her blood, beat with her heart. It was warm and comforting and felt almost sentient in the way it seemed to beg to seep out of her and into the world.

Deming longed to give it what it wanted, but after countless hours over the past two days of trying to coax it to materialize, she had nearly resigned to being the only mage on the continent that was unable to actually use their magic.

She flopped onto the ground.

The grass tickled her neck.

"Try again," Vallyn encouraged.

Deming propped herself up on her elbows and huffed noncommittally. The exasperated sigh pushed the white tendrils framing her face out and away. They fell haphazardly across the bridge of her nose when they fell.

"Try what?" Deming asked with an edge to her tone.

It wasn't that she was annoyed with Vallyn. Her friend had been incredibly helpful and supportive as Deming tried everything and anything under the sun to awaken her abilities. It was just that after two days of nothing besides one, tiny flicker of light that immediately withered, she was feeling burnt out.

Vallyn leaned back against the tree trunk behind her. One leg was bent, an arm casually hanging off it. She was wearing an outfit that hugged her body closely. Everything was all black save for the silver of her boot buckles and the gold bands accenting her hair.

"I think the slow breathing was helping," Vallyn said, picking at the chipped nail polish on her thumb. Ilysse had been painting her own nails last night and had somehow convinced Vallyn to let her paints hers, too.

Ilysse had managed one thumb before Vallyn tore her hand away and stomped upstairs, muttering nonsense under her breath.

Deming smiled at the memory. "Maybe," she acquiesced, folding her legs underneath her once more.

"Go on, then."

Deming rolled her eyes but straightened her spine and laid her hands palms up on the tops of her knees.

Slowly, she drew breath into her lungs. Her chest expanded, her chin rose, and when she could inhale no more she held her breath for one, satisfying moment before releasing air through her nose in a long, measured exhale.

Again, and again.

Each repetition brought her more focus, more clarity. With every exhale Deming could feel her magic more fully. It danced just out of reach, singing a foreign song that felt like it was on the tip of Deming's tongue.

Resting in the calm that this exercise brought was easy, familiar, even if the feeling of her power rolling in her veins was not.

Despite it being so close, her magic remained out of reach.

She called to it. She begged and pleaded but it was no use.

Deming opened her eyes and felt the sparkling ecstasy fade away to a simmer.

The weight of Vallyn's hand fell on Deming's shoulder. "Keep at it. You'll get it."

As Vallyn walked back towards the house, Deming's gaze drifted across the lush landscape.

The beauty of it all took away the sting of failure.

Arsaela still held her heart, and she desperately missed being cocooned in the rocky embrace of the Telaciens, but there was something so serene about this little patch of evergreen land. The way the tree line melted into the fields was like out of a painting. Soraya's home was nestled in the center, cozy and full of character with its hammered glass windows and smoke billowing out of the chimney. Horses nickered from the paddock and sunlight beamed down on it all, Kielle's warmth eternal here in Bascade.

A flurry of grunts drew her attention towards the south lawn.

Nikita was sparring with Ilysse.

Their toned bodies spun around each other in practiced, clean movements. Nikita's feet swept across the dirt as he ducked a punch. Deming swore she saw a glint of bone shining in the afternoon light. Would they be sparing with Ilysse's claws out?

They swapped hits and dodges and circled around each other, both equally predator and prey. Ilysse feinted to the side, then spun and struck.

She watched as Nikita fell for the feint and took a blow to the chin.

He was losing, Deming realized with a hint of playful satisfaction.

Nikita laughed and wiped at his bleeding lip with the back of his hand.

She walked towards them and sat down on the rickety back stoop to watch the rest of the training session unfold.

Deming bit her lip. She was close enough now to see the sheen of sweat glistening across his brow and the individual fluctuations of feathers as his wings cut through the air.

The material of his pants molded to his thighs like it was a second skin.

How someone this magnificent could ever be interested in someone as plain as her was simply beyond comprehension.

She wished they had the luxury of peace. She wished they had more time to learn about one another, to explore one another and whatever this was between them.

Deming felt physically drawn to him like they were being pulled together by some unknown force. She had always gravitated towards him, but it was more intense the past couple weeks. It was getting progressively more challenging to ignore the desire to be with him, but she did her best.

This was not the time. Nikita had so much on his mind, being so close to his father. She didn't want to overwhelm him.

With a swinging kick to Nikita's ribs, Ilysse sent him crashing into the dirt.

Nikita exhaled roughly from the ground. His wings were splayed like an ink spill behind him. "I saw that coming."

Ilysse's feline smile showed off sharp canines as she helped him up. "Whatever you say."

Deming gave Ilysse a curt nod as the female dipped inside the house then stood.

Nikita was unwrapping the bandages around his knuckles. After his hands were free, he grabbed the nearby glass of water and placed the edge to his lips.

"Why didn't you use your wings?" Deming asked. "You could have flown out of reach."

He gulped down water and pushed sweaty pieces of hair away from his face. "Part of the drill." His breathing was heavy. "No aspects."

He tilted the glass back, swallowing the rest of the water. His throat was fully exposed and Deming had the impulse to press her lips to the pulse point that beat beneath his skin. His shirt was rumpled and torn at the hems. It clung to the corded muscles of his chest and abdomen.

Deming hugged her arms around herself in an attempt to slow down her racing heart. "Ilysse was using her claws."

Nikita barked a short, gruff laugh. "Yeah, I saw that. Her emotions are running high." He arched his back, stretching, and his wings flared out. He rolled his neck, set the empty glass down, and crossed his arms. A smirk played at the corners of his mouth. "If Ilysse liked males I'd say it was my irritatingly good looks that pushed her over the edge but alas, she's probably just annoyed that we've stayed in the same place for so long."

Deming frowned at that. She was looking at her open palms when she said, "I'm trying my best."

"No, no," Nikita tipped her chin up, "she's not annoyed with you, or anyone."

"You just said—"

"I didn't mean you. I promise."

He held his finger under her chin until she nodded in acceptance. When he withdrew, she immediately missed his touch.

"A piece of advice," Nikita continued, "whenever you think Ilysse might be mad at you, just remember that she is generally irritable and her attitude is almost never because of one particular incident."

Deming laughed begrudgingly. "Okay, fair enough."

"How did your training go?"

Deming's neck tilted and she hung her head dramatically backwards and groaned. "Calling it training is a gross overstatement."

"That bad?"

"I'd love bad, bad implies something happened. But no," she drew out the word as her eyes rolled, "I can't make my magic do anything I ask."

Nikita's head cocked to the side, inquisitive. "You're still healing, though, right?"

"Over time, yes. But it's not because of anything I'm doing voluntarily. Vallyn thinks that meditation is helping." She twirled her hand in the air. "She thinks I'll be able to feel my magic better if I'm calm, still, or something."

"Nothing about you should be tamed," Nikita said, stepping closer.

Deming's stomach flipped at their proximity. Her mind tunneled back in time to the last time they were this close, this alone. The kiss they shared under the moonlight was imprinted on her soul. It crept into every dream, every wandering thought.

"I don't—that's not what Vallyn meant, I don't think—" Deming stumbled over her words until she faked a cough and pressed her lips together.

A mischievous spark played between the shades of gray in his eyes. "Does my presence unnerve you?"

Unnerve, placate, excite, calm.

Pick nearly any adjective.

"Yes," she growled low and slow, "you know it does."

He leaned in closer. Waves of cardamom and salt washed over her, the underlying, heady scent of him made more potent by heat and sweat.

His hand traced the curve of her hip.

Deming could feel his lips brush against the shell of her ear.

"I like knowing the effect I have on you," he whispered.

His nose grazed her temple and she felt him inhale deeply. The action was so personal, so intimate. His breath caressed her skin like a lover.

Deming placed her hand atop his and pressed his grip harder onto her waist.

She looked up at him, lips parted, eyes pleading.

Nikita met her gaze with intensity of his own. His storm cloud eyes were ablaze. Streaks of want tore through them like lightning.

Her back arched beneath his touch, sending her hips forward and her mouth all the closer to his.

The softest whimper escaped her lips.

That sound must have snapped something with Nikita because the moment it fell he closed the distance between them.

The kiss was firm and eager, soft and perfect.

Deming nipped at his bottom lip and he groaned.

This is what she wanted. This, and more.

Heat pooled in her stomach and an ache began throbbing between her legs.

Her hands found their way up his neck and into his hair, threading themselves into the dark curls and tugging him closer to her.

Nikita kissed her with fervor and Deming felt more alive than she had felt in months.

Then, far too quickly, he stopped.

Her mind swam with thoughts of his mouth. The only sound was their shared panting.

Deming's lips felt swollen, her cheeks felt flushed. There was an insatiable need for more—more kisses, more touching, more of him—swirling in her.

"Why did you stop?" she asked breathlessly. Her heart pattered with the worry that she had somehow pressured him to more than he wanted.

His eyes darkened and when he spoke, there was a husky edge to his voice. "Because if I didn't stop now, I wouldn't be able to stop at all."

A shiver, as delicate as lace, trickled up her spine.

He pressed his mouth to her neck and spoke into her heated skin. "And when we finally have each other that way, I want to be able to savor you."

Gods, she had never wished to be alone with him more than she did in this moment.

He was right, though. They were dry kindling to the spark of their desires and now, standing in the backyard of Soraya's house with all of their friends on the other side of the door, was not the time to give in to the fire.

Their foreheads rested against each other, the tips of their noses touching.

Together, they put distance between want and reality until they were both breathing normally.

It was only when she reluctantly slid her hands out of his hair that she realized her palms were aglow.

Warm, buttery light shone from them like a mirage against the afternoon air.

"Kit," she breathed.

He inhaled sharply, taking her hand in his and cradling it gently.

The light dimmed slowly until it was no more than a droplet in her palm, then it blinked out of existence.

"I think we've been going at this wrong," Nikita mused.

Deming looked up. "What do you mean?"

"You've been trying to drag your magic out by either force, cutting yourself, or serenity, meditation. But Soraya already gave us the key." He looked at her with curious awe. "Heightened emotions can trigger magical responses."

Realization dawned in Deming, clear and bright. One look at Nikita and she knew he was thinking the same thing.

"You think it'll work?"

"It's worth a try, isn't it?"

Paris lay on the bed, unmoving.

His blonde hair was brushed away from his ashen forehead. A white sheet had been pulled up over him, covering most of his body, and a thick, colorful blanket was folded neatly atop his legs.

Deming rubbed her thumb along the back of his hand, which was limp in her own.

"Hey, Paris."

Her voice cracked on his name. Seeing him so still—so quiet with no curiosity or apprehension or emotion of any sort animating his features—was undoing Deming's sanity bit by bit every time she visited his bedside. She would continue coming back, though. She would rather fall into madness than abandon her friend.

Every morning she came and spoke to him.

Every morning she watched the dawn soak into the sky like watercolors outside his window.

And every morning she cursed the crushingly beautiful periwinkle sky as it heralded in yet another day that Paris remained unchanged.

The golden rays of late afternoon that drenched the bedroom now did nothing to ease Deming's trepidation.

"Kit thinks my emotions are the key to my magic. He thinks that if I focus on how I feel about you, I may be able to heal you."

Steam wafted from her cup of tea. It was perched perilously close to the edge of the simple wooden nightstand but Deming paid it little attention.

"You don't even know I can do that." Her face pulled into a frown. Her fingers stilled. "I'm not who you thought I was. I'm not who I thought I was."

Deming sighed and watched Paris's chest rise and fall in the steady rhythm of his breathing.

"I am…not human." The words clung to Deming's throat like too thick honey. She forced them out despite the way they dug their claws in, terrifying her. "I'm a mage."

It was the first time she had said it out loud. The words fell like dead leaves.

It felt permanent, now, as if acknowledging it aloud bound it into the fabric of the world.

Silly, that feeling, since it was true no matter if she said it or not.

She wondered if Paris could hear her at all, if she would need to say it all again if he woke up.

When he woke up.

"I don't know what it means for my family. I don't know what it means about my parents."

Emotion choked her at the thought of Silas and Samira. Though, that was the point. If she could tap into her emotions, maybe she would be able to heal Paris.

So she twisted a spade deeper into her soul and unearthed everything she had buried.

"And do you want to know what the worst part is? I don't even care that I don't know. I can't find it in myself to care anymore about whose blood I share because all I can think about is what this means for me, for my future." The laugh that cracked out of her was stunted, manic. "How selfish is that? I learn that the man I thought was my father was just another piece in the long string of lies fed to me since birth and all I can think about—"

Deming's throat closed up.

"All I can—"

Her chest felt like it was cracking in two.

Deming folded in on herself, the weight of all she carried suddenly too much.

Into the crumpled fabric of her shirt, she admitted to Paris what she had kept hidden far within herself ever since she found out she was a mage. The terrible truth that she had not been able to face until now out of fear of falling apart completely.

"All I can think about is that I will never get to be a mother."

Her heart splintered with the words she had barely let herself think, let alone speak aloud. Miriam's heart pendant was clutched in her hand, the metal smooth and cool and comforting against the tears that sprung forth.

A cracked whimper escaped her throat. She squeezed her eyes shut and curled onto her side.

That, more than anything else, was the deepest wound the treacherous nest of lies surrounding Deming had caused. Deeper than finding out Miriam was a mage, deeper than the loss of never knowing who her birth father was. The fact that she would never have children of her own cut deeper than it all.

Mages could not sire nor bear children, and that truth shattered the one hope Deming had always carried for her future.

"We used to dream about that, remember?"

Through teary eyes Deming looked at Paris, lost in memories of when they were young and naive and in love. It didn't matter they were no longer together, everything they once were was preserved in amber.

"A little girl with red hair and blue eyes. Quiet but joyful, wary but proud. The best of both of us."

Deming held Paris's hand tightly and closed her eyes. Her lashes spread the tears across her cheek as her face pinched with loss.

"She will never exist."

The hurt of saying goodbye to that dream was made more painful by the fact that she may lose not just an imaginary daughter, but Paris, too.

They had been through so much this year. He wasn't perfect, but neither was she. They were not meant to be together romantically, she knew that now. But she also knew they were meant to be in each others lives. He and Colette had built her girlhood brick by brick and Deming was not ready to say goodbye to them, too, in the wake of all the other changes to the world as she knew it.

She shoved the errant wish for Colette away. Her feelings about her cousin were too complicated to parse through right now.

Paris was here, now, and he needed her.

Taking a steady breath, Deming sat up straighter and wiped away her tears. "I can live without a daughter, but I don't know how to live without you."

She placed her hands on his chest, closed her eyes, and focused on her magic.

It was there, warming her from the inside out. It rolled and moved with the emotions crashing through her like waves. Turbulent and ready, it was there.

Deming called to it, begged for it to come when she beckoned.

A flicker of orange painted the backs of her eyelids and she opened her eyes to see soft light pouring into Paris from her hands.

She nearly cried. It was working, she had done it—

The light started to fade.

"No, no, no..." The pleas tumbled chaotically from her lips.

Just as quickly as it had appeared, the light collapsed into nothingness.

She lifted her palms, cursing them and the fickle light magic they held.

Paris looked exactly the same.

"Wake up," she implored him.

Paris remained resolute in his unconsciousness. Still as a corpse save for the rise and fall of his chest, he rested in the bed.

She had failed.

Disappointment and fear threatened to swallow her whole.

Her fingers dug into her scalp, pulled at her hair.

She had been so close. Why would her magic not obey her?

How much longer could Paris survive in this state?

"Come back to us," Deming whispered, "please."

She tried again and again until the stars in her vision had nothing to do with her magic. Then, with nothing left to do but let dread lap at her sanity like waves on a beach, she kissed his palm, placed it on his chest, and left the room that was beginning to feel more and more like a tomb.

CHAPTER NINETEEN

DEMING

THE AIR SMELLED OF copper and hung heavy with self induced suffering.

Blood licked its way down Deming's arm, pouring from the freshly opened wound on her forearm. The knife lay discarded in the grass. Its blade was covered in layers of blood in various states of freshness. She gritted her teeth and squeezed her eyes shut against the waves of sharp pain that rolled through her.

Too deep, she had cut too deep that time. It was impossible to parse through the pain to try and find the thread of healing magic that was racing through her body to the source of the injury. She could feel no warmth, no spark in her veins, no hint of the magic she knew she possessed. The only thing her mind could focus on was the screaming of her torn flesh.

A metallic tang flooded her mouth. She had bitten her tongue.

Again.

After failing so miserably to heal Paris yesterday, Deming had thrown herself into practice at the break of dawn. She was determined to get this. The need to grasp her magic, any part of it, felt more intense than ever. Her emotions clearly played a role in her magic, but they were too unpredictable.

Paris needed her now, and Deming would do whatever it took to heal him.

The result was that she had been slicing shallow cuts into her arms for too long with too little active magic produced and was now wound so tightly she felt she might snap.

The broken dreams she spoke aloud were like shards of glass in her soul.

"You need to take a break," Nikita said.

"I'm fine." The lie tasted rotten in her mouth.

"You're getting sloppy. That was too deep."

Deming reached for the knife but Nikita beat her to it. She glared at him through the haze of pain. "I asked you to help and you refused."

"You asked for me to cut you open repeatedly," he growled, his lips pulling back into a snarl. "That's barbaric and unnecessary."

Deming grabbed the roll of gauze and ripped off a piece. She dabbed it around the wound then wrapped it tightly around her arm. In the hours that she had been at this, she discovered that while her body would heal itself on its own, the process went faster when aided by pressure.

"How else do you suggest I locate my magic, prince?" The title was spat like an insult, though her heart wasn't in it and she immediately regretted it. She knew he meant well. In fact, if the roles were reversed, she knew she would be acting the same way. Even the thought of harm coming to him sent a malicious shiver down her spine.

"Sorry," she mumbled, "that was uncalled for." She shut her eyes tight and watched stars dance across the backs of her eyelids. "I need to be able to help him."

Nikita's sigh was heavy and full of frustration.

Her voice softened at the sight of him. "I wish there was another way, trust me."

"I know," he said, the words muffled from behind the hands he had brought up to rub his face. "Be done for tonight, though. Please. If not for me, then for Paris. You are no use to anyone, especially him, if you bleed out."

Nikita was right, she needed a break. They had been at this for hours. She was losing blood faster than her body was regenerating it. Her incisions had gotten sloppy. Rest was as important to growth as effort.

If she wanted to find the threads of magic within her, she needed a fresh mind. A well-rested mind. She would try again tomorrow. For tonight, she was finished.

"Okay."

The relief Nikita felt was palpable. Every muscle relaxed, his wings dropped slightly.

Deming smirked. He was every bit the territorial Fae royal. Always needing to protect what he thought was his.

And yet, he hadn't demanded that she stop. Only pleaded.

She could get used to him begging.

Blush crept up her neck at the thought. It had come on so quickly she hadn't had time to prepare for the onslaught of daydreams that accompanied it.

Nikita kissing her.

Nikita on his knees before her.

Nikita begging her to touch him.

Her hand winding through his hair, across his skin, through the feathers of his wings.

"Deming?"

Her eyes shot to his, alarmed and pulled from the recesses of her mind. To her horror, her breath came in ragged pants. She struggled to push the images of the male before her down and regain control of her sanity.

He stared at her intensely, the gray of his eyes dark and stormy as if he could read her mind. She felt the heat of her blush creep further up her neck, onto her cheeks.

"What are you thinking about?"

Her lips parted to speak but no sound came out. She cleared her throat. "Nothing, I was thinking about nothing."

"If you're going to lie to me you'll need to do a more convincing job."

Deming found she could not come up with a more convincing lie, so she said nothing.

Nikita chuckled knowingly to himself and Deming glared at him.

Then he pushed himself up from his chair and gestured towards the kitchen window. It was lit brightly. Deming saw Hartford pass by, smiling back towards someone.

"Tea?" Nikita asked.

"That would be great, thanks."

Deming watched as he walked away. His shoulders shifted with the weight of his wings. The arch of them curled gracefully over his head and cascaded down in a waterfall of iridescent feathers until just above the ground. She could see the muscles in his back shifting as he walked and she wanted nothing more than to drag her nails down them.

Her eyes drifted lower, catching his ass just before he slipped inside.

Deming fell back against the grassy knoll, groaning.

He was so attractive. It wasn't fair.

She threw her arm over her face and yelled—short, sharp, and muffled by her coat.

Her restraint was hanging on by a thread.

She had marginally collected herself by the time he returned with her tea, though the graze of his hand against her as he passed her the cup sent a sparks dancing across her skin.

Deming brought the cup to her lips and blew. Steam wafted away in delicate curls. She took a sip and jasmine filled her senses. Heat trickled down her throat, pooling in her belly and warming her pleasantly.

"Thank you."

"Of course." Nikita settled onto the ground beside her. He bent an arm behind his head to rest on and stared up at the sky. "How's the arm?"

Deming extended her arm, turning it and flexing her bicep to test the muscle. There was a small twinge of pain but nothing more. She would bet her crown that if she removed the bandage, it would be close to healed already.

"Good. Even though I can't do it myself, every time my body is forced to heal itself it happens a little bit faster." She cursed the magic that lay in her veins, seemingly inaccessible to her.

"Makes sense I guess." Nikita nodded, considering. "Like anything, the more practice the better." He looked in her direction. "And you're okay? Not lightheaded or anything from the blood loss?"

She shook her head.

He grunted, satisfied, and they both relaxed in the warmth of a Bascade afternoon.

It was peaceful in this little corner of the world. Divine rays of sunlight poured through the clouds. Birds flitted from tree to tree. Jasmine from her tea perfumed the air.

It was so beautiful Deming could almost forget the weight she carried.

They lay there, shifting imperceptibly closer to the other with each shift and adjustment of their bodies in the grass, until she was laying atop his wing. Feathers tickled her cheeks and twined with her unbound hair. Their pinkies touched and without thinking she reached just enough to curl hers fully around his.

Without missing a beat, Nikita turned his wrist and slipped his fingers between hers.

Deming's heart thudded in her chest. She knew her erratic breathing belied her attraction but there was nothing she could do to control it. His presence undid her.

"I was thinking about you." The words that had been perched on her lips like a bluejay on a branch suddenly spilled out.

Nikita propped himself up on an elbow, looking at her with intrigue.

"Earlier, when you asked what I was thinking about. I was thinking about you."

He smirked, eyes lighting up with mischief. "Is that right?"

He stared down at her with those storm gray eyes and she swore she saw desire swirling in their depths, mirroring hers.

Deming felt blush creeping back up her neck. There was so much heat in his gaze.

"I'd love some more specificity."

She hadn't admitted to anything yet. She could still get out of this unscathed. She could water down the admission, say she was thinking about something less intense.

But Deming decided rashly that she didn't want that at all.

"I was thinking about what you might look like on your knees before me. What it might feel like to kiss you again—to touch you—but not have to stop."

His reaction to her honesty could only be found in the details.

His nostrils flared. His hands tensed. His wings lifted.

Deming barely noticed any of that. She was focused on the way his eyes darkened at her words, on the way her body warmed under his gaze.

"Say the word, Deming, and we can do whatever you desire."

"Take me somewhere we can be alone."

She was wrapped in his arms in seconds, the grass and her tipped over cup of tea a distant memory as the sky enveloped her.

They landed in a field of wildflowers.

The stalks swayed in the wake of the beat of Nikita's wings, their scent rich and full and fresh, exactly like the wildflowers in Laey.

Nikita folded his wings neatly behind his back but only barely loosened his grip on her as she slid from where she was nestled in his arms from the flight.

The petals were soft under her bare feet.

She turned in his embrace and relished the feel of his hands on her waist.

He leaned into her, pressing his forehead into hers. Their noses were almost touching, their breath mingled.

"What do you want, Deming?"

Everything, all of him.

She looked up and caught his gaze. "I want to forget everything, just for a moment. I want to relax." The heat from his body seeped into her and she could feel how hard he was already as he pulled her closer. She felt like she might melt into a puddle at his feet. "I want you to finally do what I've dreamt of for months."

His grip on her waist tightened. "Anytime you want to stop, we can stop," he murmured into her temple.

"We haven't even begun."

"I just want you to feel safe."

He was the embodiment of security to her. He was comfort and peace, safety and home. He was at once the fire that kept her warm and the earth that kept her grounded.

"I have always felt safe with you."

His hum of approval into her neck sent shivers through her. She felt the vibrations ripple across her skin and muscle. His lips were pressed into her, firm but soft, urgent but impossibly steady. He nipped at her neck, causing the memory of the last time they were in this position to rise through her consciousness like smoke from a fire.

Even the smallest of his touches made her wild. What would something of substance do to her?

She let her hand trace nonsensical patterns on his back. Each swirl and dip wove closer to where his wings hinged from his shoulder blades. The echo of their last kiss guided her movements. She was eager to recreate that moment, to feel him shudder against her. She was eager for more.

He hissed into her neck as her fingers teased the downy edges.

"Kiss me, Kit." She sounded as desperate as she felt. "Please."

"I thought I was supposed to be the one begging."

Her laugh was cut off by Nikita's mouth on hers.

His lips were soft and the kiss was passionate and deep, instantly heating her and coaxing her desire to the surface. His tongue parted her lips and she met him stroke for stroke.

One of his hands cupped the back of her neck, the other remained firmly on her waist. She felt his fingers dig gently into the soft skin on her hips and tangle into her hair. Her own were spreading feathers, feeling the texture of them slip against her skin like silk. He pulled her so close to him that she swore there was no space at all between their bodies. Where he ended, she began.

They moved in tandem, a give and take of heat and lips and hands gripping waists and necks and hair. It was beautiful and chaotic and Deming had never known that kissing someone could make her feel this joyful and free, and suddenly she was laughing, the sound pealing around the colorful flowers like a bell.

"Is this amusing to you, princess?" Nikita growled, playfully nipping at her ear.

She took his face in both hands. "You make me feel alive."

And it was true. The very existence of him sung to her like a melody. She wished she could dance in this feeling, bottle it up and sip it like wine.

Nikita's eyes were aflame with desire and reverence. "You make me feel everything, Deming." He spoke her name like a prayer.

Deming felt pressure on her back, he was guiding her to the ground. She let him hold her weight completely as he dipped her slowly to rest in the bed of wildflowers at their feet. He joined her, their legs a tangle of limbs and the desire between his hips pressing delectably into the apex of her thighs.

Nikita peppered her skin with kisses. One forearm rested beside her, holding him up, but the other hand was free to roam. He ran a finger over her lips, swollen from kissing, and parted them just enough for Deming to lean into the impulse that surged through her and take the finger into her mouth.

She sucked, hard, then swirled her tongue around him. He swore and buried his face into the side of her neck. When he returned, his eyes were near black.

"You have a wicked mouth, princess."

She smiled sweetly up at him, releasing his finger and relishing in the wanton desire that filled his heated gaze. She slid a hand in between them and palmed him through his trousers. She gave him one, two strokes. "I can do so much worse."

He grabbed her hand and pinned it above her head. "In time," he leaned in close, his breath hot on her neck, "I want you to do all sorts of wicked things to me." He sealed his promise with a slow, methodic thrust of his hips.

The friction sent Deming off the edge. Her back arched, her hips moved of their own accord. With wild abandon she moaned and panted his name, desperate for more contact, more touch, more anything.

"Please," she begged.

"Please what?"

"Please touch me."

Nikita's smile could have outshone the sun. "As you wish."

He lifted himself off her, only to reposition himself so he laid on the ground beside her. His mouth kissed her neck and shoulders and arms and his hand traced an invisible line from her jaw, down her neck, around her chest.

Though she still wore her dress, every touch of his was electric through the fabric. With one finger, he circled both breasts painstakingly slowly, making sure to tease her nipples. He flicked one unexpectedly and Deming cried out in pleasure.

"Like this?" His voice was like the thickest velvet.

Deming closed her eyes, desperate to sink as far into the feeling as possible. "Yes," she whispered hoarsely. "More."

He was all too happy to oblige.

Time swayed like saplings in the wind. How long she lay in that bed of wildflowers being caressed by Nikita was completely lost on her. His touch was languid and deliberate, coaxing soft sounds to crest her lips and decorate the air between them like stars until her body was as pliant and eager for him as her mind was.

He stopped and Deming's eyes opened slowly, as if moving through molasses or waking up in the middle of a dream.

"Why did you stop?"

His eyes burned like molten silver as he responded.

"I don't think I can bear to live another second without knowing how you taste."

Deming's heart skipped a beat. She splayed her knees.

"Words, princess," Nikita murmured against her skin.

"Yes," Deming said, "I am yours."

"And I am yours."

He kissed his way down her body, pressing affirmations into her with each one.

Her neck. "Beautiful."

The crook of her elbow. "Vexing."

Each breast. "My queen."

He pulled the skirts of her dress up and let them pool atop her stomach. The next two kisses were pressed onto her bare skin and Deming felt she might die of pleasure before he had even begun.

Her left thigh. "Captivating."

Her right. "Worthy."

The ember in her belly had already been stoked to a flame but feeling Nikita's breath in between her thighs ignited her entire being. She was an inferno of desire. Everything fell away except the delicious, tantalizing, excruciating sensation that was building in her core.

Her hands slid through the leaves and grass and into his hair. She tugged him forward, begging him to close the gap between them, to place his mouth on her, to have her in a way no one else ever had.

"Impatient woman," he breathed out, collecting her wrists in one hand. "Be a good girl and keep your hands above your head. Can you do that for me?"

Deming nodded fervently, clasping her hands together and burying them in the wildflowers above her. She would do anything he said if it meant he kept going.

She cried out when he finally slid his tongue in and gave her a deep, deliberate lick. Then another, then another.

"You," he said, voice muffled as if he was loath to part from her even to speak, "are unbelievable."

He slid a finger into her with the next pass of his tongue and she gasped at the feeling of him inside her. He moved deftly, stroking her again and again as his tongue swiped up and across the bundle of nerves nestled at the top.

Her breathing was ragged, pants came out unevenly. He had brought her so close after so long of teasing her body with his touch it was shocking to have so much direct stimulation.

Without stopping the motion of his hand he looked at her. "Is this what you like?"

It was hard to comprehend his words, she was so deeply immersed in the sensations pooling within her. It was harder still to imagine that anything could be better than this.

Yes, she liked this. It was a ridiculous notion to consider she didn't enjoy the feelings he was giving her. She was heat and desire and passion under his touch. She felt everything. Her skin was prickling with pleasure from her head to her toes and yet...

"Slower."

Her voice cracked on the word. She had nearly forgotten how to speak.

Nikita slowed instantly and Deming could once again breathe.

He replaced his tongue inside her with gentle kisses on her inner thighs. He sucked her skin into his mouth, grazed his teeth against her. He gave her the lightest bites he could manage and each nip sent lightning shooting through her veins.

His finger had remained inside her all the while. He curled it against her belly from the inside and pulled out with painstaking slowness. Only when she was aching and empty and yearning for him to fill her once more did he slip inside her and repeat the motion.

Deming's back arched and her hips moved with him, emphasizing the path his fingers created within her. Her breathing, too, became synced with the movement of their bodies. The repetition and leisure with which he stroked her blew a gentle wind on her desire, lighting it aflame. Before it had been such a whirlwind of sensation that she couldn't focus on taming the desire into release. This was far different.

She broke his rule and released her grip on the wildflowers. Only the gentlest nudge from her fingertips and he understood.

Gentle as the petals crushed beneath them, he pressed his lips to her and gave her a long, slow lick that culminated in him sucking on the bud of nerves that sat atop her like a crown with the care one only gives to something deeply cherished.

She gasped and heat flared in her. There. That. More.

"Again."

He obeyed.

"Again."

She was so close, pleasure was cresting in her like a wave. Again, please. She begged in her mind, unable to speak as every muscle in her body tightened in desperate anticipation.

He added the slightest bit of additional pressure to his fingers, stroking her from the inside and the most sensitive part of her in his mouth once more, though this time he didn't release her. He sucked and licked and worshiped her endlessly and did not let go as the pressure inside her built and built until it finally came crashing down like thunder in the midst of a storm.

Her hands dug into the ground as her head tilted back and an uninhibited cry of pleasure escaped her as release barreled through every part of her with the crackling energy reserved for stars and suns and magic—

The backs of her eyelids were painted red as light flared out from her in abundance. Stars filled her mind and vision, and she couldn't be sure what was from pleasure and what was from her magic.

After seconds or years or days Deming returned to her body, earthliness settling into her bones with a heaviness that felt relaxing and grounding and reminded her of who she was.

Her first thought was that they hadn't even taken their clothes off.

Her second was that Nikita was still buried between her legs, licking up the remnants of her pleasure. It felt good for a moment then was instantly entirely too much, the sensitivity of that region having been turned up immeasurably in the wake of her release.

She squirmed beneath him. "Kit."

At the sound of his name he surfaced, meeting her gaze for a moment then breaking into a grin as wide as the continent.

"What?"

He propped himself up on his elbows and she could see his mouth was slick with her. Mirth and surprise laced his voice. "I've never made someone literally glow with pleasure before, that's all."

She looked down and sure enough, every inch of her skin was glowing with a faint, soft light. The sight sent a shiver of awe through her and the light flickered with her for it was her and she was it and they were one.

She raised a hand, turning it over and flexing her fingers. She had magic. Whether it was the lingering joy from being with Nikita or the beautiful form her magic displayed for her now or for some other reason entirely, the fact that light flowed in her veins just as blood did filled her with eagerness and excitement. Looking up at her hand shimmering with a similar glow to the moon and stars that hung in the sky behind it was humbling. She didn't just have magic, she was magic.

Something akin to pride kindled in her chest.

Nikita had moved up to lay on his side next to her. He leaned over to kiss her cheek but she turned and caught his lips with hers.

She could taste herself on his tongue as they melted together.

When they pulled apart Nikita brushed her bottom lip with his thumb and a deep, pleasured rumble echoed from him. "Was that the way you imagined us?"

"It was everything and more." She kissed his shoulder, then his neck, then his cheek. She would never tire of feeling his skin beneath her lips. "Though," she looked at him coyly through her lashes, "I never did get to see what you looked like on your knees for me."

"Next time and forever more. I will fall to my knees before you for the rest of my days."

CHAPTER TWENTY

DEMING

THE BERRIES WERE RIPE and irresistible. Deming plucked another from the chipped ceramic bowl and popped it into her mouth. She savored the vibrancy of its natural sweetness and wiped the juice that stained her fingertips onto the blue linen folded on her lap.

She had felt calm and in control when the bright morning light sprayed into her room and woke her up this morning. There had also been instant butterflies flitting about in her stomach at the memory of what her and Nikita had done yesterday.

Pleasant, toe-curling butterflies.

Her eyes flicked to his from across the table.

Smoldering gray clouds told her he, too, was thinking about their coupling.

Deming clenched her thighs together and placed another berry in her mouth to avoid melting into a whimpering puddle of need over breakfast.

"You're going to be more berry than blood and bone if you keep that pace up," jested Nikita. His wings twitched in time with the corner of his mouth.

Deming flipped her hand vulgarly at him.

"The prince is right," Vallyn added, "stained fingers is one thing but your tongue is purple and that is concerning."

"It's not my fault that Runne grows berries that taste like summer." Deming took one more from the bowl, sucking the juice off her thumb this time rather than wiping it away. She looked directly at Nikita while she did it. His nostrils flared and she smiled demurely.

"Do you not agree?" Deming asked him. "If I had spent months eating the inferior fruit in Laey I would be devouring these jewels for breakfast everyday."

"I enjoy them as much as the next but..." Nikita's comment drifted off as he looked to Ilysse, who was washing dishes in the basin near the door.

"I can't eat them, actually, so I wouldn't know if they taste any different here than elsewhere on the continent," Ilysse said.

Deming balked. "What do you mean you can't eat them?"

Ilysse shrugged, soapy bubbles shimmering in the air above where her hands worked to clean a plate. "My throat closes up. It's been like that since I was a child."

Vallyn, barely restraining the glee in her voice, rested her chin in her palms and said, "Do you mean to tell me that the fierce Fae captain can be taken down by a summertime berry?"

Ilysse's ears flattened as she bared her canines at Vallyn. "Watch your tone, human."

Undeterred, Vallyn slapped a palm on the table. "Oh, this is too good! Next time you threaten me I'll just dice up some berries and mix them into your oats. Think of the tales that would be sung. The ferocious Ilysse Cane, taken down by a piece of fruit."

Ilysse growled, dipped her hand into the basin, and flung a cupped handful of water at Vallyn, splashing everything and everyone in the process.

"Not the berries!"

Deming wasn't sure who said it—Vallyn, maybe—but laughter from everyone, even a tight bark from Ilysse, bounced off the walls of the room.

The sharp staccato of hooves on wood announced Hartford. Soraya followed closely behind, though Deming would have missed the second female if she hadn't been looking in Hartford's direction. Where Hartford's footfalls were crisp and clear, Soraya's were silent as snowfall. The pads of her furred paws splayed gently into the wood with each step, muffling her movements like the predator she embodied.

The laughter simmered away naturally as the two females descended the stairs.

"Oh, good," Hartford said upon seeing the gathering before her, "you're all here."

It was then that Deming noticed what Soraya held in her hands.

"You have news on the parasites?"

"Yes and no." Soraya shrugged. She slid into an open chair. Hartford remained standing behind her mate, placing a hand on Soraya's shoulder. Her thumb rubbed gentle circles into Soraya's skin. The casual touch, so full of love, sent a pang of longing through Deming's heart.

"I've spent days observing these things," Soraya continued, gesturing with frustrated horror to the jar, "and still I can't say with confidence what's happening here."

Soraya loosened the lid and shook out one of the wriggling abnormalities onto the table. Deming could feel her face mimicking the disgust rippling across the faces of her companions. The worm-like creature undulated back and forth across the wood. Its veins and organs visible through the translucent skin that held it together.

It would have been impossible to tell which end was the head and which was the tail had it not been moving clearly in one direction.

Soraya pulled a hairpin from her bronzed bun and drove it into the body of the parasite.

Deming watched in horror as the worm thrashed back and forth, desperate to escape the sudden threat. It moved so violently it was sawing itself in half. A thick, clear liquid pooled underneath it as it succeeded in its venture and both halves of itself shot in separate directions away from the pin.

The halves lay still for a moment, softly twitching in a way that sent a chill up Deming's spine, then the severed ends slowly but surely began stitching themselves back together, the wound closing with efficiency and accuracy until what was once one parasite, was two.

Deming had to intentionally tell herself to close her gaping mouth, lest she look more like a fish than she already did.

"Healing magic?" Ilysse questioned.

Soraya shrugged. "I have no idea. It looks similar to what Deming's magic has shown us, but I've never heard of living things other than mages possessing magic like that." She brushed both worms into her palm, then back into the jar. "The only way I've been able to kill them is by fire, and hot fire at that."

Nikita picked up the jar and twirled it. The movement sent the parasites into a flurry. "Have you found any reason to believe they would cause the leodins to form packs and attack unprovoked?"

"No," Soraya said, clearly disappointed. She looked over her shoulder to Hartford, who nodded for her to continue. "Which is why I have to ask something of you all."

Deming cocked her head, curious.

Ilysse turned around and stopped washing dishes, though her hand remained submerged. The water sloshed against the walls of the basin at lower and lower heights until it settled and only lapped gently against her wrists.

"I need you to find another leodin and track it."

Deming felt her body tense. They had barely survived the last encounter. To seek one out intentionally seemed...

"That is unreasonably dangerous," Nikita said.

Yes, that.

Soraya shrunk into herself, a movement so uncharacteristic to the predator she embodied it made Deming uneasy.

"I know its a big ask—"

"Paris is slowly succumbing to his fever because of the leodins," interrupted Vallyn, "is it really worth the risk?"

Hartford stepped forward, hands clasped together in front of her stomach. "We came here for answers. We will not have any unless we learn more about this," her nose scrunched, eyes peering at the parasite, "unknown magic. Find a leodin and discover if the pack that attacked you and their parasites were an anomaly or a symptom of something more dangerous. The other option is to be content with not knowing what lies in front of us."

Her eyes swept the room, prodding silently.

The illusion of choice was just that—an illusion.

They left that afternoon.

CHAPTER TWENTY ONE

NIKITA

EXPANSIVE BLACK WINGS CARRIED the Prince of Runne high above the world. Like the bird of prey his wings were fashioned after, Nikita flew through the air.

He spun and swooped, his wings tucking and curling and flaring through the currents. Up here, with the wind teasing the edges of his feathers, it felt like the sunlight was made simply to shine on him. He felt carefree and careless and for a sliver of time, he allowed himself the luxury of leaning into the pillowy embrace of the clouds.

He drew his wings in close and the muscles along his spine tightened. He dipped his shoulders down and laughed with pure joy as he began the free fall.

The wind bit and tore but it didn't realize that he himself was wind and freedom. The wind didn't know that its roaring song was woven into the very fabric of Nikita's being. The prince whooped into the empty sky and cherished the seconds he plummeted through the air before flaring his wings and arcing back towards the sun.

A flicker of emotion shivered down the golden bond connecting him to the woman far below and only then, when he could taste iron in his own mouth from Deming's fear, did Nikita level out and fly steady.

A smile tugged at his mouth.

The mating bond had been changing lately, strengthening. Ever since they had lain together in the wildflowers, Nikita had felt glimpses of Deming's emotions trilling down the bond like a songbird through the trees.

He wondered if she could feel anything from him. He wondered if she had thought any more of the night the bond snapped into place. She had told him she felt it call to her, though she didn't know it by name, but she hadn't mentioned it since.

Whether or not to tell her was what Nikita mulled over before closing his eyes at night and what he pondered as light streamed into his bedroom in the morning.

Over and over, he questioned if keeping something this life altering to himself was morally wrong. However, it was the very fact that this would upend her world that kept him coming back to the same decision.

Keep quiet for now.

Deming was dealing with too many other changes in her life. He wanted to be a steady presence for her, someone she looked to for comfort when everything else was shifting under her feet.

Nikita landed gracefully a few yards away and Vallyn, Ilysse, and Deming all halted their horses.

"No need to stop on my account," he said, hiking himself up onto the broad back of Pascal and settling himself into the worn leather saddle. He winked at Deming and pleasure rolled through his core when her nose scrunched up to hide a laugh then winked back, blushing.

Gods, she was beautiful.

He shifted in the saddle, adjusting to accommodate the rush of blood that flooded between his legs at the sight of her flushed cheeks.

The shadows were long and the air held a nip of chill as dusk approached.

He closed his eyes and took a deep breath. The warmth of his horse under his thighs and the worn leather reins in his hand were feelings he knew well after all their travels. Despite his previous misgivings towards the animals, the sway of Pascal was making him drowsy. But just then, a distant roar sounded.

Pascal nickered and shook his head, agitated.

The Telaciens rose high and mighty around them, the tallest peaks still far away.

Between them and the mist-shrouded mountains dove two amphitheres. One cobalt, one a grayish green that nearly blended into the density of pine and rocky surface behind them.

They spiraled around each other in a winged dance, so close their tail feathers seemed to tie them together as one. They tore apart suddenly and roared again. The sound reverberated through Nikita's bones though the beasts were miles away.

He nudged Pascal forward, falling in line beside Deming.

"Are they always this active?" she asked.

Since they had arrived at Soraya's, the sound of wingbeats and the song of amphitheres had been a constant presence. There had not been a sighting as close as that first day in Bascade, but Nikita had seen plenty of them pepper the distant skies wherever he was outside for training or gathering food and water.

The frequency with which they appeared in the skies was indeed at odds with what he knew about them. The thought chilled him.

"No." Curt and to the point, Nikita's lips twisted downward. "Many come to Bascade for our high holidays," he continued, "and their leather winged cousins from the coast are seen often—"

"Sorry," Deming leaned over to catch his eye, "what?"

"The amphitheres that nest on the Draconic Isles have bat-like wings. Not feathered."

Shock colored Deming's expression and Nikita wondered—not for the first time—what kind of second rate education system Laey had in place. He pushed forward, answering her question. "The Telacien amphitheres roost in the uppermost peaks and can occasionally be seen in the distance but never come this close, this often."

His frown deepened at the admittance, his grip on the reins tightened.

"Do you think it's tied to the leodins?" Deming asked warily.

Nikita shrugged. "There seems to be a lot of unrest in this region. I wouldn't doubt it, though I hope not. If we are dealing with something the amphitheres have decided to get involved with we should be very, very concerned."

From ahead, Ilysse called out, "We should camp near here for tonight. I picked up a leodin hunting trail nearby. We can follow it in the morning and track those feral cats." Ilysse dismounted, not waiting for anyone else to chime in with their opinion. "I need to eat or I'm going to start getting unpleasant."

The gold adornments in Vallyn's braids tinkled together as she tilted her head. "Start?"

Ilysse bared her canines, then slung her bow over her shoulders and stalked into the woods.

Their dinner, courtesy of Ilysse, were rabbits—gamey but satisfying.

Nikita tore a bit of thigh meat away from the leg he was eating. Juice dribbled down his chin and he wiped it away with the back of his hand.

Vallyn and Ilysse had already retired and across the dying fire, Deming was playing with sparks made from her magic. Within the last day, she had figured out how to bring light to her fingertips consistently. Unfortunately, that was all she had figured out. The healing abilities they all knew existed within her remained out of her reach.

He was happy she was here, though, and proud that she stuck up for herself back at the house.

Initially, it had been suggested that she stay back with Soraya, Hartford, and Paris. She wasn't a fighter, though she was improving every day, and she had such a connection with Paris it hadn't seemed fair to ask her to leave him.

But, to everyone's surprise, Deming was adamant about going with them.

She claimed that with the group splitting up, she would be sitting around worrying for one party or another no matter where she physically was and at least here, traveling through the forest, she could learn tracking skills and continue her training with Vallyn and Ilysse.

Selfishly, Nikita wanted her as close to him as possible which was why when the last of his rabbit was gone, he walked over and settled in next to her. Their thighs touched and she leaned into him with an ease that made his heart ache.

Nikita nodded to the light. "Looking good, princess."

Sparks danced across Deming's fingertips like shooting stars. "I can't hold it for more than a few seconds. What good is a bit of spark going to do."

"Don't belittle your accomplishments or undermine the value of your magic. Neither is becoming of you."

She glared up at him through her lashes. Then, with a flick of her finger, sent a spark flying towards him.

It sizzled into the bridge of his nose and he sneezed. The tingling sensation of the spark lingered like a mini lightning strike under Nikita's skin. It was delectably unnerving.

Deming laughed, the sound pure and free as it echoed through the tall trees before being swallowed by the brush.

He elbowed her and she yelped, caught off guard.

Her focus wavered enough that the rest of the sparks disappeared. She frowned. Furrowed her brows. She stared at the pads of her fingers, willing them to return.

She looked adorable with her face scrunched in concentration.

Deming huffed in annoyance when the sparks remained quelled. "You scared them away."

Incredulously, Nikita pointed to his nose. "You started it."

She mumbled something unintelligible under her breath but snuggled into him again.

He slung an arm around her shoulder. "That's what I thought." Pressing a kiss into the crown on her head, he asked, "What does it feel like? Your magic."

She hummed thoughtfully, then said, "Bubbly and sharp, almost like static. Then it's warm. So, so warm all the way to my bones." She craned her neck upwards so she could look at him. "It feels a lot like what I feel when I'm with you."

Nikita's heart skipped a beat. In order to keep from telling her that what she felt was their mating bond, that what they had should feel like magic because it was magic, he leaned down and kissed her. Just once, soft and slow, like a promise.

A promise that one day they would know peace and ease instead of this broken world.

A promise that he would never leave her side.

A promise that one day he would tell her they were fated.

Just not tonight.

Chapter Twenty Two

Nikita

When dawn rose and the birds began singing, they had packed up camp and were on their way again.

Nikita scouted from the sky, ensuring they stayed true to the hunting trail Ilysse believed she had found yesterday. According to her, it would lead them high into the peaks of the mountains.

Leodins ranged all over the Telacien's, so it wasn't entirely unusual that they would have been spotted at this altitude. The oddity came from the fact that this was almost certainly a hunting trail the pack was using, and none of the prey leodin normally ate was ever seen this high up save for the occasional elk.

Nikita peered through the wilderness. There was certainly not enough elk in this rocky, craggy section of the mountains to sustain a pack of beasts as large and ferocious as the leodins seemed to be.

The movement of the amphitheres made more and more sense the closer they approached the peak. If leodins were encroaching on the nesting space of the amphitheres during their mating season, it was all that could be expected for the winged creatures to investigate and defend if necessary.

Like almost every living being, amphitheres were protective of their pregnant and young.

Then, out of the corner of his eye, he spotted motion through the brush.

Immediately on high alert, he signaled down to Ilysse.

She jerked on her reins, halting her horse and throwing a hand up in the air to tell Deming and Vallyn to still.

Deft and quick, Nikita landed on near silent feet next to Ilysse. He tucked his wings in too swiftly, though, and some of his feathers brushed against the rump of Ilysse's horse.

It spooked, rearing slightly, and Ilysse leaned close to its mane and stroked its broad neck slowly as she asked him quietly, "What is it?"

"Three leodins, two miles north."

"Are you sure?"

"Yes."

"Another pack?"

"It would appear so, yes."

Her face contorted into a grimace that Nikita felt echoed in his very soul. It had been an unspoken hope that the pack of leodins they encountered earlier were an anomaly. One pack of infested creatures was an issue, without a doubt, but as they had killed all of them the issue would have been more or less dealt with. Now, with confirmation of another pack, the door of conspiracy had swung wide open.

Nikita addressed Deming and Vallyn, gesturing towards the horses. "We need to travel on foot from here, the horses will be too loud."

Everyone dismounted and tied their steeds up to neighboring trees. They would track the leodins on foot, then return to this location before nightfall to camp.

Ilysse looked back only once to check everyone was ready before plunging into the brush.

Vallyn followed after, and Deming trailed behind her.

A flurry of red, white, and pink drew his eyes to her.

Deming cocked her head in question.

"I'm coming," he said, patting Pascal's hide and securing the reins.

Nikita couldn't shake the feeling that the further they dove into this mystery the further they were getting from the promise of peace he wished for himself and Deming.

There was nothing to be done about that, though, so he turned on his heels and followed everyone else into the woods.

Other than seeing Deming collapse over Miriam's dying body, the sight before Nikita stoked fear in his belly like nothing else ever had.

Five leodins prowled the clearing, large and quilled and snarling. Two more had joined up with the three Nikita had spotted. They had tracked the pack for an hour as the cats prowled through the woods and were now watching the animals interact in the clearing ahead with grotesque interest.

The leodins bit at each other periodically, when one got too close to another. The sound was rumbling and deep, not unlike the call of the amphitheres but far more foreboding.

The amphithere call was ancient and echoed through time and space. It demanded reverence.

The growls that escaped the jaws of these animals were nothing like that. These noises were not of this world. Untenable and skin-crawling and, though Nikita knew it was melodramatic to say, evil.

Horrendous sounds aside, they weren't acting like a pack.

Nikita wasn't sure what he had expected. Leodins were solitary creatures, pack behavior was abnormal to them. That was part of what was so off about the ones that attacked them. But given that they were, in fact, grouping up, he assumed the leodins would adhere to a pack mentality similar to wolves. A family system, maybe, where food and responsibility was shared.

This was clearly not the case.

To start, none of them were behaving naturally, even taking away the oddity that was five of the beasts within striking distance of one another. They were not acting like animals, even wild ones. They were acting manic, almost.

Rabid.

One was rolling around in the dirt, back and forth, back and forth. Quills were periodically breaking with sharp snaps. When exposed, Nikita could see its spine was bloodied and raw. Through every movement the leodin's eyes remained glassy and despondent.

The smallest by far—though that was laughable to say since it was larger than any leodin had the right to be—was pacing in circles around the edge of the trees. Its tongue lolled. Its head swung side to side.

The second largest in the pack, a husky beast with scorched fur and scars covering one flank, dug its claws into the earth and bellowed at the runt for seemingly no reason.

Even from where they hid, Nikita could see spittle flying from its maw.

Even without what happened next, Nikita would have said there was something deeply unsettling and wrong with these animals. With it, he was at a loss for words.

The larger leodin lunged at the smaller.

The action was faster than his eyes could track and when they finally caught up to the animals, they were rolling atop one another.

Angry roars and hurt yips and warning snarls echoed so loudly through the woods that all other sound was momentarily drowned out.

Claws flew and teeth flashed.

Blood sprayed, arcing through the air like a morbid rainbow.

One of the bodies—the runt—tried to rip itself away from the fight but its throat was caught firmly in the jaws of the other and its blood was everywhere. It fought on, swiping claws as large as knives at its attacker, but it had lost the second the artery in its throat had severed.

Blood pooled beneath them, coating their fur as they rolled and bit and slashed.

The scarred leodin took both hind legs and kicked hard into the other's stomach, sinking its claws in and ripping downwards in a final blow.

Guts spilled and the battle was over.

The leodin released its kill, roared, then shook its head and body to rid itself of the wet blood that coated its fur.

The whole ordeal took mere seconds.

From where she was nestled into his side, Deming asked, "Have you ever seen one act like this?"

Nikita forced an answer out through the gruesome horror coiling within him. "No."

"Should we engage?"

Ilysse looked at Deming, genuinely curious if not appalled. "You want to engage with that?"

Deming shook her head fiercely.

"We wait and see where they go next," Vallyn spoke, sure and steady.

The whispers shared between the four of them were hushed.

The group spoke no more as they waited.

It took a long while before the leodins made any move to leave the clearing but when they did, it happened with speed and intensity.

One second the quilled big cats were pacing and growling as they had been for half an hour, the next second all four that were left snapped to attention.

Paws settled into the dirt. Ears flicked up. Quills bristled.

Then they tipped their head back and yowled before darting into the woods.

"Follow them," Nikita commanded.

Thorns bit at his ankles and branches whipped at his face. He was lightly bleeding in more than one spot, he was sure of it, and he was also fairly sure he had twisted his ankle on a bulging root half a mile ago.

Nikita did not slow his pace.

There was no time to consider an alternative. His legs ached at their pace, but it was a pleasant ache.

He breathed in the cool air, slow and steady, despite the speed at which the four of them raced through the mountain range.

They were no match for the speed of the leodins, but they were not falling behind enough to lose their trail completely.

Ilysse led them. The elongated points of her ears were constantly flicking, though her eyes remained set on the path in front of them. They had paused only briefly and only twice to confirm the trail.

After half an hour of intense tracking, it was clear that their initial understanding was correct.

The leodins were leading them to the peaks of the Telaciens. To the amphitheres.

Nikita was both thrilled and terrified at the idea.

The peaks of the mountain loomed above them, awe-inspiring and grand in a way they couldn't be when seen from far away. The castle his father reigned from in Bascade was not far from here, a day's ride, perhaps, but even that distance was enough to diminish the grandeur of the Telaciens.

He had admired the looming presence the mountain range provided in Arsaela. Reynes Castle was nestled into the foothills of one of the western most peaks. But not even from the highest window in the tallest spire of that castle were the mountains as impressive as they were now.

Ilysse slowed and the rest of them followed suit as they approached a cliff face. She jogged down and back, eyes scanning both the rock and the forest to their right. Finally she slowed to a walk, then stopped completely.

"The trail ends here."

She spoke as if she had just woken up, not run multiple miles. Nikita grinned. He was constantly impressed by her.

Running a hand through his disheveled hair, he asked, "Nothing into the forest?"

"No."

"Well they didn't just disappear," said Vallyn.

Ilysse snarled, the exact way she always did when Vallyn said something unnecessarily snarky just to annoy her, and didn't respond.

Nikita turned to the rock face, catching Vallyn smile at the Fae as he did. He placed a hand on it, its surface cool despite the sun beating down on it.

Snarky or not, Vallyn was right. The leodins didn't disappear. There were strange things afoot, but the pack disappearing into thin air was a step too far for Nikita to accept.

He looked around to find Deming and saw her running her hand along the rock. Her eyes skimmed the broad expanse that extended into the clouds.

She stopped in her tracks, then took three large steps away from the cliff face.

Her breath hitched and Nikita felt alertness shimmer down their bond.

He was beside her in seconds. "Did you see something?"

She didn't look at Nikita when she responded, instead keeping her eyes trained on the mountain. "Not yet..." Her voice, quiet to start, trailed off into the breeze.

Then a wide grin splayed across her face. "They didn't go back into the forest, they went up."

Every pair of eyes swung to where Deming was pointing.

Nikita stepped forward, examining the rocky surface. His eyes went from Deming's finger to the mountain. Brow furrowed he was about to question what she was looking at but suddenly it clicked.

There.

Once he saw, he couldn't unsee it. The treacherous path formed by crags in the mountain leapt off the side of the mountain as if lit by lanterns.

Up and up it went, ending in a small cave that, without scrutiny, would have appeared as merely a shadow.

Nikita looked at her with glee. "You clever girl."

Deming shrugged, but pride was plastered all over her face.

"I hate to break it to you all," Vallyn said inspecting the path, "but I would rather my death not be because I fell and snapped my neck trying to scale a rock face meant for mountain goats and, apparently, unnaturally large leodins."

Nikita sketched a bow, flaring his wings. "At your service."

Vallyn groaned, Deming grinned, Ilysse rolled her eyes.

"Let me scope it out first," the latter offered.

Nikita wasted no time scooping her up and soaring to the cave entrance.

As it turned out, the cave was not at all small and could certainly not be mistaken as a shadow once they were level with it.

It was cavernous, yawning. Rugged and natural, the edges looked like teeth as the darkness within beckoned.

A chill settled onto Nikita's shoulders like a cloak and he set Ilysse down.

"Be careful."

She waved him off and prowled inside, weapons out.

Unable to hover but wanting to stay nearby, he flew in small lazy circles waiting for her. After a minute or two, Ilysse reappeared.

"It's just a tunnel but the area up here is safe for now."

Content with that, Nikita darted to the ground to grab the others.

He extended a hand to Vallyn next.

She shook her head. "I'd rather not leave the princess unattended. Take her first."

Nikita's head swiveled to Deming and she stepped forward.

He bent slightly to slip one arm under her knees. The other snaked around her waist. Her body was warm and comforting, the weight of her like a blanket easing the chill the cave had brought.

The second her own arm was secured around his neck, he shot into the air.

Before either of them could appreciate the beauty of the forest from high above the treetops, Nikita was touching down at the lip of the cave. He pressed a kiss into her temple, his hands squeezing her into him.

"You two are disgusting." Ilysse snorted.

Deming whipped around in Nikita's arms. He knew that if he could see her face, it would be scowling.

Ilysse was leaning against the wall of the cave, shaking her head and smirking.

At the sight of Deming's annoyance Ilysse added, "Respectfully."

"You can't just tack on a word and make it so."

Ilysse pushed off the wall. "Apologies."

Deming muttered something about that not sounding very genuine.

"I'll be back with Vallyn," he said.

Once the four of them were gathered together once more, Ilysse stalked into the cave commanding, "Weapons out."

She needn't have said anything. Deming's hand was already firmly gripped around the hilt of her dagger and the blade of Vallyn's sword glinted ahead of her.

As for Nikita, he had his faithful scimitars. Their curved blades were sharp and menacing.

The tunnel was poorly lit. The only light came from the entrance far behind them and some far off glow down the path whose origin they couldn't make out. Their steps, no matter how carefully placed, sounded impossibly loud in the hollow space. Occasionally water dripped from the ceiling, the plunk of it hitting the stone floor with a high pitched echo.

For a long time, the deeper they traveled the more oppressive the darkness became. Then, so slowly Nikita thought he might be imagining it, the tunnel began brightening.

They approached the torch with apprehension. The wall mount was rusted, ancient, and sat high on the rocky wall directly in the middle of two branching pathways.

Vallyn's sigh bounced off the walls. "Stay together or split up?"

There was safety in numbers, but they could cover more ground if they separated.

Risk for knowledge.

"We split up," Nikita said, "Deming should go with the most skilled which would be me—"

"Me."

"Me."

"The ego on the lot of you is astounding," Deming muttered.

"She's certainly not going with you," Ilysse said, pointing to Nikita. "Rationality goes out the window when you two are together. She'll go with Vallyn."

Every fiber of the golden thread tying him to his mate grew taut.

He opened his mouth to protest but Ilysse cut him off.

"Nikita," her eyes were soft, understanding, but firm, "no."

"Think I'm incapable of protecting her, prince?" Vallyn asked.

"That's not what I said," he growled.

Ilysse pushed forward with a plan. "We split up, learn what we can, and meet back at the entrance in an hour. No risky moves, no confrontation." She looked around their small group. "Understood?"

Nikita made to argue further but Deming stepped in front of him. She placed a hand on his chest. Her fingers trembled though her voice was steady.

"It's okay. I'll see you in an hour, right?"

He ground his teeth.

It felt wrong to separate from her, to let her go into the unknown without him. His vision blurred at the thought of anything happening to her—

Which was exactly Ilysse's point.

He would do anything for Deming, including throwing himself into danger or risking the entire mission.

He placed his hand over hers. "See you in an hour."

He watched as Deming and Vallyn vanished into the darkness, then turned around.

Nikita clutched the hilt of his weapon so tightly his knuckles blanched.

Unease seeped through him like blood from a cut vein as he followed Ilysse into the tunnel.

CHAPTER TWENTY THREE

NIKITA

FOR AS ROUGH AND unaltered as the initial tunnel had been, this new one was carefully curated.

The ground was flat, easy to traverse and absent of the jutting rocks and tripping hazards that littered the entrance. The walls were smooth and cold to the touch.

Nikita ran his fingers along one side and suppressed the urge to shiver. It felt like marble. Polished, refined.

This was no mountain lair for beasts of fur and claw and quill.

There was certainly no way any of the leodins could have fit their hulking bodies down here, not with the shrinking width and height of the tunnel.

This was deliberate, planned.

Someone had made these tunnels.

So where were they?

Ilysse had been prowling ahead of him through the torchlit tunnel for nearly twenty minutes now and they had yet to come across a single indication of life, a single sound save their own movements.

With each minute they walked, the path grew increasingly narrow. What had once been cavernous was now crushing. Nikita squeezed the muscles in his back and shoulders to keep his wings from touching the walls.

Every time a feather brushed the edges of the space something slick and chilling slithered up his spine. Like shimmery oil, the shadows here seemed to shift and move and glisten abnormally.

"We should turn around," he said. His voice echoed eerily down the tunnel.

Ilysse flicked him an amused look over her shoulder. "Scared?"

Nikita rolled his eyes though she had already trained her gaze forward.

As his feet propelled him through the darkness, his mind wandered elsewhere.

The tether on his heart was strong. Warm and ethereal, it reached out through stone and rock and ether towards Deming.

She was safe, Nikita was certain.

Through the bond, he could feel hints of emotions. Spikes of curiosity, a subtle throbbing when her heart rate increased.

He wished he could hold her, see her, speak to her.

They didn't know what awaited them in the tunnels and as much as he trusted Vallyn to protect her, he trusted himself more.

His hands tightened on the hilt of the scimitar.

Ahead, Ilysse had paused.

Frozen like a predator, she waited, listening. Her slim, pointed ear twitched where it poked out of blonde hair.

"There's running water up ahead," she said.

Sure enough, within a minute or two Nikita's lesser hearing picked up the rush of water. A lot of water, if the roaring pounding through the tunnel was any indication.

Weapons at the ready, they approached the end of the path.

Nikita squinted against the sudden change in light.

It was brighter here. Marginally, but brighter.

He blinked at the sight before him.

Thrice as tall as it was wide, the cavern spread out across a massive, rocky floor. There were more than a dozen other tunnels that dumped out into the space and in the far corner, all the way across the cavern, was a set of stairs.

Towards the back wall the ground disappeared under the edges of lapping water. A lake. And pouring into that lake was a powerful torrent of water.

Craning his neck, Nikita trailed the waterfall in reverse until he caught sight of the opening in the wall where some underground river was coursing out and into the cavern.

"Some space, huh?" Ilysse whispered.

Nikita was about to respond when something prodded at his consciousness.

It was soft, gentle. Like a shadow, it crept along the corridors of his mind and curled inside him like a cat.

Everything else fell away the moment it arrived.

The cavern, the waterfall, the leodins—Nikita forgot it all.

Nothing seemed to matter except burying further into the comfort of the shadows decorating his mind.

He had the distinct impression of feeling warm and safe.

It reminded him of Deming.

His mate's name tickled something at the edges of his consciousness. There was something about Deming that he was supposed to remember. Was he supposed to meet her somewhere? Was she in danger?

A blanket of shadow settled over his entire soul, soothing him. The spike of fear was quickly doused.

No, she was safe. She was...where was she?

Nikita asked the shadows and they whispered to him.

Home.

She was back home.

He should return to her.

Yes, he should be with his mate.

Cocooned in the cloud of safety the shadows provided, Nikita glided to his mate.

Time was a mirage. He felt like a piece of driftwood in the ocean. Rocking and swaying with the rhythm of the world. Slowly, the current drifted him to shore.

Like fog as dawn bled into morning, the shadows lifted.

Nikita blinked and the warm, pleasurable feeling was instantly replaced with sheer terror.

Fear like he had never known, so strong it made him physically ache, lanced through his heart.

They were no longer in the tunnels.

They were no longer near the mountain at all.

The sun dipped low and the shadow of pine and birch trees reached languidly across the grassy clearing. The Telaciens were peaks against the sky in the distance and planters full of wildflowers and herbs decorated a plain cottage just ahead.

Nikita spun, frantically taking in his surroundings.

To his right lay his scimitar.

To his left stood Ilysse.

And directly in front of them was, impossibly, Soraya's house.

CHAPTER TWENTY FOUR

DEMING

THE TUNNEL TO THE right had so many rooms and passageways attached to it that Deming and Vallyn were nearly paralyzed with indecision.

It would be impossible to investigate every branch into the mountain in the hour they had. Less than that, really, if they were to make it back to the top in time to meet Nikita and Ilysse at the cave entrance.

The quantity of tunnels to investigate was annoying, but making the process absolutely retched was the smell. The scent of burnt flesh began to tease the air after a couple minutes and only got stronger as Deming and Vallyn descended. It hung in the air like a physical entity, clinging to Deming's skin and clothes and clogging her nose enough to make her gag every few feet. Eventually, it began mixing with the scent of rotting things and waste.

The only saving grace was that it seemed no one lived or worked in this hollowed-out mountainside. Every tunnel, every room, every corner was empty.

It was eery.

Everything about this place was eery, Deming supposed, but it was particularly chilling that this expansive tunnel system was unguarded and seemingly unoccupied.

Where were the leodins?

Where was the abysmal smell coming from?

Deming was on edge with every corner they turned. Her and Vallyn both were waiting on pins and needles for someone, anyone, to show their face. They knew someone had been here recently because, though the tunnels were empty, the rooms were full.

Each varied in size, ranging from a cupboard to washroom to storage spaces and even, once, a hall longer and taller than the throne room in Reynes Castle.

And each of them clearly served a purpose. Shelves were lined with potions and bones and rare flowers and books. There was one that was, somehow, a rich and thriving greenhouse with crawling ivy and fruit-bearing trees and flowering bushes. There must be some underground spring that fed into the mountain to sustain such a garden.

Still, they encountered not a single living soul as they maneuvered through the mountain.

Vallyn rounded a corner and halted.

Spilling before her was a staircase. Down, down, down it spiraled until the disjointed, rocky steps disappeared into pitch black shadows.

Deming looked at her hand, bringing pin pricks of light to life at the tips of her fingers and waggling them at Vallyn.

Vallyn looked at her skeptically.

Annoyance flared in Deming's gut—not at Vallyn, Vallyn was right—but at herself. This would be the perfect opportunity to use her light magic if only she could produce more than sparks.

Cursing her inaccessible power for the millionth time, Deming jogged back a few yards and grabbed one of the torches that had been sporadically lighting their journey thus far.

"Sorry," Vallyn said, taking the torch.

"No, it's fine," grumbled Deming, "the torch is better."

It was still and quiet at the beginning of their descent, but as they approached the bottom, a cascading sound of water built louder and louder. And atop the sound of rushing of water, sending chills up Deming's spine, were notes of low growling and claws scratching into stone.

They had found the leodins.

Vallyn slid the torch into a sconce on the wall and held a finger to her lips. She motioned for Deming to stay put, then snuck down the remaining steps.

Against her better judgment, Deming followed.

Her heart was beating out of her chest, but she wrangled her breath into slow, deliberate inhales and exhales through her nose. At the last step, she tiptoed up behind Vallyn and tapped her once on the shoulder.

Surprise flitted across her brown eyes for only half a second. In its place slid pure, unadulterated annoyance.

Deming winced and mouthed an apology.

She peered around the corner and stifled a gasp.

A huge cavern yawned before her. Up and up it went, so high Deming could barely see the ceiling. It must have been triple the size of Reynes Castle. The floor stretched out far, rocky and natural. A multitude of tunnels peppered the base of the walls.

How expansive was this tunnel system?

Out of the far wall, about a quarter of the way up, was a massive waterfall. Water roared from the opening, pouring down in a billowing torrent into a large, underground lake.

It was so loud Deming could barely think, though she was grateful for the noise because between them and the waterfall were seven leodins.

The cats lounged on the cavern floor. Some prowled the perimeter, some lay asleep on the stone. Two were at the lake's edge, lapping water and cleaning their quills.

Deming's mouth was suddenly very, very dry.

Then, with the same, unnatural behavior they displayed in the clearing earlier, the pack froze as one and looked down a different tunnel. One of them yipped, its tail slashing across the floor, then sprung into motion.

Deming tensed, fearing they had scented her and Vallyn, but the leodin ran away from the two women, not towards them.

The rest followed, disappearing down the tunnel that bore into the middle of the cavern wall, and within seconds the only sound was the roar of the waterfall.

Where were they going? Was someone—something—calling to them?

Vallyn grabbed Deming by the arm and dragged her back up the steps.

A dangerous, impulsive thought flitted across Deming's mind. "I have an idea. And before you say no," she pressed her palms together in faux prayer, "don't say no."

Vallyn waited, face pinched and doubtful.

Deming pulled a small vial out of her satchel. "We should get a sample of that water."

Vallyn scoffed. "No."

"We can't go back empty handed. Maybe that's where the parasites are coming from. Soraya could run tests on it."

"The leodins just left, Deming. Who knows when they'll return. We can't go back at all if we're dead."

"You're really hung up on us dying."

Vallyn threw her hands in the air. "Dorthrum forbid I try to avoid situations where the rightful and only heir to the Queendom of Laey doesn't die on my watch, I'm so sorry." The last bit was dragged out, long and sarcastic.

Through all the theatrics, though, Deming could see Vallyn agreed. She perked up as Vallyn looked back down the stairs, then eyed her.

"Stay fucking here," Vallyn growled, "you understand?"

Deming nodded, rolling her eyes.

Vallyn's pointed finger pressed hard into Deming's chest. "Not a joke. Tell me you understand."

"I understand," Deming said impatiently, "I'll stay right here, I promise."

She may be impulsive, but she was not one to break a promise. Deming did as she was told. She sat on the steps and drummed her fingers on her knee while she waited.

It took Vallyn less than a minute.

The sound of boots on stone announced her arrival. When she appeared, Vallyn held the vial out for Deming to see.

Crisp, spring fed water sloshed around the glass. And swimming within, if Deming looked close enough, were parasites.

"You were right."

Deming beamed.

Vallyn pocketed the vial. "We've got to start making our way up and out, come on."

The ascent through the mountain went without trials until they were nearly back to the fork in the road.

The distinct sound of snuffling behind one of the doors they hadn't checked earlier stopped Deming in her tracks. "Vallyn," she hissed.

Vallyn turned impatiently.

Deming nodded towards the door. "I think an animal is in there."

"And we've had such great luck with the animals inside this mountain so far?"

"Why is it behind a door? How did it get there?"

Vallyn bit her lip. Her eyes darted towards the end of the tunnel. They were less than a hundred yards from where they split with Nikita and Ilysse.

"Fine," she said sharply.

The door opened on surprisingly silent hinges when Deming tugged on the metal ring.

It was a small room, poorly lit.

It took Deming's eyes a moment to adjust.

She blinked through the darkness, confirming what she thought she saw when the door swung open.

Thick, metal bars rose from the ground to the ceiling, cutting the room in half and creating a cage.

A pig stood within.

Deming squinted her eyes at the source of the snuffling. Not just any pig, or a pig at all, really. If the curl of the small, developing tusks protruding from the corners of its bottom lip were any indication, it was a baethor.

Native to the Kingdom of Monstakar, baethors were much like the leodins in that the Monstakarrian royalty claimed it for their crest and the beast was larger and more unique than its common counterpart, the wild boar. A full grown male baethor could weigh as much as a horse and bore two tusks that jutted upwards from its jaw.

The tusks were actually two of the baethor's teeth, which Deming had always found rather entertaining, and were poached for totems and good luck charms, which Deming had always found rather repulsive.

Those, supplemented by the additional two massive horns that began at their forehead and grew to circle around their entire face, made the baethor the most dangerous animal on the continent.

Without fail, they killed more people than any other animal every year. This was in part because they were naturally aggressive and in part because humans and Fae tended to underestimate them. Regardless, they were not to be trifled with.

This one, though, was small—an infant. It was pawing at the ground with its hooves and repeatedly nudging the side of the cave, its nose sniffling wildly.

Deming looked to other parts of the cage and stifled a gasp when she saw what lay in the corner.

The flickering light of the torch cast the body of the mother baethor into stark relief.

Laying on its side with its belly towards the bars made it so the gruesome remnants of the birth were on full display to Vallyn and Deming. It's belly was flayed open from the center to the tip of its tail, entrails scattered around her like a gory ritual. Flies buzzed around the carcass like vultures though rot and decay had yet to eat away at its flesh.

Based on the state of the mother, this birth happened a few days ago and yet—

Her eyes flashed back towards the baby. Based on her knowledge of the animal, a babe born only days ago would not be that large or have tusks of any kind. They were born bare faced. After all, Deming's eyes drifted back to the mother, who would want to give birth to something with sharp, cutting tusks.

Deming eyed the baby. Its near black eyes stared at the wall in front of it and its mouth opened to bray once more. It knocked its burgeoning tusks against the stone over and over and over and then with a crack that shattered Deming's heart, a piece of it chipped off.

"I wish we could save it," mourned Deming.

"The best we can do is kill it."

Deming spun around. "Kill it?"

Vallyn was already kneeling at the bars of the cage. She reached an arm inside, curling her fingers and coaxing the baethor to her. "We could dismiss the pool as naturally occurring. Chalk the parasites up to some new type of infestation."

The baethor walked forward, intrigued. The fur of its nose looked soft as it prodded at Vallyn's fingers.

Deming felt sick.

"But this," Vallyn continued, voice low so as not to scare the animal away, "the cage, the food and water...There is someone behind this. Someone is playing god and experimenting with the natural world." She shuddered, looking over her shoulder at Deming. Half of her face was shrouded in shadow. "We have no key to free it. This is a mercy."

Then, quicker than an arrow, Vallyn drew her dagger and sank it into the thick hide of the baethor's neck. It squealed and bucked, but Vallyn held onto its barely there tusks until it fell limply to the ground.

The silence was oppressive.

Vallyn's shoulders rose and fell slowly with one, giant breath, then she pocketed her dagger and rose. "Let's go. We're out of time."

Deming could do nothing but nod and follow her out of the tunnels.

Despite the lingering sadness over the baethor, Deming let relief wash over her. They had done it. They had more knowledge than before and had samples to take back to Soraya. They had played a risky game and came out of it unscathed. All there was left to do was wait for Nikita and Ilysse—

"Hello, niece."

CHAPTER TWENTY FIVE

DEMING

PAIN LANCED THROUGH DEMING'S heart and she was taken aback by the feeling until she realized her chest was physically hurting because her pulse had spiked so quickly. Her heart hammered in her chest. Her nails dug into her palms.

Dresden Penrose stood before her.

He was many things to Deming—uncle, High Steward of Laey, once beloved—but only one trilled in her head as she looked at his impassive face, staring at her with condescension.

Miriam's murderer.

The song of steel cut the air as Vallyn drew her sword.

The person before her slit Miriam's wrists and left her to die.

"I knew we would meet again," Dresden took a step towards her and Deming bristled, "but I would have never guessed the first time would be here. Tell me, how are you finding our experiments?"

His head cocked to the side as if he was genuinely interested in her response but the hardness in his eyes remained.

Our experiments. Who was he working with?

He began walking towards the pair of them. Deming looked frantically around the hallway for a way out but it was too skinny to attempt slipping by him.

She drew her dagger, bent her knee.

Dresden laughed.

The walls narrowed in around him and the edges of her vision turned blurry and tinged with red.

"You killed Miriam!" Her grip tightened. Vallyn was saying something but she couldn't hear her. Deming's voice rose. "You stole my throne!" The words ripped from her throat in a guttural scream that pitched and shattered against the walls of the cave and she was suddenly, violently, back in Miriam's bedroom watching her bleed out.

Her heart racing as she tried to staunch the bleeding.

Her voice pleading with Nikita to help, to do something, anything.

Her chest heaving with sobs that left her choking.

Miriam's last words whispering affection for the daughter she had not carried.

Dresden shrugged with indignant nonchalance. "I did what had to be done for the good of the realm."

The good of the realm? Miriam was the good of the realm. She was the light that brought Deming back to life. She was warmth and safety and home.

Her lips pulled back into a snarl.

This man was a monster and he deserved to die for what he did.

Deming lunged.

Dresden's eyes widened in shock and he stumbled backwards, tripping on loose stones.

Good. Let him underestimate her. Let him believe what he wants to believe about her.

That she was weak and tiresome and unfit for rule.

She struck without hesitation.

That she didn't care about her people.

She thrust the dagger forward, with little plan other than to hurt the man in front of her.

That she was flippant and careless with her heart.

The blade sank into the soft tissue between his collarbone and shoulder.

That she was goddess-damned.

She pulled on the hilt and skin tore and the scream he let out sent waves of sadistic pleasure rippling through her because this was what he deserved.

His scream turned into a roar as he gathered his senses and pushed her off and onto her back. From within the folds of his clothes he pulled a knife.

She whipped her head to the side just in time, the blade nicking her cheek as he slammed it down.

They flipped over each other, rolling on the ground with rocks stabbing into their backs and forearms and knees. Something hard hit Deming in the jaw and pain burst to life in her. Thick warmth welled in her mouth. Her tongue tasted iron and her teeth were coated with blood.

Dresden managed to pin her down, his hand finding her wrists and holding them above her. He grunted, wrestling the dagger from her grip and succeeding when he let his weight fall even further, expelling all the air from her lungs.

His body was hot and heavy atop hers and for a brief moment she was back underneath the leodin in the forest suffocating. Her chest heaved for air but none came. His forearm found her throat, further cutting off circulation and air and pressing so hard her windpipe constricted and crushed and all she knew was pain.

Stars filled her vision and the rest of the world fell to black.

Someone would help her. Vallyn would help her.

Vallyn was right behind her. She was a warrior, she would help.

Where was Vallyn?

Vallyn didn't come.

No one came.

Deming was alone and dying. She didn't want to die. She would not die.

She would not die, she would not die, she would not die.

With the last remaining whisper of consciousness and strength she could muster, she drove her knee up as hard as she could.

It connected between his legs and he keeled over, groaning.

Deming gasped.

Bruised and burning, her body filled with precious air.

She coughed, then coughed again. She scrambled out from under him, dizzy and unbalanced. She shook her head, trying to clear the haze.

They crouched there, panting, staring at each other, catching their breath.

Malice dripped like venom from his gaze.

"You fucking bitch. You'll die for that."

Deming spat blood onto the floor and charged at him once more. Tunnel-visioned in her rage, the dagger was left by the wayside as her muscled thighs propelled her towards her uncle. She swung hard and he dodged her, her movements too obvious.

Slow, she remembered, patient. Anticipatory.

Dresden shuffled forward, knife glinting, and made to kick out her legs.

Deming jumped, landed, feinted to the left then swung to the right. Her fist connected with his face, and though her knuckles screamed pain, she felt none of it. The satisfaction of seeing him stumble backwards and clutch his face filled her with bubbling, golden, vicious pride.

Perhaps she was vicious.

Perhaps that was what he made her.

Perhaps that was a good thing.

She had been reborn in fire and death and betrayal. She was no longer the meek girl he used to know. His passive, naive niece was gone.

The woman stalking towards him was someone new entirely.

Without waiting for him to catch his breath, Deming leapt into action. She spun and ducked his incoming fist, then advanced.

He was taller and stronger but she was quicker and full of vengeful rage. The tunnel collapsed and sounds faded away as all her focus turned to finishing this, finishing him. He landed a punch on her shoulder. She absorbed the blow and retaliated, jabbing him quickly in the stomach, then the wrist, then the neck.

While he was choking on air she paused, breathed, then spun forward like a whirlwind.

Deming had never been more thankful for the hours spent training than she did the moment her foot kicked hard into his thigh and he tumbled to the ground, his head hitting the stone floor with a crack.

Her body was on top of his before she could register her own movements. She threw all her weight behind her closed fist and swore expletives at the bloodied face below her as her knuckles smashed into his nose.

It broke with a satisfying crack.

Dresden's chest rose and fell erratically.

So much blood was smeared across his puffed and agitated skin that he hardly looked human.

Ironic. Deming cocked her head. She was the one who could no longer claim to be human and yet here her uncle was, laying in his own sweat and blood because of the inhuman actions he chose to take.

She may be a mage, but she was more human than he.

She raised her hand again. Anger coursed through her like lightning. Fast and impatient and blinding—

"Enough."

That voice. She hadn't heard it in years.

Deming's fist froze inches from her uncle's brow.

Nothing save for the shock of that familiar voice ringing in her ears could have drawn her from the frenzy she had whipped herself into.

Her heart stuttered to a stop.

He was here.

Khalil.

"I had hoped for a jovial reunion."

Deming drew stuttering, stunted breaths in through her nose and turned around slowly to see the tanned skin and soft smile and crow's feet that she associated with curiosity and love in front of her for the first time since she was a child.

Her father's best friend.

Miriam's brother.

He was here, alive. Not dead. Not burned in the fire that took her parent's lives like she had believed her entire life.

He had abandoned her.

He had left her alone to mourn the loss of her parents—

No, she corrected herself, bitterness and anger mixing in her belly to create a dangerous, heady emotion that left her feeling spontaneous.

Everything that Miriam had confessed in those last chaotic days in Arsaela barreled through Deming. Miriam may have hidden her magic from Deming and used her shadows to hide the city in fog, but that was nothing compared to the betrayal Khalil inflicted.

Khalil had been the one to set fire to the apothecary when she was a child. He had wanted her parents dead because they refused to bend to his will. They refused to go along with his outlandish ideas and he had killed them for it.

And now he wanted her. Miriam's warning was like a bell in her temple.

Khalil had been working with someone to get to her. It was clear now that someone was Dresden. Deming's fist curled further into her uncle's bloody shirt. Dresden had staged the coup not only for his own selfish reason but because Khalil needed her. He thought she was the key to whatever he was working on.

"You're supposed to be dead." Her voice cracked. She hated that her voice cracked.

It was after she spoke and not a moment before that she realized with icy horror why Vallyn had not intervened during the fight.

She was laying on the ground before Khalil, limp and unconscious.

Panic took over, making her heart race and palms sweat.

Was she dead? She couldn't be dead.

Deming found it hard to breathe. Her eyes flicked up to Khalil's once more and opened her mouth to beg and plead and trade her life for the woman beneath him but he cut her off before a single sound escaped her lips.

"Alas, here I am," Khalil said, looking at her with genuine sadness. "I'm sorry to see you aren't pleased with this development."

Then he whistled and two leodins leapt from the shadows of the stairs. Shadows that moved like oil, unnaturally curling like they were—

Magic.

Deming stumbled backwards.

Khalil was a shadow mage, just like his sister. Miriam had told her that in the hidden apothecary all those months ago but seeing it in person, seeing milky gray shadows twist and bend and melt towards him, sent a sinister chill through her.

Darkness bloomed around him like a cloak.

"Bring her to me," he commanded the leodins. After a moment he added, "Alive."

The quilled beasts snarled. Hot, reeking breath leaked from their jaws. Then they pounced.

CHAPTER TWENTY SIX

DEMING

SHE COULDN'T OUTRUN A leodin.

The thought pounded in her head with every step, every heartbeat, every breath.

She sprinted down the tunnel. Every lick of anger was instantly quelled by the howling of the animals and impending death they offered.

It hurt her soul to leave Vallyn behind, to not know if she was alive or dead, but Deming couldn't save her if she was captured, too.

It was close enough to Vallyn's constant warning about her own safety that tears gathered in the corners of her eyes only to be ripped away by the wind passing over her and she darted through towards the cave entrance.

She screamed in frustration and pain.

A queen was supposed to save her people, not condemn them to die.

She yelled into the abyss again, if only to relieve the building pressure and panic in her bones, and then came to a skidding halt.

Pebbles clattered off the edge of the cave entrance.

She stood on the cliff face above the treetops, stared at the ground far below, and swore.

Deming swung her head behind her.

Fear, not relief, fluttered in her stomach when she saw no leodins on her trail.

Where were they? Had he made them wait? Was this a game to him? A game to the leodins?

Her mind swum with the possibilities and they threatened to drown her.

As if timed, growling rumbled towards her from the darkness.

Deming's eyes flew wide open. She scanned the tunnel, peering aggressively into the black pit she had escaped from, but saw nothing but shadows.

Another growl sounded, this one sounding closer. The screeching sound of claws sharpening on stone sliced through her like a blade.

"Oh, gods. Oh, gods. Oh, gods," Deming babbled to herself. She was trapped. There was nowhere to go, nowhere to hide. She had no wings to fly away and the only pair she knew had no idea the peril she was in.

He was far away and she might die without ever seeing him again. She might die without seeing any of her friends again.

A pitiful sob worked its way out of her.

She had the distinct impression of being a mouse in a trap, unable to escape as the metal jaws swung towards her to snap her neck.

She whimpered. Bile climbed up her throat and she got sick over the ledge.

She couldn't just stand here. She had to do something, anything.

It was either death by leodin eating her alive or death by blunt force trauma from falling from fifty feet. At least if she fell on her neck she might die instantly.

She hopped from one foot to the other, gathering her courage, then, avoiding the slickness of her vomit, she slipped over the edge on her belly.

Her feet scrambled for purchase on the craggy lips of stone below her. Her toes slipped, once, twice, but on the third try she felt confident enough to release her fingers from the lip of the cave.

Her heart hammered in her chest so loudly she feared the beats would push her chest away from the cliff face and to her death but they did not and after giving herself one, singular second to collect her wits, she looked.

The vertigo was intense and instantaneous.

Her vision swam and she leaned against the cool mountain, closing her eyes. She couldn't stop, there wasn't enough time, but the panic rising like the tide in her belly told her that if she didn't slow her pulse she would pass out and that would be the death of her far more surely than risking the climb down.

Five things she could see.

She cracked open one eye. Moss. Lichen. The sky. The stone. The ground.

Quick and without reflection. There was no time for anything more. She swallowed once in fear and again for courage but kept her eyes open and scanned for the next available jutting rock to step on to.

As she bent her knees and reached one foot down, she listed off more.

Four things she could feel. The cool rock. Something wet under her fingers. Her chest rising erratically. Her pounding heart.

They weren't the four most calming things in the world, but the exercise was still doing its job. She needed to focus on the task at hand and in order to do that, she needed to be grounded in reality, not panic.

Her foot touched the next landing. She felt exposed and precarious in this position, one leg extended down and out and the other bent at an odd angle but to be still was to panic and to panic was to die so she pushed off her left foot and fell into limbo.

The seconds before becoming steady again were of another world. They passed both slowly and with speed. They felt both restricted and freeing. It was like the old adage—an apple placed in a field and left alone was both eaten and whole. Time suspended and the years that slipped by in which Deming was perched atop the side of a mountain, anchored by five toes gripping for her life, she was both dead and alive.

She laughed when all four limbs were in contact with the mountain once more.

Time resumed.

Three things she could hear. Her labored breathing. The crumble of gravel and small stone beneath her feet. Wingbeats.

Wingbeats? She shouldn't be able to hear wingbeats this high up. No bird flew this close to the mountain.

She turned her eyes upwards, scanning the sky and momentarily pausing her journey to the ground. She couldn't see anything. There were no larks or bluejays in sight, let alone a bird of prey with wings large enough to hear.

Her face scrunched in confusion.

In her focus to find the source of the sound, Deming had nearly—nearly—forgotten the reason for her hasty descent and while she was searching the skies the predators had found their prey.

She heard them before she saw them.

A rumbling began, low and slow enough that Deming thought, for a moment, it was only her imagination. The noise grew, though, and so did her anxiety.

Two things she could smell—

Pebbles skittered down the mountainside. One hit her forehead, snapping her attention and sending her gaze towards the entrance of the cave.

The moment her face tilted upwards a hot, slick droplet splattered against her skin and she met the eyes of a panting, growling leodin.

It pulled its lips back to show its teeth and growled again before snapping them at her.

The second prowled up next to it, both of them leering down at her with undiluted hunger.

She was as good as dead.

Deming glanced down. She had only made it two ledges, the earthen floor was still eons away and if she leapt she would break her legs if she were lucky or, more likely, send her femur shooting through her gut. Both of those options still sounded more appealing than being eaten alive by rabid leodins or tormented by Khalil. Before she could seal her fate though, something far larger and far more fierce than the leodins arrived.

An amphithere tore through the sky, banking hard seconds before it crashed into the cliff face that Deming clung to, and shot straight in the air.

A roar sounded through the treetops like the gods themselves were bellowing.

Deming clutched the mountainside so hard her nails cracked.

Wind blustered and branches cracked into each other, snapping and whipping at their proximity to the thunderous wingbeats that accompanied the roar.

Deming dared a glance up, risking speed for awareness. She couldn't very well continue climbing down if the legless beast decided to whip the air into a frenzy again.

For a brief, awe-inspiring moment, feathered wings blocked out the sun. Everything fell into shade and a hush fell over their small area of the world before the amphithere dove once more.

This time, its jaws were open wide and Deming had the pleasure of seeing each and every knife-like tooth glisten menacingly before it snatched one of the leodins off the mountain.

The leodin had been in mid leap towards Deming, but its body was picked out of the air like a salmon from the river and before it could bite or tear at the amphithere's scales with its claws it was bleeding out. It roared in pain, briefly, before the amphithere snapped its jaws shut completely, crunching its spine with a crack that Deming felt from her head to her toes.

Wind rushed over her, unraveling her braid and sending her hair snapping into her cheeks and neck and shoulders with pinched bits of pain, and within two humongous beats of its wings the legendary beast was above the trees once more.

To its credit, the remaining leodin had the wherewithal to appear leery. Eyes flicking to the skies to track the alpha predator, the leodin crept towards the lip of the cave.

If at all possible, Deming panicked further. She had not finished her calming exercise and even if she had, the situation demanded far more than chewing on a mint leaf.

The leodin growled and placed a paw on the vertical face of the mountain.

Deming looked to the skies, praying the amphithere was still hungry.

The amphithere circled the sun—watching, waiting.

Then the leodin launched itself towards Deming, claws glinting in the afternoon light, and she had no choice but to leap off the mountain to certain death.

Chapter Twenty Seven

Deming

DEMING COULD HEAR NOTHING but the wind roaring as it tore at her skin, the thin air doing nothing to slow her. Her eyes were open against the gusting wind, her lashes were tickling the thin skin of her eyelids, and her heart raced when she realized she had already tumbled into the wrong direction. She had made the leap too much of a dive and her head was leading her body towards the earth.

She tried to orient herself in the air but her body was twisting and squirming as she fell and it was so difficult to move when there was nothing to push off of but air and desperation.

She would hit the ground in seconds, and if she didn't get her feet somewhat under her she would either crack her skull and bleed out and die or crack her neck and bleed out and die.

She yelled and pried her chest up, forcing her legs below her just in time for them to brace her impact as she crashed into the earth.

Bones shattered, muscles tore, and Deming screamed.

The leodin and the amphithere and the loss of Vallyn and everything else in Deming's entire world faded to black with the snap of the bones.

There was nothing but the searing pain in her legs.

It felt like she was being flayed alive and drowning in a frozen lake and smoldering over hot coals. There was nothing comparable to the intense pain radiating from her lower half.

She couldn't breathe. Her chest was heaving and her lungs were on fire but she couldn't bring any relief to them as she gasped and gasped.

Her hands shook like leaves in a storm. She tried to steady them against her chest but they would not stop trembling.

Deming closed her eyes. She needed to reach her magic. She could heal herself, she had done it before. She needed to do this if she was going to survive. A woman with two broken legs alone in a forest was as good as dead.

She felt for the golden thread of her light magic but could sense nothing but the flashing red and white of pain. Everywhere, all consuming pain.

Her eyes flashed open though she didn't dare look at the mangled mess her legs had become. She rested her head against the ground.

She must master the pain. There was too much riding on this half-baked, hair-brained plan she had put together while clinging to the slide of a mountain in a panic.

Who knew what would become of Vallyn if Deming couldn't alert the others—

She shifted and pain tore through her anew, bone jutting from where her shin should be.

She grit her teeth against the scream that barreled through her chest.

Her magic, find her magic.

All that pooled within her was horror.

"Settle your mind."

Deming's eyes flew wide at the unfamiliar presence in her mind. It was deep and cool, like the underbelly of some ancient coursing river.

She tried to ask who was there but all that came out was a hoarse croak.

"Calm your mind and heal yourself. Your magic is you, there is no need to search for something that is inherently yours."

Deming gasped. The pain was blinding. Perhaps the voice was a figment of her imagination. She certainly felt delirious enough. Waves and waves and waves of pain worse than she had ever felt before crashed into her.

She was wrong, she would not survive this.

"I..." she panted, eyes wide then pinched close, "It hurts."

"And yet your light is still there. Pain cannot take away your magic. Even death cannot do that."

Deming heard without understanding. She could feel herself slipping away. She had lost so much blood. She searched her body for any ray of magic or flicker of healing ability and found nothing but searing pain.

"You have much to learn," the voice rumbled. Something that could only be described as a disgruntled sigh accompanying it despite it still existing within the confines of her mind.

Then, just as the sparks and shadow began to creep into Deming's vision, trees cracked in half, felled by wings that stretched as wide as a galleon was long, and an amphithere landed. The same one that was circling above, Deming noted with the last slivers of consciousness.

The ground shook as it did so. Leaves fell, ripe fruit was shaken from branches.

Deming's sense of self was slowly withering away as she crept towards death and therefore could not and did not appreciate the grandeur of the amphithere's wings as they folded out of the sky and into its scaled, snake-like body.

She felt it wind its way to her. She felt its tail curl around her body, lifting her head. The scales were hot. Or maybe she was hot.

"Be still."

As if she had any control over anything.

The amphithere lowered its great head, resting its nose on her legs. The scales around its nose were surprisingly soft and warm. The breath that it exhaled through its nostrils was warmer.

"All magic is connected."

Warmth flooded through Deming. It was pleasing at first, then it was too hot. She was bubbling, simmering, boiling—

Then it stopped.

The last thing she remembered before she fainted was the amphithere scooping her up into two terrible jaws and taking off into the sky.

Chapter Twenty Eight

Deming

"Wake up."

The command tickled Deming's consciousness, teasing her from the dreamless sleep she had fallen into.

Sensations came to her in waves.

Her shoulder pressed into something firm, a wetness transferring from it to her skin.

High pitched whistling echoed around her.

It was the pulsing heat that woke her fully, though.

Steady gusts of air so hot some of it felt more like steam rocked against her left side like waves against the shore. Her whole body was drenched in sweat. The heat clogged her nose and throat and each breath she took was heavy and slow.

Blinking the remnants of sleep away, she felt the pinch of something sharp on her arm and opened her eyes fully to see what had caused the disturbance.

Fear, familiar and piercing, shot through her at the sight of her arm cradled against two fangs the size of her thigh.

She was inside the mouth of an amphithere.

Her body went rigid, every muscle taut and locked up but before she could so much as think to panic, the same rumbling, feminine voice that commanded her to wake up entered her mind once more.

"We near your home. Prepare yourself. Death hangs heavy in the air."

The warning was ominous, vague.

Her heart clenched at all the possibilities, each more devastating than the last.

Deming rallied her confidence to speak. "Who are you?"

Her voice was snatched by the wind rushing by but the amphithere heard her regardless.

"You may call me Rendrel."

The name sounded like a polished stone when the amphithere spoke it and when Deming repeated it, it tasted like fresh snowflakes.

The further into consciousness she swam the more she realized she was in no pain. Not even the twinge of a bruise could be felt.

She tried to peer at her legs but Rendrel's jaws were too wide.

With caution, Deming flexed one foot, then the other.

Awe and confusion blending her tone into something close to reverence she said, "You healed me."

"You need to live," Rendrel responded cryptically.

Soraya's house came into view before Deming could prod further.

Soraya was pacing on the porch. Her eyes flashed in recognition of the tri-colored hair that was strangling the fangs of the beast and her pacing stopped for a moment as she took in the unbelievable sight. But seconds later she was back to constant movement.

It set Deming on edge, the repetition a clear sign of nerves. Something was wrong. Even without the warning given to her moments ago, instinct made the hair on Deming's arms prickle.

Death hung heavy, Rendrel had said.

Who's death?

Deming wanted to scream the question until her voice gave out.

The second the shadow of Rendrel's wings touched the grass of the hills around her home, Soraya yelled something through the window, sat down on the bench, then stood and continued pacing.

They landed, Rendrel laying Deming on the ground as gently as she could, and Soraya flung down the steps and ran to them. Her hair was unbound, her face was flush. Concern and anxiety swirled in her eyes. She dipped her head in reverence to the animal that was more god than anything to the Fae, but Rendrel uncoiled herself and took flight before Soraya could address her. Dust blew in mini storms in the wake of the amphithere's departure.

Deming didn't see where Rendrel flew to because at the same moment, all of her attention swung to the body bursting from the front door.

Nikita looked frantic, manic. His hair was tangled, his eyes were wide and wild. In his hand was a dagger, though the moment he saw Deming it clattered to the ground.

His wings twitched and flexed and moved like they itched to be in motion and suddenly they were. He half ran, half flew to where she stood and scooped her into a vice-like embrace.

He ran his hands over her head, through her hand, across her shoulders. All while murmuring into her neck over and over, "You're alive, you're alive, you're alive."

Ilysse appeared over Nikita's shoulder. "Where's Vallyn?"

Deming met the female's golden gaze, her own eyes brimmed with tears.

Ilysse's face contorted into vicious disbelief. Her canines flashed. "Where is Vallyn, Deming."

"She was unconscious," Deming said, shaking in Nikita's arms, "the leodins, they attacked. I had to jump—"

"You left her?" Ilysse snarled.

"I couldn't—I didn't have a choice—"

"You always have a choice!"

"Shut up, Ilysse!"

All heads snapped to Soraya.

Tail swishing, paws planted firmly on the ground, she stood just beyond the three of them. Her hands were balled into fists at her sides. Her furred ears were tall, alert.

"We can talk about this later. Deming needs to know. Now." Soraya looked to her, sorrow coating her voice like a mourning veil. "Paris is…" She swallowed hard and started again. "Paris is dying."

Death hangs heavy.

The breath was knocked from Deming's lungs. "What?" she managed, though she had heard Soraya clear as day.

"He took a turn for the worse. The fever spiked and nothing I've given him has helped." Soraya looked pained, genuinely distraught. This was her specialty, after all, healing. She was supposed to be able to help. That was the whole point of being here.

"The leodin claws must have some new toxin on them or something. Or the parasites are transferable or his body isn't taking to my herbs because he's human."

She rambled, each word getting higher and higher pitched until the last broke into a sob. "I'm sorry, I'm sorry…"

Deming pried herself from Nikita and left Soraya's apologies behind. She swept inside quickly, taking the stairs two by two, and thrust herself into Paris's room.

The door cracked against the wall and swung back to hit her on the shoulder. She didn't feel it. Didn't feel anything. All she could see was Paris's limp and pale body slouched into the bed in front of her.

Dying.

Just like Miriam.

She froze, her body cold as ice and her breath like frost in her lungs.

Paris was white, so white. The blood had drained so thoroughly from his face Deming worried it would never return even if he was able to climb back from the brink of death. His chest rose and fell, which was the only solace. Although each inhale was shaky and labored, the exhales rattling like each might be his last.

She forced herself into motion. She took one step, two. The third brought her to her knees and she half slid half crawled the rest of the way to his bedside.

His hand felt like a corpse in hers and that, more than anything else, frightened her.

"Paris?" Fear crept into her voice. "Paris, you're okay. You're fine." She swept her hand through his blonde hair, messy and tousled from laying in bed for so long. "Paris, please." She was barely speaking at this point, her voice small and scared. The plea left her lips and was immediately swallowed by the devastation that hung in the room.

When Rendrel's voice slipped into her mind, Deming was too lost to anguish to feel any morsel of surprise.

"You can help him."

"I can't," she yelled into the air, "I've tried but I can't!"

Deming felt hopelessness sinking into her bones.

"You can either try, or let him die, Light Heart."

Deming's head lifted, the last two words were a key to a lock inside her she hadn't known existed.

Rendrel's voice was resolute, firm, commanding. She repeated what she had said before healing Deming's legs. *"All magic is connected."*

Deming didn't know what to do with that. She needed her magic, not a philosophy lesson.

"You healed me," she pleaded to Rendrel, "you can heal him."

"I cannot intervene with fate." Despair washed through Deming like a flood but just before her head hit the mattress Rendrel spoke again. *"But I can show you the way."*

Pressure built in Deming's head and before she could truly comprehend what was happening, Rendrel had placed a memory in her mind.

It felt foreign, cool and smooth, against the familiar hallways of her consciousness. As Deming examined it, she realized it was less a memory and more a pathway, a guide.

"All magic is connected," Rendrel repeated.

Then her presence disappeared.

The door behind her opened but Deming barely registered the creaking hinges. She certainly didn't hear Soraya's paws on the wood floor, nor the brush of Nikita's feather's against the walls.

She had fallen deep into the drop of knowledge Rendrel had given her.

It was not made for her mind, the colors and words and emotions were so at odds with her perception of reality that Deming struggled to make sense of anything at first. Then, slowly, threads of understanding began taking shape.

It was not separate, magic, from anything in the world. It was infinite, it was everything. There was no finding it, no controlling it. It simply was.

With little more than a whim and a hope that she had interpreted Rendrel's advice correctly, Deming pulled out of her mind and settled beside Paris.

Time felt slippery. Sound and sensation, too. The sheets between her fingers were like water. The air tasted of iron.

Deming placed her palms as gently as she could on Paris's chest. His skin was hot to the touch and felt slick with sweat.

She had removed his shirt and bandages and he now lay on top of the bed, skin bare to the air. Seeing the mauled flesh in such a serene environment, with light streaming in from the window and the starchy whiteness of the fresh linens he lay upon, made the wound look so much worse.

Deming focused not on the wound she was to heal, nor the state of her friend. She didn't think about the pull in her gut drawing her towards the winged male behind her and she didn't think about the amphithere that had given her this knowledge.

Worry nor fear nor distraction would not help her here. Instead, she focused on the rise and fall of his chest, watching her hands move with his breath. His breath may have been labored, but it was there. He was still with her and she was determined to keep it that way.

She closed her eyes, let all her focus siphon to her own body and the one below her.

She felt the steady if faint drumbeat of his heart and looked inward to her own pulse. Slowly, with care, she matched their breathing. Where Paris rose, she rose. Where Paris fell, she fell. They moved as one, breathed as one.

Connected.

Once she felt a semblance of peace, she began looking inward. Her magic responded to her, was a part of her, and had risen to the surface rushed and chaotic when her emotions were unchecked. What she was about to do could not be manic.

She felt the breath move in her body, felt the blood course through her veins, felt the warmth of her magic twinkle and spark to life. Golden and shining.

Instead of trying to bring it to the surface, she lived with it. Breathed with it. Knew it.

It was not just in her blood, but the bone and muscle and sinew that built her. It was in her mind and her thoughts. It was in her heart and in her soul.

The longer she sat with it, caressing the threads of light and coaxing them to come play with her, the warmer she felt. Her skin felt like she was wrapped in steam, like the sun was licking at her in high summer.

When she opened her eyes, her palms glowed.

She drew her attention to the wound that was sucking the life from Paris. It was substantial, crossing much of his chest. Skin and muscle protruded from the opening, peeling back and away from the wound like the poison it was.

Constant pain and fever was a horrible, slow way to die.

But Paris wouldn't die.

She wouldn't let him.

Deming felt magic at her fingertips. It warmed her, and Paris's skin flushed under her palms, too. At first, nothing happened.

Then the torn flesh...relaxed, almost. The edges that were flayed open to the world gently moved towards each other once more. The blood leaking from it slowed to a drip, then stopped completely.

Sweat beaded on her forehead behind her ears, at the nape of her neck. Tears fell freely from her eyes but Deming refused to think of anything except the thrum of magic in her hands and the way Paris was ever so slowly being knit back together.

She kept her breathing steady with his.

In and out.

Rise and fall.

Beginning and ending.

Life and death.

They were one. Connected. Flowing together as Deming's magic flooded his system.

His collarbone was healed first, the skin pink and fresh like a newborn, and the rest followed.

Minutes or hours or days could have passed and Deming would have been none the wiser.

Then, as the last hint of tender skin disappeared and the wound fully sealed itself under her palms, Paris gasped.

His eyes flew open.

He took one breath, then another, then he looked at her.

Love and longing and kinship and hurt and desire and understanding and gratefulness crossed between their eyes. Lifetimes and galaxies and misunderstandings. Friendship, pure and undiluted.

"Hey, Deming."

His voice cracked, harsh from lack of use, and Deming sobbed, the sound raw and wild.

"Hey, Paris."

And then they were laughing and crying and tangled in each other's arms and Deming felt whole for one brief and shining moment.

CHAPTER TWENTY NINE

DEMING

DEMING WALKED THROUGH THE forest alone.

She was unsure why she was here—she couldn't even place where here was—but she felt something pulling her deeper and deeper into its depths. Curious and only reasonably afraid, she followed the call.

Her skin felt flush. Sweat beaded on her brow though she wore only an ivory slip made of layers of lace. A breeze whistled through the leaves above. One broke free and fluttered to the ground. Deming thought it looked rather whimsical. She looked skyward. She wanted another to fall.

A tug on her heart.

Her feet propelled her forward, following whatever was calling to her on their own accord.

Fog drifted down from the heavens. It wove through the branches, light and misty.

Still she walked.

On and on.

As she walked, the fog grew. It thickened, darkened. Deming's mood soured. It was so beautiful before, why did the weather have to become such a heavy blanket on the forest?

She sped up.

Twigs snapped beneath her feet. Bushes rustled as the hem of her dress snagged on leaves and thorns. One pricked her ankle. She frowned.

Deming gathered the thin material in her hand, bunched it high on her thighs, and picked up her pace once more.

Something ominous crept through the forest. The fog had brought it, she was sure of it.

She broke into a run.

Branches scratched at her face and undergrowth threatened to trip her but she was sure-footed and quick, darting through the forest like a doe.

Light sparkled off something ahead. She raced for it.

Deming burst from the forest into a clearing. Before her was a large lake, pristine with a glassy surface that reflected the sun's rays.

She sighed in relief. The fog had not followed her here.

She was walking towards the lake when thunder boomed behind her. She spun, panicked and surprised. The fog had thickened into a storm that rolled over the forest with black clouds. Lightning cracked, lighting the clouds from within.

Deming stumbled backwards. She fell and her hand landed in the lake. Water splashed onto her skin and her slip. She went to stand but froze when she saw red dripping from her fingertips, red staining the white lace she wore.

The lake turned to blood. It expanded towards her, the shore lapping at her wrists and waist and calves.

She scrambled away, her feet splashing blood as they stomped through the growing tide. Soon she could not lift her legs out of the lake at all, so she began swimming instead.

Blood drenched the lengths of her hair from tip to scalp. It dripped and splattered onto her face and into her eyes and mouth.

It was hot and thick and no matter how hard she swam she made no ground towards the shore. It evaded her through every effort.

Her breathing became labored.

Her arms became heavy.

Her hair melted into the blood, red against red, and then it was over.

She was pulled under the waves of blood, then fell backwards into a pool of stars.

Deming slept for two days.

Her dreams were haunted with shadowed figures and whispers of war. The voices of her loved ones sung words of hatred and betrayal that sounded so close and so real but when she turned, there was nothing but darkness.

She woke in a cold sweat on the morning of the third day, hand clutching her throat where a dream-blade had just slit her open.

Gasping, she joined the world of the living once more.

The moments before sleep took her flooded forward and the first word she said was a name.

"Paris?"

"I'm here."

He was sitting in an armchair to her right. Alive, well. Blood had returned to his face, his skin was no longer that terrifying shade of white.

It hadn't been a figment of her imagination. She had healed him. Relief poured through her, shattering all other thoughts for the smallest moment in time.

As dreams and nightmares released their hold on her mind and reality grounded her, Deming became increasingly aware of the sparkling embers in her veins.

Her magic.

She could feel it within her now easily. It was golden and shimmery like the first rays of morning light. It was warm like a bed of coals and soft like the setting sun. Right now it was relaxed, waiting. It lazed in her like a dew drop on grass.

It was astonishing that she had never been able to feel this before. Her magic was so clearly an intrinsic part of her that it seemed unfathomable that she had ever gone a day without understanding it.

Deming looked at her hands and with barely a thought, they lit up like the brightest candle. She turned her hand over, an awed smile plastered on her face. Light twinkled from every pore. It stretched and pulled, brightening the room until everything was coated in a warm glow.

A choked laugh escaped her throat.

Paris echoed the sound. "You're magic, Deming."

She was. This light was an extension of herself. It was connected to her mind and her body and the breath in her lungs.

All magic is connected.

Rendrel had unlocked this piece of her.

The light in her palm winked out as Deming closed her fist. She shifted up on the bed, leaning her back against the downy pillows. "Is she still here? The amphithere?"

Paris's hand slid up on his thighs. "Yeah, she is." He nodded towards the window. She's been waiting for you to wake."

That was not what she had expected. Though half of her wanted to speak with Rendrel more and hopefully learn more about her magic, the other half was terrified by the monstrous, scaled body and fangs that accompanied the beast. Amphitheres were not known to pay much mind to the workings of mortals, what could she possibly want with Deming?

And why had Rendrel said that Deming needed to live?

Not that she wanted Deming to live, not that she took pity on her injuries. No, Rendrel was clear. Deming needed to live.

"Why?"

Paris shrugged. "I don't know. She hasn't left the forest. She spoke to the prince once, but other than that has been adamant that she would only talk to you."

Rocks sunk in her stomach. What could that possibly mean?

Deming licked her lips, afraid to ask the other question tearing into her like the rusted edges of a thousand blunt knives. "And Vallyn? Has anyone gone back for her?"

The idea of Vallyn alone and unconscious in the darkness of the tunnels was enough to coat her tongue with bile. What would Khalil do with her? Stick her in a cage? Harm her? They didn't even fully comprehend what he and Dresden were doing under the mountain, what use could they have for Vallyn? A bargaining chip? Someone to experiment on like the leodins and the baethors?

Deming clutched her stomach to quell the nausea. Khalil wouldn't do something like that on a human, would he?

Paris's expression was taut, his skin ashen. "We were waiting for you to wake up, too." He wrung his hands, his eyes darted to every corner of the room before settling on her. "There were problems that Nikita and Ilysse faced that made us think we needed every piece of information before going back for her."

"What problems—"

"I won't be able to explain them properly," he cut her off, shuddering, and the sight of him so uneasy made Deming shift uncomfortably. "I don't think they even really understand what happened. Besides," he added, eyes shifted to the window, "I really think you need to talk to her first."

Talk to Rendrel, talk to Nikita and Ilysse, figure out how to get Vallyn back.

She could do that.

Deming pulled her legs out from the cover. The wooden floor felt cool and scratchy on the soles of her bare feet.

"Do you need help?"

She shook her head. "I'm going to get changed then I'll come downstairs."

Paris gave her a tight smile then left.

Slipping out of her cotton sleepwear and into fresh clothes felt wonderfully normal. She picked a loose fitting white shirt with billowing sleeves that cinched at her elbows and wrists and paired it with simple black trousers.

Her boots were laying haphazardly but clean in the corner of the room. Deming silently thanked whoever had cleaned off the mud and dirt that had been caked onto them.

After braiding the white strands of her hair away from her face and pulling the entire, colorful, unruly mess back with a maroon ribbon, she was ready.

The stairs creaked under her boots. For all that getting ready had settled her nerves, each step she descended cranked them back up.

She saw Ilysse first.

The female was already looking at her from the plush chair she was curled up on in the living room. Her face was stoic, her eyes cold. In her hand was a glass of red wine though it wasn't noon yet.

She took a long sip, downing half the glass without breaking eye contact, then rose from the chair, walked across the room, and shoved past Deming.

Deming reached a hand out but Ilysse had disappeared into the kitchen before she could speak.

Soft sounds of feathers on floorboards and someone saying her name turned her attention back towards the other room.

Nikita's pale face and sharp cheekbones filled her vision. "How are you feeling?"

"Okay," she said, smiling up at him, "A little out of it but good."

"Do you need anything?"

Deming shook her head. "I'm going to talk to Rendrel, the amphithere."

Nikita's hands curled into fists at his side. His wings pulled rigidly into his body.

Before she had a second to question his reaction he relaxed.

"When you're done we have to go over what happened at the cave."

Deming's shoulders fell. "I know, I'll be quick."

"Take all the time you need." Then he sat back down, albeit stiffly.

The air outside was fresh and clean. Kielle and his sun were inching their way towards the top of the blue sky that domed above her. Clouds drifted by as if pulled by a paintbrush.

The day was far too serene for all that had to happen.

Deming found Rendrel easily.

The amphithere was coiled around a birch tree like a python around its prey. Silver irises shone from serpentine eyes. Steam billowed from her nostrils, making the underbrush and fallen leaves quake and shift.

As Deming approached, Rendrel lifted her head. *'Light Heart.'*

Hearing her speak felt like being wrapped in a warm blanket, like sipping tea at dawn. It sounded like snowfall and plucking a spring flower from the ground. Delicate. Snapping. Beautiful.

Deming stopped a few feet from her, her scaled head towering over her small, human frame. Deming bowed low and waited for her approval.

"Rise."

She obeyed.

With all the chaos and fear and pain that surrounded their first meeting, Deming hadn't fully comprehended how beautiful Rendrel was. Now, though, the amphithere was before Deming in all her glory.

She was unimaginably awe-inspiring. Deming would never claim to be the most pious woman on the continent but seeing legend made flesh up close and personal was nearly enough to become an acolyte. The gods had truly outdone themselves.

Scales glistened like a million tiny emeralds. They began under her chin and trailed down what was the equivalent of her chest, disappearing from view where her tail met the ground. Each slithering shift of her body caused the crystal-like scales to slip over each other, seamlessly dipping under and out from the one below it. Feathers decorated her wings and tail.

Rendrel was green from tip to tail. Deming had never seen so many shades of the color. The sun shone brilliantly on the amphithere through a crack in the clouds. The individual scales and feathers ranged from moss to viridian to the exact shade of olives. The darkest of them looked nearly black, like the beginnings of a storm cloud. The lightest like the leaves of seedlings.

Atop her head, looking very much like a crown, were decorative feathers that swayed stunningly as Rendrel moved. Five in all, they cascaded up in length. The middle one was nearly as tall as Deming herself.

Deming stood face to face with what was as close to a god as something earthbound could achieve and asked, "Why do you call me that?"

"It is who you are."

The voice filled her mind and she thought she may never get used to the sensation.

The longer she stood in front of Rendrel, the more firmly something clicked into place inside Deming. She couldn't quite articulate what it was, but it was as if a piece of herself had been brushed off and polished. Something forgotten, buried, but always there.

Deming was hit with the strangest wave of feeling like she was back home in Arsaela, walking the beaches of Queen's Bay as water lapped her toes.

Her spine snapped straight at the sizzling sensation that shot though her as her eyes met Rendrel's silver ones. It felt like an echo of what it felt like to touch Nikita, to catch his eyes through a crowd of people.

Who was she?

What was she?

Deming's feet carried her forward on their own accord. Close enough to Rendrel to feel warmth rolling off her scales in waves, Deming paused, cocked her head. "I feel like I know you."

A pleased rumble sounded from deep within Rendrel's chest. *"Your soul knows mine."*

"How?"

"All in time."

Deming was unsatisfied with that answer but didn't have the gall to prod further. She spoke plainly and with confidence. Deming felt it was unlikely she would elaborate.

"You said I needed to live. Why?"

"You are prophesied."

Deming's heart lurched. "You know of the prophecy?"

"There are many futures ahead, Light Heart, many prophecies. You are integral to most."

The way Rendrel spoke was slippery. Her words felt that they held more than one meaning, the truth veiled.

Deming shifted her feet, sticks and leaves crunched underfoot.

"Paris told me that you stayed to speak with me."

Rendrel rustled her neck, feathers and scales jostling. She was quiet for some time, then huffed out a large gust of steam from her nostrils. Intense heat washed over Deming. The skin on her face felt pinched afterwards and she wondered how much hotter it would feel like to be within a blast of her fire.

"I thought you may want an explanation of your fate."

Her fate?

Rendrel lowered and tilted her head. One impossibly large and irreverently bright silver eye was in line with Deming. The translucent inner lid that protected her eyes during flight blinked.

"Do you not?"

"I don't understand," Deming said honestly, "What do you know of my fate?"

Rendrel looked at her, her gaze piercing.

Deming shivered. Something deep within her pulled out and away and the most curious feeling flooded her senses. It felt like her heart was being prodded at in her chest, like someone was plucking at the threads of her soul.

Just as quickly as the sensation appeared, it vanished.

A cautious rumble filled her mind. *"You have not discovered the fate tie, yet."*

Deming's brow furrowed. "I know of the prophecy."

"That is not what I mean."

Rendrel uncoiled from the birch tree and Deming had to take multiple steps back to give the amphithere space enough to move freely. She slithered through the grass and when her wings were clear of the branches she opened them wide.

"Wait!" Deming's hand shot to cover her mouth the second the word left her lips. Who was she to command an amphithere?

Laughter rumbled through her mind. Though it did little to put Deming at ease, it did give her the confidence to speak her mind before the amphithere took to the skies.

"Please," her voice as demure and quiet as she felt, "my life has been a series of unfortunate events and much of who I thought I was has fallen apart in my hands recently. If you know something of my fate, please tell me."

Rendrel twisted her spine towards Deming. Steam curled from her nose with every breath, misting the scales around her jaw. She looked at her with what seemed like curiosity.

"All in time, Light Heart. The weight of what I have to share will be heavy. I remained here because I thought you knew more. I understand the white-haired woman you left behind is to be your priority. Focus on her. Come to the nest afterwards and all may be explained. Bring the prince. No one else."

Then Rendrel leapt into the sky with a solitary beat of her wings.

CHAPTER THIRTY

NIKITA

NIKITA STARED OUT OF the window, waiting for Deming to return.

Deming had been unconscious for days after healing Paris. For more reasons than one, they had been some of the slowest days of his life. He desperately wanted to see his mate's shining eyes open and curious once more. He wanted to see her moving around, to feel her presence in every room he was in.

More practically, he wanted her to wake so they could talk about what had happened.

Because, truly, what had happened?

He and Ilysse had shared their very hazy recollection with Soraya, Hartford, and Paris, but they still had next to no information about what Vallyn and Deming had experienced. Without that, they could do very little.

"Would you stop that?"

His eyes leapt to where Ilysse was leaning against the doorframe. Golden eyes molten, canines bared. Her arms were crossed tightly against her chest and out from between the knuckles of her closed fists were every one of her long, sharp claws. If she had hackles, they would be risen.

Her sanity had been nearly as precarious as his own these past few days. It was like her emotions were dancing on the edge of a knife.

"What?"

"The incessant tapping," she snarled.

Nikita stilled his leg. He hadn't realized the nervous habit had surfaced.

He sat in the chair silently, still, for no more than a minute before the itch to move returned. He pushed out of the chair and began pacing in front of the stained glass.

Ilysse muttered under her breath. "You're unbelievable."

Ire like a red hot brand stung Nikita. "What is your problem?"

"What's my problem?" Ilysse asked incredulously, hand splayed against her chest, "What the fuck do you mean what's my problem?" She began ticking off them one by one on her fingers. "Could it be that shadows infiltrated our minds? Could it be that Vallyn is likely dead? Could it be that Deming yet again proved worthless when it actually mattered? Could it be that the amphithere that—"

Nikita cut her off before she could finish that last thought. Even he wasn't ready to think about that particular detail yet. Instead, he latched onto the attack against Deming.

"It's not her fault—"

"Not her fault? You and I got out of there just fine, didn't we?"

"We were forced out of there against our will," Nikita seethed. "I'd hardly call that getting out just fine."

"She was in—"

"No, Vallyn was in charge of protecting her."

Ilysse barreled forward with no regard for the damage her words may cause. "What kind of spineless creature leaves her friend to die?"

"Watch your mouth, Ilysse. She's—"

She was his mate.

But he couldn't say that. Not to Ilysse, not when Deming didn't know yet.

"She's the Queen of Laey."

Hatred and pain forged Ilysse's expression into something Nikita didn't recognize. "Right now she is queen of nothing."

Nikita might have taken a swing at his closest friend had it not been for Hartford stepping into the room.

Hartford's soft voice slid through the tense air like a ribbon. "Ilysse, please stop."

Ilysse tightened her crossed arms. She looked one muscle tense away from snapping. Her claws had yet to retract.

Gentle and patient, Hartford walked slowly to Ilysse. She placed her hand under Ilysse's elbow. "It hurts to lose one of our own. Vallyn means more to Deming than anyone else here. Imagine how she might be feeling, having been there when she was lost."

Ilysse ripped her arm away before Hartford had even finished and stormed upstairs like a petulant child.

The door slammed, the sound echoing loud and terrible in the silence that followed.

Nikita rubbed at his temples. The budding headache there was doing him no favors.

"Feeling out of control brings out the worst in her."

He glanced at Hartford through his fingers.

"She cares a lot," Hartford continued, "too much, probably. The shadows really terrified her. She's lashing out because she feels responsible."

Nikita slumped back into the chair. "She should pick someone else to lash out at, then," he muttered.

A shadow of a smile crossed Hartford's face. "She'll recover. She just needs time to feel everything. You know she's not the best with emotions."

"She won't apologize."

"No," Hartford laughed, "she won't. But she won't stay like this, and she won't hold it against Deming."

As frustrated as he was, Nikita knew she was right. Ilysse was fiery, passionate. She cared about those she loved but someone would have better luck catching a fish with their bare hands than getting her to admit that.

The mission having gone so awry was surely something she would take personally. Vallyn's capture would have hit hard. It was in her nature to protect others, it was why she had glommed onto Nikita all those years ago. Such blatant violence against someone she knew would have shaken her. She needed space and time to get over a failure like that. No matter to what degree she was actually responsible for it.

And that wasn't even considering how invasive their own departure from the tunnels had been. Hartford was right, loss of control was something Ilysse feared nearly more than anything else.

He shuddered at the memory of those slinking, slithering shadows caressing his mind.

A soft creak drew him from his thoughts.

Deming stood in the doorway, hand on the doorknob. Her eyes were heavy, the beautiful bow of her lips sagged. "I didn't want to leave her."

The words were no more than a whisper. Cold sorrow, deep blue and stinging, bled down their bond.

Fierce proactive instincts flooded Nikita. He rushed to her, scooped her into his embrace. His wings curled around them both so all the world was behind the black shield of their feathers.

She leaned into him but was otherwise still.

Gods, he would kill Ilysse for this.

"You heard Hartford," he said into her hair, "she's just emotional. She doesn't truly blame you."

Deming pushed her hands against his chest and Nikita reluctantly let her slip out of his arms. "She should."

A gravelly voice sounded from the other side of the room. "Playing who's more guilty will get us nowhere."

Soraya.

The female stood behind Hartford, one arm slung casually around her mate's waist. Hartford leaned into the touch.

Paris joined them moments later. "Well," the blonde said, "Deming is awake. What are we waiting for?"

With heavy hearts and wide eyes, they all listened to her account of the events.

It was harrowing.

Starting from the split in the tunnel and ending with the amphithere carrying her back in its jaws, Deming spared no detail. Her voice trembled when she described the fight with her uncle, how the sight of Khalil shook her to her bones. Her throat bobbed recounting the way Vallyn's body had lain, limp and unmoving, at the feet of that twisted man. Deming even told them parts of the conversation she had just had with the amphithere outside.

At one point she reached for his hand and their fingers had been intertwined ever since.

Through her story, then his, they held each other.

Not gripping, not with ferocity.

But soft, lingering touches. Nikita's thumb brushed up and down the back of her hand. Deming's fingers played through his own. Every contact of their skin telling the other than they were safe now, that they were okay.

After he finished explaining, the best he could, what he and Ilysse had experienced, Deming's face pinched.

"So it what," Deming struggled to find the words, "portaled you here?"

Hartford shook her head. Her full lips were pulled into a frown, her hazel eyes sharp with concern. "No, I watched them walk all the way down the road."

"It was like they were in a trance," interjected Soraya. Her tail twitched back and forth, belying her anxiety.

"Yeah," Hartford agreed, "absolutely. And then when they got close to the house they stopped walking, dropped their weapons, and woke up? I guess? I don't know. It was weird."

"They were shadows?" His mate looked at him with curiosity.

Nikita gave her a tight lipped nod. There was no other way to explain it.

Deming bit her bottom lip. "It was Khalil, then, right?"

Paris leaned forward, elbows on his knees. "Is that even within the realm of a shadow mage? To get into someone's head like that?"

"Not to my knowledge," Soraya murmured.

White strands tousled with red and pink as Deming shook her head adamantly. "We can't underestimate him. We don't know what he's capable of."

"We need to tell my father," Nikita said, begrudgingly.

"Tell him what?" Hartford asked not without softness. "That some man is experimenting on animals deep within the Telaciens? That just sounds like a madman. We don't know what Khalil wants. If we could get approval for an audience, which is a big if, your father will laugh us out of the city."

"Then we go to the nest," Paris said, gesturing to Deming, "she told you to go, didn't she?"

Deming opened her mouth to respond but before she could a cool, immovable voice sounded from the bottom of the stairs.

"No."

As one, their heads spun to Ilysse.

"Vallyn is the priority. Before we do anything else, we're bringing her home."

Beside him, Deming was frozen. The appearance of Ilysse was like a command for her entire being to still and be as small as possible.

His mouth twitched. She should never be made to feel small.

He smothered the feelings that surged in him like an ocean current.

It was getting worse, he admitted silently, the protectiveness he felt towards her. The longer their mating bond remained unaddressed the more irrational he got around her.

He would need to tell her soon.

How, though, with so much at stake? The barrage of problems they needed to deal with was only growing.

To Ilysse, Nikita asked, "How do you intend to do that?"

He spoke carefully, Hartford's words hitting home. With distance from their biting argument, Nikita could clearly see how distressed she was. Ice coated her gaze. Her cuticles were picked over, red and raw. Several blonde braids were frayed, their normal tidiness slipping like her emotions.

Ilysse didn't move from the stairs. "We know where she is, don't we?"

"Hypothetically, yes," Nikita said, "but should we really go back after everything—"

"Yes."

Deming, not Ilysse, spoke the affirmation into existence.

He turned to her, caution wrapped around his wary heart just like ivy around trees, like her fingers around his.

"Deming—"

"I know," she pulled her hand out from his and he immediately longed for that sliver of contact, "it's impulsive and brash, but we have to try." Her pleading eyes bore into his. "We can't abandon her."

"What do you say, prince?" Ilysse crossed her arms. "Up for round two with the shadows?"

Chapter Thirty One

Deming

THE ENTIRETY OF DEMING'S soul felt like it was sitting on a bed of needles.

Her skin, her clothes, her emotions, nothing was safe from the incessant feeling of prickling urgency.

Nikita and Ilysse had been gone for nearly two days.

After being properly shut down in her attempt to join them, the pair had departed from Soraya's house on horseback. They would go try to find Vallyn in the tunnel her and Deming had gone into. If they didn't return, everyone was on strict instructions to send no one after them.

Deming, in particular, had been forced to promise that should Nikita and Ilysse not return by noon on the third day, she would go with Hartford, Soraya, and Paris to the capital. The king may not have any love left for his son, but he wouldn't ignore a blatant attack on his life.

They were to plead asylum for herself and Paris, tell Trevelyan of the tunnels, and wait.

She was of two minds.

Part of her was grounded in keeping her promise. She had no family, no throne, no power save the light magic running in her veins. Her word was all she had. The other part of her, though, the one that ached to run to Nikita, was feral. That part of her would be nearly impossible to rein in if he was threatened, taken from her.

She couldn't stomach losing Vallyn. If a situation arose where she also had to lose Nikita?

She might very well break.

Her teeth ground against each other and the squeaking sensation sent a chill through her.

She tossed her cards on the table.

"Hey," protested Paris, "I was about to win."

"Sorry," she mumbled.

Paris scooped up the cards and started shuffling them. Over and over, he spread them between his thumb and forefinger, expertly mixing the deck. The sound of cards thwacking on the table was deeply satisfying.

Deming clung to that momentary sliver of peace before rolling her neck, sighing, and saying, "I don't want to play anymore."

The cards stilled.

"Okay. What do you want to do?"

Deming rubbed the bridge of her nose. She appreciated everyone's attempts to keep her occupied while Nikita and Ilysse were away, but it was too much today, the voices in her head too loud.

She shoved away from the kitchen table. "Be alone."

Deming walked with purpose through the kitchen, through the sitting area, and out the door. She sat down on the front step and looked out over the expanse of green.

From here to the edge of the woods, only the gravel path disrupted the grass. It billowed gently in the breeze. The early evening sun decorated the blades with warmth.

Strange, she thought, how she could look out on such serenity when nothing about their circumstances reflected that.

That was the duality of life, she supposed. There was always war, always sadness, always pain. And in the same breath, there was always hope, always joy, always beauty. Everywhere, all at once, there was both life and death.

Behind her, the door creaked open then clicked shut.

"I know you said you wanted to be alone..."

Deming's resolve softened. "No, it's okay," she gave Paris a close-lipped smile, "sit."

The wood groaned as he sat beside her.

He settled in comfortably, hands draping casually between his knees, and Deming leaned to rest her head on his shoulder.

"Thank you," she said, still staring out at the waves of grass.

"For what?"

"For following me out. Being alone would have bred more doubt."

One of his hands lifted, pressed into the side of her head, then fell back down.

The small winged shadows of larks and songbirds darted from tree to tree, nest to nest. Crickets chirped. From inside the house, a kettle whistled.

"Beautiful night."

Deming hummed her agreement.

"How are you feeling?"

It was the question she had been trying to answer every second since Nikita and Ilysse had left. Ever since she had woken up after healing Paris, if she was being completely honest.

She didn't want to repeat the way she had fallen into darkness after Miriam's death.

Longing throttled her chest.

It still hurt so badly to think of her.

Deming clenched and unclenched her hands.

There had been so much pain in her life recently, she didn't want to succumb to it. There was no hope in that, no life.

No vengeance, either, a small, vicious part of her whispered.

She wanted to leave the world better than she found it and the only way to do that was to live. She couldn't help others if she was lost in a fog. She couldn't take back her throne if she couldn't even bear the weight of losing a friend.

And yet, there was a deep, deep pit of terror in her chest that was constantly trying to pull her in. When she had looked back to see Vallyn unconscious, the beckoning from that pit had nearly won.

Deming had felt such profound loss in that moment she wasn't sure how to express it to someone who wasn't there. Seeing Vallyn had thrown her through a pool of time. Down, and down she went, reliving every loss dealt to her. Miriam, Colette, her mother, her father.

How much loss was one person expected to bear in a lifetime?

And if Nikita and Ilysse were lost, too, what then?

How was she supposed to deal with a soul-deep pain like that?

She was the center of all the terrible events that had happened. How was she supposed to walk with her head held high knowing that death followed her like a specter?

Quietly, she told him everything.

Paris considers her words carefully. Then, with a sadness Deming hadn't ever heard from him threading through his voice, he said, "It could have been me. Should have been, maybe." He scratched the back of his neck. "If I hadn't been injured I would have been with you guys. Maybe one more person would have tipped the scales, maybe Vallyn wouldn't have been caught off guard. Or maybe it would have been me taken instead."

Deming sat up, her frown deepening. Her hand settled on his shoulder. "We can't know what would have happened if you'd been there. And we would have gone back for you, too. Your life is just as valuable as anyone else's."

He turned, pressing a chaste kiss into her palm before removing her hand. "I know." His smile didn't reach his eyes. "I just wanted you to know that you aren't alone. We all carry some level of guilt for everything that's happened."

Deming swallowed the lump in her throat.

She was about to say more, impress on him how much their friendship meant to her not just because it grounded her to the comfort of her old life, but because it was pure. Their friendship had frayed edges. They had fought and made up countless times. They had tried to love each other and were now trying to sift through what their relationship was after heartbreak.

In the swirl of dishonesty and lies, Paris was truthful, honest. Even when it hurt.

She was about to say all of that when shadows shifted in the woods.

Two figures emerged.

Two, not three.

Deming's heart cracked in half.

Wings carried low, feathers dragging unceremoniously through the dirt, Nikita came into view first. Ilysse followed closely behind. Her eyes were downcast, hands curled into fists so tightly at her side that even from the porch Deming could see her knuckles were white with strain.

It was like she was in the midst of a nightmare. She wanted to look away, she wanted to move, but her limbs were paralyzed.

Like molasses, Nikita and Ilysse walked towards her.

The entire world held its breath as Nikita's feet dragged to a stop before her.

"I'm so sorry, Deming."

A million tiny shards of sorrow pierced her heart.

She knew he was, but even the comfort of his embrace couldn't stave off the feeling of despair that enveloped her like an old friend.

Deming had been silent, then she had screamed, then she had demanded to spar with Ilysse who gladly beat her senseless.

Her emotions had been violent, rapidly changing like the winds of a storm, until suddenly they were not.

Khalil was gone.

Dresden was gone.

The leodins and baethors were gone.

Every piece of parchment, every quill, every vial, every scrap of proof that something other than rock and water had ever existed within the tunnels was gone.

Vallyn was gone.

No trail, no broken branches. No paw prints.

Dead ends, everywhere.

They had vanished like thieves in the night.

Vallyn could be anywhere on the continent.

Eventually the feeling of helplessness overwhelmed all other emotions. It suffocated anything else until Deming could feel only the bone-heavy despair.

She let herself wallow for a day, then two.

On the morning of the third, she woke up.

She would not fall prey to loss. She hadn't been lying when she told Paris she didn't want to get caught in the never-ending web of sadness again.

She wouldn't ignore it, either.

She would take her sorrow and put it in a vase alongside flowers in her soul. She would feel it, remember it, be driven by it.

Deming would find her friend if it was the last thing she did. The moment there was an inkling in the wind about where Vallyn was, she would run to her.

Until then, she would live.

It was past dusk, the sun long since set. Nikita was laying in a patch of grass on the hill behind Soraya's house. His wings were spread out wide behind him. The black feathers teased in and out of the grass, some of them blending into the creeping darkness.

Deming let herself fall back into him. The crook of her neck fit perfectly into his shoulder. Her hair splayed out behind her. She was sure it tickled his skin.

With such perfect timing that a half smile parted Deming's lips, Nikita jostled his head and pushed parcels of her hair away from his cheek.

The night sky was like a painting. Swirls of stars and far away galaxies mingled in the deep blue. The moon hung high, shining Selene's light on all of her subjects.

Holy Mother of the Midnight.

Turner of Tides.

Queen of the Continent.

All that Selene was sparkling through Deming's mind.

She wished she could be as carefree as the moon.

Staring up at the sky, Deming let herself dream.

She dreamt of a world where all children had the luxury of growing up with their parents. She dreamt of a world where everyone was empathetic, where no feelings were hurt. She dreamt of a world where friends didn't have to sacrifice themselves for the greater good.

Then she thought of the grass from earlier. How luxurious it looked basking in the last rays of the sun. She wondered whether or not it would have seemed so beautiful if she had not been full of such worry, if she had never known pain or hurt or loss.

"Kit?"

"Yes, Deming."

"Do you think we have a fate? That our actions are predestined?"

He stilled. She let her head rest heavy on his chest and could feel his heart thunder beneath layers of muscle and bone and blood.

He withheld an answer for long enough that Deming thought perhaps he had fallen asleep.

Then, "Yes, I believe we have a fate. Though, I also believe that Kielle and Selene gave us free will. Not everything is written in stone."

Something tugged at her heart. Deming curled closer into his warmth.

"I must be fated for tragedy, then."

Nikita's arm hugged her tightly. His voice was soft but fierce. "Tragedy is part of your story, Deming, but it is not your fate."

There was something in his voice that made Deming pause. Something about his words felt like a string of pearls laid delicately against her neck.

There was only one way to know what her fate had in store for her.

"We need to see Rendrel." She threw a leg over his, further entangling them. "She asked that you come with me."

Nikita exhaled long and slow. "I knew she would." The air seemed to shift. "There's something you should know."

The back of Deming's neck prickled. Her hands felt suddenly clammy. "What?"

"Rendrel, the amphithere that brought you back, the one with scales like emeralds?"

"Yes?"

"I know her."

Deming propped herself up on her elbow. Her hair fell down around them like a waterfall. She brashly shoved the waves behind her back. "You know her? How?"

She saw the strangest mix of reverence and guilt and betrayal in his eyes as he answered.

"She is the amphithere that marked me."

Deming couldn't find the words to speak.

Rendrel had marked Nikita? She was the one that had claimed him as a Rider and then abandoned him? Taken the mark away?

Saying the mark was taken away was not quite right, she corrected herself with a grimace.

Deming could see the faded, curling, pale gray scar in her mind. How hollow and incomplete it looked. How hollow and incomplete it made Nikita feel for so long. Perhaps still does, if the thinly veiled anguish on his face was any indication.

His lips were pursed. His shoulders were tight. His free hand came up to his chest and touched where the skin beneath his clothes was marred. What should have been a symbol of honor was now the physical reminder of his failure and banishment.

Protectiveness surged in her. She squeezed his hand hard enough she thought his bones might snap.

"We don't have to go—"

"Yes," he cut her off, "we do." One corner of his mouth drew up. A shallow version of the smirk that usually graced his face. "It's okay, truly. I may never know why she decided I was unworthy, but it was my father who scarred me, not Rendrel."

Their chest rose and fell, his deep and heavy, hers erratic.

One thing was for certain.

When she faced Rendrel again she would hear not only her fate, but Nikita's. If she would be gifted clarity she would demand it for him as well.

"Tomorrow," she said with finality, "we go to the nest tomorrow."

Nikita pulled her back down into his arms. "Then stay with me here just a bit longer."

Who was Deming to deny him when that was what she herself wanted.

Nestled together under the blanket of night, Deming let herself feel it all.

The night air was warm, the stars were bright. The grass they laid upon was soft and Nikita's body under her was softer.

Deming's mind filtered through all the day had brought her.

There was much to mourn. Vallyn was lost, hidden somewhere in the shadows of the continent. The prophecy of war loomed over them like the sharpest peak of the Telaciens.

And right now, under the glow of the moon, Deming also felt at peace.

Both feelings could exist within her at the same time. She was done pretending they could not.

There could be no joy without pain, no ease without discomfort.

They stayed there, tangled in one another's limbs like roots of some ancient tree, until even the creatures of the woods tucked into the waiting arms of sleep.

Deming fought her own tiredness as long as she could.

After a time, though, her breathing grew deep and her eyelids grew heavy.

She had fleeting memories of Nikita carrying her to bed, then there was only the haze of her dreams.

CHAPTER THIRTY TWO

DEMING

THE JOURNEY TO THE nesting amphitheres was long and arduous.

Nearly a three day ride from Soraya's house, the path through this patch of forest was rugged, untamed. They needed to rest the horses more frequently, too, because the closer they got to the Telaciens, the more sloping the foothills became.

Deming and Nikita spent the days fluctuating between comfortable silence and learning about one another. They shared stories of their youth and young adulthood. Deming told him about the time she let all the horses out of the paddock because she thought Quintessential looked horribly sad and might want to play with her friends. Nikita shared that he broke his arm not once, but twice, trying to fly before his wings had matured enough to carry his weight.

It was light, easy conversation. After each memory they shared, Deming felt incrementally closer to him.

There were lingering glances and soft touches here and there. They slept in the same tent, sharing the warmth of their bodies, but the thought to do anything more never crossed Deming's mind.

With every spare second, she was preoccupied worrying about the revelation Nikita shared with her before they left.

Rendrel was the amphithere that bonded to him.

What could it mean? Why had she been there to save Deming from the leodins? Why had she called Deming to the nest?

The glimmering strands of fate pulled at Deming's instincts. Something larger than herself was at play here.

Shoal, the gray mare she rode, jostled under Deming, shaking her from her thoughts of Rendrel and Nikita.

"It'll do no good to ruminate over an amphithere's motives," Nikita said pensively, "I would know."

He pulled his mare away from Shoal, having purposely bumped the horses together to get Deming's attention. Shoal flicked her ears in annoyance.

"How did you know I was thinking about her?"

Nikita shot her a soft grin. "You're easy to read, princess, remember?"

Deming bit her lip to hold in a smile. "Yeah, I'll work on that."

"Don't." He flicked a wingtip in her direction. It brushed lightly against her thigh. "I like seeing your thoughts."

She looked sideways at him, lips closed but mouth upturned.

The path they took through the forest grew more and more dense as they rode. Brambles crept in and boughs hung low. Leaves rustled and twigs snapped and every time Deming was sure the sounds were coming from somewhere other than the hooves of their horses she tensed and grabbed the hilt of the dagger at her waist.

She had slid the blade half out of its sheath more than a dozen times today alone.

They were nowhere near the leodin sightings, those two spots lay around the western horn of the mountain they were currently riding towards, but everything about their surroundings looked and felt the same and so Deming's senses refused to fall into a false sense of security.

Her body was on high alert, even if her mind found peace in riding next to Nikita.

The sun was just past its highest point. Late afternoon rays filtered in and out of the dense blanket of trees. The redwoods and warm climate of Bascade was long behind them. The air was once again cold, the ground underneath coated in a thin layer of snow that crunched delightfully with every step their horses took. Most of the trees here flaunted evergreen needles. A few oak trees held onto their leaves but for the most part their branches were bare.

It was an interesting combination, seeing nature thrive and coexist in such unique ways. One choosing to hunker down for the colder months, shedding its beauty and waiting for warmer days to bloom. The other choosing to survive by turning sharp and defensive, its limbs coated in fierce protection that could withstand the cold.

The Telaciens rose around them, cocooning them more and more as they approached the place they would leave their horses.

As much a precaution against the lesser beings of the continent as it was to be close to the sky that called to them, the amphitheres had chosen a nesting place that was accessible only by flight or an intense and dangerous climb.

Thankfully for Deming, Nikita would be flying them the last portion of the journey.

Without much warning other than the peaks of the Telaciens no longer being in sight, no matter how far Deming bent her neck back, their horses burst from the edges of the forest and stutter-stepped as they rode up to a sudden cliff face.

The transient space between forest and mountain was small, tight. Both Shoal and the roan mare pawed at the ground, ears flattened. There was little space for them to move and Deming felt sorry to leave them tied to the rickety wooden post that was buried in the ground a few feet away.

Gray and craggy, the ascent on foot to the amphithere's nest began there. Deming's eyes traced the stone steps that were carved into the side of the mountain in a meandering, weaving pattern. They rose and rose until she could no longer differentiate intentional steps from the face of the mountain itself. Thin and crumbling as they were, Deming shuddered at the thought of having to trust only the ancient footholds and her balance to prevent her body from tumbling down to certain death.

It was a blessing she wouldn't be tested in that way today.

"Are you ready?"

Deming glanced to Nikita, who had already tied his mare to the metal latch on the post.

She nodded, dismounting.

She gave both horses a sugar cube from her pack and softly scratched under Shoal's muzzle. She patted her broad neck, warm and comforting and sturdy and wondered not for the first time how Quintessential was faring back home. "Be back soon."

Nikita smiled at her as she took his hand. He kissed her knuckles and she melted under his soft affection. Nothing seemed too daunting when she was with him.

"To the nest?"

"To the nest."

He scooped her into his arms, flared his wings, and launched them into the sky.

The nest was higher than Deming had expected.

She knew it would be the highest she had ever been—higher than flying above Arsaela with Nikita, higher than when she fell from the bounty hunter's clutches—but still, she had not been prepared for how thin the air was.

Nikita had tried to warn her, to coach her on taking slow inhales and to not panic when her lungs did not feel quite the same, but it was so much worse in action. It was like she had been swimming in an ocean of air on the earth's surface and up here it was like a spring rainfall. There was enough to dampen, but not enough to drench. Deming hadn't quite understood how drenched with air her lungs needed to be to feel safe.

Nikita's hand brushed her head, pressing her hair down and her body closer to him as they continued to fly into spaces that no living being should ever be.

Slow, shallow breaths.

Keep her heart rate down.

Deming focused on those two things as she peeked out from Nikita's calming hold.

The air was thin, but at least the view was beautiful.

Similar to how she had been unprepared for lack of oxygen, she had also been unprepared to see the world as a pinprick of color. It was like something out of a dream. The earth was an abstract mural as they soared above it. Swaths of greens and browns bled into one another like watercolors. She had long ago lost the ability to see individual trees but she could see rivers cutting through the forest, ribbons of cobalt amidst an emerald sea. Clouds coalesced around them, coating their skin in chilly dewdrops, and the mountain rose beside them, strong and steady.

Despite her lungs screaming at her that she was meant to be earth-bound, her soul sang the higher they climbed. She belonged among the clouds.

She drew her hand away from Nikita's chest and into the air, letting the wind slip through her fingers like a current. She turned and twisted her wrist, loving the feeling of being pulled by the rush of air. It was exhilarating, being this free and wild and at one with the sky.

There was no fear of falling, not in his arms. Only the pure, undiluted joy of flight.

Perhaps with practice she could learn to breathe easier here. In this moment she wanted nothing more than to have her body and mind feel equally at peace in this intangible space between nothingness and earth.

"Enjoying yourself?" Nikita pressed a kiss into the top of her head along with the words.

"Mhmm," the affirmation rumbled in her chest. She pulled her hand back, clenching it tightly near her heart.

"Good, because we're here."

Her heart skipped a beat as the cliff face vanished and the nest appeared.

Out of nowhere, a portion of the mountain leveled off. In its place was an open expanse of slate. Snow dusted everything. Craters in varying levels of depth and width marred the surface creating a dimpled, pockmarked effect. Mist shrouded peaks in the distance, gray tendrils wrapping around rock and dirt like a blanket as the mountain reached even taller still into the sky behind the carved out, gritty field.

The intrigue of the landscape was nearly instantly lost to the thrill of what occupied it.

Amphitheres. Everywhere.

Lithe bodies twined through the sky, one with the air. Flashes of scales in every color imaginable reflected the sunlight that poured through openings in the clouds. Feathered wings carried long, twisting bodies as young and old, small and large, red, green, black—

Deming blinked, reminded herself she needed to breathe.

And below, like gems in a cushion, over two dozen amphitheres lay inside their craters.

Nests, indeed.

Something about seeing these great, ancient, near mythical beasts coiled tightly against the chilly mountain air and snow, ribs expanding with drowsy breath and eyes closed peacefully, pulled on her heartstrings. She had seen them in flight before and had seen Rendrel up close, but it was the sight of them resting in their home that hit her like a punch in the gut.

They were so utterly astounding. Magnificent in every way.

"Nothing quite like it."

Deming wasn't sure if he said that to himself or to her, but she was at a loss for words regardless as he carried them to the ground.

She slipped from his arms, though he kept one hand on her back to steady herself.

Snow crunched under her boots as she stepped across the mountain. Bones picked clean and large, curling horns lay scattered haphazardly around them. A nearby amphithere raised its head drowsily, eyeing them as they walked. Its eyes were rubies, its scales like a million tiny garnets. A feathered crest of black plumes extended from its forehead, shifting delicately in the breeze, and wings of matching color stretched wide as it shook sleep from its body, screeched sharply, and careened into the sky.

Deming froze, a deer amongst wolves.

"They are peaceful creatures," Nikita reminded her, "They will not harm unless provoked."

She had the distinct thought that two strangers landing suddenly in the space where they slept and ate and birthed their young could be construed as provoking.

Her eyes scanned the earth and sky for Rendrel but found no emerald green glinting in the shrouded sunlight.

"Where is she?"

"Here, somewhere." Nikita stepped further into the nests. "We will need to be given permission from the Crest Major to stay here long enough to speak to her."

Deming's spine straightened like a sting from the clouds puppeteered her. "We have to what?" she hissed, body tense.

He had conveniently left out that little detail.

The Crest Major was the ruling amphithere of the Telacien band. Older than nearly every living creature on the continent and rarely seen, he was a figment of bedtime tales and hushed whispers around fires.

"And if he doesn't give us permission to stay?"

Nikita shrugged. "We leave."

Without knowing her fate.

She wouldn't let that happen.

"He will be in the cave. His name is Daughlr, you may address him as such." Nikita nodded towards the edge of the open space, where flat rock met the rest of the rising mountain. A large cave yawned there, edges ragged and natural.

He knew, for he had been here before. The rough grip of sympathy for what Nikita's memories of this place must entail clutched at her heart.

A flicker of silver and white flashed from the depths of the cave.

The Crest Major.

Was it fear, truly, that was stoked within her at the red amphithere taking off so close to her? The question peppered against her skull as she approached the Crest Major on swift feet. It had taken her by surprise, that was certain. And it would be silly not to have a healthy respect for the vicious rows of teeth within its maw. She wasn't sure. The amphitheres were as beautiful and awe-inspiring as they were dangerous and intimidating. They held fire in their bellies and wind beneath their wings. They were chaos. They were ethereal. They were, at the end of the day, wild.

Wonderful, but wild.

They had closed half the distance to the cave when two words broke through her mind.

"Light Heart."

Rendrel's presence in Deming's mind felt like an extension of herself. Her voice was like the essence of the earth, the warmth of a roaring hearth.

Daughlr's presence felt...other.

Deming stiffened as his mind touched hers. A chill washed over her, like she had placed her hand on marble. The edges of Daughlr's mind could not be contained nor understood. He was timeless, ancient. It wasn't unpleasant, but it did not leave her with anything close to the intrigue and comfort that Rendrel did.

The Crest Major was power incarnate.

When he spoke, it felt like the plates of the earth grinding against one another, like the rumbling ground beneath an erupting volcano.

She stopped mid step.

Her breath came in cloudy puffs from her lips.

Nikita's elbow dug into her spine and she turned to smack it away but paused, seeing him bent over in a low bow.

Shit, shit, shit.

As deftly as she could, Deming hinged at her hips. The snow beneath her was disturbed from her boots. Her hair hung loose off her shoulders, most of it having fallen out of the braid she had plaited it into prior to their ascent.

What could only be described as a throaty chuckle sounded.

"Rise."

With no small amount of trepidation, she did.

Her eyes saw his muscular coils first. Scales of ivory and porcelain and silver decorating his body in a near impenetrable natural armor. His tail was wrapped tightly in a coil and from that coil rose the latter half of his body, white wings stoic and strong. His eyes twinkled with wisdom and something Deming couldn't place.

Every scale and feather shimmered here in between sky and earth. The snow and clouds and thin mountain air blended in with the stark whiteness of him.

He opened his maw and roared.

Deming's blood froze, her bones rattled. She wanted to cry and cower and pray and exalt him all at once. It was a whiplash of emotions that ricocheted within her as the sound poured from his maw.

He snapped his mouth close. The edges of his teeth like swords.

"Prince Nikita," golden eyes like shining brass stared forward, *"it has been a long time since you graced our mountain top."*

"Yes, Crest." Nikita inclined his head once more in reverence, though he did not bow fully a second time.

Daughlr's head bobbed and weaved through the air, slicing back and forth like a snake. *"I recognize the soul beside you."*

Deming swallowed hard. Rendrel had said something similar.

Nikita opened his hips towards Deming. "This is Deming Reynes-Elyachar. Rightful heir to the Queendom of Laey. She has been visited by Rendrel."

"Yes," Daughlr rumbled, *"she told me such a curious story. I was wondering when you would appear before me, Deming Reynes-Elyachar."*

Deming stepped forward with more confidence than she felt. "It is an honor to be in your presence." Unlike Nikita, Deming did fold over into a full bow for a second time. The perfect picture of submission. As demure and nonthreatening as she could possibly make herself, Deming awaited the judgment of the Crest Major.

What could only be described as a throaty chuckle vibrated through her mind.

"There is no need for such flattery."

Straightening, Deming said, "We wish to speak to Rendrel. She said she could explain my fate. May we remain here, at the nests, while we await her?"

Snow sizzled and puddled as the Royal Crest considered her words. The world was full of soft sounds—wing beats, the whistle of the wind.

Daughlr's golden eyes observed her, then trailed to Nikita as if following some invisible string. Caution and intrigue dueled in his next question. *"Why?"*

Deming turned to Nikita in time to see his wings tense.

"There was never a good time—"

"There is always time."

Nikita cowed under the amphithere's chastising tone.

"What—"

"Don't fear, Light Heart." A heavy sigh blew through Deming's mind. *"All will be revealed soon enough."* Daughlr peered at her with intensity. *"Do you wish to know why we call you that?"*

The inability to breathe suddenly had nothing to do with their altitude. "Rendrel said that was who I am."

"She tells no lies. You have been prophesied."

Deming's response was no more than a whisper. "She told me that, too."

Warmth encompassed every inch of her soul as Daughlr slithered towards her, heat following him wherever he went. Deming wondered if that was true of all amphitheres, or if somehow more fire was cradled within his scales because he was the Crest Major.

Not daring to move, it came as a shock when something smooth and firm and blazingly hot rested on her shoulder.

Daughlr's muzzle.

Nikita inhaled sharply beside her, though Deming didn't need that to know what was happening was unprecedented.

Deming could feel the skin on her shoulder smoldering under the heat of Daughlr's scales. She bit her lip to keep from crying out, not wanting to offend him. Besides, this was an honor. She didn't know what was happening, but she knew it was significant. So, despite the pain and scarring she knew would come, she did not waver.

"You bear the pain well," Daughlr's voice poured into her mind as he pulled away.

Deming stood on wobbly legs. Nikita made to help her, but she flicked her hand up softly to halt him. She could be strong. She was strong.

"Pain and I are familiar friends."

The Crest Major looked at her inquisitively. The glint in his eyes felt younger than his years. His entire body had relaxed, coiling around and around and around itself. His feathered tail brushed back and forth across the snow to his left. His wings were tucked loosely at his sides.

"Neither I nor my forebears have given the Seal in centuries."

The Seal? Deming looked to her shoulder. The wool coat and shirt underneath had melted. Branded into her skin were four concentric circles. It burned.

Deming glanced at Nikita, the question written on her face. His mouth tugged down and he gave the slightest shake of his head.

"I don't know what I did to deserve such an honor."

"It is not what you have done, but what you will do."

Anticipation curled in Deming's stomach.

Daughlr's voice reverberated through her mind. If sound was power, his voice would be it. *"The Seal is only given to those whose fates are intricately tied to those of our kind. It is both prophecy and path. You, Light Heart,"* he puffed steam at her, sending her hair rippling behind her, *"are not only one of us. Through you, the world will be saved."*

Deming's heart felt like it might beat out of her chest. The world would be saved through her. How? It was similar enough to the seer's prophecy, but something scratched at her sanity with Daughlr's words.

And what did he mean, one of them? An amphithere? She could wrap her head around being a mage but she must not be understanding Daughlr because unless wings were about to magically sprout from her shoulder blades—gods, wouldn't that be a sight—she was no amphithere.

Another deep chuckle rolled through her mind.

"You do not hide your emotions well."

A sharp laugh burst from Nikita. Deming glared at him, but he already had a hand over his mouth, mirth dancing in his gray eyes.

"So I've been told," Deming said, returning her concentration to Daughlr, "So that is my fate? To be tied to the amphitheres and save the world? I don't understand."

"Nor I. Your fate is winding, knotted into the fate's of others. Much is shrouded even to me. I only feel the call of the Seal." Hot steam billowed from his nostrils, blowing Deming's hair off her shoulders. A shiver rippled across her skin despite the heat. *"What I can tell you is the Seal represents what will be needed during your journey."* He eyed the four circles like a ripple on her shoulder. *"The light, and the bond; the earth and the moon."*

Deming hardly had time to contemplate his words before he uncoiled, stretching his wings in preparation for flight. They took up the entirety of the cave entrance in their grandeur and Deming stifled an awed gasp. She wondered if she would ever get over the sight. She hoped not. She cherished the flighty, skittery feeling that blossomed in her chest whenever she saw an amphithere's wings unfold against the sky.

Nikita's, too, though for different reasons.

Before Daughlr could spiral into the sky, Deming reached out a hand. "Wait" he eyed her, "where is Rendrel?"

"Do not fret, Light Heart. I have called her. She will be here momentarily."

And then with two beats of his wings the Royal Crest was gone. Spiraling tunnels of snow spun in his wake.

Deming tried to pull in steady breaths into her lungs to calm her trembling fingers and frantic heart, but the thin atmosphere fought against her.

She turned to Nikita, reached out her hand.

"What does that mean? The light, the bond, the earth, the moon. What bond?"

Nikita stiffened and a wave of nausea rolled through Deming. With sudden certainty, she knew he was hiding something from her.

"What is it?"

He pressed her knuckles to his lips. "Nothing."

"Kit." A warning, hissed low through clenched teeth.

His thumb rubbed the back of her hand. "Not now, Deming. I'll tell you later, I promise."

Before she could respond, Rendrel burst from the clouds.

Emerald green scales glistened and winked, sliding over each other like water over rocks in a riverbed as the beast carved through the air towards them. The feathers gracing her wings were broad and strong, flickering in the wind, refracting every color of the forest. The five pronged plume rose from her forehead like a crown, and she stared the pair of them down with eyes like molten silver.

Rendrel landed before them, opened her fanged mouth, and roared in greeting.

Something sizzled up Deming's spine at the sound. Every nerve in her body felt alive.

CHAPTER THIRTY THREE

DEMING

RENDREL'S VOICE FILLED HER mind, winding and ancient like rivers that poured from mountain peaks.

"What of your moon-touched friend?"

Moon-touched? Deming frowned. Did she mean Vallyn's white hair?

"She was gone by the time we returned." The words were bitter on her tongue. Deming could feel genuine sorrow filter through the mental connection between her and Rendrel.

"I'm sorry to hear that, Light Heart." With serpentine movements, Rendrel wound herself towards Deming and Nikita. *"You are here to learn about your fate?"*

"Yes."

Silver eyes slit like a cat stared at her. *"Are you sure? Not all fates are well received, and not all fates come to fruition. Knowing yours can just as easily be a burden as a release."*

Deming considered her words. The past six months had been nothing but trial after trial, betrayal on top of loss. Could she handle it if whatever Rendrel had to tell her was too much? Was there a limit to what she could bear?

Did it matter if there was?

The world was on the brink of war, aflame with chaos and twisted magic. There was a chance that if she simply stepped away, buried herself somewhere in a far away forest, that the world would right itself on its own without her. She was just a girl, there were more important players in this game.

And yet, something in her knew that her place was here, amidst the ever-changing battleground the continent was becoming. Her soul felt intertwined with the destiny of the world, like the gods were calling her here, to this moment.

It was frightening, but right, and Deming found herself eager to learn what the threads of fate held in the palm of their hands for her.

She was the daughter of the most beloved monarchs her queendom had ever known. She was a wielder of magic that lit her blood and bones alive with ancient knowledge and mysticism. She was an oak amidst a storm. She was the cliffs against which seas broke.

She could handle anything. She had before, and she would continue to do so until the continent was at peace and she was sitting on her rightful throne, crown atop her head.

Deming stood tall. As if the mountain could feel the emotions swirling inside her, the wind kicked up. She had the feeling of standing against the world. Not alone. Never alone anymore. Simply strong in her belief and love of herself.

Not only did she need to hear her fate, she wanted to.

She told Rendrel so.

"Good." The amphithere slithered closer to Deming, who stood frozen in awe as an emerald form curled around her and a warm, scaled forehead pressed into Deming's own. *It will be easier to show you.*

Deming felt Rendrel press into her mind, much like when she had planted the seed of knowledge about magic there. Within seconds a complex wave of sensations flooded her consciousness.

Physically, she had the vague sense that her feet were still planted on the snowy, rocky ground of the nest. If she focused, she could still feel the wind biting at her cheeks and her hair whipping wildly. She could tell Nikita was nearby, always, his presence a grounding force not even the magic Rendrel was pouring into her could overshadow.

Mentally, though, was a completely different story.

Wings and seasons and sun and rain and scales and travelers and kings and queens darted before her, around her. The mountain top was a whirlwind of every moment that had touched it. Scenes flashed and amphitheres dove in and out of her vision. Sound was far away but somehow still impossibly loud. The wind and the roars of the beats echoing through time and space as Deming herself remained rooted where she stood.

She had the sense of seeing everything at once and nothing at all and all of time was both speeding by and nonexistent because time means nothing against intangible love and soul bonds and the universe and then, suddenly, she was still.

Atop the mountain, in nearly the same spot as they left, Deming blinked, looking at the scene before her.

A line of amphitheres stretched from one side of the mountain top to the other, an array of jewels shining in the shifting sun that would rival any collection in any court on the continent.

A whoosh of air rushed past her and with it, the Crest Major soared. He flew from one end to the other in one broad stroke of his wings that even in the memory were breathtakingly large.

With a roar he landed on a crag of the mountain face above everyone else.

They were all waiting for something. Someone?

Amphitheres of every color of the rainbow sparkled in front of her. Some were all one color, some were many. Some were nearly as large as the Crest Major, some were barely the size of a large horse.

Nearly midway down the line of amphitheres was a familiar green one. Her silver eyes inquisitive and body undulating in the dirt, eager, anxious.

Rendrel.

Deming put a hand onto the warm scales of Rendrel's body, still wrapped around her like a snake. The amphithere was here in the flesh, with Deming, not across the barren field.

This was a memory.

Rendrel's voice caressed Deming's mind. *"Yes, Light Heart. We are inside an important memory of mine."*

"Why is this one important?"

"Because today," Rendrel adjusted herself, settling in to watch the scene unfold, *"is the day I meet the prince."*

Deming immediately spun to look behind her and there he was.

Same dark hair, though the curls hung shorter. Same gray eyes, though they held only joy and intrigue. Same black wings with their iridescent shimmer, though they appeared to be still fledging. Tufts of fluffy feathers clung to where they protruded from his back.

Nikita, as a boy.

He was so little. The hand holding his father's was round and pudgy with youth. He smiled wide, tugging his father's hand and pointing at the row of ancient beasts waiting for him. The king smiled and laughed, then whispered something to Nikita that Deming couldn't hear but made the prince squeal with excitement.

He was just a child.

Deming choked on emotion for everything this precious, small, immortalized version of the male she loved was about to endure.

Nikita was all bright eyes and eager anticipation as he walked up to the amphitheres. The beasts stared him down, not cruelly, but with scrutiny. Deming would have given anything to know what they were thinking. Could they feel the bonds between them and their Riders on sight? How intuitive was it? Did they think it as high an honor as the Fae did to be chosen?

An amphithere with wings the color of lilacs in springtime ruffled its feathers and screeched into the crisp air. Young Nikita bounced from foot to foot at the sound, his grin ever growing.

They came to some unmarked line in the snow and Trevelyan stopped his son. Both royals knelt and bowed their heads.

When the Crest Major spoke, it sounded like Deming was hearing it through a veil. Rendrel, the one wrapped around her, had sounded clear and present but the voices coming from the memory had an echo, as if they had to actually stretch through time to reach Deming's ears.

"Rise, Trevelyan Magdalene, King of Runne and the Fae Territories." He did as was commanded, releasing his hand from his sons who remained on one knee. *"Who do you bring before us to be bonded?"*

Trevelyan had broad shoulders and dark hair. Not a wrinkle to be seen. His eyes sparkled. He looked happy, hopeful.

This male was nothing like the portrait of a cruel father figure Nikita had painted for her. Between this memory and the present, something within the king had turned rotten.

Nikita was not the only one damaged by his father's actions, it seems. Trevelyan had allowed the poison to spread through his own veins.

How was it possible to ruin two lives over one moment?

"I bring forth my son and heir, Nikita Magdalene, as an offering to be bonded."

Nikita rose, tiny wings trembling with excitement.

"As every heir apparent of Runne has been offered in times of strife, so too shall you," the Crest Major's voice echoed, *"If the bond has been predestined, you will become a Rider forevermore. Ever together and as one with the amphithere that chose you. A Rider until the gods come to take you home. If you are not chosen, you will leave and rule your territories with our blessing but not our bond, as ancestors through time have done before you."* His head lowered, peering over the crag where he sat. *"You may begin."*

Nikita knew exactly what to do. He walked as stoically as he could manage to the edge of the line and faced the first amphithere—a white and gray dappled one with eyes such a deep blue they verged on black.

He stood in front of the amphithere and bowed so low his face was near parallel to the ground. After a beat, the mist-colored head of the amphithere joined him.

The pair stayed like that just long enough for the breath of the amphithere to jostle Nikita's hair then the beast lifted its head, opened its wings, and flew to a craggy ledge on the mountain behind them.

Nikita rubbed his hand on his pants, smiled, and moved on to the next amphithere.

On and on it went.

Nikita bowed and was bowed to, then every amphithere one after the other fled the clearing for the mountains.

Each retreat took a fleck of joy away from Nikita's face. He was holding it together as best as a five year old could, but Deming could see the cracks beginning to show. He truly believed with every fiber in his small body that he was destined for a bond. What had Trevelyan told him about this day? What expectations had been laid down for something that, at the end of the day, Nikita had no control over?

Every time Nikita fixed his face and wiped away any trace of disappointment, a piece of Deming's heart broke.

When Nikita approached Rendrel, everything began the same. A bow for a bow, a breath held. But instead of flying away, Rendrel leaned in closer.

Nikita's eyes widened but he did not move a muscle as she sniffed at him, nudged his head.

Then Rendrel arched her back and pulled her tail forward, curling her body into what resembled half of a heart and Nikita's entire body tensed.

He was so, completely still as Rendrel lifted her maw and roared into the sky, fire licking her teeth and shooting into the air.

"Rise, Prince Nikita Magdalene," Rendrel spoke soft and gentle, *"my Rider from now until the gods come to take you home."*

Nikita straightened and looked Rendrel in her eyes. Gray and silver. Same and different. Together and never alone again.

Nikita gave her a wide toothy grin and Deming could do nothing but join in his unadulterated joy.

Then Rendrel reached her snout out and pressed it into Nikita's outstretched palm.

Deming couldn't see the mark as it spread across Nikita's chest, but she could feel it.

Warm and tingling, it felt as though it were being etched across her own skin. Curled and swooping and glorious it went on and on and on.

An echo of familiarity rang through Deming's body. She had the urge to run to Rendrel in the memory, to leap on her emerald scales and touch the sharp edges of her muzzle.

Where they stood watching, Rendrel tightened her body around Deming, feeling it too.

Laughter bubbled from Nikita. He buried his face into the crook of Rendrel's feathers and then the scene disappeared into a swirl of gray smoke.

Deming blinked away the clouds from her mind and from the haze rose a new scene, a new memory.

Still atop the mountain, there was no longer a line of amphitheres. Instead, it looked much more like the present her and Rendrel had left. Beasts dotted the sky like colored stars and curled into nests like gems. Snow fell from the sky in thick, wet clumps, coating everything in a blanket of white.

They were inside the Crest Major's cave. He was accompanied by Rendrel, and the sight of the green amphithere so close when the real one remained curled protectively around her sent a heavy wave of nausea churning through Deming.

She placed a hand on Rendrel's warm, scaled body to steady herself.

"I do not know how to advise the king," Rendrel of the past spoke aloud to the Crest Major.

At the mention of Trevelyan, Deming searched the flat mountain top for any sign of him or Nikita. Far away, almost to the drop off, she spotted them marching away.

Nikita's small head hung low. His wingtips brushed soft trails in the fresh snow. He reached up for his father's hand and Trevelyan held it for a moment before pulling away, leaving his son alone and grieving.

A pang of sadness swept over Deming as the knowing of what memory they were now inside of hit her.

"I felt the bond when we matched," Rendrel lamented, *"I wouldn't dare to make a mockery of that honor by falsifying the bond."*

The Crest Major's head swung slowly, *"I do not believe you to have done that. Indeed, if I had it would make me a fool. No one can force a bond that isn't there."*

"Why has it been lost then? I can no longer feel his thoughts. It is as if our connection wanes with the fading of his mark."

He sighed heavily, steam billowed from his nostrils. *"I do not know. Perhaps the winds of fate have changed for him. The gods bow to no one, no bond. They move in ways we cannot fathom."*

The amphitheres pondered in silence. The only sound the whistle of wind winding through the cave and the far away roars of their kin.

Then the air shifted, stilled, silenced. The Crest Major raised his head, eyeing Rendrel curiously, and Deming wondered how powerful he must be that his presence could affect the threads of nature in that way.

"Or," he mused, each word building in confidence, *"perhaps his fate has not yet been revealed."*

Rendrel tilted her head quizzically.

He wove himself to the mouth of the cave. He stared at Nikita as he and his father disappeared down the side of the cliff face and out of view. Without turning to Rendrel he said, *"It is possible you sensed your Rider through the prince. After all, there is more than one sacred bond on this earth."*

Something small and delicate kindled in Deming's chest at his veiled words as the scene before them flooded with smoke and they were hurtled back to the present.

Through time and space they spun and twisted. The journey home was quicker and soon Deming found herself on wobbly legs back where they started.

The second she had oriented herself she stared at Rendrel, not daring to hope what the amphithere had just shown her could possibly be true. The gods had never answered her prayers and this...This would be everything she had ever dreamed of and more. It couldn't possibly be true. She didn't deserve it to be true.

"What…" Her voice was as small and delicate as the ray of hope peeking through the desperation in her chest. "What did you just show me?"

Rendrel sent a flare of comforting heat towards her. *"Your fate, as you asked."*

Trembling fingers pressed into her lips. "I'm…" The words caught in her throat.

"A Rider, my Rider." Rendrel closed the distance between them once more and extended her snout.

Instinctually, Deming knew what to do.

With her left hand, she reached out, copying what she had just seen a younger Nikita do. Her fingers were a breath away from the smooth space between Rendrel's nostrils, the scales there so small they were almost indistinguishable. Heat pulsed across the space, begging Deming to touch the amphithere and twine their fates forever as was written in the stars.

She placed her palm firmly on Rendrel's snout and an inexplicable sensation began coursing through her body in waves.

It started in her fingers, then moved to her hand, her wrist, her arm. Spreading and spreading until her entire body was filled with heat so hot it felt cold and the feeling of every nerve in her being attuned to the beast beneath her palm.

It could have been seconds, minutes, or years before the feeling came to an abrupt halt.

Deming's eyes flashed to Rendrel's. Had she done something wrong?

Rendrel nudged Deming's hand, her gaze unflinching and unfazed.

Then her mark appeared.

Delicate and winding, the black line began on the pad of her middle finger and wrapped around the appendage thrice, curled once around her wrist, then began climbing up the inside of her arm like a vine.

Though it had disappeared under the thick wool she wore, Deming could feel it inch its way up her body. She closed her eyes to bask in the sensation.

It followed her veins. The lifeblood of her body and the lifeblood of her bond to Rendrel echoed one another as the mark continued to grow.

When it reached her shoulder, it curled up and onto her collarbone where it then branched out into three separate lines that wove themselves into an intricate knot directly above her heart.

The entirety of the mark was etched into her skin clear as day.

Pure and black. Strong and permanent.

When the magic of the bond settled, Deming was left a Rider.

She blinked away tears, blearily finding her amphithere's silver eyes.

"You are a Rider, from now until the gods carry you home." Rendrel's voice was soft and careful in Deming's mind, like she knew just how meaningful her next words would be. *"Though you have seen my memories, I should not be the one to speak of the second fate tie to you."* Her snout nudged Deming. *"Go to him."*

Deming twisted, looking desperately for Nikita, needing more than anything to be in his arms. She knew deep in her bones what the second fate tie was but she needed to hear it from his lips.

The thread between them tugged and she finally found him.

High cheekbones that could cut glass, hair moody and dark and curled.

And his eyes. Those stunning, storm filled eyes were rimmed with red and wet with emotion. Though the wind was loud and amphitheres roared, Deming heard him clear as day.

"My mate."

She ran to him, their bodies crashing together as he pulled her tightly into him and kissed her face a thousand times. His wings carried them off the ground. The world spun and twisted around her, snowflakes peppered her skin and far away the roar of amphitheres sounded and all Deming could think was that this was the most magical moment of her entire life.

Nikita's hand drew her chin upwards. He peppered her skin with kisses, each time his lips left her he murmured, "My mate." The affirmation sang through her blood. "I should have told you sooner. I have been and will forever be yours."

"You are everything I've dreamed of," she told him, sealing her words with a kiss.

She hadn't dared to hope it would be true. Caring for him as she did and feeling that admiration in return was more than enough. But the confirmation that the bond they shared—that golden thread she felt connecting them, guiding her to him, the way she knew where he was in any room before seeing him—was real and not something she had made up in her mind sent sparks across her vision and songs through her heart.

The most gilded, wonderfully warm, pure joy of understanding every piece of herself spread through her bones.

All the pieces of her finally fit together like they were supposed to all along.

Mage.

Rider.

Mate.

Happiness bubbled out of her in the form of laughter. Tears were streaming down her face but she didn't care because she was whole, finally. Not because of Nikita or Rendrel, but because she finally knew every part of her soul that had been sheltered or kept from her. There was no need to question anything any longer, for everything was abundantly clear. Every moment she felt less than, every moment she felt lost and broken and wondered why nothing had ever come easy or felt right or true. Her longing for the sky and flight, the knowing in her soul that she was meant to be among the clouds. This was the answer.

She simply hadn't known.

She had always been exactly what she was supposed to be.

And all of those hidden pieces were now brought to the light.

Shining, beautiful, glimmering.

Whole.

Ever so slowly, Nikita brought them back to the ground. The fall felt like descending a spiral staircase. Round and round they went, slowly and together, savoring every touch, every breath, every second.

Deming stepped onto the snow covered ground once more, beaming up at her mate. He slipped an arm around her waist and wove his other hand into her hair.

She never wanted to leave his arms, but that was impractical and altogether nonsensical.

Deming made to move towards Rendrel again, eager to speak with her, but her leg gave way under her and she stumbled.

"Deming?"

She blinked, trying to rid her vision of the spots suddenly marring it. Her head felt floaty and her thoughts were far away and difficult to grasp. She opened her mouth to say everything was fine but wobbled again instead.

Then the lack of oxygen and overload of information caught up with her. She felt her limbs collapse. Just before the world blacked out, something Nikita said echoed in her mind.

I should have told you sooner.

CHAPTER THIRTY FOUR

DEMING

THE WATER LAPPED SOFTLY against her skin.

Waist deep in the lake, Deming blinked, turning slowly.

A great forest rose around her. The tips of the trees like paintbrushes on the night sky. Stars twinkled and a full moon hung heavy in the darkness.

From the forest flew a crow. Its wings melded with the sky as it cried out. The sharp, harsh sound felt out of place in the serenity of the dream. It swooped low, darting across the lake towards her, then tilted its wings and shot towards the moon.

She raised a hand to touch it, to beckon it back, but in a blink of her eyes it disappeared.

Deming stood, arm outstretched, as a deep ache bloomed in her core. Dread and anxiety unspooled though she knew not why.

Bringing her hand away from where the crow blinked from existence, she found that her skin was soft and dry despite having been pulled from the lake. In fact, she realized, looking down, nothing about her was wet. The dress she wore hung loose and free like she was standing on dry land not the shores of a lake in the middle of the woods.

A sound like breaking glass pulled her attention to the sky.

The moon was shattering.

Fear spread through Deming in tandem with the cracks reaching, reaching, reaching to every groove and divot of the bright orb in the sky. The wound grew until the moon was a web of cracked veins that cast shadows across the world.

Then a shard of the moon fell from the sky.

The snap of it breaking away sent a chill racing up Deming's spine. The sight of it falling built layers of terror within her she had never known.

Down and down, it tore towards the ground with rapid ferocity, and as it raced towards its doom, it transformed.

Lengthening and softening, glowing and shining, the shard became a beam of light so bright it washed everything below it in swaths of white and gray. It absorbed all color and sound and nothing could possibly exist except this monstrosity of nature.

Down and down it fell.

Deming was frozen as the moon beam crashed into the lake and all the world's light vanished.

Silence as thick as darkness enveloped her.

One heartbeat. Two.

Then a voice like liquid gold and unyielding power slid through the abyss.

The time is near.

Soft singing and the warming scent of cardamom coaxed Deming awake.

Blinking the fog of sleep and dreams away, the first thing she saw was gauzy fabric draped above her, tied loosely around four tall spires of a bed frame.

A bed frame?

She squeezed her eyes shut, then opened them, blinking rapidly.

Last she remembered was being at the nest with Rendrel and Nikita and—

She shot up in bed, every revelation crashing into her at once.

The light, the bond; the earth, the moon.

Four circles scarred on her shoulder, the burning simmered into a pulsing heat.

The bond.

She was a Rider. Rendrel was bonded to her.

Deming brought her hand in front of her. The black mark was solid and bold, winding around her finger and up her arm.

Her heart fluttered at the implication.

Not implication, fact.

Rendrel had sensed their bond through Nikita because...

Nikita was her mate.

And she was his.

The singing stopped and Deming was jerked out of her thoughts. She quirked her head, peering around for the source.

Nikita lounged in an armchair at her bedside. Wings as dark and wondrous and all consuming as the void at the end of world spanning out from his back. Eyes like storm clouds, lips like a promise.

And between them, invisible but tangible to her soul, their bond. It tugged and flowed between them, a constant reminder that they were fated. Every piece of their connection made perfect sense now. She felt like she could burst with happiness despite the remnants of the dream hanging over her.

"Were you..." Deming asked slowly, "were you singing?"

That sharp smirk of his darted up. "What's it to you if I was?"

"I didn't know you did that." She pushed herself up and leaned against the pillows. "Sing, that is."

He stood and ambled to the bed. "I thought it might comfort you. You seemed restless in your dreams."

Deming frowned.

The dream felt slippery and far away now. The further she waded into consciousness the further the stone of her dream fell into the hidden layers of her mind.

"Are we," Deming looked around the lavishly appointed room, recognition ringing through her like a noon bell, "back at Soraya's?"

He swung his legs onto the bed, crossed them, and faced her, hands in his lap. "Yes. It was the closest and safest place I could think to fly you after you fainted." A birdlike cock of his head. "How are you feeling?"

Deming took a deep breath, taking inventory of her body. "A little woozy, but I'm fine." She pushed her hands over her face and through her hair. "Gods, that was embarrassing."

"It was a lot to take in."

His voice was as soft as silk and when she looked at him his gaze was as warm as embers in a hearth. He was looking at her like she was the most precious thing in his life. Maybe she was. That was certainly how she felt about him.

But...

The shiny film that had been wrapped around the reveal of their mating bond tore.

Deming sighed. They had only been given moments of happiness before reality set in.

She reached her hand out tentatively and he took it.

Nikita frowned, sensing her hesitancy. "What's wrong?"

Her other hand came up to hold their joined ones, her fingers wrapped around his like a lock. "Humans—mages—" she caught herself, slipping into the shell of her past accidentally, "don't often have mating bonds."

He shifted closer to her. Their knees knocked together and a somber smile graced her face at the sight of them sitting cross-legged together on a bed. She felt fifteen again, giddy and young and newly in love.

"It's not that they don't have mating bonds," Nikita said, "it's that their magic isn't typically strong enough to feel them."

"For good reason, though." She looked directly at Nikita, eyes burrowing into his.

She may not be human anymore, but she was still mortal. Nikita would live for centuries, maybe longer if he was lucky. Deming's body and mind would age and crumble and then she would wink out of existence all within decades, leaving him stranded and heartbroken. The tales she had heard of mated mages or humans losing their partner were heart-wrenchingly sad. Even when there were only years separating the deaths, the surviving mate lived with a constant, dull ache for their loved one. The tales of Fae who had lost their mates, when decades or centuries of loss had to be felt, were far, far worse.

Time did not heal the wound of a mating bond. That missing thread would be felt until death greeted them. A bond severed was not to be trifled with.

"We will only have a few decades together," she whispered.

"And I will cherish every bit of them."

"The loss you'll have to deal with—"

"Is nothing compared to how I feel."

Deming felt anxiety creeping in. Her heart beat erratically. The nape of her neck felt slick with sweat. How could she claim to care for him and yet stand by while death and his inevitable loss drew closer with each breath she took?

Was there a way to stop the bond? To unseal it?

She knew the answer before she had completed the thought. Their bond had been sealed long ago. They were mates before they were flesh and blood. There was no undoing what had been decided before the dawn of time.

Her existence had chained him to a fate he hadn't asked for.

She shook her head violently but the errant thoughts would not leave. "I'm not enough. I can't possibly be worth—"

He was on his knees and his hands were on her face in an instant, his lips crushing into hers and silencing her plea.

Just as quickly he pulled back. Leaning over her like this he filled her senses. His wings spread from his back like a canopy, blocking out everything from her peripherals so it was only his face she could see. He spoke slowly, evenly, and to the very core of her being.

"Breathe, Deming."

She forced air into her lungs. One long, shaky pull at a time.

His hands began gently stroking the sides of her face. He tucked her hair behind her ear and the pad of his thumb as it trailed along her neck simultaneously sent shivers up her spine and calmed her wild heart.

Her eyes flicked to his.

"I have not lived long by the standards of my people, but I have seen my share of horrors and felt my share of shame. I know what it means to be lost and alone."

Every word he said felt like it was spoken down the shining thread connecting them. Each word like a heartbeat, a promise. It was so clear, now that they knew what this tenuous, tangible, living thing between them was. How had she not guessed it before this moment? How could the way they were intertwined be anything but a mating bond?

Nikita was baring his soul and Deming was enraptured.

"And I know what it means to be found because of you. You have been the brightest soul I've ever known from the second I met you. Your tenacity and grit and capacity to care deeply and truly is a gift to the world and to me. The well of love you hold for others goes down, down, down into the marrow of your bones. I am who I am now because of the specters of my past. But I will become who I am meant to be because of you and that is something not even the gods can put a price on. I would spend a millennia missing you if it meant I got to spend even one day with you."

Deming nodded into his hands. Her hair was mussed and tangled but she didn't care about anything other than the gentle care pouring into her from the male on his knees before her.

Crown Prince.

Nikita Magadelene.

Banished Son.

Kit.

Her mate.

"I believe you," she finally murmured into the small world he had created for them between his wings.

When she smiled up at him, eyes bright and big, he relaxed onto his haunches and let his wings retract.

A soft chuckle accompanied the shake of his head. "You continue to surprise me, princess."

Deming's brows crinkled.

"I thought you would worry about what the mating bond says about us," he said with a shrug, "Though I should have known your selfless tendencies would prevail."

"What would the mating bond say about us?"

Nikita pulled his feet out from under him, clambering gracefully back into the cross-legged position he had been in before. "Since humans and mages are less likely to find their mate in their lifetime, there are often misunderstandings that arise out of ignorance. Many believe that a mating bond forces love onto two people, that their autonomy is stripped."

Deming frowned. She hadn't thought about that. It hadn't felt that way to her, it had felt like a confirmation of what she knew already. Like the gods had given their seal of approval of their union, or like what they felt for each other was so strong that they had been able to find one another before the bond was revealed.

"I don't believe our mating bond takes anything away from the way I feel about you," Deming said to him earnestly. She needed him to know that she was in for the long haul, she was in it for as long as he would have her. She had been his for longer than she cared to admit. "We may be bound by fate, but I am yours through love and choice. What the gods designed us to be is an affirmation of what I already felt for you, not the reason my adoration exists."

Nikita smiled down at her. "And I, you, princess. We are predestined, written in the stars."

Then, like the smoke from a dying fire, something rose through the blur of Deming's memories. So much had happened yesterday. So much had been shared with her. But there was something at the back of her consciousness like quiet knocking at a door.

She blinked.

She frowned.

"Deming?"

She ignored Nikita's worried voice just as she ignored his hand on her thigh, squeezing in concern. Instead, she was slipping through words changed like pages in a book.

Nikita told Daughlr that there hadn't been time.

He had told her...

What felt perilously close to betrayal darted across her mind, unbidden and crass.

He said that he should have told her sooner.

"Did you know we were mates?"

Eyes wide, she waited for his response with bated breath. For whatever reason, it would feel worse if he had known.

Nikita stilled, then withdrew his hand from her thigh. He looked pained, but he did not lie. "Since the magic-imbued stone was pulled from you."

Her head drew back. "You knew?"

"Deming, please—"

"You knew and you didn't say anything?"

"Deming I didn't—"

"After everyone, my entire life, lied to me? You decided to lie, too?"

"I couldn't force someone else to love me!"

His words ricocheted around the room. Ringing, ringing, ringing until there was no sound but the heavy panting of his breath.

He broke eye contact and held his head in his hands.

"Not you." His shoulders shook, wings trembled. "I couldn't force you into loving me."

The fight in her died a bit at his confession. Stripped bare and wounded, Deming could see more than ever the small, hurt child that lived within him like a curse.

She wanted to reach out to him.

The sting of veiled lies and hidden truths stopped her.

She wrapped her arms around her stomach. So quiet she was surprised he heard her, she said, "Can I have a moment to myself?"

Nikita's head hung heavy. His knuckles blanched, hands twisted into the sheets of her bed.

Then without another word, he left.

CHAPTER THIRTY FIVE

NIKITA

HOW COULD HE BE so stupid?

Nikita paced back and forth along the side of Soraya's house. The ground underneath was a mix of crumpled grass and mud thanks to his incessant pacing.

His wings itched, each feather feeling overly sensitive to the breeze whistling through the air. He clenched and unclenched his hands so many times and so roughly that his knuckles cracked over and over again. A cold sweat had broken out on the back of his neck.

He knew he should have told Deming sooner. He hadn't lied to her, not exactly, but withholding information was nearly as bad. And withholding something like this? How had he expected her to react?

A snarl rippled through his throat.

If only they had more time. If only he had known that Rendrel knew about their bond.

If only, if only, if only.

Deming valued honesty, it was a pillar of her relationships. And for good reason. Had he forgotten that? Had he thought she would make an exception for him?

Over and over, Nikita's thoughts tumbled through his mind like leaves in the wind. Anger at himself built and with it, as much as he was loath to admit it, anger at Deming simmered too. Why didn't she understand? He was only trying to protect her.

Could he do nothing right? He had lost so much, was he destined to lose her, too?

In a crescendo of frustration, Nikita threw a violent punch at the bricks and instantly cursed at the blinding pain that shot through his hand like a lightning bolt.

He curled over himself, cradling his arm, fingers limp and bleeding. His knuckles were sizzling with pain so fierce it lanced up his bones all the way to his shoulder.

"Well, that's broken."

Hissing through the pain to avoid biting his tongue, Nikita turned to the voice.

Deming stood a few feet away. Her arms were crossed tightly over her chest. She wore a simple brown frock tucked into white trousers. Her hair was twisted into two braids that hung over her shoulders and draped casually over her chest.

"Just my knuckles," Nikita grunted, "I've had worse."

Deming looked at him coolly. Then she offered her hand. "Let me."

Gingerly, he placed his broken hand in hers. Her fingers curled around it gently. The thin black line that marked her as a Rider twisted delicately around her middle finger. It was beautiful.

Like the first rays of morning bleeding into the sky, warmth began seeping into Nikita's hand. It was gentle, soft. Embers kindled to life in his blood as bones knitted back together and veins unruptured.

"There." Deming's hand slipped from his.

Nikita flexed his hand. Not a stitch of pain remained.

"You have more control over your magic," he stated.

She hummed, eyes still low and not meeting his. "It gets easier every day. Ever since Paris it feels like I was given a key to a lock. Rendrel helped."

Rendrel.

She was the impetus for so much of the rocky relationship he had with his father. Now, she was also one of the most cherished relationships Deming would ever have in her life. Nikita never held any malevolent feelings for the amphithere, but that was mostly because he never thought he would have to interact with her again. Now?

It seemed all three of their lives were intricately woven together.

He didn't know how he felt about that.

"Can we talk?" Deming asked.

"Of course."

They didn't move far, choosing a patch of soft grass near handfuls of wild daisies to sit down on. Nikita picked one and twirled the stem between his thumb and forefinger. He held it up in offering to Deming, who gave him a lopsided smile and nodded.

He pulled the stem through one of the plaits of her braid. The white petals looked perfectly at home nestled in her hair.

"I'm frustrated," Deming began, "because I don't understand why you didn't tell me."

She picked at the grass by her side, not looking at him.

"I wanted to tell you, Deming. I was going to."

Her face was scrunched, her brow furrowed. "Something this personal," Deming sighed deeply, "should have come from you, not Rendrel."

"If I knew Rendrel was going to tell you I would have—"

"Would have what?" Deming's entire expression was one of incredulity. Her emotions were already heightened, her tone already escalating into anger. "Told me sooner? The only reason you would have thought to tell me about this life altering fact would be the risk of someone else telling me first? Do you hear how self centered that sounds?"

Nikita groaned in frustration. Palms grinding into his eye sockets, he hit his head lightly against the ground three times in rapid succession. This is not how he wanted this conversation to go.

"No," he ground out, "of course that isn't the only reason I would have told you."

"When, then?" As quick as the heat in words appeared, it vanished. In its place was pleading desperation. "When were you going to tell me?"

When was he going to tell her? After they found where Vallyn was being kept and rescued her? After she was more comfortable with her light magic? After they retook her throne?

There was always going to be something.

"When you had less on your mind," he offered limply.

"Less on mind," she echoed, then huffed, "not vague at all."

Nikita sighed. He understood her, he truly did. If the roles were reversed he would feel the same way. There just wasn't a good alternative. He tried to explain himself, hoping she would understand.

"You were in such a dark place," he said softly, "for so long. There was always something that seemed more important. Your grief over Miriam, the leodin's and Paris's injury, your magic and finding out you were sired by a Fae. I wanted you to be able to feel all of those emotions properly, to be able to process them without worrying about us. I was never going anywhere, with or without a mating bond, I wanted to be with you. I still do, more than anything. So telling you about the mating bond always seemed like a lesser priority."

He tried to imbue just how sorry he was that she found out this way into his words. He had never wanted to be on the list of people who had hidden truths from her. He only wanted to protect her. "I never wanted to lie to you, Deming."

She pulled her knees into her chest. "It doesn't feel like that. It feels like you're sorry someone beat you to the punch."

The truth felt slippery, ever changing and impossible to pin down. Had he wanted to tell Deming? Of course. Was he annoyed that Rendrel told her instead of him? Yes.

Still, Nikita didn't feel like he was completely in the wrong.

"I just didn't see a world in which you found out about the bond and it went over well."

Her archer's bow lips turned down. "And I don't see a world in which I would ever be okay with you keeping something this big from me."

They stared at each other, an ocean of differing opinions between them.

What did it mean to argue? To disagree? Where was the line between healthy differences and insurmountable opposing opinions?

Nikita had never had to have conversations like this before. His father was painfully straightforward. Besides, it was difficult to argue with the king of a realm. The power dynamic there was so lopsided. His mother had only ever been a positive influence. And Ilysse was really the only other close relationship he had in his life. They bickered like siblings, but it had never felt like this.

"I don't know how to compromise here, Deming," he said in a low voice, "I can't take back my decisions and to be honest, I stand by them anyway."

She arched an eyebrow. "You'd lie to me again?"

"It doesn't feel like a lie to me," he implored, "I only ever want to make life easier for you. You may disagree, but I don't believe you were ready to hear we were mates at any point during that past few weeks. It would have been too much."

She muttered something he couldn't quite hear.

"What?"

She rolled her shoulders, sighed, then flopped onto her back. "It wouldn't have been too much. You are one of the only constants in my life right now. To know that your presence is assured, promised, would only have been a good thing."

"That's not how the mating bond works," Nikita said carefully.

"I know. Choice, free will. It's important." She rubbed her hands on her face. "I just don't see how the bond could be anything other than positive. It's an affirmation of what we already feel for each other." Her eyes were inquisitive and pleading as she looked at him. "Isn't it?"

His heart splintered. "Yes, it is. I was overwhelmed with joy when I found out. It made me immensely happy."

"It makes me happy, too," she said with a frown, "which is why I'm sad that our first moments together as mates feel tainted."

That crushed Nikita. It was the last thing he wanted.

She had all but confirmed his next question already, but there was a seed of doubt in his mind placed there by all the loss he had already endured. He had to make sure she wanted this. He needed to hear her say it.

"It doesn't have to be life altering," Nikita said quietly, calling back to her earlier comment. "You don't have to accept the bond. It would be fine if you didn't," he swallowed hard against the lie, "nothing has to change between us."

Deming closed her eyes. She reached over and threaded their fingers together. The smallest sliver of relief cracked through Nikita.

"I want to be your mate, Kit. I felt the bond before I knew what it was and have always found it comforting, natural. " She rolled her head to the side and looked at him through forlorn eyes. "I just wish you would have told me when you knew. I wish we could have had the extra time together on the same page."

He gave her hand a squeeze. "I know."

A songbird trilled in the distance.

"Miscommunication is like rotting wood for relationships," Deming said, looking at the sky, "our foundation will collapse before it's even built if we keep this up."

Nikita watched as she chewed on her bottom lip. "I don't want us to collapse."

Emotions sparkled in her amber eyes. "I don't either." She curled onto her side and shuffled closer to him. "I also don't want to fight."

"I don't either. I'm so sorry that I held this from you. I hope you know, though, that everything I do, I do for you."

"I know."

"I will honor your wishes moving forward, Deming."

"No more lies, no more hiding."

"Never again, I promise."

As both peace offering and appeasement for his own curiosity, Nikita sent a thrum of affection down their bond. Bright like sun streaming through the window, warm like shared heat between bodies. The golden thread very nearly purred with adoration.

Deming perked up marginally.

Nikita smirked. "Did you feel that?"

She quirked her head at him. "Can I do that?"

He shrugged. "I assume so. I've been able to feel your emotions more and more recently. Now that you know we're mates I bet something similar will start happening to you." He tipped his chin towards her. "Try it."

Her face pinched in concentration and Nikita had the overwhelming desire to flick her nose. He restrained himself, of course.

Like a raindrop into a puddle, something rippled down the bond. It felt distinctly like running fingers through the soft petals of wildflowers. It was stuttering and faint, flickering in and out like a candle wick in the wind, but it was there.

Nikita grinned. "Just like that, princess."

Deming crawled into his lap. He wrapped her in his arms.

"I'm sorry, Kit. For everything. I didn't mean to yell."

He pressed her body tighter to his.

"I didn't mean to, either."

They stayed like that, breathing as one and bundled in each other's warmth, for a long while. When Deming pulled away, for Nikita had refused to be the first to do so, they remained close. Bits and pieces of their bodies touching causally. His hand on her thigh. Hers on his knee. Their legs twined together like a braid.

CHAPTER THIRTY SIX

DEMING

THE PAST WEEK HAD been the best and most challenging of Deming's life.

The absolutely unbridled joy of discovering Nikita was her mate set her soul ablaze. There were so few opportunities in life for the fabric of the universe to speak with someone, through someone, and the mating bond was one such way. Understanding that the tug in her chest, the closeness she felt to him, was not a figment of her imagination but a very real consequence of their relationship was as relieving as it was invigorating.

Nikita had told her that the initial days after a bond settles could be intense, and he hadn't lied. She wanted to be with Nikita—touch him, kiss him, fly with him—at all hours of the day and every second of her dreams.

Conversely, the weightlessness she had felt atop the mountain had dissipated. The twin prophecies tying her to the continent and to the amphitheres now sat like stones in her gut. She felt no different than she had a week prior. She was still a woman ousted from her throne, wandering the wilds. It felt impossible that she was linked so closely to the fate of the continent.

And then, there was the underlying turmoil in her relationships.

She and Nikita had talked endlessly about what their expectations were of each other. Over breakfast, in between training, before they drifted to sleep. Peppered throughout every day were small moments that attempted to solidify how shaken she had felt finding out Nikita had kept the bond from her.

She knew he cared for her. She knew he wanted to protect her. She knew that everything he said about her fragile emotions had been true. From mourning the loss of Miriam to the threat of losing Paris to actually losing Vallyn—Deming had been a mess. Was still a mess. There was simply not enough room in the day for her to process the sheer volume of change happening around her and yet still she wished he had told her.

Honesty was always the right choice.

They were not fighting anymore, neither of them wanted to. She understood him, though she disagreed with his choices. And he remained resolute that he had done the right thing, though he vowed to not hide anything from her again. There was nothing more to be done about it other than move forward, stronger and together.

Deming scrubbed harder. Soap bubbles shimmered in the hot water.

"I think it's clean."

Deming flashed Paris a smirk over her shoulder before pulling the plate into a towel and drying it. It was cream, like all the others, and a pattern of ivy decorated its edge. "How was training?"

The plate clinked as she set it onto its matching stack.

Paris heaved a sigh, running a hand through his thick mop of blonde hair. "Good."

She looked at him pointedly.

He rolled his eyes, pulled out a chair, and sat down on the kitchen table.

Deming filled a glass of water for him.

"Ilysse is a hard ass."

"I heard that," a feline voice drawled from outside.

Deming leaned back to peer out of the cracked window above the sink. Sure enough, Ilysse was a few yards away, cleaning her weapons and putting away the shields she and Paris had been using.

"Damn," Paris swore, chuckling lightly, "forgot about the whole Fae heightened senses thing."

"I think it's got more to do with her lioness aspect than being Fae," Deming corrected.

Paris mumbled through a shrug, gulping his water.

Deming wrung the towel and slid it back into place on the brass hook nearby. Crossing her arms and leaning against the counter, she found herself in a small bubble of normality. Passing the time with Paris was just about the most comforting thing she could imagine.

As to be expected, it was disrupted immediately.

"Hey Deming," Ilysse called, "you've got a visitor."

Deming could feel it faintly now, something tugging gently on her soul. The second bond within her. Silver, wispy, and ethereal.

Rendrel.

A pleasant breeze and the faint aroma of wildflowers greeted her as she stepped outside.

Ilysse put the last blade on the rack, metal shining and polished, and nodded to the sky.

Deming looked up, one hand on her forehead to shield her eyes from the sun.

Curling through the air like smoke, green scales reflecting the sun's light like the jewels they were, was her bonded.

Anxiety and excitement sparked to life inside Deming. She hadn't seen the amphithere since she fainted at the nest. Each morning she wondered whether that day would be the day Rendrel would grace Soraya's house with her presence.

She jogged out to where Rendrel landed. Giant, feathered wings beating into the air as her massive, scaled body slithered onto the ground. Dirt and grass and flowers were disturbed by the movements. It was all Deming could do to stifle her ear-splitting grin.

"Welcome back."

"I would have come sooner," Rendrel's voice cascaded into her mind, *"but there was a disturbance at the nest."*

Deming was sure her confusion was written all over her face. What could possibly cause a disturbance to a nest of amphitheres? They lived at such a high altitude, could anything other than their kind last up there for long enough to cause a scene?

"What kind of disturbance?"

Rendrel coiled around herself. Her tail feathers brushed in agitated motions against the ground. Pebbles skittered in its wake. *"Weirfenn has not returned."*

Deming was lost.

She must have looked it, for Rendrel clarified. *"A member of our band. He has not returned from the hunt."*

The silver thread between Deming and Rendrel thrummed with agitation.

"And that isn't normal?" Deming pressed.

"No. We worry for his safety."

What could harm an amphithere? Deming shuddered.

"That is not why I have come. It is past time for our bond to be sealed."

Oh. Deming looked down at where her hand was inked. She rather thought she had already done that. "I accept the bond," she said slowly.

Laughter rumbled through Deming's mind. She blushed. Had she said something wrong?

"It is not so easy a thing," Rendrel's head lowered so her eyes were nearly level with Deming's, *"to accept a Rider's bond. It must be sealed through flight."*

Deming's heart fell through her stomach.

Rendrel uncoiled herself just enough so that her wing joints were clearly visible, roughly the first third of her body in one, long line of shimmering scales. "Between the wings," she commanded.

Deming balked. She unconsciously took a step back. "There's no saddle."

"I'm no horse."

"Where am I to hold onto you?"

Feathers rustled. *"Where my wings meet my body. Quell your fear, Light Heart. You will not fall. Come to me, feel."*

Deming approached Rendrel. Trembling in anticipatory concern, she placed a hand on the vast body of the amphithere. Rendrel's scales were pleasantly warm, like blankets that had been sitting by a fire for a while. The heat seeped through Deming's skin and into her bones.

Then, a million tiny pins pricked at her palm.

Frowning, Deming flipped over her hand. Nothing.

"Our scales are designed to hold a Rider, no matter how infrequent the bond may be."

She looked to Rendrel's scales. Deming had to squint to see them, but protruding from the emerald scales were miniature barbs. Thinner than a needle, thinner than thread, but everywhere. They coated the entirety of Rendrel's body.

"I promise, Light Heart, you will not fall."

With nothing left to do but trust Rendrel, Deming heaved herself over her massive, scaled body. The pinpricks were muffled by the fabric of her clothes, but they did indeed keep her steady as Rendrel began to move.

Riding an amphithere was nothing like riding Quintessential.

Rendrel was all but a giant snake with wings and Deming was smacked in the face with that fact, not for the first time, as the amphithere wound herself a few feet through the tall grasses and flowers. The motion of her body made Deming sway like the ebb and flow of the ocean. Rendrel's scales slipped over each other beneath the palms of her hands like water over stones at the bottom of a river and it was all Deming could do to not fall into a trance watching them.

"Keep your body loose, and your grip tight," Rendrel advised.

Deming plunged her hands into the dense thicket of downy feathers at the base of Rendrel's wings.

She leaned into the amphithere's body just as Rendrel shot into the sky.

Higher and higher and higher they rose. Beyond the tops of the swaying trees, beyond the smoke rising from the burning chimney, beyond the clouds painting the sky with dashes of white and ivory.

The house was a pinprick beneath them in seconds. Wind tore at Deming's hair and clothes and skin. They melted into the clouds and left feathers swirling in their wake. Rendrel had taken flight so quickly Deming had little time to think let alone scream so when her mind caught up to her body she found herself laughing into the crisp air high above everything she knew.

Deming tightened her thigh's grip on Rendrel's body but kept her spine supple and loose. She gave into the motion of flight, moving as one with her bonded.

Flying was glorious. There was no other way to describe it.

Whether it was being in the sky with the wind in her hair, or having Rendrel's ancient and glorious wings beating so close to her that feathers were whispers against her skin, or all of the chaos that had unraveled finally catching up to her, Deming found herself clutching at her chest, overwhelmed by emotion.

"This is amazing. Thank you." Her words were snatched away by the wind but Rendrel heard her all the same.

The wind did not matter for Rendrel's voice, for, as always, it sung only in Deming's mind. Soft and sweet as a spring flower, flowing gently like the rippling edges of a river. Deming thought Rendrel's voice was the most precious lullaby she had ever heard. The comfort it carried spoke to mothers and daughters, warm bodies nestled together, the feeling of sleeping at home after a long journey.

"There is nothing to thank me for. Your soul is in balance and at peace, as it should be."

A rumble passed through Rendrel, along with a flash of heat. Deming pressed her hands harder into her scales, trying to chase the comforting feeling.

"In balance?"

"You have finally found who you are meant to be. Mine and his and yours. The three veins of your soul now flow uninterrupted."

The past week had indeed felt like an undoing of her past, an untangling of herself. She had been tugging away at the knot within herself ever since meeting Nikita. Her mate, far before she knew what he was to her, had stoked a small fire back to life within her. The mess of guilt and shame she had worked herself into had already begun to fray before the flight to the amphithere's nest, but Rendrel's snout touching her palm and the Rider's mark spreading down her arm like a promise was the final piece to the puzzle.

Her life had cracked when her parents died, shattered when Miriam was murdered, and crumbled into dust when Deming let herself wither away. But now, winding through the air above the Fae Territories farther away from home than she had ever been with her bonded amphithere beneath her and her mate waiting for her on the ground, Deming felt the truth of Rendrel's words.

She was whole. Uninterrupted. She always had been.

The understanding she came to was as freeing as it was painful.

So many years she had spent wasting away in the ruins and rubble of her grief. So many people she had let walk over her, lie to her, die for her.

She was here, now, and that was a miracle.

But there was so much death and destruction in her wake.

Something deep within Deming broke for good as her and Rendrel raced through the sky. The rocky exterior of who she once was cracked wide open and, like a geode, magic and mayhem emerged.

Deming clung to Rendrel and screamed into the wind.

She screamed for her parents and the family they had lost. She screamed for Miriam and the love that carried on after death. She screamed for Vallyn, lost somewhere in the continent. Most of all, she screamed for herself.

As wretched, broken, enraged screams tore from deep within her, Deming felt every single wrong that had ever been done to her pierce her heart all over again. Every betrayal, every attempt to silence her. Every loved one torn from her grasp. Every moment of doubt cast in her. The pains that were the sharpest, however, were the ones she inflicted on herself. She had allowed herself to shrink into a shell of a woman. She had let her life slip away under the guise of grief. She had turned a blind eye to her queendom. She had been so flippant about her destiny that she had all but given it away on a silver platter to her family.

Her uncle and cousin may have dealt the killing blow, but she had willingly laid her neck on the block and given them the axe.

The world had hurt her, there was no doubt.

But she had hurt herself too.

Never again.

Deming threw her palm forward and out shot a brilliant beam of light. White and pure and scorching it barreled through the air ahead of them. Rendrel twisted her body and flew in a tight corkscrew around her magic. Sparks bit into skin and scale.

Deming relished the feeling. She laughed, wild and uninhibited, and the sound was so clear and pure she could almost hear the gods laugh with her.

Rendrel let loose a roar to accompany her and the sky was lit aflame. The clouds became fire, the air became heat. They flew through billowing waves of orange and red and yellow and Deming felt her soul forging into something new in the cauldron of fire and magic they were drowning in.

Only when her throat was raw did she stop her screams and settle into the new version of herself she had allowed to come forth.

She had been burned and born anew all those years ago, but she had let herself stay trapped within the confines of her grief. She had let others make decision after decision for her all in the name of safety and youth. She had been happy to let them, happy to fade into the darkness and wait for someone to save her, never knowing that all this time she held the key.

All this time, her cage hadn't even been locked.

Now, amidst the clouds, she was finally waking up.

The invitation came the next morning.

A sharp rap on the door and everyone froze.

When Nikita swung it open, whoever had knocked had vanished, leaving behind one a small scroll of parchment tied together with a thin, satin ribbon. A wax seal embossed with the royal crest of Runne was pressed into one side.

Ilysse handed the parchment to Nikita.

He took it with trembling hands. The missive didn't stop shaking in his grip for a second as he read the words scrawled there. When he spoke, it was in a voice Deming had never heard from him before. Small, cowed, unsure.

"My father's penmanship. There's to be a ball at the castle." He flipped the parchment over, looking for more information, then handed it to Ilysse. "In my honor."

Ilysse read it through once, twice. Rare worry glazed her eyes.

Dread pooled like an oil spill in Deming's stomach.

CHAPTER THIRTY SEVEN

NIKITA

THEY HAD LEFT FOR the castle as the sun spread across the horizon and still it took them until well after midday to reach the city proper.

Everyone came. Hartford and Soraya, Ilysse and Paris, Deming and himself.

They left their horses at an inn close by, opting to walk to the gates.

Nikita knew he had been incorrigible the entire morning. Curmudgeonly and quiet. He couldn't help it.

He could count on one hand the number of times he'd been back in Bascade since he was banished and none of them had ended well.

There was the time shortly after he was banished that he ran away and cried to the nearest townsperson that he missed his family and needed to go home.

There was the brief blip when he was ten, when his father informed him he was trying for another heir. Nikita had traveled a day and a half both ways to hear that pleasant piece of news because the king didn't want any letters to be stolen. The mirage of a family must remain intact.

He had visited shortly in his teen years when his great uncle passed away. Even his father wouldn't take away burial rites.

And finally, his most recent visit. Not six months ago, he was summoned so that the seer's prophecy could be explained. He and Ilysse were given the task of protecting Laey's crown to maintain stability in the region.

Given his history with Bascade, Nikita felt he was more than justified in feeling on edge as they walked through the city.

A ball.

Nikita scoffed under his breath.

In his honor.

What a joke.

The king wanted something. Nikita simply hoped they could find out what it was quickly and leave before any of the city's memories tainted him further.

The only thing keeping him tethered to some semblance of sanity was watching Deming as she walked through the city for the first time.

Her eyes were wide as if she couldn't possibly take in the city quick enough. Her mouth was open just slightly. Gossamer awe coated the bond between them.

While Nikita himself was too tense to appreciate Bascade for what it was, he could appreciate Deming.

To her credit, if all Nikita had ever experienced of the world was Arsaela, Bascade certainly would be something to admire.

Where Arsaela had cobblestone streets, Bascade had packed dirt. Where Arsaela had courtyards and straight roads that tended to intersect at regular intervals, Bascade had interwoven streets that curled and spiraled and spilled into each other creating an almost maze-like feeling.

It was the City of Eternal Summer, nicknamed as such for the gardens surrounding the castle. Even outside the palace walls, Bascade was lined with greenery. There was an abundance of grasses in every color spilling from the cracks on the side of the road. Thin, brittle looking yellow stalks swayed rigidly next to purple grasses topped with bristles.

Deming floated a hand over top of them as they walked and Nikita watched surprise unfurl across her features as she realized the bristles were as soft as silk.

The pine trees of the Telaciens seemed a world away. Towering trees, a completely new variety local only to Runne and concentrated in and around Bascade, poked into the sky from behind buildings and on street corners. They had trunks thicker than boulders and branches full of leaves that extended wide, resting on roofs and shading the roads. The giant boughs appeared weightless despite their impressive girth.

"Do they have a name?" Deming asked him.

Nikita smiled, anticipating her question before she had even spoken. "We call them redwoods."

Deming ran a finger on the bark of one as they walked by. It was shaded like a poppy, but it absolutely had a reddish tint. She laughed, shaking her head in disbelief. "Original."

He joined her, his laughter surprising him. A small respite by way of the nonsensical naming of trees was just the kind of light-hearted conversation he needed.

The people here, too, lifted his spirits slightly. He had no qualms with them. They had no say in his banishment, most of them were completely unaware that the royal family was on bad terms. They simply believed Nikita had been sent away to complete his studies in other countries, other cultures. It was not so far off from what would be expected of him as heir.

So as he meandered through the winding streets, Nikita let himself feel the sliver of comfort that came from being around so many of his own kind.

Just as Laey was predominantly occupied by humans, Runne was home to Fae. Humans rarely visited, let alone lived here permanently, so the animal aspects of the Fae were on full display in Bascade.

Wings took up their fair share of space here. Fae flew through the air on wings that spanned every variety he knew, and some he didn't. Black, tan, colorful. Some feathered, some leathered like a bat. Spotted for camouflage or iridescent. No pair was the same.

Nikita spotted a boy flying through the sky on wings so impossibly similar to his own, hand in hand with his mother, that he very nearly fell into a pool of memories.

He drew a spade and buried the thought. Any memory of his mother felt too prickly to think about right now.

The streets were just as full as the sky. A girl with a russet fox tail disappeared down an alleyway. A female with shining silver fish scales rather than skin perused a shaded fruit stall.

A gaggle of children ran through the crowds, pushing and shoving their way through the heated mesh of bodies and laughing all the while. Two with furred hind legs led the pack, giggling breathlessly. One at the back fluffed out a pair of dove gray wings and soared above his playmates.

Most had aspects that were easily seen. Nikita spied only two during their walk that had the pointed ears of the Fae but nothing animalistic about them. Much like Ilysse, some Fae had a more subtle aspect, or one that could be hidden in some way.

His eyes flicked to the blonde female.

She swaggered ahead, stone cold silent. Her mood had been foul for some time now.

They wound their way through the streets, Ilysse in the lead, Nikita and Deming walking together, Hartford, Soraya, and Paris bringing up the rear. They rounded yet another winding corner and suddenly the castle was before them.

Nikita's feet stopped on their own accord.

Towering walls of white stone reached towards the clouds they were colored to match. Long slashes had been cut from the stone to create open air windows, too many to count, and none of them held glass. The weather was always so pleasant, most structures were built without window panes. It was one of the things Arsaela did better than Bascade, in Nikita's opinion. The beautifully intricate glass work that adorned many of the windows in Reynes Castle were inconceivably beautiful.

This monstrosity before him was nothing more than stone and mortar.

A slim arm slipped into the crook of his elbow. "Hey," Deming said. Her eyes were full of understanding.

"I'm scared," Nikita said with a hint of shame. "I don't know what we're walking into."

"Whatever it is, we'll face it together."

Together. There was that promise again.

Nikita pushed forward.

A large iron gate, manned by two burly guards, greeted them when they neared the entrance.

Nikita handed over the summons. "We're here to see the king."

One guard looked over the parchment. The other stared stoically ahead. Neither recognized him, though one did a double take.

Nikita found that it didn't bother him. He preferred to blend in when it came to this particular castle.

He frowned as the gates of the castle opened with a groan.

They were flanked by guards as they walked through the hallways. For all the ways that Bascade was different from Arsaela, the castle layout was surprisingly similar. There was a grand staircase center-fold when they entered. Hallways lined with braziers and torches stretched in all directions. Portraits and murals decorated the walls while thick, intricately woven rugs padded the floors.

To a certain extent, wealth and royalty was wealth and royalty.

They stopped in front of a set of large wooden doors. They were carved to depict two amphitheres, one on each side. Their bodies twined in a mirror image of each other.

The throne room.

A horn sounded from the other side. A muffled voice followed, likely announcing their arrival.

The doors opened and Nikita blinked against the light.

The throne room was vast, longer than it was wide, with ceilings that reached dizzying heights. There were raised benches on either side but every plank was vacant. The only people other than the male they were walking towards were servants with their backs stiff as a board against the outer walls. One near the front held a clear pitcher of water and a tray with a selection of vibrant fruits and soft cheeses.

It was so, superbly quiet.

His feet propelled him forward. Without realizing it, they were suddenly within spitting distance of the throne.

It was solid wood, polished until it shone. Even from where he stood Nikita could see the firelight flickering clearly on its surface. The seat was twice as wide as necessary and the back stretched far above the tip of the crown perched upon it. Every inch of it was carved, like the doors opposite it. Battlefields and births and amphithere blessings covered the wood. Runne's past and future, according to the seers.

The King of Runne sat atop the throne, resplendent in a fur lined seafoam green cloak.

His grin was as lazy as his words, his eyes were sharp and clever, trained on Nikita.

"My son," he drawled, "welcome home."

Chapter Thirty Eight

Nikita

"My King."

Nikita forced the words out and fought against the desire to sneer. His emotions demanded to be felt. They raged in him like a storm, but he ignored it all. He wrapped the cyclone of aged pain within him in wool and stifled it until only a dim roar sounded from the corners of his mind.

He only had to get through this first interaction.

Nikita knelt, his movements stiff and structured. His knees hit the marbled floor too hard and a zing of pain sizzled through his bones. Ilysse and Hartford followed suit on either side of him. Behind them, he knew Deming, Paris, and Soraya would join them.

He clenched his teeth, waiting for permission.

Trevelyan took his time. Nikita ground his teeth together.

Finally, they were bid to rise. Nikita's joints cracked as he did.

King Trevelyan Magdalene looked every bit a Fae King. His mustachioed face was impassive and strong. A wide set jaw and heavy shoulders gave him the build of an ox. His hands were decorated with rings of iron and gold and an inked depiction of an amphithere graced his neck, most of it disappearing under the slippery shirt he wore. Elongated canines, brutal and sharp, flashed when he spoke.

Even without the thick, gold circlet that rested in his dark curls—which were the only trait he shared with his son—no one could ever think he wasn't made to sit on a throne.

Years had passed, but he looked exactly as Nikita remembered him.

His eyes did a second cursory scan of the room. His mother was nowhere to be found.

The thought of Sabel Magdalene set his teeth grinding again, though for different nuanced reasons. His mother loved him more than life. She had been his biggest champion, until she wasn't. Sabel had done nothing when Nikita was banished. He was five, barely fledged enough to fly, and she had done nothing. Her son was ousted from the castle he was to rule from and she stayed quiet. Nikita had always wondered why. In the end, he assumed, even maternal love was not enough to stand up to the whims of the king.

"How have you been?"

The king's voice was booming, even when speaking at a normal volume. It was fitting of the burly stature he owned. The corners of his lips upturned as he spoke.

The flare of his nostrils was the only sign of distress that Nikita allowed himself. When he responded to his father, his voice was low and cool, but respectful.

"I have been well, my king."

"Such formalities twice now. Perhaps your time away has made you forget that I am your blood and bone." He raised his arms as if attempting to welcome Nikita into a hug. When they fell, his hands gripped the edges of the throne. "Are you not my loving and devoted son?"

A muscle feathered in Nikita's jaw. "I have been well, father."

White hot fury singed the edges of the mating bond. Deming was furious. Had he not been preoccupied, Nikita may have smiled. She was a spitfire when it came to the well being of those she cared for.

"And my dear Hartford, how are you?"

Hartford tensed beside him. "I'm happy to be back on Runne soil, and to be with Soraya again."

Trevelyan drummed fingers against the polished wood. "I'm glad to see you reunited with your mate." His tone pitched down. "Though, I am more interested in the road that led you back home. My instructions on your involvement in the Laey situation were quite clear."

Nikita's stomach flipped at the undercurrent in his voice. The threat of punishment was clear as day. Before he could defend Hartford, she spoke.

"I apologize for the instability in the region. With respect," she inclined her head and the strings of stones and gems tied to her antlers swung, "there was nothing we could do to keep the heir in her seat of power."

Ilysse stepped forward. "I can attest to Hartford's claim, my king."

Trevelyan studied her, the captain in his army skilled enough for him to know personally but young and disposable enough to let go when she fled to Nikita's side.

"Hello, Ilysse. Claws still as sharp as your tongue?"

"Always."

"Good." He smirked, waved his hand. "Go on."

Ilysse padded forward, hands behind her back, spine straight. "The steward of the Queendom of Laey and a former member of the Laey court, thought to be dead, staged a coup to unseat the heir. It was thoroughly planned and caught us off guard, despite our awareness of the prophecy."

"Laey is in a state of unrest?" he asked his captain.

"There have been substantial efforts to delegitimize the heir's claim to the throne. From my understanding, the people of Laey do not object to the installed ruler as she is of royal blood."

Nikita couldn't stop his lips from curling at the mention of Colette. He hoped, for Deming's sake, that she was an unwilling participant in the coup. But with each day that passed, that reality felt further and further away. Where was she, if she opposed the coup? Why had she not come forward?

Trevelyan's frown deepened. "This is concerning. You were to prevent something like this happening. We cannot allow the prophecy of war to come to fruition."

Ilysse dipped her head. "I understand the consequences of our failure. However, the coup has quickly been overtaken by a larger issue."

The king bent forward. With a twitch of a ring-clad finger, he beckoned her to continue.

"The two aforementioned individuals established a base deep in the Telacien mountain range. We have first hand accounts that they are performing testing on creatures of the continent," Ilysse swallowed hard and shifted her weight, "with success. These creatures pose an immediate threat to the safety of not only Runne, but the continent as a whole."

Trevelyan pulled at the corners of his mustache absent-mindedly. "The prophecy will be fulfilled then. War is to come. Creatures of what nature?"

"Leodins, primarily."

His eyebrows shot up, audibly hummed, then mused, "This is all rather curious." He looked to his son. "I imagine the level of unrest through the continent is why you've been regifted the Rider bond."

Confusion rippled through the room.

Sensing the change in the air, Trevelyan prodded, "Your bond has finally been realized, has it not? There were reports of a green amphithere in the sky, Rider astride their back. The amphithere's description was identical to the one that marked you all those years ago. Was that not you and Rendrel in the sky?"

All the pieces fell into place.

The ball in his honor was because the king believed Nikita had lifted the shame brought on his family. Trevelyan believed his son was a Rider once more. The ball would be to announce the bond.

Nikita felt sick to his stomach.

"A Rider has indeed been chosen," he began.

Silence permeated the very stone of the room.

Hope, fickle and flimsy, flitted across his father's expression.

Nikita took a deep breath before finishing, "But it is not me."

Every muscle in his father's body froze at that one, small sentence.

"Who, then?" the king breathed.

Nikita caught his father's eyes dart to his chest, where they both knew the discarded remnants of his tattered bond lay tattooed on him like a brand. In his father's eyes, Nikita's worth was tied to that mark.

Nikita stepped aside, revealing Deming fully. "Her."

All eyes snapped to her. Deming bore the weight well. She did not falter. She did not wilt. Nikita was so proud of her.

Calm and steady, Deming walked to Nikita's side. Subtlely, he grazed the edges of his feathers along her lower back. There was little else he could do to comfort her now.

Deming's voice did not tremble as she addressed the king. "King Trevelyan, I am Crown Princess Deming Reynes-Elyachar, heir to the throne of the Queendom of Laey and Rider bonded to the amphithere, Rendrel." Deming twisted her hand up and towards her chest, showcasing the curled black line around her middle finger. "She waits outside the city in case you wish to speak with her."

All decorum left Trevelyan. His jaw hung slack, his eyes were round with curiosity and disbelief. "How did this come to be? The mark has never been bestowed to more than one individual."

Deming looked at Nikita. Her eyes begged the question of how much they should share.

He took her hand, then turned to face his father.

"I was never meant to be given the mark, it had always been destined for Deming. All those years ago, Rendrel sensed Deming through me."

"How is that possible?"

Nikita gripped Deming's hand tighter.

Trevelyan looked at Nikita with the oddest mix of sadness and desperation. Then he answered his own question. "You're mated?"

The golden thread tying Nikita to Deming sang with the proclamation.

"Yes," Nikita answered.

Trevelyan said nothing for a long while, then, "Leave me to consider all you've said."

"Your Highness." Ilysse stepped forward.

The king raised his hand loosely by only his wrist but at the slightest flick of his fingers Ilysse halted. "I have spoken," he said hoarsely, "You are dismissed."

And so they were led from the throne room without another word.

The suite was quaint but well appointed. Four doors, one to the hallway and three to modest bedrooms, graced the walls of the common area. Every inch of the walls were covered with still life oil paintings, each nestled within the same style of heavily carved, gold foiled frame. A soft carpet lay beneath a two-seated couch, an armchair, a velvety chaise. Vases of flowers sat scattered on table tops, scenting the air with rose. A trio of large, open-air windows let a gentle breeze and dusky light cascade into the room. Swaths of thin cotton hung from either side, shifting delicately.

His old bedroom.

Nikita inhaled shakily and forced his hands to uncurl. He had not stepped foot in these rooms for well over a decade. Like dusting off cobwebs from an old shelf, walking through the room rustled memories long since buried.

His mother reading him his favorite fairy tales on the chaise.

The way the wind howled through the turrets.

Crying into pillows the first night his mark began disappearing.

Everything had been preserved perfectly. Nikita wondered whether his mother had any say in the matter. Leaving his things untouched seemed like something she would do.

His mind felt frayed, used. He desperately wanted to be anywhere else. Any corner of the continent would be better than here.

A knock on the door sounded.

Nikita knew who would be on the other side before the door so much as creaked on a single hinge.

Amber eyes and white curls brushing pale cheeks and lips curved like the most delicate bow and all around her—all around every-thing—was shimmering gold.

He pulled Deming into his arms.

CHAPTER THIRTY NINE

DEMING

NIKITA'S ARMS WERE WRAPPED around her like a ribbon around a gift.

Her face was pressed into his chest. Her hands slid up his back, resting at the edges of his wings. The downy feathers near the wing joint tickled her skin.

She made no move to pull herself away.

Finally, his head lifted. Limbs still wound with his like roots of a tree, Deming looked up. "I came to see how you were doing."

He chuffed and peeled away from her body. "About as well as could be expected."

Nikita dipped back into the room. He wandered to the window and leaned against it. Deming followed tentatively.

The height of their suite gave them a completely unobstructed view of Bascade and its plethora of redwoods and winding roads. From here Deming could almost make sense of the city, though she knew the second they were back on the ground she would lose all sense of direction once more. In the distance rose the Telaciens, tall and mighty. Bascade was not nestled into the mountain range as

Arsaela was, it had none of her city's altitude or pitched streets, but the Telaciens spanned the continent and graced the skyline all the same. Deming thought she spotted a pair of amphitheres circling one of its peaks, but they were too far away to be sure.

"This," she asked, "was your room? When you lived here?"

"For a time."

"How does it feel to be back?"

Nikita rolled his shoulders. "Like I never left."

Deming frowned at the way he said it, his tone lonesome and far away. "Do you have any happy memories here?"

A whisper of wind tugged a curl out from behind his ear. Deming's fingers itched to put it back in its place. Instead, she shuffled closer, leaning against the other edge of the window.

"Yes, many," he admitted. The ghost of a smile played at the corners of his lips.

Deming waited to see if he would share more. She knew more than most how difficult it could be to talk about memories and the thorns they carried.

"The first time I flew," he offered.

"That was here?"

"Mhmm," he pointed out the window towards the direction of the stables, "right over there. I climbed to the top of that tree, the crooked one with squirrel nests littering the branches? Do you see it?"

"I see it."

Nikita crossed his arms. His wings rustled. "I climbed all the way to the top and leapt. My mother was below, ready to catch me, but she didn't need to. It was wobbly, and my landing was atrocious," a short laugh escaped his lips, "but I flew. I can still hear my mother's whooping cheers."

The image of a young Nikita learning to fly for the first time was so endearing to Deming she found herself grinning ear to ear. "I'd like to meet her."

A shadow flickered across his face, but his smile remained. "I think you'd like her." Nikita turned. What little light that was left of the day filtered through the window, illuminating half of his face. "Thank you."

"What for?"

"For helping me remember that there is good here, in this castle."

Deming said nothing, opting instead to close the gap between them and kiss him softly.

As she pulled away, he looked at her, eyes unreadable. "Would you sleep in my bed tonight?"

Deming's neck pulled back, head tilted.

He rolled his shoulders, trying to shake the weight of the day off, maybe. Or maybe just trying to muster the courage to bear a vulnerability. "I just don't want to be alone."

His voice broke on the last word.

Something swelled in her, a feeling she couldn't place but felt strong enough to knock her over or take her breath away.

In that moment, the mating bond between them had never felt so strong. The world had been too cruel to him, too cruel to them both. They were shattered pieces of who they were meant to be, mirroring one another's familial trauma like broken twins from different parts of the world. If someone's mate was their equal, there could be no more obvious mate for Deming than Nikita. She only wished their mimicked pasts could have been more gentle.

Why the rippling of time and fate brought them together she wasn't sure, but she would be eternally grateful. He held her together and maybe, by some miracle, she held him together too. She never wanted to be parted from him. She hoped he knew that. Perhaps she should tell him.

She took his hand and let him lead her to the four poster bed.

"Can you untie me?" She was perfectly capable of untying this particular corset. Nikita's smirk told her he knew that too.

"Of course, princess."

She turned around, pulling her hair over her shoulder as she did so. He walked to her and before long she could feel the soft pressure of his fingers on her back through the fabric and boning. She resisted the urge to lean against him.

He worked to loosen the ribbons that laced up the corset. Each motion easing the pressure on her lungs and chest. Beautiful though they were, Deming resented the tightness in her chest they caused. In all her years she had never gotten used to the feeling. Colette was always the one who appreciated the sacrifices that came with high fashion.

Deming frowned and pushed thoughts of her cousin far away.

"Are you okay?"

She must have tensed.

"Yes," she turned to face him, the corset having been successfully unlaced, "sorry, my mind drifted to sour thoughts for a moment."

He hummed, dragging a thumb along her jaw. "I don't want any sour thoughts here tonight."

Deming shook her head ferociously. "Nor I."

She put space between them, enough to shimmy out of her corset and overskirts. They were nothing compared to what she used to wear in Laey, but the feeling of peeling off layers of clothes felt just as freeing.

She was in only a thin slip now. It was white and silky and she knew it clung to her curves delicately. Her hand lifted to her neck and the gold locket hanging there. A thin slip, and Miriam's necklace. She never took it off.

"You are…" His entire face softened as he took her in. "There are no words to describe how beautiful you are."

Feeling coy, Deming batted her eyes and leaned into a part of her that rarely reared its head. "You could try."

He laughed, and she was instantly glad she had tried to keep the air light.

Nikita crossed his arms, his expression contemplative.

"Looking into your eyes is like swimming in pools of honey." He cocked his head to the side, a glimmer of amusement flickered in his own eyes. "The bow of your lips and the quiver of words that shoot from it are the finest weapon I've ever known."

Deming smirked, liking that one.

"Your hair is gossamer," he continued, stepping forward, "spun from silk and painted the likeness of summer blooms." He twirled a pink strand between his forefinger and his thumb. "Your heart is so golden it shines from you like the sun." His face was inches from hers. "How was that, princess?"

Deming shrugged but the breathiness of her voice undermined her attempt at nonchalance. "That was passable."

"Passable," he chuffed, "you have high standards."

"As we all should."

"As we all should," he echoed just before closing the distance between their lips.

The kiss was soft and slow, the both of them languid in their exploration of each other. It felt as natural as breathing, to be kissing him, Deming thought, and at the same time it felt shimmering and new, exciting, even though this was far from the first time they had shared each other in this way. Nerves and desire fluttered deep within her.

His hand found the back of her head. Hers settled on his waist. They pulled each other closer at the same time and smiled into the other's lips.

Nikita backed up, drawing Deming with him into the bed. She sank into the downy plushness and relaxed, watching him undress for her. He was succinct and within moments his shirt was on top of his trousers on the floor and he was kneeling on the bed in front of her looking like he was carved from stone.

Deming's eyes followed the curve of his neck, the broad expanse of his chest, the sharp panes of his stomach. The faded curls of his Rider's mark that had connected them before they knew of each other's existence.

Her fingertips traced corded muscle with awed reverence and when they trailed to the band of his underwear she swallowed a groan. The one article of clothing he kept on left little to the imagination.

He made a noise of amusement. Deming dropped her hand, glancing up to his eyes. They were dark and knowing.

"Like what you see?"

There was little point in lying. "Yes, very much."

He lowered himself next to her, his wings folded behind him like kites, wafting rich cardamom across the sheets. His gaze roamed her body beside him. "I know the feeling."

They stayed there, bodies close enough to be touching anywhere they wanted but for some reason they restrained themselves. Deming's fingers twitched. She buried them in the sheets. Nikita's eyebrow arched, lips tugging upwards. She scrunched her nose at him.

Their chests rose and fell in time with one another. It was peaceful, this liminal space between the posters of the bed.

Deming pressed a kiss to the tip of his nose. He swatted at her and they laughed and the heaviness of their day, their months, eased for a moment.

It was lovely, to lay next to each other like this. They had so rarely had moments alone while on the road and even fewer moments of comfort. The sheets of their bed were soft against her skin.

His bed, Deming reminded herself. She felt her cheeks heat.

Nikita's smile reached his eyes. "What are you thinking about?"

She shrugged. Her mouth opened to speak a half truth, then closed it. Again, there seemed little point in lying. "I enjoy sharing a bed with you." He nearly preened at that. "I think I would very much like to share a bed with you every night."

"Crown Princess, what a tantalizing proposition." He leaned forward and kissed her so softly the feeling melted away before she could savor it. "Are you truly that enamored with me you'd chain yourself to the posters of my bed so quickly?"

"I mean," Deming said, rolling her eyes in feigned deference, "I'd prefer silk, rope even, to chains, but if that's how you play I'm more than happy to try."

Nikita rolled onto his back, laughter bursting from him. The sound felt like embers in a hearth, tasted like summer rain. Deming knew without looking that the skin on her chest held the faintest glow. Right above her heart, a part of which was now and forevermore held in the cupped hands of the male beside her. She could no more take that piece back than move the earth beneath her feet or live without air in her lungs. She wouldn't have it any other way anyway.

"Kit?"

"Yes, princess."

"I am yours. I have been for a while," she spoke quickly, trying to get her thoughts out before she lost her nerve, "but I don't think I've been clear about what I feel for you."

He stilled, every part of him down to the last feather frozen in anticipation or eagerness or something completely other. It was a rare moment in which Deming could not read him. She pushed forward with her declaration anyway.

"You have become someone I can't imagine living without. I crave your presence and your words and I love the way you treat others. I love a lot about you actually. I love your tenacity and will. I love your dedication. I love your spirit."

She was rambling. She needed to stop rambling. Reel it in, Deming.

"I guess what I'm trying to say is..." Deming bit her lip. Her heart was beating so loudly in her chest she feared the whole world could hear it.

Nikita lifted her chin, forcing her eyes up, and the second she met the depths of those gray eyes the words tumbled out of her mouth on their own accord.

"I love you."

Oh, fuck.

Panic surged through her instantly, instinctively, horrendously. She inhaled sharply but all the breath in the world couldn't reel in the words that hung thick like honey in the air between them.

She hadn't meant to say that. She couldn't love him. She cared for him but she didn't love him. Love was sacred and delicate and everyone she had ever loved had been taken from her or hurt because of her or betrayed her and shattered her world into a million pieces. Their faces flashed before her eyes—Silas, Samira, Miriam, Paris, Vallyn, Colette, Dresden. Cruelty and death and broken hearts lay in shards at the foot of her love.

Oh gods, he would be taken from her too.

Darkness swept in, hard and fast.

She could take it back. She couldn't let her love hurt anyone else.

"I—" Her voice broke. Something wet fell down her cheek. Gods, was she crying? Why was she crying? "I didn't mean to say that, it just slipped out, I don't—I mean, I can't—I don't love you. I care about you, like I said I don't—" More tears fell as she rambled, heart beating in panicked, stuttering pulses that made it hard to breathe. Her chest heaved, lungs fluttering within frantically.

"Deming."

Her name snapped her attention back.

"Breathe," he commanded.

A calloused thumb brushed the tear away and when Deming met his eyes she saw waves of emotion crashing in that vast gray sea.

"I am blessed beyond my worth to be known and held and wanted by you and I am honored—honored—to be loved by you. I will carry your love with me through distance and pain, through trials and joys. It will be the most meaningful action of my life, to hold your love, not just because your love is precious but because it is reciprocated."

Deming gave up on holding her tears back. She curled into his chest, sobbing into his skin and he spoke those three words over and over into her hair.

I love you.

I love you.

I love you.

He held her until she had no more tears left to cry, until her breathing had calmed, until the heavy peace of a cathartic release settled around them like a blanket.

They lay there, intertwined. His fingers played gently with her hair, her cheek warm against the skin of his chest.

"Deming?"

"Mm?"

He shifted her out of his arms, resting his head on the pillow and looking at her with such care and devotion Deming's heart broke and healed all at once.

He palmed her face as he spoke, his voice soft as feathers.

"We should all be so lucky to love and be loved. Love emboldens and ties and strengthens and yes, sometimes, love hurts but we cannot deprive ourselves of what makes us who we are. You love so much," he stroked her hair, kissed her shoulder, "your people, your queendom, your friends. You love more deeply and truthfully than most are capable of understanding. It is a gift, to have that much love to give, not a curse."

She heard his words, knew them to be true, and still could not find it in herself to trust them completely. It was terrifying to love.

"I'm scared," she whispered into his skin.

"I am too," he whispered into hers, "but not of us. This is right. Whatever happens next, we will face it together. That is where we belong, I with you and you with me."

Deming nodded, still buried in his chest.

He pulled her closer until there was no space between them at all. They were a tangle of long limbs and careful caresses and hopes and fears and new love. They cocooned themselves in each other and Deming had never felt as safe as she had in that moment.

Chapter Forty

Deming

Deming woke to the peaceful sounds of slumbering breath over her shoulder.

Nikita's arm was thrown over her waist. They were spooned together like nesting dolls. So much of their bodies touched including—

Deming shivered, swallowed.

He was hard against her.

Her stomach was suddenly full of sparks. Heat pooled in between her thighs. Never had desire come on so fast for her.

She squeezed her thighs together to relieve some, any, of the ache between them but all that did was add delicious friction.

A moan slipped out of her, and Nikita woke.

Rustling of sheets and feathers filled the air.

Then, as if Deming's desire was a physical presence in the air that he sensed, Nikita stilled.

Her heart thudded in her chest.

Nikita hummed and pulled her ever closer into him.

He nipped at the skin on her neck then whispered into her ear, "I dreamt of you."

"What of me?" Deming hardly recognized her voice.

Nikita's middle finger traced delicate circles into the skin on her stomach. "The memory of us. Laying with you in a bed of wildflowers. The way you felt. The way you tasted."

Each word sent a flushed flutter through Deming.

"It's a shame I woke you up."

He slowly shook his head, lips barely lifting from her skin as he said, "This is much better than any dream."

Deming felt they were on the precipice of the final piece of their relationship. The last, desperately intimate details of each other they had yet to learn.

With her hand, she guided his own away from her hip. Lower and lower, until his fingers rested lightly atop where her body was aching for him. She arched her back, pressing her ass into him.

He groaned and rolled his hips into her.

Deming licked her lip, begged her heart to slow even slightly. It was already beating out of her chest and she wanted to be calm and present for this moment that she had dreamed about and longed for for months.

The edges of his wings trembled. His breathing was irregular, heavy. It wasn't just her, then. That was a relief.

"Are you sure?" His voice was soft as butter and quieter than snowfall.

"Yes," came her breathy reply, "There is nothing I am more sure of than wanting this."

He turned, then, meeting her honeyed eyes with his cloudy gray gaze. Sun and storm, light and shadow. Emotions barreled down their gaze, their connection felt tangible, like Deming could reach out and feel golden, warm thread between her fingers.

His gaze held hers for a moment, then trailed down, tracing her entire form. She felt his eyes on her neck, her shoulders. She felt it on her chest and the flat pane of her stomach. She squirmed underneath his gaze as he lingered on the apex of her thighs, taking his time as if remembering what she tasted like.

He took his time, drinking the sight of her in as if he were trying to paint the image of her laying in bed waiting for him in every corner of his mind.

"Stand up," he said, voice rough with desire.

Deming shifted towards the edge of the bed, pushing off the soft duvet to stand on bare feet in front of him. The floorboards were smooth and cool beneath her.

She looked up and whispered, "Why do you need me on my feet?"

"Well," his hand slipped under the sleek nightgown she wore, "it's only fair that I help you out of these clothes."

"There isn't much to remove. I could have done it myself."

"Oh, I know." His hand tightened on her waist, pulled her closer. "But why let you have all the fun?"

She couldn't hold back the full body chill that shivered through the marrow of her bones as he trailed his hands across her skin, taunting, teasing.

He grabbed the lace hem of her nightgown and tugged it up over her hips, over her chest, over her head. She let the fabric slink across her shoulders and arms and relished in the feel of the breeze coming from the courtyard window on her skin. It was just cool enough to temper the flush beginning to bloom and brought in soft, hidden scents of roses and darkness with it.

She wore nothing underneath the slip. The instant it pooled on the floor beside her, she was bare before him.

Nikita's eyes softened, taking her in. "You are glorious."

Her spine straightened, preening at his compliments. Heat crept across Deming's cheeks, then down her neck, then through the knot of ink that graced her chest until the entire mark felt licked by flame. Her hair falling in loose curls down her back, white tendrils framing her face, backlit just slightly by the glow of the moon. The skin below her eyes was tainted a soft purple from exhaustion, but her amber irises shone bright.

She reached out a hand, finding his. The pad of his thumb stroked her palm, her forearm. She shivered. He pulled her hand to his mouth and placed the most tender kiss she had ever been given onto her knuckles.

He pulled her close and Deming felt the desperate, carnal need to feel his skin against hers. She reached for the band of his boxers to tug him closer but he caught her wrist.

"Patience, princess."

Deming growled half-heartedly and Nikita laughed as he tilted his head and whispered.

"I also needed you to stand," he kissed her neck, her earlobe, " because I made you a promise."

Then Nikita Magdalene, Crown Prince of Runne, fell to his knees before her.

The words tumbling from his lips coupled with the sight of him kneeling before her like she was a goddess fanned the flames of her desire. She wriggled in his grip, anxious, anticipatory. Had anyone ever wanted someone this much? It seemed hard to fathom.

His body fell, but his hands remained. His fingertips dug into the softness of her hips in the most delectable way, strong enough to be felt but soft enough to be comforting.

He kissed her calves, her thighs, her stomach. He peppered his lips everywhere except the place she most wanted him to be.

She watched him, breath coming out in pants already, feverish with desire to take his head in her hands and move him to the center of her.

But this was just as much about him as it was about her and when their eyes caught Deming saw a fire in his that mirrored her own.

He wanted to savor this.

So she let him.

It wasn't too difficult an ask, when it came down to it, being worshipped slowly and completely. Each brush of his lips against her skin heightened her senses. The world around them quieted and the ecosystem of heat and breathy sighs and subtle touches enhanced until it was all Deming knew.

He guided her to the bed. She leaned against it, perching on the very edge and her elbows sinking into the sheets to support her upper body.

"Lift your legs," he murmured into her upper thigh. His breath tickled her and she squirmed, sighed, arched her back, then did as he asked.

He slipped underneath her thighs so her legs were draped comfortably across his outstretched arms and back. His hands found purchase on the bed on either side of her and he inched his knees closer.

Then he ran his nose up the center of her, teasing, and she cried out in delight as a pleasurable shiver raced up her spine.

"Do you like that?"

"Yes," she breathed.

He did it once more, then replaced his nose with his tongue and began languidly pleasuring her in a way that made Deming sure he was finding pleasure in this too.

Her eyes had long since closed. She let herself fall into intimacy and desire, succumbing to the feelings he brought out.

He had taken what she said all those weeks ago to heart. He was slow and deliberate with the strokes of his tongue. He nudged her closer and closer to release with patience, giving her long, consistent licks before taking her bundle of nerves between his lips and sucking.

Her head fell back, neck rolling as she groaned.

Her body felt electric, tense and ready in the best way.

"Don't stop," she begged, "please."

He hummed his approval into her and the vibrations made her gasp.

With each stroke of his tongue her desire curled tighter and tighter until it was so taut Deming felt she might fracture into a million shining pieces—

Then she did.

All she knew was fingers grasping sheets and stars in her eyes and every muscle tightening around the pure, undiluted, pleasure rippling through her, trying to hold onto it for as long as possible.

Panting, she opened her eyes as her release receded from waves to ripples to a simple, soft heat that pulsed within her to the beat of her rapid heart.

Nikita had risen from the floor. His chest was heaving, wings were trembling. He looked at her with a reverence that humbled her all the way to her simmering, satisfied core.

"Come here," she whispered, too limp from her release to move quite yet.

He leaned over her, dark hair curling around his face like a silken frame.

"You are beautiful always," he said, voice husky, "but seeing you come undone for me is a beauty I didn't know existed."

She smiled into his lips, pleased.

She hummed and reached for his boxers once more, meeting no resistance this time around. She tugged them off his hips and down his thighs and swallowed hard when they fell to his ankles.

He was magnificent.

Lithe but strong chest and shoulders. Skin begging to be touched. Muscles that dove on an incline into his trousers.

Deming swallowed, tracing the curves of him with her fingers. She never wanted to stop touching him.

He was perfect.

She told him so and he smiled.

She beckoned him back to her and he obeyed, scooping her into the center of the bed and straddling her in one fell swoop.

Looking up at him, with his dark hair and dark wings and dark eyes and desire simply pouring from every inch of him, Deming had the distinct feeling of being in the presence of an immortal being. He was other, powerful, more. Dangerous, even, though she knew he would never hurt her. He would hurt others for her, though.

And she loved it.

Wanted all of him, now.

She reached out, grasping his length, and relished in the feeling of control and power as he shuddered beneath her touch.

Slowly but with purpose, she began stroking him. He had been hard already, his desire for her and pleasure at bringing her release clear well before, but as she moved her hand it felt as though he were steel beneath her.

He moved his hips in rhythm with her, bucking against her palm, encouraging her without words to move fully from base to tip, then shuddered to a stop. He placed a hand on her stomach.

"Fuck," he hissed between clenched teeth, "you're going to have to stop that, princess, or this is going to end earlier than either of us want."

Deming glowed under his praise, literally, and they both laughed at the sight of her magic as it flared then faded.

She relaxed her grip, but guided it towards her.

Nikita pulled back and tensed. "Are you sure?"

"Yes, I'm sure," she confirmed, "I don't think I've ever wanted something more than I want this, right now, with you. Please." She leaned up and sealed her last word with a kiss, swiping her tongue along his bottom lip.

He kissed her back as he guided himself into her.

Deming's head fell back, her eyes closing instinctively as she felt him enter her with such ease and care it made her want to cry.

"Is this okay?"

"Yes," she breathed, the word like a prayer on her lips.

As their hips joined, he let his weight fall just slightly onto her, the pressure and heat making her feel cocooned and safe and wanted.

His hand grasped the back of her head, his fingers twining with the colored ribbons of her hair. He took her lips in his as he rocked in and out of her slowly. Every slick movement gave Deming reasons abound to moan and relax into the sheets.

While she knew from experience that she would not find a second release while he was inside her, this kind of pleasure was not focused enough on the areas most sensitive to her, she found herself present and enjoying the roll of their hips like she had never before. Was this what sex was supposed to feel like? A continuation of her release, like she was coasting on the high he had just given her? Easy and soft and pleasurable regardless of whether or not she was building to an orgasm herself?

Her hand lifted to her chest on its own accord, Deming's sense of self long lost to the feelings Nikita was bringing out in her. Her fingers trailed over herself, circling her nipples until they were stiff peaks.

A low growl rumbled from Nikita as he watched her. "Do you like touching yourself, princess?"

"Yes," she nodded, circling herself once more.

"Does it feel better than when I touch you?" His thrusts were leisurely, intuitive. He found a rhythm that matched the speed of her hands and breathing and Deming had never felt so in tune with another in all her life.

"You've not touched me nearly enough to say," she managed to get out, eyes fluttering open to meet his briefly.

His teeth nipped lighted at her skin as he said, "We'll have to change that."

Deming hummed her agreement, arching into his touch, trying to pull herself closer to him though they were nearly one body already. They moved in tandem, ebbing and flowing like the tides. Kit's breath was hot against her neck and her hands roamed his body, eager to touch every part of him. They skimmed his chest and shoulders, they twisted languidly in his hair, they traced the curved lines of his muscles as they tapered from his chest to his waist to where he was thrusting into her.

She needed to be closer to him, closer to the friction between her thighs. She wanted more of every lick of feeling coursing through her.

Her legs wrapped around the back of his thighs, urging him faster and harder and their breathing became ragged as he listened to her cues and surged forward with renewed vigor.

"Fuck, Kit. That feels so good."

An understatement, to be sure. The sparks coalescing in her belly and the tightening of every muscle in her body felt unbelievable. It was undiluted pleasure, to be beneath him, around him, touching him. She never wanted him to stop and at the same time needed him to find his own release more than she needed to breathe. She wanted him to share in the pleasure of coming as she had. She let her hands settle on his hips and tugged him closer, faster, harder into her.

Her words and hands ignited something in Nikita. He groaned, eyes closed, his hands curling tightly into the sheets near her head. His pace increased, chasing the high he was barreling towards.

"Look at me."

His eyes flared open, dark and wild, and caught hers as he tumbled over the edge into oblivion in rapid thrusts and elevated breathing. His hands moved from her waist to the pillow she lay on and only when his hips slowed then stopped altogether did the fire in his gaze begin to settle.

Their hearts raced as one and Nikita leaned to seal their union with a kiss, deepening it with his tongue and holding one side of her face like she was the most precious thing he had ever laid his hands on.

"I love you," he told her.

"I love you," she echoed.

Emotion surged in her and suddenly an unbidden whimper escaped her lips.

"Deming?" Immediately on alert, Nikita tensed and gently brushed the tear from her cheek.

She shook her head, not wanting him to misunderstand. "I'm fine, everything's fine." She looked up at him and hoped the pure joy she felt was reflected in her eyes. "I just didn't know it could be like that."

He bent down and gave her another kiss, softer and quieter than the last but Deming loved it the most of any kiss she had ever received.

"Neither did I," he said when they parted.

With one last stroke of her hair, he rolled off her and Deming instantly missed the heat he took with him.

She watched from the comfort of the bed as Nikita padded to the bathroom and found herself biting her lip at the sight of him walking away. His back was glorious—muscled and strong, wings on full display. And lower...She huffed a laugh, throwing an arm over her face. It was ridiculous how attracted she was to him.

He returned, a towel loosely tied around his waist, a glass of water in his hand, and a small embroidered hand towel wrapped over his forearm.

He came to her side of the bed, offering the glass. "Thirsty?"

Deming took a sip and set it on the table. "Thank you."

Nikita nodded, then handed the small towel to her.

The fabric was soft and warm. Deming stared at the offering now in her hand and smiled. "That is," she tilted her head, looking up at Nikita curiously, "very thoughtful. Thank you."

He chuckled, "You don't need to thank me for doing the bare minimum, but you're welcome."

Deming thought he was selling himself rather short. The way someone acted after the physical act of sex was finished was just as important as the way they acted during it. From the second Nikita had closed the door to now, Deming had felt like his absolute priority.

She smiled to herself, awed again that she was blessed with a love like this.

What had once felt precious was beginning to feel more and more tangible, more and more real. Nikita was not going anywhere.

She cleaned her thighs and folded the used cloth neatly on the floor. After relieving herself in the adjoining bedroom to avoid any unwanted discomfort, she found Nikita was back in bed lounging. Deming was more than happy to join him.

The light of the stars and the moon danced across his wings. Every minute movement refracted shimmering light and highlighted the nuanced colors in his feathers. To call them black was to do a tragic disservice to the multitude of jeweled undertones that winked in and out of existence with every shift of his body.

Deming thought they looked particularly magical this morning. Though, everything seemed particularly magical in their post-coital glow.

It was peculiar, the feelings that washed over someone during intimacy.

The world felt all at once insular and profound, like the earth revolved around two beating hearts. Like the heat that kindled as fingers touched the curves of bodies was the sun and the breath shared between fervent kisses was the wind. The softness with which love manifested itself physically was impossible to quantify. How was one supposed to explain the way their blood rushes to meet another's? The way language becomes less about words and more about the arch of their spine?

Time was a beautiful medley as seconds began ticking once more and their senses widened to allow the sounds and sights of the world in again.

All Deming knew was peace in that moment.

The sheets and hair were mussed, sweat lingered on their skin, and all she knew was peace.

She lay next to Nikita, watching him watch her breathe, and was overcome with a sense of contentment. Everything that made her alive and real let out an exhale in the aftermath of intimacy with him. She hadn't even known the tension she had been holding, the fear of being alone, of being unworthy, of being a curse. The sticky syrup of dread had soaked into her pores so thoroughly and for so long that she hadn't realized she was drenched in it.

But here, laying in postcoital bliss, all of that melted away.

She was not so naive to think those fears would stay away, but as Nikita drew her close and took her bottom lip between his, she felt something golden and warm seal inside of her. They were here, together, in love. He would protect her, and she him. She no longer had to carry the weight of her past alone and the relief she felt at finding someone who not only understood her pain but held it as if it was their own was overwhelming and resolute.

He was everything that was good in this world.

She promised herself that they would survive whatever this war threw at them even if it took defying the gods or sheer force of will.

Cardamom filled her nose as he shifted his body to accommodate his wings more comfortably and Deming inhaled deeply before blinking thrice as an epiphany hit her.

"What do I smell like?"

His eyes crinkled joyfully. "What?"

The sheets made soft sounds as Deming shuffled herself closer to him. "You smell like cardamom and the air at the coast. What do I smell like?"

"You," he kissed her forehead, "are something else."

She raised her eyebrows expectantly.

"And you smell like daisies and fresh linens."

"Daisies," Deming echoed, mouth pulling downwards, eyes flicking to his, "I smell like daisies?"

"To me, yes."

Deming hummed. She resisted the urge to bring her wrist to her nose and smell herself, but she knew that wasn't how things like this worked.

Satisfied, she kissed his cheek.

Joy rippled across his features like a raindrop falling into a puddle.

Her touch lit up his eyes. Her kisses ignited his spirit. Her body was a flame and he was the moth.

He became undone by her.

It was a new feeling, having that effect on someone. She relished and cherished and wanted to explore it and more than anything hoped he knew she was the same with him.

"I don't deserve you."

His words came out quiet, mumbled, and then his head pulled back just slightly as if he hadn't meant to say them out loud.

Deming opened her mouth to protest then paused. She had been about to refute him, and though she wanted to, what she wanted more was not to invalidate his feelings or push him away. They had done that to each other too much these past few weeks. Nikita had familial trauma buried deep in him, in different ways than Deming but just as painful and lasting all the same.

As much as she loved them, Deming had hated when Paris and Colette had spoken to her in ways that made it seem like she was wrong for hurting, wrong for being scared or angry or insecure. Nikita was far more than her friend, and that made maneuvering this conversation even more important. Her words carried more weight with him than almost anyone else. She wanted to wield the sway she knew she had with him positively. Neither of them needed to be further hurt, there had been enough of that between their two lives to go around.

And besides, who was she to tell him he deserved her when she herself thought she didn't deserve him? It was a double edged sword, caring for someone that was grieving in similar ways to yourself.

So she swallowed her initial reaction in favor of something softer.

Deming took his hand in hers and kissed each fingertip, then held their joined hands and cradled them against her chest.

She pushed his hair away from his face, left her palm on his cheek. "You have been taught that love is painful, that it should be felt from a distance. You have been shown that the bonds that tie lives together tie so tightly that parts of yourself must die to keep the peace."

He watched her, entranced. Lives and loves swirled in his gaze. He was unnaturally still, not a feather so much as twitched as she spoke.

It was as if he was drowning and she was speaking air into his lungs.

"I know it is not easy to unlearn what has been etched into you since birth," she sighed heavily, feeling the weight of her own past press against her spine, "but I want you to know that the way your father loves you is not the way you have to receive love for your whole life. I want you to know that I will never hold you at an arm's length. I will never treat you as a means to an end. You are worthy of so much more than that, and I will spend my entire life proving that to you."

Deming choked up thinking about dying and leaving Nikita alone on this earth, but pressed forward.

"We may not be owed anything in this life, but if there is one thing I am certain of it's that we are all deserving of love. That includes you." Tears were brimming in his eyes. Deming pushed on. "You are deserving of love. You are deserving of the way Ilysse loves you, honest and with honor. You are deserving of the way Hartford loves you, quiet and assuredly."

Deming took a deep breath because it still felt daunting to bare her soul, even though she had done so before and even though she knew her feelings were reciprocated. Loving someone as she loved him and feeling the same kind of love in return was new to her.

"And you are deserving of the way I love you, soft and fierce, nuanced and all-consuming. My love for you contains multitudes, and you are deserving of it all."

Her voice faded out and a light, whistling wind filled its space. An owl sounded, far away.

Nikita looked at her like she hung the moon and the stars, like maybe she was the moon and the stars. He squeezed her hand, the both of theirs still pressed into Deming's chest above her heart. He poured everything he was into the words he said to her next, and Deming heard it all. Every kernel of gratitude, every wound, slowly healing, every ray of hope.

"You are deserving of my love, too."

"I am deserving of your love, too."

And to Deming's surprise, she found she believed it.

Emotions welled in her as she finished speaking, as Nikita's words in response melted into the evening air. The truth of her words sank like a stone in her mind. It was as if she had been speaking not only to Nikita, but to herself.

She thought, perhaps, that this was what being loved was supposed to feel like while healing from trauma. Not the absolution of guilt and perceived sin and profound sadness, but the embracing of it as a part of you. Everyone was gifted scars through their lifetime, but in the same way that a brass statue became more beautiful as it aged because of its tarnished surface, not in spite of it, scars did not make someone less worthy of love. It made them more.

Chapter Forty One

Nikita

THE ROSE HIP OIL Deming had rolled onto her wrists complement-ed the floral scent of the gardens wonderfully. Between that, the delectable breeze whispering through his feathers, and the lingering postcoital bliss, Nikita was the happiest and most content he'd been in months.

He and Deming had stayed in bed for hours that morning. They shared kisses and hopes, touches and dreams. They laughed through stories of past relationships and all the fumbling moments of their first times.

Nikita had thought that hearing about Deming sharing a bed with another man would breed jealousy, especially since that man was here with them, but it hadn't. All he felt was closer to Deming. Every piece of her, every sliver of memories or tales of who she was before they met, felt more precious than gold. He drank in everything she shared eagerly, and she did the same for him.

When they couldn't justify laying in bed a moment longer, Nikita had offered to show her the gardens. It was a thinly veiled attempt to avoid his father, but Deming accepted nonetheless.

As expansive as they were beautiful, the gardens were comprised of acres on acres of land that sprawled all the way from the edge of Bascade to the formal border between Runne and Laey, a great river that poured in blustery rapids from the Telaciens all the way down the edges of the two countries until it became a gentle stream before becoming a lake oasis all the way in the desert at the center of the continent.

The gardens were both wild and highly curated, a curious mix of foliage that represented nearly every varietal known to the continent, and even some that were foreign. As Nikita walked Deming down the path cobbled together with stone and marble and brick, they saw orchids and daisies, ivy and roses. Deming had stopped at a row of delicate pink peonies. She voiced gingerly all the wonderings that the familiar flower brought.

Where she would be, what she would be, on the next anniversary of her parents death. Would she be back in Laey, a queen crowned? Would she be in Laey at all to lay a bouquet of peonies on their grave? Would there be another grave to visit? Another headstone to add to the ever growing array of people she loved that found themselves six feet under?

It was altogether possible that Vallyn was already dead. The continent was vast and they had no idea where Khalil and Dresden had relocated. They all wanted nothing more than to leave no stone unturned in the search for Vallyn, but Nikita knew that without a lead, they would be searching blind.

Neither of them had answers, but his company seemed to ease her discomfort.

Deming exhaled slowly through her nose.

The peony slipped from between her fingers, swishing back to its place within the bush with a flutter of leaves and petals.

The further they walked through the gardens, the more exotic the flora became.

A fruit bearing tree rose from rich, earthy soil. Round stone fruit weighed down its branches, the skin a deep purple in the shadows but a startling magenta wherever light filtered down through the broad leaves.

They were admiring a conical flower with stiff, pointed petals of vibrant orange and yellow when, impulsively, Deming arched onto her tiptoes and placed a kiss on his lips.

Or, she tried to, anyway. Nikita caught her movement from the corner of his eye and leaned down to greet her, but they were misaligned and she ended up catching only half his mouth. He tried to correct but knocked his chin into her nose and they pulled apart in surprise, eyes wide and grinning like fools.

Laughter spilled through the air.

Deming was keeled over, hands on her knees. Her curled hair fell in loose waves over her shoulder and bounced with every laugh that shook from her chest.

Nikita admired his mate with such adoration it made his heart hurt. He, too, was chuckling through closed lips. The feathers of his wings wavered with the sound.

"Is something amusing, princess?"

She cupped his face in her palm, still smiling brighter than the sun. "Can we try that again?"

He leaned in so close to her that when he nodded, their noses rubbed lightly. "We can do anything you want."

Deming's breath hitched. Six little words and the entire atmosphere shifted. What was once bubbly and light was now thick and heated. She blinked up at him, lips open just so.

"What do you want, Deming?"

"I want you to kiss me."

Nikita wasted no time following directions.

His hands were on her instantly, pulling her body to his. He pulled gently at her hair, tipping her head back to get a better angle at her mouth.

Her lips pressed into his with a fierceness he hadn't felt from her since that first night in the middle of the woods. Her tongue parted his lips and danced with his own like they had memorized the steps together in another lifetime.

His heartbeat quickened in tempo with her eager movements. Blood rushed south. He had the overwhelming urge to fly her straight back to his bed. There would never be enough time in the world to worship her body the way he wanted to, the way she deserved.

Petals rained down around them as they collided with the trunk. Every shade of purple imaginable drifting from the flowering tree. Lilac and amethyst, lavender and periwinkle. The world was showering them in softness and beauty.

Nikita inhaled sharply when she trailed her hand lightly up the seam of his pants and she smiled into his mouth, clearly pleased at the effect on him.

He pulled away slowly, panting and out of breath. One hand was on the tree behind her and one was tangled in her hair. Deming gazed up at him with an expression that made every inch of him burn. It was tender and soft, but singed with such deep-seated want the edges of it curled like parchment in flame.

He pulled his hand out from behind her head and stroked her cheek.

"It's unreasonable how much I want you." Nikita nuzzled her neck. "Let's go back to my room."

She tilted her head back, laughing. "We can't!"

"We could, though."

Deming's hand slid up his chest around the back of his neck. She hummed as he pressed his hips suggestively into her.

Just then, muffled voices filtered through the trees. Deming froze. At the definitive click of heels on stone, she leapt out of his arms completely.

Eyes wide and cheeks flush, Deming giggled nervously. "And we certainly can't get caught!"

"I'm the prince," Nikita said, "who could possibly be coming that could tell me what I can or can't do?"

Deming's smile was snuffed out as she spied someone rounding the corner behind Nikita.

Her spine straightened, her eyes widened. Then she fell into the crispest curtsy Nikita had ever seen.

A feminine voice trilled through the gardens. "Oh, Nikita. I hadn't thought I'd find you here."

Memories flashed across Nikita's eyes. Stumbling into arms when he was hurt. Forehead kisses as he was tucked into bed. Carefully curated lessons on monarchies and kingdoms and how to be a fair and just ruler. Unconditional love until there was silence, instead.

Nikita turned to face his mother.

Sabel Magdalene was a painfully beautiful waif of a woman.

Chestnut hair pinned neatly into a chignon at the nape of her neck, the Queen of Runne wore a brocade corset over a simple gray dress. Rings of silver pierced up pointed ears. Her crown perched perfectly on her head. A thousand tiny crystals decorated the delicate arch that came to a point from which a pear-shaped diamond hung. Tawny eyes slit like a cat blinked curiously at him.

Nikita's chest contracted with emotion. "Mother."

"I'm sorry I was unable to be present when you arrived." Her voice was gentle, warm. "The king—your father," she corrected, "requested to welcome you alone."

Nikita tried to parse through her words, to find some other meaning, but came up short. Why had she not tried to seek him out on her own? She had clearly not meant to find him in the gardens.

It was only when Deming elbowed his hip that Nikita realized he hadn't responded.

"I'm happy to see you, now."

"And I you." Sabel's eyes slid to Deming. "You are Rendrel's Rider?"

"Yes, Your Highness," Deming replied demurely.

"My husband is much more formal than I," Sabel's mouth twitched, "there is no need for titles. Please, call me Sabel."

"Yes, Sabel," Deming repeated. "My name is Deming. I'm the heir to Laey and am recently bonded to Rendrel." She looked to Nikita then back to the queen. "And I am—"

"My son's mate." Some distant emotions flickered across Sabel's face, but she quickly smoothed it over. "Yes, I heard. I'm sure the members of court will have all sorts of questions for the two of you at the ball."

Surprise flared Nikita's nostrils. "He's still hosting it?"

"Oh, yes."

"Why?"

The king had summoned them to Bascade because he thought Nikta was once again blessed to be a Rider. Now that he knew that wasn't the case, Nikita had been sure that any events in celebration would be canceled.

"He believes honor has been restored," his mother's gaze drifted again to Deming, "however different the bond may look from how he imagined."

She met Nikita's gaze as she said, "He believes that without you, Rendrel would have never found her Rider." Then, more flippantly, "I don't pretend to understand the inner workings of his mind."

The gardens were quiet save for the skittering of animals through leaves and the occasional bird call.

Nikita simply didn't know what to do with this new development. Had his father truly forgiven him? Was it all a ploy to get something?

"Well." Sabel clasped her hands together. They melted into the folds of her skirt. She gave him a tight, distant smile. "I'll leave you both to enjoy the gardens. It was a pleasure to meet you, Deming."

Her handmaids split to opposite sides of the path to let the queen return from whence she came. At the corner, she stopped and looked over her shoulder. "I'm glad you're home, son."

Emotions burned at the corners of Nikita's eyes. "I'm glad, too."

He was shocked to find the words weren't a lie.

Then she was gone.

The sigh that escaped Nikita's lips was drawn out and heavy.

Deming placed a hand on his arm. "Are you okay?"

"I don't know," he answered honestly.

There was so much to unpack with his mother. In a way, his relationship with her felt more fraught than the one he had with his father. With the king, Nikita knew where they both stood. He knew what his father believed and what he valued. It was straightforward, regardless of how cruel hating a child for something they had no control over was.

Though, now, maybe even that relationship had changed.

Nikita had no idea.

With his mother...

Nikita ran a hand through his hair. "She was the best mother. I loved her so much. I do love her so much," he corrected quickly, "it was just hard to not have her on my side when it mattered."

Deming nodded slowly. "Your father is an opinionated male. Strong-willed."

"Very."

"Perhaps she did fight for you. It may have felt like she didn't," Deming took his hand, "but memories rust with time. And as a child, you wouldn't have been privy to the conversations your parents had behind closed doors."

His heart cracked at the thought. "Maybe."

Deming looked to where Sabel had disappeared. "She clearly loves you."

"She does," he agreed.

He should talk to her. No more running away, no more wondering. He should walk right up that path and find his mother and ask her what had happened all those years ago.

His feet remained planted.

Perhaps another day.

Perhaps when there was less in the world to worry about.

Perhaps when he felt more prepared for her to deny Deming's idea, to say that she hadn't fought for him at all.

Nikita was not ready for that reality. "Tell me something joyful."

Deming mulled it over. Then she looked up at him with delight sparkling in her eyes. "The ball."

Nikita cocked his head. "What of it?"

"I'll be wearing something magical, I'm sure. Wouldn't you love to twirl me around in a gorgeous gown?"

He grinned at her.

Yes, he very much would love to do that.

Chapter Forty Two

Deming

THE BALLROOM WAS DRIPPING with diamonds.

Small, glittering strands of them decorated the chandeliers that hung on polished chains from the rafters. Large clusters of the gem, uncut, studded the walls. Clasped around every neck were diamonds of varying sizes, accompanied by jewels in a multitude of colors. Gifts, from the king to his guests. A shining diamond the size of a fist was nestled between the breasts of a female with the skin some poisonous reptile. A delicate chain with rubies interspersed with diamonds looped thrice around the neck of a male with a twitching, spotted tail. A female with small, plain wings of dusty brown donned a collar of diamonds cut into flat planes and sharp angles. It stretched from jaw to collarbone.

In the midst of it was an obsidian slab larger than entire rooms. Marquise cut diamonds were inlaid to the black stone in a swirling pattern that resembled a starry cloud.

It was breathtaking. The level of wealth displayed was beyond comprehension. How long had it taken to amass this quantity of the gemstone? From what she knew of mining, which, to be fair, was limited, Deming believed diamonds to be rare.

She hid in the shadows of a curtain, observing it all. Her hands had grasped at the skirts of her dress so often during the first hour of the ball that the taffeta had permanently wrinkled.

Deming frowned down at the fabric. The generous skirt spilled out from a snug bodice. It was a simple gown, no detailing, but the nearly invisible stitching and way it hugged her waist and chest so impeccably made Deming confident it was worth a small fortune. Thin, silky gloves slunk up past her elbows and her shoulders were bare. No straps to ensure that the Seal Daughlr had given her was on full display. Four perfectly concentric circles scarred into her skin.

Deming sighed.

At least the gown was black. The color hid the winkles well.

"The king certainly knows how to host."

Deming yelped and nearly fell into the swaths of thick, velvet draping adorning the tall window next to her.

Ilysse's hand gripped her wrist, preventing the tumble.

"Jumpy little thing, aren't you."

"Sorry," breathed Deming, "I was lost in thought."

Ilysse released Deming's wrist in favor of smoothing a crease in her lapel. She wore an impeccably tailored suit of deep maroon. Gold sparkled from her cufflinks, the tiny buckle on her heels, and the threading of the jacket. A thin stripe of gold ran down the sides of either pant leg. Glittering in the candlelight, pinched into various placing around the intricate weave of loose blonde braids spun into a bun high atop her head, were small, gold accents.

Deming opened her mouth to comment on them but Ilysse cut her off.

"I used to enjoy this room. It's so glamorous."

Deming's eyes swept over the ballroom. Glamorous was one word for it. Ostentatious, another. Obscene, a third.

"What changed?"

Ilysse crossed her arms. She leaned against the wall, one ankle crossed over the other. "Nikita's banishment. Changed the whole way I viewed the royal family." Her eyes tracked the bodies spinning across the floor but her gaze looked far away. "I grew up here, you know. It was my first home. But once Nikita's Rider's mark began fading, everything changed. The castle never felt quite like home after that."

Deming barely moved, barely breathed. This was the longest Ilysse had ever spoken to her. And it was certainly the most vulnerable she had been. "I can't imagine what that must have been like to live through."

Ilysse shrugged curtly. "I was young. I don't have a ton of explicit memories from then. Just feelings. Impressions. I remember thinking the hallways felt empty after he left. It was just as busy as before, but, without Nikita, life here withered a bit. I don't think I was the only one to feel it, either." Her eyes landed on the queen.

Sabel was sitting on her throne, hands in her lap. She looked upon her subjects with what could only be described as deep ambivalence. The cream organza gown she wore seemed to swallow her.

"When I was old enough," Ilysse continued, "I found Nikita again. Everything was a bit better after that."

"I thought my ears were burning." Nikita strolled towards them, a lopsided smile gracing his face. There was a mischievous twinkle in his eye. "Singing my praises, Ilysse?"

Ilysse shoved off the wall and brushed non-existent lint off her jacket. "You wish."

"How's the dancing?" Deming asked, nodding her chin towards where opulently dressed couples were bowing to each other. The brass band in the corner had just finished another ballad.

Nikita had been on the floor nearly all night, a stipulation his father had required. It was clear that while Nikita was welcome within the castle walls, his presence came at the price of renewed vigor in princely duties. He was to speak of his travels and time away from Bascade to anyone who wanted his ear with absolutely no mention of resentment towards the crown or king.

That was something that still perplexed Deming.

Trevelyan had wanted nothing to do with his son, banished him from the castle, yet somehow managed to convince his court that Nikita's leave was for his son's benefit? That a five year old wanted to be raised away from his mother and father? Away from the seat of his future throne?

Annoyance prickled at the skin on her neck.

To his credit, Nikita was seemingly handling the attention of the lords and ladies of Runne rather well.

"Pleasant, if not tiring," Nikita answered. He looked at Ilysse, cocking an eyebrow. "Not interested in partaking tonight? I usually have to drag you away from the dance floor."

Ilysse stilled. "A rowdy bar is far different from a royal ball." Her hand touched one of the gold accents in her hair. "Besides, I was just leaving. There's no one here I want to dance with." She sketched a bow to Nikita, eyes flashing to Deming as she did so. "Enjoy the revelry."

She was lost in the crowded room before either of them could protest.

"Is she okay?" Deming asked.

"No," Nikita frowned, "though I suppose none of us really are."

Deming hummed in solemn agreement. Vallyn's face flashed through her mind, bright and fleeting.

The violinist let their last note fade from a trill into nothingness and after two heartbeats of silence, the King of Runne's booming voice commanded everyone's attention.

It was time.

Deming swallowed hard, her heartbeat like a hummingbird in her chest.

Nikita interlocked their fingers and pulled her towards the dias.

"Citizens of Runne," Trevelyan addressed the room, "thank you for a wonderfully pleasant start to our evening of celebration and debauchery." The king exuded power in his black trousers and matching pin stripped vest. Diamonds studded down the seams of both, and amethysts the size of plums were set into a gold crown atop his head. "It is now time to reveal the true meaning of our gathering."

Hushed whispers of interest rippled through the crowd. Deming found Paris amidst the revealers, arms crossed leaning against the back wall. He gave her a nod of encouragement. She squeezed Nikita's hand tighter.

"The Magdalene line has long presided over Faekind. Through peace and war, our blood has stewarded the great Kingdom of Runne. Today, I am the herald of inspiring news." The king paused, surveying his court. A crafted smile lifted his lips as he continued. "My son and heir, Prince Nikita, has returned home after long years of travel and with him, he brings divine confirmation of the Magdalene line. The woman at his side, Deming Reynes-Elyachar of Laey, is my son's mate."

Spines straitened, eyebrows raised. Murmurs of curiosity rumbled through the room.

Deming willed the blush in her cheeks to go away. She locked in on Paris's eyes, something to steady her in the wake of the entirety of Runne's court now looking at her. The king had told them this announcement would be quick, unobtrusive. His grandiose speech said otherwise.

"Through the mating bond," Trevelyan continued, "we found that not only is this woman my son's mate, but she is prophesied. On her shoulder you will see proof that the Crest Major gave her the Seal."

At that, decorum was lost. Lords and ladies alike jostled for position to better see the ring of scars on Deming's shoulder.

Deming breathed through her nose, she shifted from foot to foot.

Trevelyan's smile reached his eyes this time. "More will be revealed in time. For now," he spread his arms wide, "bask in the joy and comfort of knowing that the Magdalene line is amphithere blessed. To ring in their union, Prince Nikita and his mate will lead the next dance."

Deming's stressed hands wrapped around taffeta once more.

Nikita whispered, "Help me forget our woes for a night?"

With a gentle crinkle, the fabric of her dress uncurled from her hands. With a slight nod to Nikita, she stepped into the throngs of spinning bodies.

Her heels clicked delicately against the obsidian. She had expected the floor to be slick—it shone brilliantly like it was freshly polished—but she found her footing easily. Perhaps that had more to do with the steady arms that encircled her.

Deming met his eyes and instantly felt calm. Sparkles like the gems surrounding them pierced through the swirling tempest of gray. She inhaled sharply. He was so beautiful.

"As are you."

Her cheeks flushed as she realized she said that out loud. Nikita was preening, his wings fluffed out.

"Though," Nikita mused as he maneuvered them expertly around the room, "black is too stark. You belong in jewel tones. Emerald and ruby and amethyst. Colors that drip with decadence."

Deming thought back to Arsaela, to the gowns that were crafted specifically for her. "Those colors are so bold. I always preferred blending into the background more."

"You couldn't blend into the background if you tried."

Deming cut off the undignified laugh that barked out of her. "You didn't know me before. Believe me, I was a wallflower."

The music swelled and Nikita dipped her so low her curls pooled on the floor. Her heart skipped a beat. Midwinter played across her memories like a living painting. They had been here before, his hand splayed across her back, dipping and spinning her in tune with music. It was suddenly to easy to forget that their mating bond had just been announced to the prying ears and eyes of a hundred strangers.

He pulled her up and around, leading her in through choreographed steps. "Do you still feel like a wallflower?"

"In some ways," she admitted, "but mostly, no. I think that part of me died with Miriam."

Her eyes burned. Her grip on Nikita's hand tightened.

"We are not meant to stay the same our entire lives."

"No," she said softly, "I suppose not."

Subtle piano notes lingered in the air as the song ended.

"Should you entertain someone else now?"

Nikita pulled her closer and leaned in. "No," he whispered into her ear.

His breath tickled her skin, sending a shiver of pleasure through her like an arrow.

The musicians started playing something faster paced and without a beat of hesitation Nikita whisked Deming around the floor.

In and out, he pushed and pulled her in tune with the music. He spun her away, clutching her with only one hand, their arms completely extended, then twirled her into his arms. The skirt of her dress was a flower blooming over and over, petaled fabric skimming the stone below that was such a similar color the two bled together seamlessly.

Laughter like sparkling wine bubbled from Deming's lips.

Nikita drew her into him so tightly every inch of her body from chest to hip was touching him.

One hand remained firmly on the small of her back, the other held her hand close, casually. Their fingers were threaded together fiercely. The delicate hold formal dances required long discarded.

They danced through song after song, lost in each other.

During the reprieve of a ballad, long into the night, Deming found herself swaying gently in Nikita's arms. She felt warm and happy, safe and desired. Nikita's hands had touched nearly every part of her as they danced. They skimmed the bare skin of her shoulders, pulled at her fingers, slid up her neck and through the curls of her hair. They guided her through the glittering room through perfectly placed pressure on her back.

Each touch built the fire inside her until now, as she inhaled the sharp cardamon and salt scent of him, her entire belly was warm with pleasure.

"Have your woes been thoroughly cast aside?" she asked breathlessly.

"Nothing chases the shadows away completely," he kissed her neck, "but you do a wonderful job of making a male forget."

"Mmm," she murmured into him, "shadows are no good. I'm sure I have a few more tricks up my sleeves."

He pinched her hip playfully. "You aren't wearing sleeves."

She drew her gaze up. "Gloves, then."

Intrigue lifted the corners of his mouth. "You make it sound like there is something else you wish to do."

Deming took a stuttering breath. She placed a hand on his chest. His heart thudded under her fingertips. "I'd like to be away from prying eyes."

Deming watched as desire kindled in his eyes. She pressed herself ever closer to him, desperate to feel that he wanted this as much as she did.

The thick layers of taffeta made shifting her hips difficult, but Nikita understood.

"You look quite tired, princess." His eyes darkened, his voice a hoarse rumble. "Would you let me walk you to your rooms?"

"Please," she begged.

CHAPTER FORTY THREE

NIKITA

THE RETURN TO NIKITA'S room was a flurry of hushed laughter and hungry anticipation. When they burst through the doors, it was mere moments before they fell onto the mattress.

Deming swung her weight to the side and Nikita joined in her laughter as they twisted in the air, his back collapsing on the bed instead of Deming's.

Mischief twinkled in the warmth of her amber eyes. She adjusted her legs so she sat comfortable atop him. Her weight on his stomach was pleasant and when she leaned down to kiss him, the peaks of her breasts dragged against his chest. He swore he could feel his own heart beat pulse within the inked knot above her heart.

She mumbled into his lips, "My turn to be on top."

Nikita's body tightened in anticipation, a low groan escaping his lips. "Whatever you say, princess."

He relished in the sight of her above him. She was smiling softly, happiness shone through her eyes. These moments between them were fleeting and new and special and he knew she loved them just as much as he did.

Expressing his love through words and openness was something he was working on, something they were both working on, but here, in between the four posters of the bed and blanketed by the quiet of early morning, he felt at ease.

Nikita closed his eyes and sighed as she slid her hands under his shirt. His muscles tensed beneath her touch. Up and up she went, dragging her fingers across his stomach and chest. She tugged at his shirt when she reached his shoulder and he lifted his arms without prodding, helping her pull the fabric off.

He helped Deming make quick work of everything else. The need to feel her skin on his skin, nothing between them, was overwhelming. Once his clothes were a pile beside the bed, Deming lifted herself off him and stood on the hardwood floor.

She was so beautiful. Nikita felt his heart physically skip a beat as he looked at her.

Deming didn't take her eyes off him as she slipped out of the dress she wore and let it fall to the floor. Its absence revealed a thin slip dyed such deep blue it was more akin to the midnight sky than any ocean. Thin lace trim decorated the hem and two slits cut up each side, letting her legs slip out like sunbeams through clouds as she stepped out of the pool of fabric her dress now was on the floor.

It felt like every lick of blood in Nikita's body rushed south as desire gripped him. He needed to touch her, taste her. He needed all of her.

He reached down and gave himself two long, slow strokes. He groaned, eyelids fluttering.

Through the fog of lust and love that coated his vision, Nikita saw Deming watching him. She shivered, licked her lips. Pleasure raced down his spine.

"Like what you see?"

She nodded, her voice long lost.

His teeth bit into his bottom lip and his chest rose and fell in controlled breaths.

Thankfully, for his patience was holding on by a thread, Deming pulled herself back onto the bed and straddled him.

The sight of his mate atop him stoked his simmering desire into a frenzy.

She rolled her hips against him. Nikita knew she could feel just how hard she made him. With nothing but her thin nightgown and underwear separating them, each motion drew them closer and closer together until the fabric had slipped to the side.

"Take those off," he growled.

"So needy."

Deming grabbed his wrist reaching for her hip. Lust crawled from her gaze down his body.

She nuzzled into his neck, pushing onto her knees so Nikita could peel her underwear off her body.

His hand grasped the fabric and pulled. His fingers found their way to her center and dipped in. Instantly, his head craned back, eyes closed in pleasure at the evidence of her desire.

"So wet." His words were barely a growl between clenched teeth.

Deming tilted her head back and whispered into the air, grinding lightly on his hand, "For you, always."

She moaned as he pressed his finger deeper within her. He curled it softly as he exited, then added a second. Always slow, always deliberate. Everything carefully curated so she had enough time to adjust.

He'd had sex in this position before, and assumed Deming had too, but it was clear that being touched this way was new to her. She shifted her legs, trying to find the right way to straddle him while he was inside her like this. Her movements guided his own, every subtle shift or luscious pinch of her nails finding purchase in the soft skin on his thighs told him what she liked.

The bite of pain was a welcome relief, too. The heady atmosphere of sex covered them like the heavy silence the late hours of a winter night brought. Her nails digging into his skin brought him a sense of control, a tether to reality.

Her thighs tightened, moved. Her body swayed like a serpent above his and he swore she looked more goddess than woman.

"Take whatever you need, Deming."

She moaned, her neck rolling to the side and sex clenching around his fingers.

"Do you like when I say your name?"

She hummed her approval and bucked her hips against his palm.

Nikita hadn't been sure at first if she would be able to find her release this way, but with each passing stroke of his fingers her back arched and belly tightened and eyes fluttered.

The pad of his thumb rubbed gently at the apex of her thighs. Each motion timed perfectly with the strokes of his fingers.

Her hips started moving on their own accord, like she was chasing the feeling.

Nikita felt feral with need to please her, to satiate every whim of her desires.

One delicate hand reached to his face. He leaned into her touch, her fingers clutching at black curls. She pulled gently and Nikita felt everything near his hips tighten.

Her head flung back as she bucked her hips against him, begging with the motion of her body for more friction, more touch, more strokes.

Nikita heard her as if she had yelled it to the heavens.

He pushed into her over and over, matching her pace and keeping the pressure exactly where she liked it. "Come for me, Deming."

The moment her name left his lips, she shattered around him.

Nikita watched her, wild and free, bright and beautiful, through the entirety of the fleeting moment.

Deming gasped, panted. She blinked through a pleasure soaked gaze at Nikita. Her eyes were smoldering like a bed of coals.

Nikita could feel the heat in his gaze echo her own. "I will never tire of seeing you like that," he told her.

Deming kissed him slow and deep, then rose with a contented sigh, sinking her hips back on top of his.

"I'll never get tired of any of this."

Nikita gripped her waist tighter at her words.

He knew his eyes belied how much he wanted her, wanted this. He was still painfully aware of the challenges a future together would come with, but the way she held him and loved him and looked at him made it a future he needed desperately.

He needed her like he needed to breathe and wanted her like he had never wanted anyone else before.

Anything the gods wrote into the fabric of the stars was worth fighting for.

She placed a hand on his chest. His heartbeat thundered under her fingertips.

"You're mine and I'm yours," she told him, "and that will be true long after my bones are ash in the wind."

He sucked in a breath, unable to respond as she grasped his length and began pumping her hand slowly.

"Deming."

Her name was a hope, a dream, a promise, a prayer.

She lifted her hips and pressed his tip against her. With delicious slowness, Deming sunk onto him and their voices mingled together in a shared, primal groan.

She sat on him, still for a moment as her body adjusted. The deft work of his fingers had made her pliant and wet and ready. Within moments she began using her legs to move up and down along his length.

Nikita's fists dug into the sheets. The silky fabric twisted messily and was left as much when he brought his hands to her waist once more, guiding her movements with the slightest change of his grip.

The temptation to lose himself in the moment, to urge her to ride him fast and hard until their muscles burned and he was screaming her name was so overwhelming he nearly succumbed—but that wasn't what he wanted. He wanted this to last. He wanted the only world that mattered to be the one right here between him and his mate.

A muscle feathered in his jaw. He was close.

Desperate for this not to end quite yet, Nikita took a steadying breath, gripped her waist, and slowed the rolling of her hips.

She smiled down at him with such admiration.

Nikita was overwhelmed by how unbelievably stunning she was. The curve of her waist. The delicate column of her neck, cocked now and begging to be bit. The daring sparkle in her eyes. The way her hair hung in waves, obscuring her chest teasingly.

She placed her hands on his chest.

"I love your hands on my hips," she whispered into the space their breath shared.

He swore he could feel the golden thread connecting them hum.

If there were any doubts about the mating bond reacting to her words, there could be none about the way he tightened his grip on her.

"I love your hands on my chest."

Where her praise came in breathy pants, his came bracketed by guttural groans.

"Yeah?"

"Yeah," he sighed, relaxing further into the bed.

She kept her hands there as she began moving again.

Every movement highlighted the ebb and flow of the pressure her hands put on his chest and Nikita felt grounded, secure. Her hands like this, pressing into him, added a layer of closeness. His heart beat and skin heated beneath her palms. They moved in tandem, as one.

Always together, never apart.

Exactly what he wanted.

Wherever Deming was, was where he was meant to be. He was most free beneath her touch, most at peace. The world blacked out and for once all that mattered was what he wanted, what he needed.

Nikita tensed under her. "I'm close."

Deming leaned forward. She kept one hand over his heart but slid the other one up the backside of his neck. When she nipped at the corner of his mouth he took her lips in his, kissing her with a ferocity that delighted them both.

She pulled away and his eyes snapped to hers.

Wild and reckless, lust and love. He was her undoing and she was his.

"My mate," he panted, everything he felt and hoped laid bare in his gaze.

"My mate." She leaned in close, writhing on top of him to the rhythm of his hips. Faster and faster he pumped into her and she met him stroke for stroke.

They were heat and friction and pleasure and when she whispered her final command into the space between their lips, he obeyed with vigor.

"Come for me."

His head pressed back into the pillows and undeniable pleasure rippled through his entire being. It was a lightning strike, a crashing wave against cliffs. It was the culmination of desire and love and want and need.

It was ecstasy.

Deming leaned down and pressed kisses on the pulsing veins in his neck as Nikita gripped her hips tight and pushed into her one last time.

He relaxed beneath her and their bodies softened into each other and the sheets. Nikita's world was all skin and breath and sweat slicking down his back and thighs. He stayed there, beneath her, for as long as he could. He held her close, murmuring her name in her ear over and over.

When their breathing returned to normal and the sensation of sweat coating their bodies turned from erotic to uncomfortable, he lifted her away from his chest and flopped her onto the bed beside him.

Looking at him through long lashes and heavy eyes, she asked, "Bathe with me?"

"Of course, princess. Then we should rest."

Before they could move, the insular world they had built between breath and sheets and soft kisses shattered as screams burst from the edges of the city.

Chapter Forty Four

Nikita

Ilysse threw open the door with a crash.

She halted and cast her eyes down upon seeing them tangled in the sheets. "Fuck, sorry," she growled. "Get up, now."

"What's happening?" he asked urgently, throwing a blanket over Deming's naked body.

"Amphithere attack."

Nikita, who had tensed the moment they heard the rising voices outside, downright shot out of bed at that. "That's not possible."

"Look for yourself."

He pulled trousers on and flew to the window.

"Amphitheres have never attacked a human or Fae settlement in the history of the continent." His words were breathless as he threw himself against the edge of the window with such force the stone nearly creaked in protest.

Below, the city of Bascade was burning.

Fire raced across rooftops and wound up trees. Families and children screamed as they ran from falling limbs and doors and walls.

How could this much damage be done so quickly?

An ancient, bellowing roar sounded.

When Nikita found the source, icy fear flooded his veins.

A massive black amphithere cut through the clouds, flames spilling from his jaws like lava.

Ilysse spoke low. "Your father will want you to go to the internal chambers."

Nikita shook his head. "My people are dying and my city is burning, I will not hide." He turned around, already throwing on a vest of thick hide. Not armor, but it would have to do. "Get a horse from the stables and find whoever is leading the defense. Is Merritt still in charge of the city guard?"

Ilysse nodded. "I believe so."

"Find her. I'm sure she will be working to secure the perimeter of the city. Send any injured or young to the castle. Anyone of age is to either douse the fires or band together and drive the threat from the city."

He looked to Deming. She was still in his bed, sheets twisted around her legs and waist. Her hair was wild, her face flush. She had slid a shirt over herself and was buttoning it up with trembling fingers.

"I can't ask you to fight for—"

"I will fight." The words were strong, sure. "I am not a liability," she said directly to Ilysse, who had opened her mouth to protest.

"We don't have time to argue," Nikita said, silencing his captain. "Ilysse, the perimeter. That's a command."

"Yes, Prince." She inclined her head and darted from the room.

Nikita turned to Deming as they both rushed to finish dressing. "Where is Rendrel?"

"Nearby."

"Can you ride her well enough to fight astride her?"

"Yes."

Nikita bit his lip. He resented the doubt that grew like a weed within him but Deming and Rendrel had only flown together once.

"I can do this." Fire burned in her eyes. "Let me help."

After a tense second, Nikita nodded. He offered a hand and she took it.

He swept her into his arms and leapt into the sky in one fell swoop.

There was only the one amphithere. It circled Bascade like a vulture. The moon illuminated black feathers and scales that matched the darkness of the night sky. Smoke spilled from its maw. Its eyes glowed like burning suns. There was an aura about this one that alerted Nikita's senses. Its flight was erratic. Its call harsh and cruel and foreboding.

And Rendrel was indeed nearby.

Before Nikita had a chance to scour the skies for her green form, she had burst through the treetops, screeching wildly and racing towards the black amphithere.

"Rendrel!" Deming's petrified voice shot violently through the air. She reached towards her bonded, pressing against Nikita's grip on her despite the fact that he was still carrying them high above the ground.

Whether Deming's voice reached Rendrel or something was shared through their bond, the green amphithere dove up and around the attacking beast and turned towards them instead.

"Bring me down, please!"

Deming pressed her hands firmly on his chest and for the first time, Nikita fully realized the extent of the Rider's bond that his mate and Rendrel shared. It was new, but potent. Deming may not fully understand it yet, but she cared for the fearsome creature flying towards them just as much as she cared for him.

They landed and Deming leapt from his arms.

Rendrel roared in greeting and lowered her thick chest and neck close to the ground. Deming ran towards the amphithere and pulled herself in between her expansive, feathered wings as if it was the most natural thing in the world.

She murmured something to Rendrel as she quickly tied her hair back. It was tangled and knotted. Deming's face was pinched with concentration as she shifted into a more comfortable position between Rendrel's wings. She flexed her hand, testing her magic. Light flared and simmered beneath her skin.

Then, with both hands grasping at the downy feathers where wings bled into scales, Deming looked back to him.

Such unbridled love barreled down the bond connecting them that Nikita was nearly knocked back by the force of it. She was too far away to say anything to him, but Nikita understood the message as if she had spoken it directly into his ear.

I love you. Be safe.

He sent a mirror of her emotion back to her.

She smiled before melding into Rendrel's spine. The amphithere took to the skies in a tight spiral with a roar.

Nikita beamed with pride. That was his mate.

He had no time to admire her further as the earth rumbled like it was on the verge of collapsing.

Nikita bent his knees, absorbing the shock, and turned to the commotion.

A redwood had fallen.

Bark and leaves blazed with orange flames. Screams of pain and terror filled the air. Fae, young and old, carried buckets of water from the wells scattered through the city to try and save their homes and storefronts and gathering places.

So much destruction, so quickly committed.

Nikita barked out commands as he ran, guiding people to the areas of the city that had yet to fall into disarray and ordering the injured to the castle. He had little time to hope that his father had enough humanity to let them in.

From the corner of his eye, he saw the familiar glint of the royal crest. His hand jerked out, grasping into the rough cotton of the standard issue jacket all castle guards wore.

"Who is commanding you? What are their orders?"

Startled brown eyes widened. "Captain Merritt, sir. We have been commanded to sequester as much of the city into the northern quarter as possible. If you are missing a loved one they may be in the castle." Recognition lit the guard's face and he stumbled over his next words. "Prince Nikita, I didn't know you were on the ground. If you have a different command—"

"No," Nikita interjected, "follow your captain's orders. Where has the city been hit the hardest?"

"The southern half with a focus on the trade district."

Nikita thanked the guard gruffly, expanded his wings, and took off into the air. The corridors of his city were laid out below him and he followed them like a map. Away from the opulence of the castle and towards where the guard said help was needed most.

Ash puffed up in clouds when his feet touched ground.

The chaos of bodies and voices was dimmer here, giving way to the oppressive heat of the flames. In fact, Nikita couldn't see a single Fae in his immediate surroundings.

"Is anyone here?"

The crinkle of flame eating away at wood was the only answer.

Then, a scuffle up ahead. Boots on rubble.

"I am here to help!" Nikita called, walking towards where the sound originated.

He turned a corner and suddenly a blast of fire landed where his feet had just been.

The impact of the fire blast sent him crashing to the ground. Heat so intense it felt as if his feathers should combust and his skin should melt off his bones rolled over him in waves. Rocks and dirt and broken pieces of building bit into his clothes and stomach and face and palms as he skid across the ground. He only stopped when his back smacked into a wall.

Nikita's vision blurred. The edges of the world darkened and wobbled. He blinked. He tried to inhale and coughed out smoke.

He raised a hand to the back of his pounding head. It came away stained red, though Nikita's attention was quickly drawn away from his injury and to the limp body beside him.

Caught in the same blast, thrown into the same wall, was a dark-skinned male. His tawny eyes slit like a cat's stared blankly and unblinking at the stars above. Blood seeped from where his head had connected with a jagged, broken stone.

That could have been Nikita. A few inches separated their fates.

As gently as he could, Nikita closed the males eyes. The thudding in his skull no longer seemed all that important.

The black amphithere curled away from the wake of its destruction and back into the sky.

What was prompting this? Amphitheres were peaceful—if not elusive and powerful—creatures. It made no sense—

A low growl reverberated through the flames.

Nikita's stomach sank.

Not again, not now. Wasn't a raging amphithere enough?

Like a demon from the pits of the underworld, a snarling, quilled, muscled leodin pawed through the flames.

Nikita unsheathed the sword he had snagged from the floor of his room. His feet ground into the dirt, stance firm. And when the leodin attacked, he was ready.

They were a flurry of claws and teeth and metal and limbs.

Nikita sank deep within himself as he fought the beast. There was nothing else but the breath in his lungs and the sword in his hand. It was an extension of himself as he danced with the leodin.

Nikita threw all the force he could upwards, catching the leodin in the jaw with the hilt of his weapon. Quills scratched at his arms. Fighting in close quarters with an animal like this was a horrid experience.

His blow landed soundly though, and the leodin jerked backwards, stumbling over the jagged ground and hitting a wall.

Only then, when he had a short reprieve, did realization crash into Nikita.

They knew the aggressive leodins were a product of Khalil's parasites. If one was here—

His eyes darted to the skies, tracking the black amphithere. Rendrel's green scales glistened as she chased it through the clouds.

Horror like poison spilled through him.

Was that even possible?

The leodin pushed itself away from the wall, shaking its head. Golden eyes full of predatory precision honed in on him.

Nikita steadied his grip on the sword.

The flames had stopped raining down on them, though the drum-like beat of wings and bellowing roars still filled the air. One look upwards and Nikita saw why.

Rendrel, with Deming on her back, was wrapping around the black amphithere in a tight spiral. Up and up and up they soared, Rendrel's body acting as a cage as she nipped at the other beast's wings. Light flared—Deming's magic—in spurts towards the black scaled head and open maw.

Terror seized through Nikita's spine.

His distraction cost him.

The leodin leapt off its hind legs and launched itself towards him.

Nikita moved a millisecond too late and the knife-like claws that were unsheathed snagged into the muscle on his bicep. Searing pain lanced through him.

He hit the ground, sword knocked loose from his grip. His hand flew to the injury on instinct to staunch the blood. It leaked out of him with dangerous consistency.

With a growl and a twist of its spine, the leodin stalked towards him.

Nikita scrambled away. His wings opened, ready to fly. He was not prideful enough to try to finish a battle he knew he had already lost but just as he propelled himself skyward, the leodin pounced and batted him out of the air. This time, its claws tore through one of his wings.

Nikita yelled in pain as he was dragged down to the ground again. He grit his teeth through the agony in his wing and twisted on the ground to face the quilled big cat.

A screeching yowl pierced the air.

Nikita reoriented himself just in time to see a sword slide through the ribs of the leodin. The animal fell, jerking and writhing on the ground as blood pooled out of its chest.

He looked up to see who had saved him.

"Paris?"

Shield cracked down the middle and soot smeared with blood across his face, Paris stared down at the Prince of Runne. He extended a hand and lifted Nikita to his feet.

"What are you doing here?"

"Saving you," Paris said bluntly, "apparently."

Nikita took a moment to steady himself. The leodin lay dead at their feet, blood seeping into the grass and the leather of their boots. No one else seemed to be present. Any noises of chaos were farther away. "The rest of the residents in this quarter?"

"Evacuated."

"Have you seen Ilysse?"

"No," Paris wiped his blade on his shirt, "but I have seen another leodin. Hartford and Soraya are close to the castle helping the injured."

"The leodin's presence—"

"Khalil," Paris interrupted with a grimace, "yeah, I had the same thought."

"I need to tell Deming. Her and Rendrel can track the amphithere to him. We might have a chance to save Vallyn."

Emotion crested in Paris's blue eyes like a wave. Nikita had the fleeting thought that perhaps Paris, more than anyone, felt alone here.

"I'll track the other leodin. Check for more survivors."

"Paris," Nikita called out. The blonde turned to look at him. "Thank you."

"Any time."

Then they parted ways.

Nikita allowed himself a full minute to catch his breath and wrap a ripped piece of fabric around the wound on his arm before he turned his attention to Deming.

His eyes darted to the sky.

Where was she? Rendrel was nowhere in sight.

Had they fallen?

No, he would have sensed any pain or injury through the bond.

The sky was charred with smoke and ash. There was no flicker of green or light magic to be seen.

The black amphithere, though, was still there. Its flight was choppy, stunted. Rendrel and Deming must have injured it.

He needed to get to Deming, needed to tell her about the leodins. This may be their one shot to find Vallyn. If she missed it, he knew she would never forgive herself. His teeth ground at the thought.

He sent a pulse of urgency down the bond and hoped Deming felt it.

His wing too torn to fly, Nikita ran through the streets of Bascade. He needed to get outside the city limits, he needed to find somewhere that Rendrel could land.

His eyes flashed to the skies.

The black amphithere was retreating.

He pumped his arms. His lungs burned, his thighs ached. The wound on his bicep dripped blood as he ran faster, faster.

He pushed another thread of desperation to Deming.

A flicker of curiosity and worry was sent back immediately.

If Nikita had spare breath to speak, he may have sent a prayer up to the gods.

With every ounce of clarity he could muster, he begged down the bond for Deming to find him.

The city was little more than ash around him. The further he got from the castle, the less stone there was. Out here, houses were all wood and thatched roofs between massive trees. Everything was flammable. Destruction was rampant.

At that exact moment, a shard of alarm singed down the bond and a roar echoed through the skies.

Deming and Rendrel.

Nikita looked up just as the serpentine shadow of Rendrel's body fell over him.

"A leodin," he yelled up to Deming as her and Rendrel landed.

"What?" Deming lifted her leg, making to dismount.

Nikita threw his hand up, "No! Don't dismount." Breathless and side aching, he pushed through the explanation. "There were leodins in the city. The attack," he heaved in air to his lungs, "was Khalil's doing."

Understanding sparked in Deming's eyes. She looked to where the black amphithere was retreating.

"Go," Nikita urged, "track it, find Vallyn."

Rendrel flared her wings and with two powerful beats of them, they were airborne.

Chapter Forty Five

Deming

DEMING'S PULSE WAS A hummingbird in her veins. Twitchy, quick. Adrenaline had raised her heart rate to levels she had never experienced before as she and Rendrel fought the other amphithere and then the sight of Nikita ragged and bloody and injured—

"He will live, Light Heart."

Deming leaned closer to Rendrel, finding the slimmest ray of comfort in her amphithere's voice and the warmth of her scales.

"I am tired of seeing my loved ones hurt. I want this to be over."

"The only way out is through."

Rendrel wove through the sky like thread through needle at such a speed that wind tore at Deming's face and hair. She loved the feeling. Even the soreness in her fingers from gripping Rendrel's wings was a pleasant ache. When she told Nikita that she could do this, ride Rendrel during battle, she had spoken more to a hope than a known truth. Perhaps her bones had known. Perhaps whatever part of her had already been stitched to Rendrel through their bond had known. Whatever the case, it was true.

Deming could ride. She could ride well.

It was the most natural feeling in the world to sit snugly between Rendrel's wings and soar through the air. The barbs of Rendrel's scales kept her secure, but Deming thought that even without them she would feel safe.

She had always known that she belonged in the clouds.

So now, though they were racing through the air at top speed towards an amphithere that had just laid waste to an entire city, Deming felt in control.

Anxious for those she loved—Nikita with his torn wings, Paris in a city at siege, Vallyn lost—but in control.

Rendrel banked and gravity tugged at Deming's body. She frowned against the wind. She had been almost certain that Khalil and Dresden would have gone somewhere completely different but based on the direction Rendrel was flying...

"He's heading north?" She asked Rendrel.

"Towards the western Telaciens, yes."

The western Telaciens.

That was Laey.

"Faster," she urged Rendrel.

For nearly an hour, they tracked Weirfenn.

Deming knew his name because Rendrel knew his name. He was the missing amphithere from their band, the one that had disappeared near the time that Deming found out she was a Rider. Nikita's comment early was accurate. Amphitheres had never attacked human or Fae in the history of the continent. With the presence of the leodins in Bascade, it was all Deming could do but hope that their hunch was wrong and Khalil hadn't somehow gotten his parasites into Weirfenn.

Rendrel held out no such hope.

"What will you do with him?" Deming had asked.

"That is for the band to decide together." Unfamiliar worry had coated Rendrel's voice. *"This is unprecedented and unacceptable."*

The insinuation was clear. If the evil power controlling him could not be removed, Weirfenn would have to die.

That was a problem for another time. One that Deming was not likely to have a say in despite being a Rider, despite her bearing the Seal.

What she did have a say in, however, was Vallyn.

As they followed the wavering path of Weirfenn through the clouds, anxiety spiked sharp and pointed in her gut. It had been weeks since she had last seen Vallyn. Though she wanted to believe that she would know if Vallyn had died, that she would feel some shift in the universe, Deming knew that was a fool's belief.

They had no idea what had happened to her. They had no idea if she was alive.

All Deming could do was grasp this thin thread of hope that Weirfenn had given them and pray that Vallyn was at the end of it.

The Telaciens loomed in the distance. Slowly, the peaks grew closer and closer until Rendrel was soaring over the mountain range and into the wilderness beyond.

As vast as the pine forests in and around Arsaela were, they were nothing compared to what sprawled out below them now. The valleys of the mountains here were so thick and lush it looked like it was coated in a layer of dense moss instead of trees. The greenery climbed up the rocky edges of the peaks, gradually becoming smaller and less vibrant, until only steep, inclined rock topped with glistening snow and ice remained.

Deming looked out at the wilderness, her gaze trailing from where Rendrel's wings beat at her side to straight ahead, above the amphithere's feathered crest. On and on, the mountains went. They touched the horizon, and then went beyond even that.

This was the true north. Home to no monarch, no country. The terrain was harsh, the weather and beasts that roamed the land harsher.

It was remote. Inhabitable.

Perfect for a place to hide.

So when a nudge of recognition flared down the bond and Deming finally saw what Rendrel had minutes prior, she was only marginally surprised.

Hidden in swaths of pine and the shadows of the mountain stood the ruins of a castle.

Weirfenn circled a turret and roared before diving behind the crumbling building and into the depths of the forest beyond.

They flew closer, cautious and slow.

The gate was rusted and bent. The windows were long since shattered. Half of the building was in disrepair, ivy draped across fallen and secured stones alike. And there, darting through one of the hallways open to the elements because the walls had collapsed, was a flash of fur and quills.

At the sight of the leodin, urgency blared through her like a horn. Vallyn was here, she was sure of it. They had found her. "We could go in now. Weirfenn is injured and I've seen you snap a leodin's spine with ease." Her thighs squeezed into Rendrel. "I have more control over my magic than I did before. I could—"

"Simmer your fire, Light Heart."

A feeling akin to a towel soaked in ice water being laid on her forehead enveloped Deming through the silver bond between her and Rendrel.

With an adjustment to her wings and a coil of her body, Rendrel dove down sharply, banked, then soared into the clouds back in the direction of Bascade.

Deming was seconds from protesting when Rendrel sent another soothing wave of emotion down the bond.

"We know where she is. Sometimes the best thing we can do is wait."

Deming bit her lip. "It doesn't feel good to do nothing when my friend is in there. We've been waiting for so long already to find out where she is and now..." Her voice trailed off limply because she knew Rendrel was right.

"We will need the rest of your companions to rescue the moon-touched human. We need a plan, and time to recover from Weirfenn's attack."

Deming loosened her grip on the feathers and muscle underneath her. Rising up in her seat like she would do in the stirrups of a saddled horse, Deming looked back at the crumbling winter castle.

Cold and forlorn, it stared back.

She swallowed hard and prayed that Vallyn could last a little longer.

"We will find her. For now, the people of Bascade need your magic."

Deming settled down against Rendrel's scales. At the mention of her magic, light pulsed from her palms.

They would rescue Vallyn, but they would do it right this time.

CHAPTER FORTY SIX

DEMING

DEMING HELD THE KNOWLEDGE of Vallyn's location close to her heart as they reentered Bascade hours later.

She could scarcely believe her eyes as they flew to the nearest cries for help. Though she could see no leodins prowling the streets and Weirfenn was long gone licking his wounds, the city was still drowning in tragedy.

Thatched roofs smoked and crackled, falling in on the houses they were supposed to protect, raining ash and embers onto the Fae within.

And everywhere, screams.

Screams of panic. Screams of grief. Screams of terror.

Her heart clenched. Not everyone had been able to evacuate.

The din of voices swallowed her own, though Rendrel always heard her.

"There," she yelled, pointing to a mass of people crowding around a fountain. They were trying to use the water to put out a row of houses on fire. A string of Fae lay huddled against the trunk of a grand tree nearby, either oblivious of or too hurt to move away from the flaming branches above them.

Rendrel got as close as she could to a nearby roof and slowed down just enough for Deming to leap off her back. The roof crunched and crackled under her weight, causing her to stumble into an over the shoulder roll.

"I will return once I speak to the Crest Major about Weirfenn."

Rendrel coiled away into the sky too quickly for Deming to respond. Instead, she shimmied down the side of the house, feet reaching for window sills and hands on drain pipes, then joined the fray.

It had looked gut wrenching from above, but the chaos of the fire was so much worse on the ground.

Mothers ran through the streets with children in their arms, clothes torn or burnt and ash and bruises littering their skin. Guards yelled words that no one heeded. The heat rose and rose and rose until it was nearly suffocating.

Someone collided into Deming's shoulder and she spiraled to the ground, hitting the dirt hard. A grunt of pain breached her lips as she tenderly rose, trying desperately to get to the towering tree and mass of Fae beneath it.

"You have to move!"

Her voice was drowned out by the din of panic. Why was no one else warning them? Faster, she needed to get to them faster or they would burn.

She raised her hands above her head, waving them as she yelled again, "The limbs are on fire! You have to—"

A deafening crack sounded through the courtyard and a wide, flaming limb of the giant redwood fell.

Deming watched through bleary eyes, tears having sprung to them the instant the wood split. She heard refreshed screams, knew that her own voice mingled with those under the tree who were scrambling away from near certain death.

Seconds stretched out impossibly long. Each inch the limb fell felt etched into the very core of her and suddenly she was violently thrown back a decade.

Flashes of fire swirling, climbing, licking up her skin. Pain and heat and fear. Heavy beams crashing from the ceiling. Embers like fireflies swirling around dead bodies—

Deming blinked away the memory and found herself kneeling on the ground, breath ragged, fingers digging so hard into the dirt two of her nails had cracked.

Her neck snapped up.

The scene before her chilled her straight to the bone,

A girl, no more than seven, lay crushed under the weight of the bough. Her eyes were wild with fear and pain, her mouth open in a bloody scream. The flames had claimed one side of her hair, diminishing the blonde strands to crackling ash. Tears stained her pink cheeks.

Her hip was stuck under—

Her stomach, gods, oh gods.

Her stomach was flayed open. So much worse than Paris's wound had been. Blood was already pooling underneath her, staining the grass and soaking into the dirt.

A child shouldn't feel pain like this.

A child shouldn't be a victim.

She was too young to die.

Deming's head felt fuzzy and heavy as she crawled the rest of the way to her. She took the girl's hand. Her grip was tense and panicked at first but even within the first seconds Deming could feel her grip slackening. The light in her eyes dimmed, the intensity of her pained screams receded.

"Stay with me," Deming begged, "I can help, I can heal you, please stay with me."

This close to the tree, the heat was oppressive. The fallen branch had not caught yet, thankfully, but the trunk was now swallowed in waves of red and orange and yellow.

"Help me," she croaked to anyone who would listen. "Water," she yelled louder, looking behind her. "We need water!"

Someone, somewhere obeyed and both Deming and the girl were doused in a chilly splash, the flames kissing her skin extinguished.

"Lift the branch!"

Strong hands rolled the smoking limb off the girl, leaving her free for Deming to crawl closer and hover her hands over the open wound.

She willed her hands to stop trembling but couldn't manage it.

Deming turned her attention to the girl. The girl's eyes were blue like the sky. "What's your name?"

"Danae." Her voice feathered and cracked. Her eyelids fluttered heavily.

Deming swallowed hard. "Okay, Danae. I need you to stay awake, can you do that? I'm going to help you but you have to stay awake, okay?"

Danae nodded her head just so, but its weight sank further into the grass all the same.

"Stay awake," Deming pleaded once more, then began.

The whispers behind her faded to oblivion as Deming sank into her power as fast and controlled as she could, reaching for the healing warmth that threaded itself throughout her like a vein.

It answered her call willingly, springing to her fingertips with an ease that Deming would appreciate once this nightmare was over. Warmth filled her from head to toe as she concentrated her power on Danae's abdomen.

The skin was torn and burnt and bloody. Deming tucked her horror far away into the depths of her mind. Shoved the stench of burning flesh down, down, down. She would not let this girl die. Could not let her die.

She started with the internal damage and worked her way out, staunching blood loss and cleaving blood vessels and stitching flesh then skin back together piece by piece like embroidery.

Deming's eyes closed as she fell into the trance her light magic brought on. This need not be a conscious effort. She knew what to do. Her body knew what to do. It was as natural as breathing once she let the magic guide her.

Each breath in and out was like a wave rocking with her power. Ebbing and flowing, light poured from her hands and into the child until Deming knew without opening her eyes that the wound was healed.

Coming back to earth was sobering. Her limbs felt heavy with life and exertion. But it was worth it.

Danae's abdomen was smooth and fresh. Blood stained her skin, but the wound was sealed.

She had done it. She had healed her.

Deming wiped the tears away from her cheeks and looked up to Danae, eager to reassure the girl that she was okay and would live and had a long, long life ahead of—

Danae's crystalline blue eyes stared up at her unblinking, lifeless.

The pool of blood beneath her had grown. When did that happen? How quickly does it take to bleed out?

Deming's throat locked up. She looked to Danae's chest for one, two, three long seconds only for the fragile cage to remain still and unmoving, no breath within.

No, that couldn't be possible.

She had healed the wound. It was fine, Danae was fine. She was alive and could run to find her mother and father.

She shook the small shoulders in her hands and something inside her crumbled watching her body shift limply back and forth.

Deming forgot how to breathe herself, how to move, how to think.

What use was her light magic if she couldn't save those who needed it most? She had been right there, she couldn't have gotten to Danae sooner, couldn't have done anything more. Her power leapt to her fingertips like it never had before and it still hadn't been enough?

The thought seemed impossible.

Deming scooped the girl into her arms and let muffled cries escape into her unbearably small body.

She deserved so much better than this.

It was only when a hand gripped her shoulder that Deming remembered where she was and why the little girl in her arms had died.

Bascade was burning.

"You just used light magic."

Deming looked up, eyes bleary, to see a female with spiraled horns gazing down at her with an awed and hopeful expression. Pure, honest hope shone from the female's expression. She looked at Deming like she was a deity.

With the rarity of light magic, she supposed she was close enough to that.

Deming must have looked blankly back at the Fae because she clarified, "You're a healer?"

Deming nodded, blinked away the all encompassing grief that was rising within her like a storm, threatening to pull her under in a way that felt utterly familiar and foreign at the same time.

The female's face collapsed in relief. She gestured toward an elderly male, likely her father if the shared sharp, almond shape of their eyes was any indication. She was speaking to Deming but her words went in one ear and out the other. All she could hear was the crashing of waves that didn't exist.

Deming stood and followed the horned female across the courtyard.

Danae's body slipped from her arms, and Deming knew the wet clothes had nothing to do with how chilled to the bone she felt.

The male was leaning against the dirty wall of a shop off the main street. His tail flicked slowly through the dirt as Deming knelt next to him.

His shoulder was dislocated, that was easy enough to see. He shifted and grimaced against the pain. He wasn't bleeding. A small gift.

His daughter was still speaking and Deming was still unable to grasp any of the words coming from her. She heard them, knew they were from the common tongue, and yet could not retain any meaning.

It didn't matter, not truly. The female's father was injured, and Deming could heal him.

Deming felt like she might cry but no tears came.

Her chest felt cold and still, a frozen wasteland amid the scorching fire around them.

She lifted her hands and called to her power. It rose within her easily, like whatever knot it had been tangled up in before had come undone with one perfect tug of a string. Warmth flooded her senses, though this time it didn't reach her heart. That was locked away from reality.

She did not need her heart to heal.

Didn't need to feel to help.

Instead, she fell back into the newfound ease of her magic and put the Fae out of his pain.

It was easy, uncomplicated. Nothing like stitching back together organs and layers and layers and layers of muscle and skin.

She turned away from the pair, ignoring their cries of thanks as they shuffled away from the courtyard, and faced the chaos once more. There was more fire than there had been before, if that was possible. How would they possibly stall the flames from leaping through the wooded city? Did they have no precautions to this eventuality? If not an amphithere attack, then a forest fire or a fallen festival lantern.

Useless thoughts.

They were here, now.

Every inch of Bascade was littered with the injured and dead. She couldn't do anything for the latter or the loved ones that were draped over their bodies, but she could help the former.

Deming moved through the crowds unhurriedly. There was no need to rush. Every step she took there was someone to aid. Her hands warmed and glowed as she healed burns and broken bones and torn muscles and more burns and burns and burns. So much scorched skin. The air was filled with its smell.

She spoke to no one, saw nothing but the injuries as they appeared before her.

No other bodies died in her hands as she worked.

Only Danae.

Deming thought that name would be branded into her soul for the rest of her life.

Chapter Forty Seven

Deming

"Deming?"

Her name sounded foreign. No one had spoken it in years.

She shook her head. Hours, not years. This was, somehow, still the same day her and Nikita had been thrust out of bed and into battle.

Though she blinked away the fog in her mind, the sun's rays were peeking over the horizon. The second day, then. And what a life altering second day it was looking to be. There would be countless families waking up in grief over loss. Lost lives, lost homes, lost sanity.

Where Deming fell in all of that, she wasn't sure. These people were not her people and yet her heart ached for them as if they were.

She pulled herself away from the young boy whose leg she had just repaired from the nasty burn that a collapsed thatched roof had inflicted.

Nikita stood before her.

He was bloody and bruised. Ash coated every inch of him from his face to his clothing to his wings. His bicep was still bandaged. Dark, dry blood stained the fabric. His normally iridescent feathers were dim with soot and one hung lower than the other.

A pang of love rattled through her hollow chest and she supposed that whatever was his, was hers, too. Whatever he loved, she loved. Whatever he fought for, she fought for. This city, these people, they were dear to him so they were dear to her.

He closed the gap between them and took her into his arms.

The solidity of his presence snapped something into place inside her.

Everything these past few hours had blurred together in a mess of wounds and ticking clocks and blood and fire and draining, draining, draining magic. She was tired to her bones and when Nikita wrapped his arms around her she allowed herself to feel it all for the first time since Danae died in her arms.

"It's okay," he hushed, cradling her head close, "It's okay, it's over."

"She died." Sobs wracked her body, the loss fresh and pain fervent.

Nikita stilled, curious and careful. "Who died?"

"Danae."

He didn't recognize the name, why would he? She had been one lonely child in the midst of a blustering capital city but somehow she was simultaneously no one and everyone. Every lost girl, every hurt girl, every broken piece of Deming's own past and present and future. And though, rationally, Deming knew it to be false, a small, vicious part of her felt that if she was unable to save Danae she would be unable to save herself.

She had been doing so well.

It was demoralizing, feeling the deep pull of tragedy trying to sink her once more.

She looked to Nikita with wide eyes, silently begging for a lifeline.

"Talk to me," he said softly, "what happened?"

The memory was so fresh, so new that it felt like poking a raw wound but Deming dug into the pain, desperate for anything to distract her from the siren call of profound sadness and guilt. "She was trapped under a tree. The branch was on fire. I tried to warn them but it was too late." Her voice came out in chunks, linking labored breath with words that felt more piecemeal than sentences strung together. "It was like Paris. But worse." She shook her head violently, trying to pry the image of the girl's mauled and charred flesh from the inside of her mind. "I healed her body but it…" Her throat closed up. The words she was attempting to say were physically choking her.

Nikita pulled her upright as she coughed.

"I healed her body," she started again, "but she had already died. I wasn't fast enough. I wasn't good enough."

He kissed her hair. "You helped so many people tonight—"

"Not enough."

It would never be enough. Unless Deming could protect everyone, save everyone, it would never be enough. And that was impossible, she knew it was impossible, but still it rang true in her bones.

While she had healing magic coursing through her veins, no loss of life in her arms would ever be acceptable.

Did he understand that?

She looked at him. His eyes were cloudy with exhaustion. Shame flooded her. Utterly foolish of her to think only of herself, once again.

"How are you?"

He leaned into her hand, closed his eyes in a brief moment of reprieve. "It was difficult to fight something we have never had to fight before. Armored hide. Flight. Unending fire." He opened his eyes. "We lost many already, and more will succumb to their injuries."

At the mention of injuries, Deming's eyes flashed to Nikita's.

"I'm fine, really—"

But Deming's hands were already on his arm, sending warmth and healing magic into the torn muscle. She grimaced when she turned her attention to his wing. As delicately as she could manage, she threaded her fingers into his feathers. Most were bloody, many were bent and broken.

"Ilysse?"

"Ilysse is fine. A few scrapes and a nasty burn on the back of her calf."

The three of them had survived. That was a blessing.

Deming sighed in relief and exhaustion. She pulled her hand away from Nikita's now healed wing. He tested it gingerly.

"Thank you." He pulled her in close. "I'm sorry you were alone." The press of his lips into her pulse grounded her. Then, after a pause, "How old was she?"

Blue eyes. Gangly limbs. Blonde, wispy hair, half burnt to the scalp.

Flashes of her darted across Deming's mind. She blinked the image away but it remained burned into her, like the impression of the sun when you accidentally look directly at it. She wondered how long it would be until Danae's tiny, limp frame wasn't the first thing she saw when she closed her eyes.

Maybe it always would be.

"No more than seven."

A deep, soul-tired sigh filled Nikita's lungs, then left. Deming rose and fell against his chest with the movement. He clung to her tighter, pulling her fully into his lap. She relished the contact. Even if he said nothing, and he did say nothing for a while, the more he touched her, the calmer she felt.

The sun rose on Bascade and in the light, everything seemed less dire. Smoke was still curling from rooftops and trees, but the flames themselves had been extinguished long before. Fae roamed the streets. Most were already beginning the process of rebuilding. Branches were being collected, sidewalks were being swept. One middle aged male was holding a front door up while his son fiddled with the hinges.

Of course, there were also the angsty calls for loved ones lost in the chaos, or ones who had left to battle the beast and had not returned. Those cries had slowed to a drip as the sun rose, most had given up hope long before dawn.

The few straggling people still searching for their young added a layer of somberness to the morning and Deming felt a sense of belonging with those grieving so outwardly.

Bits and pieces of the air could have smelled lovely and comforting, like a campfire or logs burning in a warm room during winter, but all Deming could smell was death.

The sun was rising and the survivors were leaning into hope but today, for Deming, hope would be tucked away. She needed time to mourn.

That was okay, she thought. It was okay to feel deeply. To feel was to live.

"I'd like to go back to the castle."

Nikita stood, lifting her body with his own. He kept an arm on her shoulder and a wing curled around her body as they walked back to the castle.

"I'm sorry that she died," he said quietly, "That must have been horrible to experience."

Not because she knew her personally, she didn't. Not even because it was a failure of her magic, though it was. But because the tragedy of watching someone so young die was an affront to everything the world was built on. Children were not supposed to die. They were supposed to be the future. What had Danae dreamed of? Who had she loved? What would she have become if death hadn't snatched her away too soon?

It was horrible too, because Danae felt like a mirror to Deming's younger self. Watching her hurt and burn was like watching herself hurt and burn. Watching her die was like watching herself die. It hit too close to home. Holding Danae in her arms as she died had torn open wounds long since stitched shut. She felt bare and raw.

It was all Deming could do to nod and let him lead her back to the castle.

No amount of hot water and soap could wash away the feeling of despair.

Deming sighed heavily and rose from the bath, wrapping herself in one of the many fluffy towels provided to her by the servant assigned to their rooms.

Danilyn. That was her name. Golden hair like spun sunlight. Soft lips and sad eyes that had been wet and red this morning. She hadn't had to say she had lost a loved one. It was written across her face boldly for all to see.

Almost everyone wore a similar expression.

Those that didn't—the lucky ones—may have shed less tears but were altered all the same. To see such devastation was sure to change a person. To see so many die...Deming wasn't sure how a city was meant to recover.

War hadn't touched the continent in ages. Even with the lifespan of the Fae, many in Bascade had never had to defend their city against a normal attack of foot soldiers and archers, let alone against a full fledged, fire-breathing, iron hide amphithere.

What could have possibly provoked the beast?

That was what Nikita and his father, along with their royal council, were discussing right now.

He had been whisked away the moment they returned to the castle, swept into meeting after meeting without so much as a second to change his clothes or wash the blood from his face. He had given Deming a look that told her to take care of herself and then was pulled into the duties of his station as if his father had never banished him at all.

Tragedy had a way of bringing people together, as morose as it was.

Deming wondered if the inclusion would hold once the danger receded.

Ilysse attended most of the meetings with Nikita, but Deming had not been invited. Despite her and Rendrel's discovery of the crumbling castle and their hunch that this was Khalil's new hideaway, the king had been adamant that she was not to be present in his council meetings. Deming wasn't sure if the decision was based in policy, foreign affairs, or simply spite, but she hardly cared. Nikita knew what she knew. He would relay all of the information and tell her what they decided. Besides, this wasn't her court, this wasn't her kingdom. No matter how deeply she cared for their Crown Prince, she was an interloper in these lands.

So she had been guided back to their rooms, given fresh linens and clothes, and left alone.

She pulled the fine-toothed brush through her hair one more time, teasing out the last of the knots, then twisted the lengths back away from her face and secured them with twin, pearl encrusted pins.

It felt particularly off-putting to pad rouge onto her cheeks and curl her lashes given the ravaged state of the city outside the castle walls. However, there was little else for her to do and if the past months had taught her anything, it was that she was always worse for wear if she succumbed to the current of grief that buried feelings and called her to curl inside herself.

She selected a beautifully pale, seafoam green, organza gown from the trunk of clothes that had been provided for her. It was the same color as the cloak Trevelyan had worn when they arrived, and many of the staff wore similar colors. Deming imagined it was a color of the royal family, though she was less sure why it had been presented to her.

Perhaps simply out of convenience.

She doubted that the King of Runne cared enough about her to deliberately honor her with clothes of the royal color. More likely they had been the only things available.

Something precious and beautiful, like butterfly wings, fluttered in her heart.

Perhaps Nikita had picked them out for her.

She hoped that was true.

Regardless, they were beautiful.

Even through the film of depression that covered her every thought, Deming could recognize that the clothes inside the trunk were stunning.

She would even go so far as to say it felt good to slide the soft fabric onto her skin. It had been so long since she had worn anything resembling anything worthy of the station stolen from her. Though the horror of Danae dying in her arms lingered, Deming was, ashamedly, calmed by the presence of royally curated clothing.

Deming swallowed bile as she clasped a small strand of pearls around her neck. The string lay delicately at the hollow of her neck, high above the locket's chain, and matched the pearl studs already pinned in her ears.

She sighed, taking in her appearance.

Aside from the hollow gaze of her eyes, she looked every bit a part of a consort to the Crown Prince of Runne. Every bit the part of a queen, if she were being honest.

The loss of her throne cut deeper than usual, peering into the mirror.

Would she see her homeland again? She certainly hoped so. Though every event since leaving Arsaela had taken her further and further from her crown and her people. Even if they were able to quell the threat brewing in the Telaciens, would the people of Laey take her back? Would they believe her story or had her uncle poisoned them against her too thoroughly? Would she have to kill him to take back her queendom? Kill Colette?

The thought of her cousin cold and dead chilled her far more than expected. Could she live with herself with her kin's blood on her hands? Would she have the strength to end the life of someone who had all but breathed life into her own soul after the trauma of her parents death?

Shame flushed through her as she realized that, no, she didn't believe she had it within her to deal the killing blow to Colette.

She should be able to. And still...

Deming winced, tasting blood. She had bitten her tongue.

Colette's friendship was entrenched in Deming's soul. It was as much a part of her as the pain of losing her parents, or the bonds she shared with Nikita and Rendrel. Colette and her may not be written in the stars, but they had been as close as two people could be. Two sides of the same coin.

Deming may hate Colette, but she couldn't kill her.

Dresden, though?

White hot fury flashed through her.

Yes.

She could kill Dresden.

It mattered not what that said about her morality. She would easily and instantly grasp at the chance to end his life. He was a blight on her life. On the history of Laey. He had played a role in Vallyn being stolen from them. He had murdered Miriam in cold blood. He would pay for everything if it was the last thing Deming did in her cursed, death-filled existence.

She had tried, after all. She had thrown a knife at his head only for it to sink into the wooden edge of the door instead of the soft skin of his face.

She had tried again in the tunnels and was thwarted by Khalil and his leodins.

She would not miss a third time.

Deming ran her tongue across her teeth. This line of thinking would not serve her. She could not afford to be rash. Ignorance had been her downfall in Arsaela, impulsivity would not be her downfall in Bascade.

She filled her lungs with air that lacked the bite of winter's chill. The City of Eternal Summer certainly lived up to its name.

"Ma'am?"

Deming turned to Danilyn.

"It's been suggested that you walk the gardens."

Deming wondered by who as she considered the offer. It would be refreshing to walk through the royal gardens. Nikita had sung their praises and Deming knew that if he thought she would enjoy them, she would. But she rather loathed the thought of walking through them alone.

Her mouth pulled down. "No, thank you, Danilyn."

A bob of her head sent blonde hair shimmering in the morning light. "Is there anything I can get you?"

Deming opened her mouth and sent the girl away.

It took two full days for Deming to find the desire to leave her rooms.

The blade sunk into the target with a satisfying thunk.

Deming let out a breath and wiped the singular bead of sweat from her temple.

She had been here, in one of what she assumed was one of many training grounds scattered around the castle, for almost an hour now. Danilyn had brought her here without question, though the girl's hands had trembled, wheeling the rack of finely crafted weapons over to where Deming now stood.

She certainly hadn't needed to stay with Deming, something that Deming made sure to explicitly state, but after a few warm up throws Danilyn found a seat nearby and watched, entranced. She asked what it felt like to throw the sharp blade in a small, awed voice. Deming hadn't known how to answer.

How did it feel? Powerful, she supposed. Hopeful, maybe. In control, certainly. But in the same breath it felt helpless and frustrating. She held the potential to wield pain and death but was unable to master it when she needed to.

She landed on a non answer. "It makes me feel a lot of things."

"Have you killed someone before?"

The question knocked the air from Deming's lungs.

She had wanted to kill someone. Was that worse? No, not worse. An equal sin, then? The desire to end someone's life and the act of doing so?

Where was the line between justice and vengeance?

Deming twirled the dagger between her fingertips. "No," she answered slowly, "I haven't killed anyone. I have been surrounded by death my entire life, though."

Danilyn dropped her eyes and nodded knowingly.

"We've all seen death."

Deming spun to the familiar voice.

Ilysse was prowling on silent feet towards them. Something glinted in her golden eyes. It told of sorrow and pain, long buried but never forgotten.

"You don't have a monopoly on tragedy," Ilysse added with blunt honesty. She came to a halt a few feet before Deming, arms crossed, blonde hair braided and twisted into a low bun. A sword hung low on her hips and heeled black boots climbed up the entirety of her calves, laced as tightly as the smile she gave Deming.

Deming sucked on a tooth. Her tongue clicked as she released it. "I know, you're right."

Ilysse looked at her curiously. She waved a hand between Deming and Danilyn. "Have you asked her who she lost in the battle?"

Horror and shame coiled like twin snakes in Deming's stomach. How could she be so self-centered? She knew in her heart of hearts that she did care and she was a good person but there was a small voice whispering that no good person would ever have forgotten the pain of others.

Deming whipped to Danilyn, who was standing and holding her hands in front of her chest so tightly it seemed she was trying to fold into herself.

Her eyes were large, her voice was steady. "My brother," Danilyn said, "I lost my brother."

"I'm sorry," Deming said, taking Danilyn's hand in hers. It was rough from manual labor. Danilyn squeezed back in response. "What was he like?" Deming asked.

Danilyn sighed, smiling. "Clever and brave." Her smile wobbled. "I mostly told him how much he annoyed me, though. I hope he knew I loved him. I hadn't told him that in a while."

Oh gods, that hit Deming straight in the gut.

Flashes of her last moments with Miriam raced through her mind. Miriam's last words caressed her consciousness like a ghostly hand reaching back from the grave.

My love.

Ilysse, too, took a staggered breath and Deming realized soberly that she knew very little about the life Ilysse had led prior to their paths crossing. Had she also lost a mother? A father? Had she lost a sibling tragically and too soon or was the grief on her face now for a friend? A partner?

Was death as close a friend to her as it was to Deming?

And then Deming had the thought that there may not be anything worse in the whole world than losing a loved one without a proper goodbye.

Deming's jagged nails, cracked from overuse during the attack and left without filing or tending to, dug into her palms. She focused on the physical pain instead of the hurt throttling her heart at the thought of all the goodbyes that had been stolen from her.

Her mother, her father.

Miriam.

Vallyn.

Gods, she missed Vallyn. That wound was fresh.

She wondered if she would ever see her friend again.

She wondered if she was even alive.

Her eyes stung and Deming clenched her hands tighter.

"He wasn't even supposed to be in Bascade." Danilyn bit the inside of her cheek to stop the onslaught of fresh emotions. "He lives on the coast. He was visiting me, a surprise for my birthday."

Deming breathed out slowly through her nose, holding Danilyn's hand even tighter.

Ilysse placed a hand on Danilyn's shoulder, squeezed once. "I am sorry for your loss. I mourn with you. Too many lives were lost."

"No more innocent people will die." The words flew from Deming's mouth before she could stop them, her eagerness to alleviate even a smidge of pain from the hurting female before her overriding sensibility. She heard the reprimand from Ilysse before it had even left her mouth.

"Do not make promises you cannot keep." Her voice pitched down, thickened, even. "Life is not that fair. Not everyone can be saved."

Deming didn't know how to respond to that, didn't want to. The truth was cruel and she hadn't yet had the chance to wrap her mind around it.

Not that it mattered. Ilysse had already turned on her heels and left.

Chapter Forty Eight

Deming

SHE SLID OFF RENDREL with flushed cheeks, a racing heart, and the sound of the wind and sky still echoing in her ears. Her grin was so wide her face felt like it might split.

In the aftermath of the attack, there were few ways to pique her happiness. Riding Rendrel was one. Being with Nikita, another. And the knowledge that soon they would be rescuing Vallyn was a third.

Nikita's wings had nearly healed and the citizens of Bascade along with the king's soldiers were well on their way to repairing the city to its former glory. That meant that sooner rather than later, they would be racing to that decrepit castle in the north.

Breathlessly she ran up to where Nikita was waiting for her. However, when she got close enough to see the details of his face in crisp relief, everything inside her tightened.

Worry and concern hung off him like a veil.

Deming was on high alert in seconds. Dread cooled her skin, anxiety spiked her heart rate.

"What's wrong?"

Nikita winced preemptively as he said, "Your cousin is here."

Deming's heart stopped dead. Her breath hitched. Her neck prickled.

"What?" The word trickled out of Deming's mouth in a voice she hardly recognized.

Nikita's face remained pinched. "Colette is here. She arrived just after you left to see Rendrel."

For a brief, fleeting moment in time Deming felt like weeping from relief. Her best friend was here. Colette was always level headed, good in a crisis. She would help Bascade heal. She would have advice on how to rescue Vallyn. She would hug Deming and the embrace would feel like coming home.

Like a star shooting across the night sky, those feelings vanished before Deming could blink.

In its wake, white hot anger flurried inside her, whipping around like a storm of betrayal and hatred and hurt so deep Deming was momentarily blinded by the feeling. She could see nothing except Miriam bleeding out on her bed, hear nothing but Dresden's wicked laugh as he fled, feel nothing except the pressure of her dagger on Colette's throat during their last interaction.

It was like she was being torn in two. She desperately wanted that piece of her old life back and at the same time wanted to burn the entire Penrose legacy to the ground for what they had taken from her.

In the end, the knowledge that Colette was poised to benefit from Miriam's death won out.

"Where is she?" Deming roared, head whipping to the castle gates.

Hands gripped her upper arms. "Deming—"

She tried to wrench herself free. "She will answer for what she stole!"

"Deming!"

Vision hazy and chest heaving she locked eyes with Nikita. "Let me go."

"No."

"No?" The word was more of a growl than anything else. Her hair hung wildly over her eyes, slashing Nikita's frame with ribbons of white.

"No," he said calmly, lowering his head so his eyes were even with hers. "You need to hear what she has to say."

Nikita sighed and the noise set Deming's nerves on edge. What was he doing? He was there with her that night, he knew intimately what her cousin and uncle had stolen from her.

"She brings evidence of Dresden's transgressions. And his collaboration with Khalil. She is here to support our cause, not fight against it."

Deep within her, so far buried that Deming hardly felt it, a crack appeared in the armor of her hatred. Through it shined a smallest ray of hope.

Could Colette be innocent?

The walk to where Colette was sequestered felt painfully long.

Deming and Nikita's steps echoed through the empty halls of the castle.

Her cheeks felt flush but cold sweat trickled down her back. Her pulse had exploded, blood coursing through her veins faster and faster with each step, but her fingertips felt frigid. Her body was an enigma—a paradox of feeling—as if it, too, was waging war over the motivations of Colette Penrose.

"Deming."

"I'm fine."

She may love Nikita but she absolutely could not deal with his placations right now. How he wasn't just as worked up was beyond her.

Her mind oscillated between the same thoughts over and over. Colette was lying through her teeth, Colette was here in good faith. Colette had deceived Deming into believing they were closer than sisters, Colette was more than a sister.

Hope and hatred were two sides of the same coin that Deming rolled between her knuckles. If she flipped it, how would it land?

When they arrived, she flung the door open and let it slam into the wall.

Deming expected to be brought face to face with Colette and be blinded by her rage on sight the second she walked into the chamber. She opened her mouth to bark out a challenge to face her.

Instead, a flash of silky black fur shot towards her and the most peculiar wave of relief and confusion and pure, unadulterated joy crashed over her, washing away her tumultuous thoughts and cooling her heated core momentarily.

"Hollis!"

Deming collapsed onto the floor and sobbed into the wriggling ball of fur in her lap.

Hollis lapped at her face and spun in circles, pressed her little body as close to Deming as possible and pawed at the ground, at Deming's legs, her chest. Her sharp claws dug into Deming's skin but she didn't feel a single scratch in the wake of holding her beloved pet once more. Hollis's tail whipped back and forth and Deming laughed as it smacked into her face over and over again.

Deming scooped the squirming pup up into her arms and pressed kiss after kiss into her soft fur. This small piece of home unlocking a longing and sadness she hadn't known was festering inside her heart.

With every lick Hollis gave her, she was hit with a memory.

Holding Hollis as a puppy for the first time, bright red bow tied around her neck.

Curling up in bed together, sharing warmth night after night until Hollis got too big and was relegated to the chair.

Crying into her fur on the anniversary of her parent's death.

Hunting in the Telaciens.

Romping in fields.

Feeling love freely given in the way only an animal can offer.

Deming wiped the tears from her face and squeezed Hollis tight. "I missed you, girl."

A familiar voice rang from the corner. Tinkling, bell-like. Horrendous. All at once, the glass bubble of happiness encasing Deming and Hollis shattered.

"I brought her as a peace offering."

The owner of the voice emerged from the shadows and Deming's blood cooled.

"And Quintessential," Colette added, flame red hair twirled into an intricate bun atop her head. Braids wove in and out of the hairstyle like a crown. She walked into the room like she owned it, like she always did. Hands clasped in front of her, Colette glided across the floor. The dark brown skirts of her gown brushed against the marble, their soft sounds and the sharp click of her heels the only sound echoing through the room. Auburn accents laced through her bodice and gauzy sleeves billowed from her shoulders before collecting into frilled cuffs at her wrists. Rouge painted her cheeks and stained her lips. Freckles dotted her cheeks the way stars dotted the night sky.

She was stunning.

Violence thrummed in Deming's veins.

The claim that her horse was here, in Bascade, healthy and alive and here for her to embrace and brush and ride, barely registered as Deming rose.

Before she could spew vitriol at the woman, or worse, throw a punch, Nikita was beside her, pulling her to her feet and keeping both hands on her. One on her wrist to steady her, one on her back to let her know he was there with her.

Deming steeled her nerve, straightened her spine, and locked away the vicious thoughts of spilling Colette's blood all over the pretty marble floors with a key in a corner of her mind.

Hollis, oblivious, continued to jump and paw at Deming, pink tongue lolling out.

Deming absentmindedly scratched under the dog's chin. Ice laced her veins and her voice. "How nice to see you, Crown Princess Colette. Or is it already queen? We've been on the run quite a bit recently. Not sure if you knew, but I've been branded a traitor. News of the queendom has been hard to come by."

The tension in the air felt tangible, like too hard a breath could shatter the entire castle.

Colette flinched at the frigid tone. "I understand you feel angry—"

"I'm sorry," Deming silenced the room. "Angry? No." She shook her head. The laugh that escaped her lips was hollow and terrifying. "I'm not angry." She glared at her cousin, pouring every ounce of fiery rage boiling inside her into the snarl she gave her. "I am incensed. You pretended to love me only to betray me, you pretended to advise me only to steal my crown—"

"I didn't—"

"You pretended to care about my wellbeing and then your own father murdered Miriam, leaving me motherless for the second time in my life!"

The chandelier shook at the violence in her words.

Fists clenched and panting, Deming swallowed hard. "Do not tell me what I feel. Do not speak to me, do not touch me, do not look at me. You warned me, that night in Arsaela, you warned me that your father would kill me. You knew he was a threat to me and my crown and my loved ones. You knew!"

Her voice exuded confidence, passion. She delivered her lines with a cutting tone save for the way it traitorously cracked on the last two words. But Deming couldn't help feeling like she was playing a part.

Under all the rage, the sight of her cousin made her feel like shattering into a million tiny pieces and collapsing onto the floor in a pool of all she had lost. A component of which was the friendship with the red-haired woman in front of her.

From the far end of the room, another voice split through the air and Deming was reminded that they were not the only two people in the room.

Far from it, actually.

Ilysse, hand on the hilt of her sword and claws piercing through the soft flesh between her fingers, stood primed to intervene mere feet from them. Three males she didn't recognize sat along one side of the long table in the middle of the room. They wore fine clothes and jewels flashed from their hands and wrists as they shifted uncomfortably in their seats. The king sat at the head of the table, stoic and regal.

Sabel Magdalene sat beside her husband. A thin, bronze circlet rested atop her golden hair. Her posture was impeccable and her hands were folded in her lap. She was dazzling in a long sleeved dress the color of polished amber.

"I will remind you all that this is my kingdom and my rule is law," Trevelyan spoke firmly. "The visiting princess—"

"She is no princess," spat Deming, finding her anger again, "She is a liar and an accomplice to murder."

"Whatever she may be," Trevelyan said, unflinching in the face of Deming's heated emotions, "she is under my protection while in the confines of the castle. Outside the city limits, she is yours to do with as you please. Kill her, for all I care," he waved a hand flippantly, "but here, in this chamber, you will show decorum."

Deming clenched her jaw, breathed out her nose, and looked at the king.

It was odd, staring down a mirror image, albeit older, of the male she loved. All of the signs of family ties were there. Silky black hair, sharp cheekbones, the aura of someone destined to lead. But the eyes that stared back at her bore no resemblance to the gray ones she loved. No, Trevelyan's gaze was unforgiving, uncompromising, and cold.

"As you wish," she ground out.

If she had an ounce of awareness to spare, she would have felt the warm trickle of blood leak from her palms where her nails had cut into the skin.

Trevelyan flicked his eyes to his son and nodded his head towards the seat beside Sabel.

Nikita held Deming's hand the whole way, unbothered by the blood smearing his skin. He gripped her tightly, not even letting go once they were seated.

Ilysse and Colette took the final chairs. The air was tense, heated. One of the nobles coughed. Another couldn't stop his eyes from darting around the room. No one said anything as they marinated in the tension that Colette's existence and proximity to Deming brought.

She bit her tongue to keep from reigniting her anger. Nikita squeezed her hand. One wing arched protectively around the high back of her chair.

"Let's not dally. Speak." He directed his command at Colette, and she withered under his tone. Perhaps his thinly veiled ambivalence about her survival had shaken her.

A rather large piece of Deming hoped it had.

Eight pairs of eyes burrowed into the de facto Queen of Laey with varying levels of distaste, distrust, curiosity, and ambivalence. No one moved a muscle and the silence while they waited for her to elaborate was thick with anticipation.

Colette cleared her throat. "Not long ago, my father staged a coup against the rightful heir to the Queendom of Laey." Her eyes met Deming's and found nothing but simmering rage. She swallowed hard, darting about to find anyone else to look at. "He believed she was unfit to rule. When the opportunity presented itself to work with an old friend and place someone else on the throne in the process, he took it. Together, they schemed to have her removed, her advisors killed, and her queendom poisoned against her with lies."

Trevelyan scoffed. "I did not come here for a history lesson. I'm well aware that your father and this other man from Laey's royal court were working together. I was told you had valuable information for us."

Colette stiffened, but continued without so much as a wobble in her voice. "I do, King Trevelyan."

Deming could see the change in Colette as only someone who had grown up with her would be able to. Her lips twitched, tightened, smoothed. Her eyes focused on the king. Her demeanor calmed.

She had been thrown off by Deming's anger, but this version of Colette was one Deming was all too familiar with. The one that wooed lords and ladies. The one that always knew what to say. The one that thrived in political courts.

Regal and poised, her cousin faced the King of Runne.

"My father knew Deming would prohibit him from bringing new advancements to Laey."

One of the Fae nobles leaned forward. "Advancements are the backbone of any successful society."

"Yes," Colette nodded, "but the types of advancements that Khalil, the man he was partnered with," she added for the benefit of the Bascade noblemen, "believes in are vile. Anyone who has seen what they are doing would agree it is an affront to nature and the gods. To label it advancement would be a terrible misrepresentation."

"I'm going to stop you there." The king sighed heavily, rubbing his temples. When he brought his attention back to Colette, his gaze was equal parts annoyance and disappointment. "We know what your father and Khalil are working on beneath the mountain. They," he waved a hand towards Deming and Nikita's side of the table, "told us of this development."

Colette dipped her head respectfully. "I'm glad you know of the experiments on the leodins and amphithere. I was aghast when I was made aware that Khalil had found a way to replicate the Rider bond."

She kept drawling on, but everyone in the room froze on those last four words.

Replicate the Rider bond.

A chill skated across Deming's skin, prickling at the hair on her forearms. The circular scars on her shoulder pulsed. Her mind went to Rendrel, to the delicate silver bond connecting them.

They had guessed as much that Weirfenn was afflicted with the same odd infection that the leodins had contracted and that was why he had attacked Bascade. But a Rider bond? Who was riding Weirfenn? Dresden? Khalil? There hadn't been anyone riding him during the attack. Was it even possible to fabricate something that only fate and destiny was meant to weave?

"Stop," Nikita rapped on the table with his knuckles, "go back. They have created a Rider bond?"

Colette blinked. Her blue, doe-like eyes wide and perfect bow lips slightly open in surprise at being cut off. "Oh, yes, was that not clear to you?"

"No," growled Trevelyan, "that was not clear to us."

She physically shrank under his ire. "Oh, well, yes. They forged a Rider bond with the amphithere—"

"Weirfenn."

Nikita stilled beside her as Deming spoke. She hadn't meant too, his name just slipped out. If he was indeed being coerced, it seemed only fair to treat him with dignity and use his name.

"Weirfenn," Colette repeated slowly, "they have bonded with Weirfenn."

"How?" An incredulous noble asked the question they were all thinking.

Stray red curls twisted down the sides of her face as Colette answered. "Khalil has found new ways to innovate with his shadow magic. He is able to infiltrate the mind of another and bend their will."

She said it with such banality that Deming half thought she was joking. Deming may have even laughed had the memory of her mate's experience in the tunnel system beneath the Telaciens not risen through her consciousness like poisonous fumes.

With the wariness of someone facing a truth they did not wish to acknowledge, Deming turned to Nikita.

Disbelief was laid bare on his features. "The shadows," he whispered, eyes looking both at and past Colette as if he was back inside the tunnels.

"What was that?" an advisor asked.

Every feather on his wings shuddered. Nikita squeezed Deming's hand where he still held it under the table. "When we were inside the tunnels, there were shadows." He looked to Ilysse, begging her to disagree, but she merely pressed her lips together in a thin line of concern. "They crept into our consciousness, pleasant and warm. They spoke to us. They convinced us to turn around."

"Did you?" the same advisor prodded, hands clasped tightly together on top of the table. The dark metal of his rings was stark against his pale skin and the whites of his knuckles.

"Yes," Nikita's sorrowful gaze turned to Deming, "we did. And then Deming was attacked and Vallyn was taken."

Sabel Magdalene slid a delicate hand across the table in the direction of Colette. "This was your father's work?"

"No," Colette shook her head, "my understanding is that my father was an opportunity for Khalil to destabilize Laey so he could get to Deming. He wants her desperately. Khalil is the shadow mage. He is the target here, not my father."

Deming ground her teeth together so hard she was surprised a molar didn't crack. "Your father is a target. He slit Miriam's wrists."

"That's not what I—"

"Stop." Trevelyan's fist hit the table and silenced the room. Calmly but with command imbued into each word he looked Deming straight in the eyes and said, "My son's mate or not, I will remind you only once more to not antagonize our guest or I will have you removed from the chambers."

Colette gasped, hand flying to cover her perfectly painted lips.

Deming didn't give her the satisfaction of acknowledging her. In her eyes, Colette lost the right to know about Deming's love life the second she accepted her place on Laey's throne.

Seemingly satisfied that Deming would remain a passive listener for the remaining conversation, the King of Runne once more turned to Colette. "You speak of these men as if you were in the room with them when decisions were being made."

Colette exhaled deeply. She pressed her shoulders back. "That's because I was. I have been privy to many of their conversations, they see me as an ally, someone that will rule a throne from which they can enact their plans."

Deming closed her eyes and tried to slow her heartbeat.

The king leaned back in his chair. "Well," he crossed his arms, "I would hope that you wouldn't be stupid enough to walk into my city if that was truly the case. Now would be the time to explain why we shouldn't throw you into the dungeons."

Succinct and emotionless, Colette did just that.

"It was not until after I was installed as heir to Laey that I met Khalil. At first, I was deeply impressed with his devotion to his craft. He speaks of magic—all magic, not just his own—reverently. He believes magic is the way to true peace, and he its guide. When he first showed my father and I his shadow magic, it was during a surgery. A young child had broken a bone, and Khalil sent shadows into his mind to take the pain away while the healer set the bone. It was wonderful. A practical, innovative use for shadow magic. I was eager to see what else he could accomplish."

Colette's mouth twitched, the only indication that something disturbing was coming.

"It was soon after that he showed us something more sinister. He spoke often of taking away pain and fear away from the world, to create a utopia with no discord. He had been experimenting with a parasite that he had imbued with his own shadow magic. He started with leodins. When infected, the animals's wants and needs were stifled and something of a hive mind took its place."

Deming's skin crawled, remembering the leodins and the way they paced and prowled and acted as a disillusioned pack instead of the solitary creatures they were meant to be.

"Unfortunately," Colette continued, "the effects were stunted. Khalil explained that the parasites alone were not powerful enough for him to control them. The leodin's acted rashly, often out of turn. He needed something else." She took a deep breath. "That was when he tried using his shadow magic directly on the mind. My mind."

Deming felt her eyes go wide. Colette herself had been experimented on? Horror, slick and prickling, slid down her spine. And though she hated herself for it, there was also a terrible satisfaction at hearing that Colette had also known pain by the hands of the men she had emboldened and worked with.

Heavy was the price of power.

The room was enraptured, every set of eyes were trained on Colette as she continued her harrowing story.

"His shadows slunk into my mind while I slept. I fell asleep one night and then had no memories of the week that followed. My father told me after the fact that I held court, spoke to citizens, and walked the cobblestone streets of Arsaela with my handmaid. I remember none of it."

Colette looked well and truly shaken. She had been a picture of stoicism up until that moment but something about reliving the experience of having her free will taken away was impossible for her to recount with a stable voice.

"It was then I knew I had to leave."

"So you abandoned ship once the price you personally had to pay was too high."

The scathing remark came from Ilysse.

Colette eyed the female. "I know the consequences of my mistakes." Turning to the room at large, she finished her tale. "I regret not coming to you sooner. However, if I had, I would never have heard the depths of Khalil's true plan and all would be lost. As a result of his success on me, he plans to use his shadow magic on every living being on the continent."

"That's impossible," Nikita breathed, "no one has that kind of power."

Colette's already pale skin lightened a shade. She looked like a ghost. "He has already had success on a mass scale. The army of Laey is under his command."

The words sank like an anchor into the room.

"He means to march on Bascade?" Sabel broke the silence.

"Not march," Colette shook her head, red curls bouncing from side to side, "invade. And he plans to do so with nothing but his shadows. There will be nothing to fight against, nothing to swing at with a blade or hide from in the dark. There will be no escape once he amasses enough power to spread his shadows."

Deming thought she had known fear. She thought she understood it like she understood loss or love or pain. But sitting at that table in Bascade, listening to Colette lay out Khalil's intentions, Deming realized she had never truly known fear. Not like this.

"That cannot happen," she whispered to no one in particular.

"No," Trevelyan responded in an unusually quiet voice, "it cannot. I propose we strike preemptively."

Deming leaned forward slightly. This is what she wanted to hear. She wanted action. She wanted retribution.

"We attack the abandoned castle with the force of Runne's army." The king was definitive, sure, in control. His voice threaded through the air like spun steel. "We go in three waves. The first will be the smallest, a targeted force of five to ten soldiers that will destabilize any defensive measures from the inside."

All eyes were trained on Trevelyan. He was decisive and confident and the strength of his conviction was easy to trust in despite Deming's inherent distrust of the male. He may be a horrid father, but he knew war.

"The bulk of the army will follow. As soon as the signal is lit, we will push into the mountain pass and take whoever and whatever is inside by force." He punctuated the second prong of attack with a fist slammed on the table. "Any leodins will be taken care of by our ground forces. The amphithere will, admittedly, be a larger issue but we will flush it into the skies where our third and final contingent will be waiting for it. Runne's archery division is second to none. Coupled with the amphitheres led by Daughlr, Weirfenn will succumb."

It was a solid plan.

But Deming knew more than most that the best laid plans can still crumble.

And apparently Sabel Magdalene had already seen the first crack in theirs.

"My love."

Those two words ripped Deming out of her thoughts and hit her like a punch to the gut. Instantly Miriam's last breaths flashed across her mind. It was jarringly sudden and violent. All she could see for unending seconds was the pale pallor of her face and the jagged cuts up her arms and the maroon stains soaking into every inch of the sheets beneath her dying body. All she could hear was Miriam's raspy, shallow breaths as she tried to drag air into her failing lungs and those words whispered to Deming as she passed into the next realm.

All it took was two words and Deming was free falling towards a darkness she never wanted to return to—

Nikita's hand gripped her thigh and the descent into madness stopped.

She focused on the feeling of his thumb skimming her leg through the fabric of her pants.

Forcing breath into her lungs, Deming reeled herself slowly back to reality. The well of loss that Miriam left in her wake was deep but inch by inch Deming grounded herself.

She would not spiral again. Miriam's death could not be avenged by wallowing in sadness. Healing through time and memory had its place but Deming had done that for too long. She wouldn't go back. She would do right by Miriam.

Jaw set and emotions in check, she blinked at the speaker of the words, angrily brushing the lone tear that had fallen.

Sabel Magdalene had broken her silence and everyone else had already trained their eyes on the reclusive Queen of Runne.

Her voice was melodic and soft like rolling hills of wheat or wildflowers. Truth be told, it reminded Deming of Rendrel's.

"Placing aside the fact that we believe Khalil now resides in the northern Telaciens—somewhere our army cannot traverse—Weirfenn nearly destroyed Bascade. We are not equipped to quell his flame."

"He could be the Crest Major for all it mattered. One amphithere against ten will fall."

Sabel looked at her husband softly. "You know the band will not attack one of their own. Even Rendrel, bonded as she is, will not wish to kill Weirfenn."

Was that true? Deming thought back to the battle. Rendrel had certainly attacked Weirfenn with her fire, but had there ever been an attempt at a killing blow? Her memory was hazy due to the adrenaline of that day but she didn't think there had been.

Deming hummed. Curious. She made a mental note to ask Rendrel about it.

Trevelyan twisted his mustache. "What are we to do then? If we can't attack, what would you suggest?"

The Queen of Runne placed a placating hand on Trevelyan's. "We need to find a way to free Weirfenn from the bond."

The king relaxed and let his wife's words sink in. Something like respect played at his features.

Deming wiped the confusion from her face. She hadn't expected that.

From the far end of the table Colette piped up. "I don't know how to free him, but," she reached into the folds of her skirt, deep into a pocket that had been hidden from view, "I think that this may be helpful regardless as we plan our next steps."

She placed a piece of folded parchment on the table. It was small, nondescript, and had a broken cornflower blue wax seal atop it.

Trevelyan looked at her expectantly.

One long, delicate finger of hers tapped the parchment as she spoke. "I wrote to the Kingdom of Monstakar."

Deming perked up at that. They so rarely dealt with their southern allies. There were amicable trade routes, but the rough and tumble, grasslands nation that spanned from sea to sea and whose southern border was unknown due to the expansive, sprawling nature of the lands was not known for interfering in disputes and wars.

"Once I discovered that my father and Khalil had forced a Rider bond on Weirfenn, I began researching anything that could help." She pushed the letter towards the noble to her left. "Our neighbors to the south are extraordinarily adept at specialized weaponry. I got it into my head that they may be able to build something that could take down something as large as an amphithere."

Nikita and Sabel joined Deming in cringing at the implication of killing the amphithere. He was dangerous, that was clear. But was it justifiable to kill something that was not in its right mind?

The letter was passed around the table until everyone had read the short missive the King of Monstakar had sent back to Colette.

One of the nobles broke the silence. "How, exactly, do you envision Monstakar supporting our efforts? He says quite plainly here that he would not do anything to bring the threat to his kingdom's doorstep."

"He also said his armory was capable of crafting the weapon I described. I propose we send a small delegation to Monstakar to plead our case." Colette looked to Trevelyan. "I believe I can win him over."

"If I may," Nikita interrupted, "Runne has a far richer history with Monstakar than Laey. Perhaps we should send one of our own?"

He nodded his head to Ilysse who immediately bared her teeth and said, "If you think for a second that I'm going to miss out on a battle in favor of a plush visit to the south you don't know me very well at all."

Nikita smiled at his friend and raised his hands in defense. "I wouldn't ask you to." To the entire room he said, "I propose a slight adjustment to my father's plans. We will send a small, specialized portion of our guard to Khalil's new keep in the north, though no army to follow nor any amphithere's. They will rescue Deming's captain and collect any information that may help us understand how to counteract his shadows. That magic is the primary threat."

"Vallyn was captured?"

Deming met Colette's eyes. Everything that had happened since the last time she spoke to her cousin built a wall between them, brick by brick, memory by memory. Deming's grief. Her magic. Paris nearly dying. Vallyn's capture. Nikita and their bond. Rendrel. The Seal.

"A lot has happened since we left."

Colette looked pained, hurt, and scared.

"Afterwards," Nikita continued, "we will send a pair to Monstakar to convince their king to build a weapon capable of neutralizing an amphithere. Peaceful capture is the priority there. I don't want Weirfenn hurt if we can help it."

The proposal sat there for a few moments before a round of murmured approvals rumbled through the air. Trevelyan nodded at his son, sealing their fate.

Colette sighed happily, a pleased look plastered on her face. "So it's settled. I'll go to Monstakar with Ilysse after we rescue Vallyn."

The king let a dark chuckle loose. "Not quite. Said with all the respect I can muster, which, I'll be frank, is not much," Deming hated that Trevelyan was able to make her laugh but here she was, suppressing a smirk as his cutting words, "You won't be leaving this castle."

Colette's head pulled back and panic shot through her expression like a flare. "What?"

"You will remain here, as a guest."

"A prisoner," Colette hissed. Her hands balled tightly at her sides.

"You'll have a room and staff attending to you. I would hardly call that being a prisoner. Though you will remain within the castle until we have neutralized the threat."

Colette looked at him incredulously. "You can't possibly—"

"I can do whatever I please," Trevelyan cut her off sharply, "and I will remind you that you came into my territories, my capital city. You, the daughter of the man colluding to erase free will from the continent, walked right through our front door. No monarch in their right mind would let you walk out again."

Colette paled at that.

Trevelyan leaned back into his chair, smugness smeared so thickly across his expression it was hard to notice anything else. He raised a hand and wagged a single finger. Three guards left their post and walked towards Colette.

Deming had to admit, she was pleased with Trevelyan's decision. She disliked much about the King of Runne, but she respected the decision to keep a close eye on Colette. Someone had to.

Colette was ushered from the room. Too shocked to protest, she left, mouth agape and wringing her hands.

The king watched her leave from the head of the table. His crown worn high, his shoulders set back. He looked pleased, in control. A measured smile graced his face and he spun one of his bejeweled rings between his forefinger and his thumb. The ruby set in its gold band reflected the light from the chandeliers high above them.

Deming stalked down the hall alone with nothing but her own tumultuous thoughts.

The plan they landed on in the end was much like the mission they lost Vallyn on. High stealth, low personnel. In and out.

It did not sit well with her that they were essentially running back the exact same attempt at entering the mountain. There was grace to be given after the first failed attempt. Not for Deming or by Deming but in general. However, trying what was essentially the exact same plan left Deming with a heavy stone in her stomach.

So much went wrong the first time.

This time was more thought through, but not by much.

Deming, Nikita, Ilysse, and two household guards would fly on Rendrel to where they believed Vallyn to be. The castle was far beyond the rugged base of the Telaciens and as such, it would be impossible to send an army. Rendrel would be at her limit of weight she could carry with five, so no one had particularly wanted Deming to go. This was a fact that Deming loathed, but understood. However, Rendrel refused to bear other beings on her back without her Rider, so along Deming was strung.

There were no illusions about the ability for them to apprehend Khalil or Dresden. With Weirfenn at their disposal and Rendrel's refusal to harm another amphithere, they would need Monstakar's help.

Their goals were to rescue Vallyn and, if possible, gain any insights on how to battle shadow magic.

It was to take place in a week.

Deming was wringing her hands as she turned the corner and ran smack into a full skirt and brilliant red hair.

Anxiety and loss and fury and pain flooded her body at the sight of Colette.

"I was looking for you—"

Deming stepped towards her cousin. "Leave me alone," she growled.

"Please, Deming," Colette spoke slowly and softly, like she was navigating a hostage situation or coaxing a wounded and wild animal towards her.

Deming took another step forward.

Colette took a step back. She hit the wall, her eyes darting down the hallway then back to Deming. "I'm not lying, Deming, I swear—"

Deming thrust her forearm into Colette's throat, cutting her off.

"How much did you know?"

The need to understand why Colette would betray her like this was overwhelming. Emotion pricked at Deming's eyes.

"I—No, I didn't—I mean I knew…" Colette stammered through the excuse, cheeks flush and eyes wide. Her hands were pressed flat against the stone wall.

"At a loss for words? How unlike you." Deming pressed harder into Colette's throat. Colette cried out, sputtered, then was silent as her airway contracted under the weight of Deming's arm. "How much did you know?"

Tears started pouring from the corners of her cerulean eyes. Her nails scratched at Deming's skin, her clothes, begging for air in any way she could.

Deming pulled back just enough for Colette to speak.

"I knew he thought I would be a better queen. We wanted the ruling line to shift to me."

The admission served only to incense Deming further. The acknowledgment that everything she had feared about her relationship with Colette was true hit her so hard she nearly collapsed. Every bone pin placed perfectly into curls, every soft word of comfort, every ounce of laughter shared over mulled cider. Everything had been a lie.

It hurt Deming just as much as it angered her.

"I thought that was what you wanted," Colette pleaded, "I thought you would be happy! You didn't want to be queen. You never wanted to be queen! I thought this would be a perfect way out of the responsibilities you hated so much!"

"You thought I would want to watch the woman who raised me bleed out in front of me? You thought I would want to have my people turned against me, to be forced to run away from the only home I'd ever known?"

Colette was crying in full force now. Chest heaving, ragged breathing, tears streaking down her skin and dampening the shoulders of that pretty dress she wore. "I didn't know he was going to kill her! I didn't know! I thought he only wanted to have you step down and me sit the throne instead! You have to believe me!"

The audacity of her to ask for belief.

"How, exactly, did you imagine he would install you as queen without bloodshed?" Deming scoffed. "I thought you were supposed to be the smart one. Besides, even if I wanted to believe you, your word means nothing." She looked down at her cousin, her once upon a time friend and confidante. The raging sea of grief and lies between them could never be crossed. Even attempting to board a ship and reach a shore where common understanding may possibly exist would send her crashing into cliffs and swallowed by waves and she refused to be crushed under the weight of torn relationships any longer.

Colette simply wasn't worth drowning over.

"I will kill your father," Deming vowed, "then I will reclaim my crown. I never want to see you again."

Then she ripped herself away from the person she used to trust more than anyone else in the world and stalked down the hall. Vengeance and grief tore through her. Each step heightened the heat of the flame within her. Each stride pushed her farther away from her cousin and she could feel in her bones that everything whirling in her head also pushed her farther away from herself.

She did not have it within herself to care.

Chapter Forty Nine

Deming

Deming grunted and pressed her heels and palms hard into the dirt as she slid across the earth.

"Focus," Ilysse hissed.

Deming hardly had time to react as the lioness leapt towards her, claws and canines out. She threw her weight to the side, rolled onto her feet, and pulled her forearms up in front of her face just in time to block the incoming blow.

"I am focused." Sweat dripped down Deming's face. The collar of her shirt was long since drenched.

It was a lie.

She was disastrously distracted by the fact that Colette was here, in Bascade. Every morning a fresh wave of anger washed over her as she remembered her cousin was mere hallways away and there was nothing she could do about it. Being constantly on edge had given Deming an ever present headache.

Her stomach soured at yet another thought of Colette, but the sourness instantly transformed into pain as Ilysse kicked her hard in the gut.

"Clearly not enough."

Deming's growl of protest was cut off as Ilysse slammed a fist into her ribs, sending Deming to the ground gasping for breath.

She coughed, spattering the air with flecks of spit as she tried to draw air back into her lungs. Each inhale brought with it a wave of pain. Groaning, Deming flipped to her back.

"If we were in battle," Ilysse said, flashing her now clawless knuckles and walking away without offering Deming a hand up, "you'd be dead."

Deming lay there for a moment trying to regain her senses. The air was hot thanks to the hours the two of them had spent training in it already. Sweat coated her skin. The roots of her hair were slick and sticky. Her muscles ached. It would be so easy to end the session early and go back to her room, curl up under the covers, and forget the world.

Yet, like the sun every morning, she rose.

Avoiding life's difficulties only ever made them worse.

Deming pushed herself up and brushed off the dust from her shirt. "There shouldn't be a battle, remember?"

Ilysse shot her an incredulous look, like Deming had personally offended her by asking such a thing. "Don't be naive. It's never a good look."

"You think we should be worried?"

"I didn't say we should be worried."

Deming sighed. Sometimes talking to Ilysse was like talking to a brick wall.

"So," Deming said, following Ilysse to the array of knives hung neatly on the far wall, "what, then? You think we'll be ambushed?"

Ilysse perused the knives. She plucked several from the wall and tested their balance and blade. Some were put back, most were slipped into a thick leather band that was home to multiple sheathes.

"It would be irresponsible to underestimate them a second time. That's all I'm implying. Here." Ilysse thrust the band at Deming, who slipped it over a shoulder.

They faced the target from twenty feet away and Deming smiled. This was her favorite part of training, regardless of the fact that she was still abysmal at it.

She shifted her feet into the correct position. Pulled in a deep breath to settle herself and eyed the target. It wasn't so far away. She flipped the blade by the hilt once, twice. She could do this. Strengthening every muscle in her core, Deming let the blade fly—

And harrumphed when it wobbled violently from a chunk of wood three inches to the right of the circular target.

"Again."

Deming threw the next one.

"Again."

And the next one.

"Again."

And the next.

"Again."

Over and over, Deming honed all her attention on the red mark at the center of the target. She ignored the ache in her shoulder and the beads of sweat trickling down her neck. She thrust all her energy into sinking the blade into that gods-damned target and over and over she missed until—

The knife flew through the air and sunk deep into the middle of the target. Wood slivers splintered off in all directions from the force of the throw.

A wild grin split across Deming's face. Her body hung there for a moment, half bent over and fully caked in sweat and dirt. Satisfaction ran through her like a flood. "I did it."

"About damn time. Now replicate that." Then Ilysse stalked from the room on silent feet.

Deming trained until it was too dim for even candles to light the room effectively. She had managed to land six other knives in the center of the target but had thrown hundreds. She was far from accurate, but the power was there and she consistently hit the broader, round target, if not the center.

That was good enough to hit a person, right? How large was a chest? Deming looked down at hers, wrapped her hands around her ribcage. Slim, but a man's would be larger. Surely if she could hit the target with consistency she could lead a throwing knife to find home in the chest cavity of a traitor.

Deming had contemplated whether or not she could sink a blade into someone's living, breathing body a lot over the past week and decided that even though skill wise it was up in the air, morally she absolutely could. After all, she nearly had all those months ago in Arsaela. If she had half the training she had now she was sure that the knife she had thrown at her uncle would have hit the mark.

Miriam would still be dead, but at least he would have joined her.

Deming's fingers sunk into her hair, pulling at her scalp harder than necessary as she washed out the lathered soap.

Hone the anger, do not let it reign.

Deming repeated the mantra over and over as she cleaned the sweat and grime off her body. Only when the water was too cold to sit in any longer without shivering did she clamber out of the tub and wrap a towel around her. It had been placed by the fire and was pleasantly warm.

She dried herself and was wringing her hair out when she noticed. She looked strong.

A shadow of a smile tugged at her lips. She had never been strong before. Seeing the flex of new muscles shift and move in her arms and stomach and thighs filled her with pride.

It was like seeing a twin of herself in the mirror. There was so much she recognized. Her soft smile and bow lips. Her amber eyes. Her scars crawling up her back and chest. She gently pulled her fingers through the wet tangles of her hair. The red pieces had deepened to an auburn in the wake of the bath.

But layered over all of that like a thin film was the evidence of her dedication.

These past few months had added a new aspect of self onto her.

Deming liked what she saw.

Sighing deeply and folding the towel on the edge of the bath, Deming pulled a butter yellow slip on and stepped out into the bedroom. The fabric clung to her still damp skin and hugged the curve of her hips.

Nikita was sitting on the bed, hunched over his knees and twisting a small, curved knife in his hands.

They had all been on edge the past week. The feeling of anticipation had been hard to shake.

"Hey."

Nikita's eyes flicked to hers and softened. A warm smile she didn't think he even knew about pulled at the corners of his mouth. "Hey."

She plopped down on the bed next to him. The duvet pushed up around her thighs with an airy puff before settling back down. "Want to talk about it?"

Nikita let out a long sigh, thick with emotion. His head hung heavy. Deming let her fingers find their way to the back of his neck and began pulling them through his hair.

"I just can't shake the feeling that this is a mistake."

"Vallyn needs us."

"I know—" He sighed again and shook his head. "That's not what I meant. Of course we should do everything we can to get her out."

He stretched up then fell backwards onto the bed. His wings spread out wide. The long, black feathers at one of his wingtips curled up gently against the headboard.

Deming curled herself into his chest, nuzzling into her crook between his neck and collarbone. He wrapped an arm around her.

"I won't ask you to stay behind—"

"Good."

"—but please, Deming, don't take on the rescue alone."

Her brows furrowed. "I won't be alone."

"No," he kissed her forehead, "but you feel responsible for what happened to her."

Her hands tightened into fists. She couldn't deny that.

"So," Nikita continued, "please let yourself trust us. We are a team. We have each other's back. I have your back. Don't do anything rash."

"I wouldn't—"

"Deming."

"Fine, yeah, okay," she admitted begrudgingly, "I won't do anything rash. We go in together and out together."

"I want all the time the gods will allow with you and that doesn't happen if either of us are dead by the end of the day tomorrow. Whatever lies ahead, we will walk through it together."

"Okay," she echoed one more time. Then she leaned into the warmth of his body and hoped their dream of a future was enough to carry the weight of reality.

CHAPTER FIFTY

DEMING

DEMING PLACED ONE FOOT in front of the other, breathing in through her nose and out through her mouth on regimented counts to keep her pulse under control. The heel of her boot snapped a brittle stick. The sound threw itself far and wide through the otherwise silent forest and she winced as the air crackled with tension.

A bird cawed and flapped away from its nearby perch.

Ilysse shot her a snarl from the head of the line.

Having frozen long enough to confirm that the noise hadn't brought any unwanted attention, Ilysse pushed forward.

Rendrel had flown them just around the opposing side of the mountain, out of sight of the castle. She would wait there for them to return.

They were now closing in on the last mile to Khalil's lair. No one spoke as they stalked on silent feet through the underbrush of the forest.

Enough time had passed that Deming's thighs burned and blisters bloomed between her heels and the black calf-high boots she wore. Then, Ilysse lifted her hand and everyone halted.

Through the trees in all directions rose the rocky cliffs and peaks of the Telaciens. Deming frowned at the memories that leapt to the surface. Leodins. Panic. Fire and smoke and Rendrel. Vallyn left behind.

Her grip on the hilt of the small dagger tightened.

They were far from the tunnel system where all of that chaos ensued. History would not repeat itself.

All was quiet when they reached the edges of the abandoned castle grounds.

Deming sat on her heels as two of the household guards they brought with them searched the perimeter of the woods. When the absence of any sabotage or hidden threats was confirmed, they approached the gates.

A light pull on the bond glittering softly within her let Deming know that Nikita was close behind her. Seconds later, his hand pressed gently into the small of her back. One small, deftly hidden indication that he was here with her.

They shifted into formation and as one unsheathed their chosen weapons. Most had swords of varying lengths. Nikita wielded his scimitars. Deming held a dagger in both hands.

Then they began the long walk up the overgrown, winding path. Ilysse led them and was flanked by Nikita and Deming. The three other Fae in another triangle behind them.

Time felt drawn out, impossibly lengthened, as they made their way through the dark. Each footfall like a droplet of water in a puddle, rainfall against the stone. The air hung heavy with must and something other, as if even the essence of the nature here had been forever tainted by the vileness brewing within the castle walls.

Deming watched the braids holding Ilysse's hair together swing from the confines of the black ribbon at the back of her head. To and fro, they moved with the motions of Ilysse's feet like flower stems in the wind.

Everything was painfully silent.

Then a yowl pierced the air like lightning and time leapt into a whirlwind of chaos.

The body of a beast leapt over Deming's head. Tawny fur and fangs as large as femurs launched through the air with unnatural strength. Claws sharper than knives sunk into the chest of one of the guards behind her and he was dead on contact, body hitting the floor hard and squelching under the weight of the snarling leodin.

Deming spun to face the beast. Knees bent, core clenched, weapons at the ready.

The leodin sank into its haunches, pierced its claws into the rocky ground like it was butter, and roared.

With everything she had, Deming roared back.

The dying echoes of her scream were still lingering in her mouth as Deming leapt towards the beast, daggers out.

She moved, quick and light on her feet. The leodin was larger and stronger and altogether far more dangerous, but Deming had one thing the beast did not.

Purpose.

Vallyn lay in shackles somewhere beyond and she would rather die than leave her friend within those dank walls a moment longer.

So she dodged swipe after swipe of the leodin's claws and stayed far out of reach of the yowling maw that roared and flung spittle at her constantly. Getting too close was a mistake here, she would have to be patient, wait for an opening to strike.

One of the guards that followed her charged forward, sword drawn and pointed towards the beating heart of the leodin.

The leodin roared and swung its great paw at the guard's head and his neck snapped irreparably on contact.

His body hit the floor, unceremoniously and unequivocally dead.

A shuddered breath left her, hands flying to her lips.

"Deming, watch out!"

She spun just in time to dive out of the way of another swiping paw. One claw snagged the soft skin on her cheek and pain flared through her as blood welled.

She flung one of her knives at the leodin, catching it in the eye. Its howl reverberated through the tunnel.

Taking advantage of the leodin's yowling pain, Deming scrambled away and tried desperately to get a handle on what was happening.

"Where did that—" Her eyes flared at the scene beyond.

Two leodins lay dead. Their blood coated the ground like a macabre blanket, their pelts a few steps from fur rugs.

Two more advanced towards Nikita and Ilysse.

Five leodins. Nearly a whole—

A low growl came from the darkness behind her and without thinking Deming threw another dagger in its direction.

She didn't see where it landed but blood sprayed and a yowl sprung through the air. She maliciously hoped to have caught its other eye.

Unwilling to give it the chance to regroup, Deming dove into motion.

She dipped through the shadows and slid across the ground underneath the approaching leodin. Rocks tore at her leathers and skin, her own blood and pain mixed with that of everyone else. As she slid, she raised her other hand and steeled herself as the dagger it held snagged on muscle and cartilage. The layers of flesh from the leodin splayed open above Deming and blood rained down on her.

She hit the wall with a crunch of her knees and ankles just as the leodin she gutted collapsed to the ground.

One hand on the ground, one wielding the dripping dagger, Deming saw the fray over the body of the dead beast. Nikita was floating across the ground, feet barely skimming the dirt as he dipped and wove in tandem with Ilysse. The pair of leodins they were taking on were bleeding, but so were they. A gnarly gash graced the back of Ilysse's calf. Kit's abdomen was slowly leaking red onto his shirt, darkening the material to a shade that sickened Deming.

She pushed forward, intent on joining them, but a cry from the other direction pulled her attention.

The last guard had faced off against a leodin that had slunk out of the shadows and won. The beast was dead. Head lolling to the ground, limbs slumped, eyes vacant. But the guard was trapped underneath its weight.

Deming was transported back to the midnight forest attack at the sight. Her chest tightened and breath shrank as if it was her buried beneath hundreds of pounds of muscles and bones again.

The guard's eyes were wide with fear. He reached out a hand at the same moment that a wheezy cough expelled flecks of blood from his crushed lungs.

Despite the knell of that knowledge ringing through her with every heartbeat, Deming plunged to her knees beside the fallen Fae and tugged on his free arm. She wrenched at his body and it shifted slightly but only his shoulder peeked out from under the hulking beast.

Changing tactics, Deming slid an arm in between the bodies and tried to pry the leodin off the Fae. Every muscle in her arm ached, sweat dripped down her neck, her teeth were clenched so hard she feared they may crack, then she slumped against the beast in defeat.

It was no use. The leodin weighed far more than Deming could lift.

"Kit! Ilysse!" Her plea was wasted. They were too far away and too preoccupied to hear.

She yelled violently and slammed a closed fist into the side of the feline.

The third and final guard let his last breath go under the weight of the leodin he killed only to have it kill him in death, and for some reason that was what paused the bloodshed.

The metallic din of battle dimmed. The guttural growling ceased.

Deming swiped her daggers from the floor and squeezed them harder in her grip as if that and that alone was what was keeping her alive. She swung away from the guard, away from the blood pooling at her feet. She clocked Nikita and Ilysse, closer to her than she thought and closing in by the second as the pack of leodins prowled around them licking their muzzles and growling and breathing out putrid, heated air like they were sent from the depths of death and decay.

How were there more of them? Where were they coming from?

The three of them drew together, back to back to back. Not one of them sheathed their weapon. Everyone was ready to die today.

Tension seized everyone and a single movement on either side would have sent the scene devolving into chaos once more had it not been for the otherworldly, bone trembling, predatory screech that came from beyond the walls of the stone castle.

Deming's hair whipped around her as she spun towards the noise, tendrils of red and white and pink dancing in the sweaty, tense space. She stepped back towards Nikita immediately but even the instant warmth of his hand on her waist could do nothing to quell the dread that rose within her at the sight spreading out before her.

Wings black as night, scales more potent than poison.

The face of destruction and death.

The Bane of Bascade.

The reason Danae was dead.

Weirfenn filled her vision.

His fangs gleamed menacingly as he roared into the sky. When he landed, the earth shook beneath Deming's feet. Her heart raced, pulse skyrocketed at the sight of the massive amphithere, and no amount of knowledge that he was not in control of his own mind could subdue the hatred boiling in her gut alongside fear.

Then Weirfenn dipped his head to reveal a human astride him.

His malevolent Rider.

Khalil.

Announcing his presence in this way was no accident. He hadn't stumbled upon their misguided efforts to save Vallyn. He knew they would be here, he would have sent the leodins himself. If he knew they would be here, then they were as good as dead. This was bad, very, very, very bad.

They needed to leave.

Deming's mind raced through her options and landed on fleeing into the forest but the second her hand touched Nikita's, Khalil's voice froze her.

"Are you in such a rush? Where on earth would you go?"

Deming looked behind her.

The leodins, more than had been there before, had all relaxed onto their haunches. None were poised to attack, but there was no way past them. A living, breathing, deadly wall.

One glared at her knowingly, its lips twitching to show a yellowed, thick canine dripping with saliva. Her heart skipped a beat.

"I'm surprised, Deming," he said with a sneer. "The girl I knew in Arsaela would have rushed to her friend's aid the moment they were in trouble. What took you so long? Is that captain of yours not quite worth the effort?"

Deming growled, every muscle in her body tensed. She knew he was trying to rile her up, to get her off kilter so she would make a mistake, and was pissed at herself that he was succeeding.

It was a lie, too. That was the worst part. The girl she had been when Khalil was last in her life was young and naive. She wouldn't have known what to do if someone she loved was taken from her. The way she collapsed in on herself after the death of her parents was evidence enough of that.

"The girl you knew is dead."

Khalil keeled over laughing. "Oh, wow. So dramatic." He wiped a tear away from his eye then patted the gleaming black scales on Weirfenn's neck. "Why the venom dripping from your tone? You loved me as a child."

Her hands balled into fists, nails digging into her palm. "That was before I found out you killed my parents. Before you helped my uncle kill Miriam. My Miriam! Your sister!" Deming's voice cracked on the last word. Family bonds meant nothing to these people. "She was your sister! What the fuck is wrong with you?"

"Now, now," Khalil chastised, "You hardly know the whole story. Why don't you listen to what I have to say, Deming?"

"Keep her name out of your mouth," Nikita growled, stepping forward and placing a protective arm in front of her.

"Yes, hello, prince. Thank you for making your presence known though I promise you, I have no intention of harming her. Back to the matter at hand. I happen to know that whatever hatred you have for me pales in comparison to the loathing you have for your uncle."

Khalil raised a hand and waved nonchalantly towards where the path disappeared into darkness behind them. The leodins growled, some bringing themselves to all fours and padding out of the way. From the opening they provided, walked the one person Deming wished dead more than any other.

Dresden Penrose.

"So you'll see why I think you'll listen."

Dresden walked towards Khalil, taking a wide berth around where Deming, Nikita, and Ilysse were gathered. He turned to face the trio smugly, hands nestled into the pockets of his coat.

"Hello, niece."

"Fuck you."

"Oh, how fun," laughed Khalil, "This was exactly how I was hoping this would go."

Without taking her eyes off her uncle, Deming said, "I'm listening. Now, speak."

"That's all I wanted. As a gesture of goodwill and gratitude for hearing me out, I offer you your uncle to kill. Here, now."

Deming's head pulled back. She blinked, confused. Had she heard him right? He was offering her the chance to kill Dresden? Weren't they allies?

Dresden spun to face Khalil so fast it seemed like time skipped a beat.

"That's what you desire, isn't it?"

Words failed Deming so it was Nikita who asked, "Why would you do that?"

"He is a small man with small ambitions and has served his purpose for me."

Dresden tried to back away but there was nowhere for him to go. Weirfenn remained coiled before him, steam and licks of fire spilling from his maw, and a myriad of weapons remained pointed at him from Deming and the Fae. The leodins, too, growled in warning as he shifted his feet. Panic flared in his eyes. "Khalil, what are you talking about? We're partners!"

Khalil ignored him completely.

"He's yours to kill, and I'll even let you retrieve your friend. She's perfectly healthy and is waiting in one of our chambers. Second hallway on the left, third door." He pulled a bronze key from his pocket and waggled it in the air. "This will get her out of her chains."

"I—I—" Deming shook her head, tried again. "I don't understand."

Khalil met her hesitant eyes and smiled with what appeared to be genuine sincerity. "Because I am misunderstood. We are not on different sides, you and I. I want to gain your trust and show you all our magic can do together."

Deming looked at Kit, then Ilysse. Mistrust lit each pair of eyes. This was a trap, it had to be. But they had no other choice. They were completely surrounded, outnumbered, and outplayed.

"Fine," Deming bit out, looking back to Khalil.

"Oh, good!" Khalil clapped his hands together. The sound bounced eerily off the cave walls. "I hope this is the beginning of a lovely partnership. One condition."

Deming tensed.

He inclined his head at Ilysse. "She leaves."

"Why?" ground out Kit.

"Because she is an unnecessary part of this deal. And because I am offering so much, it only seems fair that we limit the number of people who want to harm me to two." He nodded to Deming and Kit. "Do we have a deal?"

They were too far gone to turn back now. Everyone knew it. There was no point in having a discussion.

"We have a deal."

At Nikita's words, Deming had the sense he had just sealed their fate.

"Lovely. If you would, my lady."

Ilysse barred her canines at him as she stalked towards the edge of the tall pines. Her claws remained sharp and flexed, protruding from her curled fists. "I'm not a lady."

Weirfenn slithered out of Ilysse's way, the leodins following his lead.

Ilysse backed towards the overgrown forest. Turning to look at Nikita and Deming one last time she said, "Don't die. I'll be waiting in the woods. Bring her home."

Then she was gone and Deming was left staring into the eyes of Miriam's murderer. She didn't turn to Nikita as she said, "Get Vallyn and get out."

Nikita sent a pulse down the bond and everything he couldn't possibly tell her in words was imbued in it. Hints of every memory they had together were woven into the silent message and Deming was hit with flickers of kisses and embraces and words whispered into heated skin one after another like the twin heartbeats of their souls.

Emotion swelled in Deming's soul and waves of desire and love threatened to crack her resolve. The urge to turn and look at him was overwhelming. They could make a break for it and take their chances against Weirfenn. She could ignore her uncle, grab Nikita's hands, and take off into the woods together. She could get on her knees and plead with the gods who had so often abandoned her not to do so now.

But none of that would save them. None of that would save Vallyn. None of that would avenge Miriam.

So she didn't turn to look at her mate because she knew if she saw him she would throw it all away, and that just couldn't happen. Neither of them could live with themselves if they chose to be selfish. Instead, Deming sent all her love down the bond and prayed it wouldn't be their twisted version of a last kiss.

Nikita's footsteps faltered slightly, as if he, too, was reluctant to part, reluctant to leave her in the company of these two twisted men. But they had been backed into a corner and could do nothing to change their circumstances now. So after a moment he darted towards the castle, his steps echoing in Deming's ears like a bell.

She rolled her neck, adjusted her grip on her daggers, and faced her uncle.

CHAPTER FIFTY ONE

DEMING

DRESDEN WAS NOT NEARLY concerned enough about his niece stalking towards him.

"Khalil, you can't possibly mean to go through with this? You have what you want now. Take her! She's right there! I am invaluable to your efforts!"

His pleas were layered with confusion and betrayal. He, who had turned an entire queendom against their heir, who had murdered in cold blood, who had taken his own family and destroyed it, had the audacity to act like betrayal was a far-fetched idea.

Perhaps he was fucked in the head. Perhaps he thought Khalil was a friend. Perhaps he was simply a man that had never had to face the consequence of his actions.

Well, whatever the case may be, those consequences were now barreling towards him with a heart fueled by the memory of cut veins and spilt blood.

"You don't have to roll over and die," Khalil offered, "I'd love to keep working with you. Defend yourself," he shrugged, "kill her."

She was closing in. Deming flipped her dagger and readied to launch herself at her uncle.

"But you need her!" His neck twisted back and forth between Khalil and Deming, becoming increasingly aware that he had seconds at best before she could sink her knife into his pathetic, withered heart. "I don't have a weapon!" screeched Dresden.

"That does make things difficult, doesn't it?"

And then Deming was on him.

With a guttural bellow, she jumped forward, closing the remaining gap between herself and the man who took everything from her.

Her elbow slammed into the side of his face and they fell to the floor in a tangle of limbs. The impact sent tingling vibrations through her bones but she ignored them in the face of the blind, unadulterated rage that took over her soul at the sight of Miriam's murderer pinned beneath her, primed for death at her hands.

She slammed her forearm down, trapping one of his own beneath it, and raised her hand that held the dagger high. With a scream she drove her fist down.

Dresden flung his other arm up just in time to catch the killing blow. Deming's blade sunk deep into the soft flesh of his bicep and he wailed as she ripped it out without care or consideration to the mutilated muscle she left in its wake.

She tried once more to send the dagger home but in her fury she had loosened the grip her legs had on her uncle just enough for him to buck her off. He drove his knee up, hard, and all the air in Deming's lungs was expelled when it connected with her stomach.

He scrambled to his feet, cradling his injured arm to his chest, and faced the monster he created with horror in his eyes.

Deming lunged forward, swiping with her blade and narrowly missing his thigh. She thrust herself to her feet and began circling her uncle like a predator circles its prey, corralling him to where she wanted. Around and around she went, tightening her movements until he was jittery with their proximity.

Her lack of experience was immediately made clear when he threw a punch, catching her by surprise. It caught the edge of her shoulder and she grimaced before blocking the kick that immediately followed and absorbing the blow with her forearm and core. The dagger flew from her hand, knocked away by the force of his blow. He was larger than her and he knew to use his full weight to his advantage. He may not be a fighter, but he was strong and smart.

They skidded across the floor, rocks scattered and dust billowed from where the soles of their feet scratched into the rocky ground.

Focus, she had to focus.

She closed her fist and flung a punch at his nose. She missed slightly right, hitting the cheekbone just below his eye. Her knuckles stung but the feeling of splintering bone beneath his skin breathed life into her spirit.

Deming nocked her arm back and hit him again and again and again. Over and over she pummeled his face and shoulder and neck and chest. She missed her exact target more often than not, but connected fist to body nearly every time. Her knuckles were bruised and bloody, her breathing ragged.

She was too lost to the mad beast of revenge to see his own fist coming.

This time he hit his mark with sincerity.

Deming's neck snapped back on impact and something cracked as the full force of his punch connected with her face, whatever strength he had within him funneled into that one motion. She wheeled backwards, blinking off the dizziness that threatened to take over, and placed a hand on the ground to steady herself.

Her uncle had used the time it took for her to blink away stars to regain his composure. Before she knew it, he was on her once more. A kick to her ribs sent Deming keeling over. A knee to her skull scattered stars once more across her vision.

She went to scramble away but tripped on the rocky ground.

No longer on his heels in this fight, Dresden thrust a punch from his good arm and the force of it shot through her temple like an arrow. Heat dripped from the crown of her head, blood seeping from the wound that had cracked open beneath Dresden's fist.

He launched himself at her and suddenly they were a mass of limbs. They grappled across the floor and Dresden shouted in pain as his wounded arm slammed into a protruding rock. Deming tried to take advantage by rolling him back into it but she was too small, too weak, to throw a man of his size around like that.

Her head hit the ground and she was pinned beneath him, one leg crushing her wrist and his arm pressed firmly on her neck.

She beat at his side with her free hand, tried to curl her knees up enough to make contact with his back, but it was no use.

He pressed his forearm down harder and air ceased to flow to her lungs.

He was too heavy, too strong.

She was helpless.

No.

Her vision was blacking out from lack of air and her limbs felt heavy but realization dawned just in time.

She was not helpless.

Deming thrust her hand towards him and light poured from her outstretched palm, dazzling and bright. The space burst into whiteness as her power flashed out at her attacker. Healing properties may be a portion of her magic, but at the end of the day it was pure light flowing through her veins and light could be wielded just like any weapon of steel.

Dresden screamed as he flew off her and clawed at his face.

Deming stood, coughing up specks of blood through hoarse breaths.

It took her a few dizzying moments to understand what she had impulsively done.

Her uncle kneeled feet from her, crying out in pain, head buried in his hands. When he looked up at her, he did so through clouded eyes.

"What have you done? What have you done?"

Over and over her uncle asked her what they both knew.

She had blinded him.

Deming wiped the blood trickling down her temple and flicked it to the ground. She inhaled to steady herself, the exhale shaking and stuttering out, then retrieved the dagger from where it had been knocked to the ground. Her reflection looked back at her with limp eyes from the blade. She flicked the metal, then inhaled again, as deeply as she could. No tremors rattled her breath this time.

Hearing the ting of the dagger, Dresden turned to her. One eye was bruised and bloodied. The flesh on his cheeks were torn to shreds. Crimson stains smeared his skin. Shaking hands clasped in front of him like he was pleading for his life to the Queen of the Continent Selene herself and not a mortal woman, he begged. "Deming, please, have mercy."

The word was sacrilegious on his tongue. He had no right to mercy.

Not that it mattered. She had none to give.

He should have prayed to the goddess of death.

Deming threw the blade.

Time slowed to a drip and Deming saw with perfect clarity her dagger spin end over end. Every detail of the embossed leather hilt shone in crystal clear relief. The mid afternoon light of the sun glinted off its steel and Weirfenn's black scales. Dust motes swirled in the air like snowflakes and scattered from where Weirfenn's feathered tail skated across the ground. Khalil looked on with amusement astride the amphithere. A wicked smile slowly spread across his face, the light of it reaching his eyes as the blade flipped forward.

Time rushed forwards to its normal pace only when the blade sunk in between Dresden's ribs with a sickening, wet thud.

Fear, true fear, bloomed across her uncle's features. His sightless eyes widened, pupils growing to saucers. His mouth hung agape. A shaky gasp slipped from his lips.

His fingers fumbled to the hilt protruding from his heart. Blood poured from his chest like spilled wine. He touched the wound in disbelief. It was almost as if he thought himself immune to death, impossibly immortal. Appraisal of what had happened to him flashed across his expression. Curiosity first, then disgust. Then, just as realization dawned in his sightless eyes like the sun over the horizon, he fell.

His head smacked against the floor. His limbs splayed awkwardly around him. Bloody gurgling accompanied rattling, raspy breaths and he stared at nothing as he died.

Deming released a breath.

She had done it.

She had killed him.

The small piece of bitterness and hatred she had been nurturing in her heart ever since Miriam died found a crack of relief. This part of the journey was over. Miriam could rest soundly. Her killer was dead and the world was a better place because of it.

The path to reclaiming her crown became incrementally clearer and Deming nearly cried.

Nearly, because at that exact moment Khalil pulled focus back to him by clapping and exclaiming with glee, "How lovely! What a splendid performance. You really have honed yourself into a fine weapon, well done. Now, let's move on to the main event."

Before Deming had the chance to even think about being confused, Khalil extended his hand and twisted his wrist like he was opening a door.

Shadows spilled from his palm and slinked like the arch of a cat's back towards the opposite wall where they coalesced into a whirling mass. Ribbons of pitch black and dove gray and slate wove together until it was impossible to tell where one started and one ended.

The shadows blended together like clouds and then all at once slipped away, blending into the air and becoming one with the crevices of the mountain once more.

In their place stood a woman.

Deming pulled back in shock as she saw a familiar face and a mop of white, coiled hair complete with gold accents standing before her.

Vallyn.

Vallyn was here.

Vallyn was here, which meant she was not—

Deming's shock melted into terror before Vallyn's words had left her mouth because she knew in her bones that Vallyn's existence here meant that something malicious was in store for her mate within the bowels of the mountain.

"It's a trap! He lied to you! You need to get Nikita!"

It was then that Deming felt an absence haunting her like a ghost.

Tied to her soul like a tether against the drift of worlds was her end of the mating bond. Golden and glimmering and warm.

But the other end...

Nothing.

There was no second tether, no second knot tying her to her mate. The thread reached out and out and out into an abyss.

She couldn't sense Nikita, couldn't feel him at all.

Oh gods, oh gods, oh gods—

What had they walked into?

"I have no further use for you," Khalil waved dismissively at Vallyn, "I believe someone is waiting for you in the woods."

Vallyn stumbled forward towards Deming and what lay beyond in the yawning expanse of the cave, but she only managed one step before Weirfenn roared so ferociously the ground shook. Fire spilled from his maw, flowing like lava between the captain of the guard and her heir. Unbearable heat filled the space, scorching skin and singeing hair.

Deming barely felt it. She had seen enough, wasted precious seconds already.

"Leave. Now." Khalil's command boomed through the air with deadly control.

Deming didn't see whether or not Vallyn obeyed.

She was already flying through the rusted gates.

CHAPTER FIFTY TWO

NIKITA

ILYSSE'S WORDS ECHOED IN his head.

Louder than his boots on the stone.

Louder than his panting breath.

Louder, even, than the warning bells ringing, ringing, ringing that he shouldn't have left Deming alone with those two men.

Time and time again, they had proven themselves to be the absolute dregs of humanity and yet he had left her alone with them.

A sharp sound of frustration escaped him as he tore through the decrepit hallways of the long forgotten castle.

He pacified the raging protective nature cresting in him like a wild animal by reminding himself that he was not mated to a damsel.

Deming was strong, fierce, capable. She was armed to the teeth with blades so sharp they could cut air and the magic in her veins. She was prophesied by Fae and amphithere alike. Nikita wasn't pious by any means, but he respected the gods and fates. He believed in destiny. His mate was made for more than fodder in the early trenches of war. She would not be cut down by the pitiful likes of her uncle.

So, louder than all of that, Ilysse's words sounded.

Bring her home.

Deming had her job, he had his.

He would find Vallyn and get back to Deming by whatever means necessary. He would bring the women to Ilysse deep in the woods. The four of them would return to Runne and convene with the others.

All together, all alive.

Nikita refused to give credence to any other option.

Huge swaths of stone walls were cracked, falling into disarray thanks to the strength of the ivy that crawled up and over everything.

Second hallway on the left, third door.

Second hallway on the left, third door.

Nikita spoke the directions aloud as he ran.

Faster, he needed to be faster.

Limbs flying, chest heaving, he threw himself with vigor through the castle.

From the corner of his eye he swore he saw a shadow move but he kept moving. There was no time to investigate.

Which door was he supposed—

Third door.

Nikita shook his head.

Brightness poured in through windows long since shattered. Opaque with rounded edges from time and the elements, the colorful remains of the glass littered the floor and crunched underfoot.

He had the thought to pause. They were glittering so beautifully. He wondered what they might feel like to hold in his palm.

No. What was he thinking? He couldn't waste time looking at broken glass. He needed to get to...He needed to find...

Who did he need to find?

Through the fog slowly creeping in, Nikita dug for her name. His face pinched. What was her name?

Why couldn't he remember?

Nikita's pace slowed. Incrementally at first, then with more intensity until he was completely still. There was complete silence save for the whistle of wind through the empty corridors.

His hand was just above a door handle.

Did he need to go in there?

Everything was so blurry.

Shadows bled into his mind. They were warm, comforting.

By the time he recognized the sensation, it was too late.

His mind slipped away, lost to the gentle embrace of shadows.

Chapter Fifty Three

Deming

Second hallway on the left, third door.

Second hallway on the left, third door.

The directions became a mantra that Deming lived and died by as she tore through the crumbling castle.

Her boots smacked against the stone and echoed loudly into every direction imaginable. Her lungs ached, her thighs burned, and still she surged further, faster, harder.

What evil could possibly take away a mating bond?

Or was this something more permanent—

She swallowed the bile that throttled through her throat.

She couldn't think about that right now.

Get to him.

He was alive.

He had to be.

Every flash of her light gleaming bright white in the moisture gathering on the walls and floor made her think of Vallyn.

Vallyn, who was safe and free. The one good thing to have come from this horrendous atrocity.

Vallyn, who was alive and seemingly unharmed.

If she was alive after spending so much time under the mountain and in the grasps of Khalil surely nothing too terrible could have happened to Nikita in only a matter of minutes?

He was somewhere under the mountain.

She would find him if it was the last thing she did.

Even though she knew the way, Deming raised her palm and flashed a beam of light down every hallway she passed, into every nook and cranny of the rocky interior of the castle.

Second hallway on the left, third door.

In the distance she saw it.

Every bone in her body groaned, every muscle protested as she drove her legs towards the door with speed she didn't know she possessed.

She skidded to a halt in front of the door, grabbing onto the handle to keep from sliding down the dusty hallway. The skin on her palm ripped but she paid the pain no heed as she clambered to her feet, breathless and wild, and tore open the door.

Then something smacked her in the back of the head and Deming fell to the floor.

Chapter Fifty Four

Deming

Consciousness came to her like swimming through honey.

Deming pried her eyelids open and blinked, trying to make the dark room come into focus.

Her head pounded viciously and if the warmth on her neck was any indication, she was bleeding profusely.

She tried to stand and it was only when her body was violently jerked down did she realize she was chained to the wall.

That was enough of a jolt to her senses to fully bring her mind back from the oily unconsciousness she had been drowning in.

Eyes wide and breath fluttery, Deming took in her surroundings.

She was chained to the wall at the end of a long and dimly lit room. The other side was so far away she couldn't quite make out whether or not she actually was inside a room with a door or instead a crude, dead end hallway. The walls were covered in slick wetness and the air smelled of mold. Occasional droplets of water fell from cracks in the ceiling into the shallow puddles freckling the floor below. Each plunk echoed through the empty space.

She was deep within the castle. That much was clear. But where, exactly, she was in relation to the hallway she had been running down or the doorway she had been running to was unclear. Had this place once been the dungeons? The lack of windows made Deming think it could have been.

If she could find a way out of the chains...

Deming bent over, twisted, craned her spine and neck as far as she could but nothing allowed her any visual of what kind of metal or bindings held her wrists. It felt like a cuff of sorts. Hard circlets of metal dug into her skin like malignant bracelets.

Maybe if she could dislocate her thumb she could pull a hand out.

The thought coated her tongue with bile, but she swallowed it down.

Desperate times.

She steadied her breath and focused on the little well of water reflecting what little light the dungeon held a few feet in front of her.

Three.

Two.

One.

She yanked her right arm with all the strength she had left in her sapped body. The metal cuff cut to the bone and pain shot through her hand like a lance. She clenched her teeth to keep from screaming and bit her tongue in the process, coating it quickly in blood.

Panting and dizzy from the pulsing pain in her thumb, Deming gingerly tested the mobility of her appendages and swore.

The ligaments and muscle remained intact.

It couldn't possibly be that hard to dislocate a thumb, could it?

She was preparing herself to try again when her neck snapped to attention towards a faint noise that sounded in the distance.

"Hello? Is anyone there?"

Her voice echoed down the hallway until the darkness swallowed it whole and she was left in eerie silence once more.

"Where am I?"

Nothing but the faded mirror of her question replied.

"Where is Kit?"

Frustration built in her brick by brick with every unanswered query.

"I know you're out there, Khalil! We had a deal!"

Frazzled and anxious, Deming stared into the misty gray expanse ahead of her. Surely someone was watching her. Khalil, whoever attacked her, someone was still here. She couldn't have possibly been out for that long, there could still be time to find Nikita. If only Khalil showed himself, perhaps Deming could negotiate with him.

"Where is Kit!" Again and again Deming screamed for her mate until her throat was ragged with effort.

She tore against her restraints.

She howled into the air and the damp hallway echoed her raging voice.

This was not supposed to happen.

This was not how it was supposed to end.

It wasn't panic that lit the flame within her soul but anger.

Anger that she was here, again, helpless.

Anger that once more she had lost a loved one.

How many times would she be forced to live through the agony of that kind of loss? How much must she suffer before the gods were pacified? How much must others?

Fuck that.

Everyone around her had suffered enough.

She had suffered enough.

Her screams ricocheted against the craggy walls.

Then something sounded from the depths of the stone chamber and her muscles seized. She snapped her mouth shut. Everything in Deming stood at attention on high alert as a shrouded figure emerged from the darkness beyond.

The despair in her soul deepened as the figure's features came into focus.

High cheekbones.

Wings that spread from shoulder blades like moonlight through clouds.

Eyes like the inside of a storm.

From the shadows walked her mate.

"Kit?"

The tremble in her voice scared even her as she addressed him. It was as if her body knew before her mind that something was wrong.

Everything about him remained as it had been.

He wore the same black leather fighting gear they left Bascade in. His hair was tied back in a loose knot, just as it was when she last saw him. His wings flexed and flowed with his movements. Each feather a stroke of fine paint against the crudeness of the dungeon.

His lips curved up into a smile that she had kissed over and over again.

His head cocked to the side like a bird.

Everything was exactly the same.

Then she looked at his eyes and nothing in Deming's life was ever the same again.

The expressive gray storm clouds that had taught her all she ever wanted to know about love and lust and protection and desire and honesty were dull. One dimensional. Void.

A smokey layer of dissonance coated them.

The lack of vibrancy was enough to raise the hair on Deming's arms, but after a second of meeting Nikita's gaze something far more permanent and sinister took hold of her. Fear like she had never experienced. Terror like she hadn't had the gall to imagine.

She reached inward, fumbling anywhere, everywhere for any semblance of their bond and found nothing. Silence thrummed through her veins with every beat of her heart.

He was right here. Right in front of her. She should be able to feel the thread of fate connecting them. He was right there, she could touch him if only she could reach out her hand. She could feel his face in her palm, his hair in her fingers, his lips on hers, he was right there.

She jerked against the chain so hard the skin of her wrists tore and blood welled.

A choked sob cracked from her throat and something soul deep cracked in Deming as his slate gray irises looked at her with no hint of recognition.

"Kit?" she asked again, this time through bleary eyes. Her throat caught on his name. Those three little letters seemingly impossible to speak when the male in front of her did not move towards her.

Not to hold her or free her or protect her or comfort her.

He walked from the shadows, then stood perfectly still.

Like a phantom in the night, Khalil materialized next to him.

Resplendent in crimson, her father's best friend walked into the dim light of the chamber. He wore a vest and trousers. A gold chain was pinned decoratively to the pocket that rested above his chest. His heeled boots clicked menacingly against the stone floor and he altogether looked out of place amongst the leaking moisture and mold that coated the walls.

"Apologies for the violence." His voice was saccharine as he waved in the general direction of her head, the back of which was throbbing. Each syllable dripped from his tongue like sticky syrup. "It's just easier to have you confined for the moment and it's easier to chain up someone when they're unconscious. You understand." He gave Deming a knowing look, like they were old friends sharing a secret. "I knew you would be," he mulled over the word, "volatile when it came to the prince."

"That is not Kit!" Her cracked voice sounded like glass shattering into a million glittering shards. "What did you do to him?"

Khalil only clicked his tongue and smiled.

Chapter Fifty Five

Deming

Blood pooled in Deming's mouth and she spat it on the ground. It landed with a sickening, wet sound that echoed eerily around her.

She stared at the man before her and saw nothing of the parental figure from her childhood. She saw only someone she wanted to kill.

Was this who she was now? Someone that craved violence?

"What. Did. You. Do. To. Him." Each word was sharp and direct. Her eyes never left Khalil's despite the ache in her heart to look at Nikita.

Khalil smiled. "It's rather an astonishing accomplishment, isn't it?" He looked at Nikita with fascination. "I have to admit, when I got into his mind and found that you two were not just in love but mates…" He whistled low and slow. The sound bounced around the hollow cavern. "I wasn't sure if I could do it. Of course," he said with a flourish of his hand, "masking all of his memories is impressive in its own right. Even if that was all I was able to do I would have considered it a success. But to have actually masked a mating bond? I've outdone myself." He inclined his head to Deming and finished his monologue with demented honesty, "Thank you for the challenge, truly."

A ringing began in Deming's ears until she could hear nothing but the high pitched tone and the pounding of her own thoughts. Deming's sanity teetered on the sharp edge of Khalil's words. All of Nikita's memories—gone. How was that possible? Their bond—taken away? Could that be done? Could something that was goddess blessed, divine, woven with the threads of fate, truly be taken away by magic?

She searched within herself frantically once more. There was nothing tethering her to Nikita right now. The golden thread of their bond was twisting aimlessly in a void that led nowhere. Like a rope holding an anchor to its ship, their mating bond reached out into shadowy darkness and disappeared into the depths of whatever magic was swallowing it whole. Where before she could see Nikita illuminated at the end, now there was nothing but unending gray nothingness.

The thought of losing Nikita when she had only just found him was enough to send her spiraling. He was a piece of her, and she a piece of him. They were meant to be together, to live and love without boundaries. He had promised her that they would walk through whatever storm faced them together.

Could she function in a world where Nikita was alive but didn't know her? Where he had no memories of holding her in his arms and flying above Arsaela? No memories of saving her over and over and over again with his sword and love and patience? No memories of the way their skin felt pressed together with nothing between them?

His touch was permanently marked on her. She could sing ballads about his lips on hers, she had long ago memorized the feel of his fingertips skimming her waist.

What would it be like to look at him knowing he reciprocated none of that?

Was a broken mating bond worse than a dead mate?

Then, like the first ray of dawn, the tiniest sliver of hope sang its way through the ringing dread and depression that was sinking its claws into Deming.

Khalil had said he masked the mating bond, not broken it.

Masked.

Hidden.

Lost.

And what was lost could be found.

Her eyes burned like coals as she drew them up to Khalil. Fury lit and burned in the fire of her desperation to salvage what remained of their mating bond. It pulsed from her gaze like a tangible threat.

"I mean, truly. I have tested the boundaries of shadow magic like they have never been tested before. The stories that will be told about me. Can you imagine?" A smile slid onto his face. His eyes gleamed with unchecked assurance and ego. He was completely oblivious to her rage. "I'll be remembered as a god."

Deming spat at his feet and growled, "You are a demon."

"God, demon, take your pick. The truth at the heart of it all is that I am powerful, the most powerful person walking the continent. The continent and its people may not be ready for my work yet, but those who transform the world are rarely understood in their own time. What I offer is ingenuity, freedom from the shackles of life as we know it. With my work, we will enter a new age of discovery and innovation. Think of all the good we can do once the world is free of quarrels and petty disagreements? If kings and queens could rule peacefully? There would be no more war, no more bloodshed. I offer the final evolution of human and Faekind. With my shadow magic in the minds of the masses, the good and the great will never have to wait to change the world again." He nodded to himself, pleased with his intentions and confident in their outcome. "My vision is one worth the fight ahead."

Though Colette had told them of his plans already, hearing it directly from Khalil sent a terrifying chill racing up Deming's spine. "What you're talking about isn't innovation. It's taking away free will."

He smiled at her sympathetically. "You don't quite see the vision yet. That's okay. Your mate will help you understand."

The mention of Nikita renewed Deming's anger. She thrashed against her chains, surging forward as if she could snap the metal if only she moved quick enough. With a sickening snap, a fragile bone in her wrist cracked and she howled in agony. "Give him back to me!"

Khalil walked towards her. Deming's ragged panting and the echoes of her raging plea were a drastic backdrop to the delicate splash of his boots in the shallow puddles on the floor of the dungeon. He knelt just out of reach of her swinging torso and waited for her to settle her body.

As taut and tense as the chain binding her to the wall, Deming ceased trying to tear herself away. The pain in her wrist was far away.

Nearly forehead to forehead, Deming stared down the lost member of her childhood family. Oceans of distrust and disbelief stood between them.

He was not the same person he once was.

Then again, neither was she.

"As much as I can appreciate a direct demand, I won't be doing that." Khalil lifted a hand, pausing just before touching her chin. His eyes glossed over with intrigue and desire. "I had hoped that you would be the key to my work." His fingertip barely grazed her jawline, skimming across her skin so delicately it was as if he thought her made of glass. "Imagine my joy when my suspicions were confirmed. Not. Quite. Human." He punctuated each word with a tap to her forehead, her nose, and her chin. "A light mage with healing magic. The sun to my shadows, the life to my death. All my prayers, answered and tied with a bow in one darling package."

As if on cue, darkness slunk towards him from the corners of the room. Shadows pitched and rolled along the floor, curling up his leg like a snake.

Nausea rolled in Deming's stomach. "If you think I would do anything to help you, you are more fucked in the head than I thought."

Khalil's hand retreated. He sighed and gave her a look that made every inch of skin on her body prickle. "Oh, I know you won't help me. I believe you will come around eventually, everyone will. I must earn your trust, show you the miracles we can accomplish together, I know that. No, you won't help me right now." He leaned away from Deming, resting his elbows on his bent knees. His hands draped loosely towards the ground. He was so relaxed. "But you will help him."

With a curl of his finger Khalil beckoned Nikita towards them.

The smooth confidence with which Nikita Magdalene, the Prince of Runne, her mate, walked no longer stoked any kind of admiration in Deming. Every step was hollow, every whispered movement of his feathers was tainted. Nothing felt right about the way he moved towards her and his eyes belied the truth—he was a shell of the male she loved.

Tears pricked at her eyes but Deming refused to let them fall. Her mate needed her.

"Now, at the moment our dear prince is existing in a sort of fugue state." Khalil looked at Nikita with admiration that had little to do with anything that actually made him admirable. He didn't care for his heart or his character. He didn't care about the vision Nikita had for the future of Runne. Khalil looked at him like one looks at an uncut gemstone, like he was raw possibility and untapped wealth, like he was the physical manifestation of what shadow magic was capable of. "He isn't in pain, but he won't remember this interaction. He doesn't remember much of anything at all, actually. Think of it like he's existing in a blissful dream."

Khalil scoffed like he made a joke and Deming audibly snarled at him.

"Give him his memories back."

"Again, no. I appreciate your tenacity, though." Khalil held up a finger and wagged it between Deming and Nikita. "I would add that although he is not currently in any pain, that doesn't have to be the case. And that while his memories are cradled in a nest of my shadows, all it would take is a snap of my fingers to crush those memories to ash and dust."

Khalil snapped his fingers and Deming flinched then gasped and looked to Nikita. She scanned him rapidly, panic making her eyes flick chaotically from his eyes to his hands to his lips to his rising and falling chest under which the heart that was all but her own beat. He didn't look different, she would feel if something permanent had happened wouldn't she? Oh gods, please let him still be in there, please—

The sound of Khalil's laughter chilled her blood and rotted away any last remaining splinter of sanity. "I'm glad to see I picked the right collateral. I was considering keeping the guard, you know, but this is already working out so much better than I had hoped. The things someone will do for love. Astonishing."

"What do you want?" Deming ground out, exasperated and on edge.

"Ahh, there we go. Show me your power," Khalil nodded to her broken wrist, "show me you can heal yourself, and I will restore a memory."

Deming breathed long and slow out her nose. She bit her lip, considering, but only for half a second because the truth of the matter was Khalil was right. She would do anything to help Nikita. Everything she was and would be was anchored to the truth that Nikita was hers to love and cherish and save. She would debase and demean herself, sell her soul. She would kill and maim. She would give the last breath in her dying lungs if it meant that he would live.

Healing herself, showing the monster in front of her what she could do with her goddess gifted magic, was a small price to pay when considering everything she would do to bring Nikita back to life, back to her.

Through the agony and terror and pain, Deming plunged into her magic. It greeted her like an old friend. Warm and bright, her light magic rose like a wafting steam or the currents that brought the change in weather. It wrapped itself around her soul and let Deming guide it towards her snapped bone.

Heat filled her wrist and though Deming could not see behind her, she knew it was working because of two distinct tells. One, the pain in her wrist was lessening by the second. And two, Khalil's eyes widened and filled with terrible glee.

The warmth had barely started to recede back into the well of her magic before Deming snapped her head towards Nikita.

Her eyes searched his for any hint of recognition, any proof that he remembered who she was or what they were.

The vastness of those storm cloud eyes remained veiled. Nikita was looking through her more than at her and there was nothing, nothing, that resembled knowing in his gaze.

"You said you would give him back a memory," Deming snarled.

Khalil stood and smoothed the fabric of his vest. "And I did. He now remembers the first time his father beat him. No need to worry, I'm sure you'll learn to be more specific."

Deming pulled hard against her chains, her features twisted permanently into vile hatred as her body screamed to punch the man in front of her. Only a cruel, rotted soul would give back a memory like that with nothing else to soften the blow.

Her shoulders ached from the force of her strained pulling, her knees dug further into the hard ground and pain spiked through the bones of her legs.

He had manipulated her.

He had manipulated Nikita.

"I want a good memory restored. I want a memory of us given back to him," she demanded.

Khalil smiled, straightening the cuffs of his shirt. "Well, you will just have to cooperate then, won't you?"

Chapter Fifty Six

Deming

Each step Deming took brought her closer to both saving Nikita's mind and their mutual demise.

Shackles clanked between her limbs. The chain between her ankles was just short enough to hinder her strides so every fourth step or so she tripped, misjudging the distance she was able to travel.

Ahead, Khalil prowled. To her side, Nikita guided her.

He held out an arm every time she stumbled. At first, she had taken it, eager to touch him and talk to him but altogether not understanding the depths to which Khalil's shadow magic had claimed him. When he had remained resolutely mute, her hope faltered. When she grasped his arm and felt only cool indifference, she broke.

It was torture, to have known their bond only to have it taken away. It was unending horror to have known another person's soul so intimately and completely only to watch it be ripped from their body.

When she touched him, it should feel like raw honey on a hot roll, like a hearth heating a home. Not whatever cold, passive, impartial feeling that spread through her bones when she touched him now.

She prayed to any gods that could hear her that Nikita was still himself under the quilt of magic. Khalil had said he felt no pain, but she would never again be naive enough to believe a single word that slipped from his devious, lying, self-serving serpent lips.

So she stumbled forward. The tears eventually stopped flowing. Her cheeks were dry by the time they arrived at their destination.

What had clearly been an old throne room spilled out in front of the stairs they had descended.

Layers of dust covered the checkered floor. The pattern of swirling white marble next to obsidian went on and on. Deming's chin rose as her eyes tracked the full length of the room. Cracked and bent wooden beam supported what was left of the roof. Ivy clung to the walls.

What had this place been? Who had lived here?

Whoever this castle had belonged to was long dead. Khalil's mark was all over the place, now.

Rows of tables littered with notebooks and quills and vials of liquid in every color imaginable filled the space. Fallen stones and timber had been stacked along the outer walls, given thick steel bars, and turned into cages. Animals, or what were once animals, squealed within.

"In time you'll appreciate the wonders kept here," Khalil said without turning around, "though I understand you may not be ready to see this for what it is yet."

Deming didn't respond.

He stopped in front of a massive stone slab. Sitting around hip height, the makeshift table was craggy and natural along the sides but smooth and slippery on top. It looked like a rushing river had poured over it for centuries and bent the stone to the will of the water.

Atop it lay a leodin.

Its rib cage was at least three times the size of a humans, its paws like dinner plates. Its colossal head rested solemnly against the stone and it was only when she got closer that Deming realized many of the razor sharp quills protruding from its neck and head like a hooded collar were snapped and dripping green, sticky liquid.

The beast's eyes were closed and its chest expanded and collapsed with irregularity.

"It's dying." She hadn't wanted to speak, to be a willing participant in any capacity, but the sight of one of the great legends of the continent laying inches away from death was enough to pull sentimentality out of her shattered heart.

"Yes," Khalil frowned, "they all are. It has been the greatest challenge I have faced in my research. I have mastered the art and beauty of masking the natural mind and bending it to my will but my subjects all eventually waste away. Why? Why would that be?" He had devolved to murmuring to himself. Frustration wormed its way across his face, into his hands, which he flexed and clenched. With a heavy sigh and a tilt of his head to the roof of the cavern, he brought himself back to the matter at hand. "Regardless of why, I need a remedy or everything touched by this version of my magic will die."

Horrible realization lanced through her heart. Fear tasted bitter and metallic on her tongue.

Nikita.

"Yes," Khalil said, watching her closely, "I anticipate your mate, too, will succumb to death as well. Given enough time."

The metal binding her hands and ankles clattered against each other and the stone floor as she spun rapidly to face Nikita. Light magic poured from her towards him in a desperate, frantic attempt to heal any part of him that was withering away to ash and dust but just as her magic reached him, a wall of darkness exploded, sending the light fracturing into shards.

"You won't be able to reach him. My shadows are far too strong. He is a part of something bigger than himself."

He dare threaten her mate this way? He dare to test her? To hold her mate's life above her like a weapon?

"Free. Him. Now." Each word an animalistic demand from snarled lips.

Violence like she had never felt overwhelmed her senses. She would kill him. She would rip him limb from limb. She would tie him down and pluck his eyes out then tear his fingers off. She would carve him slowly, perfectly, so that he stayed conscious as all the blood drained from him.

Khalil looked at her with exasperation. "No."

"Fuck you!"

He just sighed. "Vulgarity will get you nowhere."

She screamed the curse louder.

"If you would calm down, I have an offer."

Every muscle in her body was tensed to throw herself at him.

She swore once more, this time to the world. Was this truly what needed to be done? Was she about to justify collaborating with someone clearly evil?

Why did anyone do anything? Love was both shield and weakness.

"What is your offer," she growled.

"Thank you for asking." He walked up to the dying leodin and stroked its fur lovingly, like one would the head of a sick child. "I believe that your magic is the key to breathing life into these creatures once more. I will lift my shadows from the parasites in its mind, enough for your magic to slip in, and you will heal it. I suspect that you will have to imbue your magic into the very fabric of its being." He cocked his head, eyeing her inquisitively. "Do you think you can do that?"

She had little choice.

Instead of speaking, she walked up to the leodin in answer.

He breathed a sigh of relief, as if he genuinely thought she might refuse. Did he know nothing of love? "As a token of my appreciation, I will reward the prince with another memory once you've made the attempt—regardless of your success."

Deming looked warily at him.

He held up a palm to the sky. "Hand to the gods. I meant what I said before. I want to partner together. I do not wish to harm you or your mate. Or anyone, really. The deaths of these creatures," gesturing to the leodin, "pain me. I want to help the world with my research, not harm."

He was delusional. Lost to the grandeur of his ideas. Taking away the free will of others would never be acceptable.

She didn't tell him any of that. Instead, she said, "I will help you heal the leodin if you agree to let us go."

Khalil looked hurt and confused. "You want to go? So soon? No, no, no. That simply won't do. You're to be my partner in this work."

Despair began creeping in. How was she supposed to get both her and Nikita out of here unscathed?

Escaping Khalil's clutches would have to come later.

Nikita's mind was the priority.

She tried again. "I will help you if you continue to give his memories back. And once he has recovered all of them, you will remove any trace of your magic from his mind."

"Now that is more than fair."

A flicker of concern wavered within her—were those terms airtight? She was sure there was a way Khalil could wriggle out of his commitment if he wanted to but she had little time to care. Every second she wasted was a second that slid Nikita closer to death's door.

She sidled up to the stone slab and slid her fingers into the thick fur. Dense muscle shifted in complex layers under its skin even when it was doing nothing but breathing.

Deming closed her eyes and sank into her magic.

Warmth spread through her veins like the softest of flames, the most delicate beams of sun and starlight. She urged her magic into her palms and searched the dying leodin for where the decay was located.

Everywhere. The decay was everywhere. Flares of unintelligible pain and wounds that were unlike anything Deming had the words to describe flowed through the sinew and bones of the leodin. From tip to tail, masses of pulsing death flourished. She sent licks of her magic into one of the pain points, prodding gently. It tensed and expanded on contact and a roar tore from the leodin's jaws.

Deming flinched away, breaking contact and swallowing hard.

It was in so much pain. She had hoped, perhaps, the beast would be slinking towards death peacefully. Foolish.

Pursing her lips and exhaling out anything that could distract her from the task at hand, Deming once more entered the ambiguous state her magic lived in.

This time, she followed the tributaries of pain the shadow magic had scored into the essence of the leodin to the source, ending up at the head. Within the skull of the leodin swirled a massive knot of magic and death, poison infiltrating the mind.

Imbue her magic into its mind, that's what she had been told to do. How, though?

Tendrils of light reached out towards the shadows.

She tried to massage her magic into an orb but it was slippery and shimmery and would not hold shape. She pushed and pulled, forced it into a trembling, small, condensed kernel—

Fractals of light exploded across her vision.

She blinked them away and smacked the table. The stone stung her palm.

"I failed," she deadpanned.

"As we all do at the onset of great achievements." He patted her on the back and she flinched away, hissing at the contact. He had the audacity to laugh. "No touching, understood. Well, my word is my bond." He flicked his hand towards Nikita then looked back at her. "One memory of the two of you, as promised. A good one too, you're welcome. I could have given him a wayward glance or a memory of being in council with you, something impersonal. Remember that. I am, at my core, benevolent. And I'm nothing if not true to my word."

The thought of him rummaging through her mate's mind like a sock drawer, inspecting memory after memory and sorting them by usefulness, made her want to strangle the breath from his lungs with her bare hands but the impulse was doused by the immediate need to search Nikita's face for any sign of recognition.

Her eyes darted from feature to feature. He was painfully beautiful, even now, even in this horrid place in these chilling circumstances.

He tilted his head just so and sketched a half bow. "Enchanted to meet you. My name is Nikita."

The air was knocked from her lungs. Did he know he had spoken almost those exact words to her when they first met? Had something slipped through the vise-like grip the magic had on him or was it a coincidence?

She managed to whisper, "Deming—I—my name is Deming. We've actually met before."

He smiled and the upturn of his mouth was so familiar, so perfectly him, it almost tricked her into thinking her name was the key to the labyrinthian maze his mind was locked in. But the smile didn't reach his eyes. They remained cloudy. Hazy. Obscured like someone had draped a thin layer of gauze over them, shrouding their brilliance.

"Ahh, yes. I remember you now. We once danced under the stars."

Deming nearly fell apart at the sound of his voice. Silky smooth like fresh cream, rich as midnight, as sparkling as the stars. She shivered as it skated across her skin.

All at once she was transported back to Midwinter.

Dancing across the cobblestone streets.

His fingers splayed across her back.

His words echoing in her ears.

My praise is for you.

How he gifted her the sight of Arsaela in his arms from the sky above.

The way he bared his soul afterwards.

"Yes," her voice cracked a million times on that one small word, "yes, we did."

"What a lovely moment we shared. I hope you have been well since then."

Tears pricked at her eyes. Since that moment she had seen people die. Twice, she had watched life fade from their eyes as she cradled their bodies. She had lost love and found it. She had stitched back her tattered heart and learned what it meant to take a stand. Something had hardened within her, fueled by rage and violence. She had strengthened her mind, body, and purpose and become something to be wary of, to fear and respect. She had the missing pieces of her fate laid bare before her, finally, and felt peace knowing the two bonds she shared had always been and would always be woven into the fabric of her soul.

The woman he had danced with at Midwinter was a distant reflection of the woman she was today. She was forever changed.

"I've had the best and worst times of my life."

He chuckled, amused. "How tumultuous."

"Yes, well," she swallowed the lump in her throat, "the future will be brighter."

No matter how far away it seemed in this moment, every bit of her held onto the glimmer of a peaceful life with him. One without war and shadow magic, without constant bloodshed and having to look over shoulders for enemies disguised as family. In the same way that she had known without knowing there was something more between them than simple lust, she knew now that one day, somehow, they would be free to love each other uninhibited.

He may be lost in some far off world, wandering the cosmos of dreams, but they were written in the stars, and she would bring him home.

The angst and pull on her heartstrings slowly simmered away with each beat of her heart. What was left in its wake was steely resolve.

She was Deming Reynes-Elyachar, rightful heir to the Queendom of Laey. She was bound by fate to the Crown Prince of Runne and had a Rider's mark tattooed on her skin. She had been beaten, bloodied, and bruised. She had been scorched and burned, but from the ashes reborn.

Her future would be shaped by her hands and her hands alone. She would mould it to her liking, and nothing—not war or magic, death or destiny, mortals or gods—would keep her mate from her.

"I will make it so."

BLURBS

Acknowledgements

Writing a sequel was a uniquely difficult experience. I felt that *Light Heart* was simultaneously easier and harder to write than *Veiled Skies*. There were so many moments in this book I had been wanting to write for years, and there were also plot points that felt like I was wrangling wild horses to make work. All this to say—I am incredibly proud of this book and how far it's come thanks to the hard work of my village.

Nick, when I started writing *Veiled Skies* we were dating and now here we are, at the release of *Light Heart*, married and in our new home. Your unwavering support as been instrumental in the completion of this book. Thank you for your willingness to read multiple drafts and give nuanced commentary every time. Thank you for your belief in me and, most importantly, the way you treat my dreams as your own. I love you more than words can express.

Neena, I will be thanking you until the end of time. You are a steadfast friend and the most amazing writer. Thank you for always being there when I need help. From character growth to design choices to plot struggles—your advice is second to none. Thank you for continuing to be a source of inspiration. When I grow up, I want to be you.

To my beta readers—Chloe, Kate, and Beth—thank you once again for reading the messiest of drafts and giving me feedback.

Without you, this book would make no sense. I appreciate not only the time you spent reading my words, but your friendship.

I have had the pleasure to work with some of the most amazing professionals in the publishing industry. Gin, my map and interior art designer, your work makes my jaw drop every time. Thank you for your timeliness, communication, and beautiful final products. Laura, my cover designer, thank you for your patience and dedication to my vision. I am constantly in awe of the colorful, maximalist art you create. And Kay, my copy editor and proofreader, where would I be without you? You go above and beyond to make my writing shine and champion my books. Thank you endlessly.

To my parents, thank you for supporting my dreams since I was a little kid. I love you.

And finally, to my readers. I will never stop being appreciative that you took a chance on a small indie author. Thank you for your support and the love you show my characters.

About the Author

Jessica Santi is an NA Fantasy author. She holds a bachelor's degree in Elementary Education from the University of Michigan and a master's degree in Social Foundations and Community Education from Eastern Michigan University. Jessica lives in southeast Michigan with her loving husband, rambunctious dog, and quietly conniving cat. In her spare time she enjoys supporting other indie authors, exploring local coffee shops, and rewatching shows she's seen a million times before.

Veiled Skies is her debut series. For information on upcoming releases, including ARC opportunities and early access to content, follow @authorjessicasanti on social media.